Bounty

Discover other titles by Kristen Ashley at:
www.kristenashley.net

Commune with Kristen at:
www.facebook.com/kristenashleybooks
Twitter: KristenAshley68
Instagram: KristenAshleyBooks
Pinterest: kashley0155

Bounty

KRISTEN
ASHLEY

First ebook edition: April 18, 2016
First print edition: April 18, 2016

ISBN: 0692630384

ISBN 13: 9780692630389

DEDICATION

This book is dedicated to the memory of Greg Bullard.
A simple kind of man.
A good friend. A great husband. A loving father.
The best kind of man.
"All I want for you, my son, is to be satisfied."
You are missed.

And to his family who I hold deep in my heart.
His wife, my beautiful Bethy,
his awesome son, Jackson,
and his gorgeous daughter, Kate.

* * *

This book is also dedicated to the living spirit of Kara Bombardier.
My sister from another sister.
My gypsy.

ACKNOWLEDGEMENTS AND AUTHOR'S NOTE

MANY THANKS TO my girl Stephanie Redman Smith for a lot of reasons, but as pertains to this book, moons ago she sent me a link to Hozier's "Work Song." Upon listening, I knew that song needed to be in a book. It fit perfectly here. I hope you'll agree.

And *much* heartfelt thanks to Mark Ashley. I decided I was going to descend into the art of writing lyrics and we'll just say I didn't succeed all that well. But my Mark, he's got a poet's soul *and* the talent to make words sing. So he took my scary song that was supposed to say everything and made it into a thing of beauty. Thank you, honey!

Finally, as ever, I'd like to encourage readers to seek out and listen to the music I note in this novel. Especially this one as Justice is a singer-songwriter and she speaks a great deal through the words she sings. As I often suggest, and will do so again here, there will be scenes in this book that you'll enjoy to the fullest if you listen to the songs they refer to while reading. And to make things easier for you, these songs include Linda Ronstadt's "When Will I Be Loved" and "It's So Easy," Jim Croce's "Time in a Bottle,"The Goo Goo Dolls "Come to Me," Lynyrd Skynyrd's "Simple Man," Hozier's "Work Song" and the Zac Brown Band's "Free."

Enjoy!

* * *

PROLOGUE

The Only Man Here

Justice

"I'M NOT SURE I wanna be saved, just sayin'."

I looked at my friend Bianca. She had that glint in her eyes as she whispered this to me and Lacey before being led to the dancefloor by a biker.

This was not surprising. After three days at a local dude ranch, she was ready for a switch-up from cowboy to biker.

And the tall, angular biker who seemed determined to dance to "867-5309/Jenny" with Bianca was worth the not-so-coded message that we were on our own for the rest of the night and she'd fend for herself to get back to the ranch. This meaning she'd be doing it on the back of a bike likely sometime tomorrow morning.

I stopped watching Bianca head to the crowded dancefloor and looked to Lacey, our other friend, who had two bikers on her hook—both standing close, fencing her in at her stool at our table, taking turns buying her drinks, this having been going on for over an hour.

She wasn't blotto, as most people would be after they'd imbibed as much as Lace had. She could hold her liquor, my Lacey. We all could. That's what happened to dedicated party girls whose lives included nothing but bouncing from one righteous experience to the next, sucking all we could get out of it before we moved on.

Lace gave me a wink that indicated her approval of Bianca's dance partner then turned back to her bikers.

I looked into the crowded bar, did a scan, saw one or two guys had eyes on me, but my glance slid through them.

Nothing had changed since the last scan.

This meaning nothing there.

Nothing at the dude ranch either, except I dug the horses. We'd ridden the trails. Learned how to lasso. Sat by a campfire. Had our massages and facials at the spa. Did the river rafting trip.

The cowboys were fine as they were intended to be considering how many single women were there for vacations and bachelorette getaways.

But, as I sat in that biker bar, watching the drinking, talking, dancing, biker-style flirting, general good-time-being-had-by-all, it came to me I was over it.

Not the dude ranch.

Not the biker scene.

I was just over it.

All of it.

And I was over it because I'd been on this course since I was born, in one way or another.

Sure, I'd never been to a dude ranch but I'd been to plenty of cowboy bars, and biker bars, and clubs in New York, LA, Chicago. Festivals in Nashville and Austin. On the back of some dude's bike riding through Death Valley. In a private jet, flying to Boston just to have fresh lobster for dinner. Wandering around St. Ives on a ghost tour at midnight. Up in a treehouse in Oregon to meditate with a guru. Sitting at the side of a runway during fashion shows in Paris. On a yacht in the Mediterranean, on a speedboat in Tahoe, on a houseboat on Lake Powell, snorkeling emerald waters in northern Venezuela, partying on a beach in Thailand. Backstage at so many concerts, there was no way to count.

It was impossible in this life to run out of things to do.

But sitting in that bar in the middle of nowhere in Wyoming, twenty-seven-years-old, it was hitting me that the buzz of life wasn't vibrating as forcefully as it used to. In fact, it was beginning to seem a chore to pack up, head out, settle in (this being dropping my suitcases in whatever hotel room, cabin, boat, ship, treehouse, wherever we were staying) and rushing out to face the next adventure.

Truth be told, in the life I'd been born to, it was a testament to the love of my mother and father that it had taken this long. That I hadn't started to feel jaded at around five. What people wanted from me, what they could use me for, how they could latch on, sink their teeth in, suck me dry.

This was why there was only Lace and Bianca for me. The others we'd scraped off.

We knew.

We were all hatched from different eggs but from the same species of chick. We got the life. It had been ingrained in us.

Legacies.

In the parental department, Bianca didn't have it as good as Lacey and me did.

But no matter what, who came, who went, around the globe and back again (and again, and *again*) we had each other.

And sitting in that bar, I was coming to understand in all I'd done and seen (and don't get me wrong, it all meant something to me, it just seemed to be meaning less and less), I only had two parents who hated each other tragically slightly more than they loved each other, but they loved me, and a brother who could be an ass more often than not…

And Lace and Bianca.

And sitting in that bar, I was coming to understand I wanted more.

I just had no idea what it was because if I wanted it, I could have *anything*.

Not to mention, the feeling was uncomfortable.

This was because I had it all.

Not like, if someone was outside looking in, they wouldn't get what it was like to live my life and that it could be a downer.

It wasn't a downer.

I actually *had it all*. And if I didn't have it, I had the means to get it.

Having the feelings I was having, sitting at that bar, it made me feel ungrateful.

Because in coming to understand I wanted more, I was coming to understand that I actually wanted *less*.

I also, right then, needed to get out of there. Not cut Lacey and Bianca's fun short by heading back to the ranch (which meant one or the other would come back with me). Not leaving them drinking and carousing without a wingman who could keep her eye on things.

Just a breath of fresh air, out of that heat, the crush, the loud music.

Just…*out*.

"Lace!" I shouted across the table and, being Lacey, even with two bikers on her hook, she turned to me immediately.

"Yo!" she shouted back.

"Need a breath of fresh air," I yelled. "You good?"

She nodded. "Good, but want me to come with?"

Again, so Lace. She had two hot guys right there ready to make her every wish their command and she would ditch them to take a breather with me.

I shook my head. "No, babe. I'll be okay." I glanced up at the guys then back to her. "And I'll be watching."

Lacey gave me a big professionally-whitened-teeth smile. Even though I'd seen it frequently and the lighting wasn't great in that bar, it still startled me like it always did. What with her smooth, milk chocolate skin (a perfect mix of goodness given to her by her Brazilian mom and African American dad), high cheekbones, shining black hair and almond-shaped tawny eyes.

She was the full package, petite, a lot of curves, a lot of hair, good genes from top to toe.

But even if her folks poured good into her since birth from the genes and then some, I still felt the abundance of beauty she had inside was all Lacey.

"I'll be watching too," she yelled back.

There it was, as ever. Proof of that beauty.

I gave her a short wave and slid off my stool.

Then, trying not to catch anyone's eyes, I made my way through the crowded bar toward the hallway that led to the restrooms, kitchen and double doors that remained open to the outside for air flow. They also remained open because there was a big patio out there (with another bar) for the smokers and folks who wanted to have a conversation without shouting.

I turned that way and saw in the hallway were three tables. One was cluttered with plastic cups and bottles, clearly a set down point for people to drop their drinks so they could hit the dancefloor. The middle one had three girls and four bikers, by the looks of it from my experienced eye they were in the throes of getting-to-know-you in order to later *get-to-know-you*.

The last table, a little removed and shoved into a corner, was vacant.

I moved that way, head coming up to scan the area in case someone had the same intent and I had to hurry to cut them off at the pass.

And that was when I saw him.

BOUNTY

There was a tall chain link fence outside, closing the customers in to the patio area.

He was straight on from the hallway, turned sideways, standing at that fence. He had a bottle of beer in his hand and a buddy who was shorter than him (in fact, smaller than him in every way, which it would seem at first glance *anyone* would be).

And he had his head thrown back because he was laughing.

Seeing that, suddenly, he was the only man there.

The only man at the bar.

The only man in the universe.

The only man breathing.

The only man for me.

He was huge. Not tall. Not big. Not broad.

All of that.

Huge.

Long blond hair pulled back in a ponytail at his nape. Cut, strong jaw liberally stubbled with red-brown whiskers. Heavy brow over (from what I could tell in profile) deep-set eyes. The muscles in his thick neck standing out, the cords of his throat so defined, they could be traced on paper.

He had on faded jeans, motorcycle boots and a white T-shirt. None of it was tight, except for in good ways at good parts in regards to his jeans. But it had to be an impossibility for that big of a guy to find a T-shirt that didn't pull at his wide chest or cling to his broad shoulders or mold around his amazing biceps.

I knew with an instinct I didn't understand that what had me in his thrall wasn't about his body, even as good of a body as he obviously had and as much of it as there was. This giving the immediate feel that this guy could be a teddy bear if he was into cuddling, making you feel small and safe and warm and protected just by wrapping his arms around you. At the same time he could also be a lion, annihilating anything that might threaten to harm you.

It also wasn't the obvious fact that he didn't give a shit about what he wore, how he looked, he wasn't out to impress, and more than just the way normal bikers rocked this look. He was him, with long hair clubbed back without much care, not bothering to shave, throwing on utilitarian clothes as a chore, maybe simply because it was illegal to walk around naked, mostly because he didn't give a shit.

It also wasn't the manner in which he held his body, his fingers casually wrapped around his beer like he forgot he was holding it. Comfortable with his large frame, one with himself, unconsciously stating he did not give that first damn if anyone looked or what they thought with what they saw.

I didn't know how I knew it but I knew that he was not there to get laid. If that happened, it happened, but that wasn't why he was there. He was also not there to see and be seen, a part of this bar, a regular, a player. He wasn't about the music. *Definitely* not the dancing.

He was just there because he was a biker, these were his people and there was beer and a good laugh to be had. Hanging with his bud. Throwing one back. Trading jokes or manly barbs or whatever dudes did when they were out shooting the shit because it was better than being alone in your living room with one hand tucked in your waistband, a beer in the other, feet up, staring at mind-numbing TV.

No, it wasn't any of that.

It was the way his face looked when he laughed.

I couldn't put my finger on it even as his laughter died down and he was just smiling at his friend, which was not as good, but it definitely didn't suck.

He wasn't even gorgeous, not in a handsome way. He was too rough, but it wasn't that either. His features were not classic or rugged or striking.

Yet he was not the guy next door.

He also was *far* from average.

It was just that you'd look twice, absolutely.

Maybe because of his size.

Mostly because, with one look, I knew he was that nut a girl itched to crack. Just watching him laugh, he made you be the girl who wanted to make him laugh like that. Who wanted to pull out the teddy bear cuddler within from the rough exterior that was without. Who wanted to live her life knowing no one would harm her because he'd sweat and bleed to make that so. Who wanted to strip that, "take me as I am, I don't give a shit, my life is mine and I'm gonna live it," clean away—not in everything, only in the sense you wanted him as he was, but he *did* give a shit about what you thought, and more importantly, his life was *yours*.

In my life I'd seen many a player, rocker, club rat, cowboy, jock, biker, businessman.

And with all I'd seen, all I'd met, all I'd had...

It was him.

A man in faded jeans and a white tee at a chain link fence in a biker bar in the middle of nowhere in Wyoming, sucking back a beer, laughing with his bud.

BOUNTY

And I didn't know his name.

What I knew was that I wanted him to take me wherever it was he lived his life, plant me in it so deep I could never pull at the roots, flourish in the life we built together, and wither to dust by his side.

I also knew this would never happen. No way in hell.

That man would not touch me with a ten-foot pole. He'd find out who I was and cut me so quickly, I wouldn't feel the bleed until after he was long gone.

As I realized I'd stopped dead to stare at him, and I didn't want him (or anyone) catching me staring at him, I tore my eyes away, casting them to my feet, and moved quickly to the vacant table, around it, putting my ass on a stool with my back to the corner. I tossed my purse on the table and set my drink there.

And I felt the bleed.

He'd never speak to me.

I'd never know his name.

It was him. Only him. But even if there was another him in the miracle of life, I couldn't have that him either.

I'd never have that him.

I was what I was, who I was, and finally having that knowledge that the less I was thinking I wanted actually was more, much more, and I'd never have it...

Yeah, I felt the bleed.

I sipped my Jack and Coke and then did the only thing I knew how to do to staunch the flow when it all got too much. When what my dad called "the curse of the Lonesome" reared its head, making me think things like I thought about that man, just at a glance. Making me feel deeper than was healthy.

Making me bleed for no reason that was every reason.

I pulled out the tiny notebook in my purse, sucked back more Jack and Coke so it was nothing but ice, tugged the band from around the embossed leather covering the notebook and opened it to a fresh page. The page where I always kept my pencil at the ready for times like these.

I bent my head and began.

Wither to dust
Crumble like rust
Do it at your side
Fresh air

Cold beer
Root myself in you
Together kiss the morning dew
Breathless to bring on the night
Memorizing you, the only thing that's right.
Wither to dust
Crumble like rust
Do it at your side
You, the only thing I need when I have everything
You, the breath I breathe I only get when you're laughing
Chain links
Worn jeans
Wither to dust
Crumble like rust
Do it at your side

It didn't flow this time. I had to work at it.

Sometimes it did. This time, it didn't.

There were strikeouts. Written over words. Lines blackened, a new one added at the side.

For this, it had to be perfect.

On that thought, my head shot up when a plastic cup with an iced beverage that looked like Jack and Coke was slid across the table toward my notebook.

I looked sideways. My gaze hit a white-T-shirt-covered wall of chest, my back went straight, my head turned fully that way, and I looked up, up and *up*.

And then I was mired in somber hazel eyes.

The man at the fence.

I forgot how to breathe.

A deep, coarse voice assaulted my ears.

"Pretty woman like you shouldn't be suckin' the dregs of a drink."

I said nothing. I couldn't. I was frozen in time, never wanting to be thawed.

Those hazel eyes dropped to my notebook then came back up to lock on mine.

"Pretty woman like you shouldn't be sittin' in a bar alone in a corner writin' in her diary, either."

"It's not a diary," my mouth blurted, fortunately working since nothing else on or in my body was.

"Then what is it?"

I had no reply to that because I knew it wasn't a diary but my brain had quit functioning so I forgot what it was.

His gaze stayed locked to mine.

I remained silent.

His brows shot together over narrowed eyes.

My heart skipped once, luckily pushing blood through my veins, but then it halted again.

"You in there?" he asked.

God, I was being an idiot!

"I…uh, write thoughts in it," I told him.

"Like a diary," he returned.

"Not those kinds of thoughts. I mean, they are, but they're not. If you know what I mean."

"I don't," he shared brusquely.

"Lyrics," I admitted, it came out soft because I didn't give that to anyone and I had no clue why I gave it to him. The only ones who knew I still did that were Dad, Lacey and Bianca. "Kinda poetry, I guess," I finished.

His brow stayed knit over narrowed eyes. "You're sittin' in a biker bar writing poetry?"

That was so ridiculous, my mouth remembered how to form a smile.

This it did and it continued to do so, except frozen, when those hazel eyes dropped to it.

I had to force my lips to move with, "It's just, I learned, when the spirit moves me, to get it out."

He looked back into my eyes. "Even in a biker bar at one in the morning?"

"Even in a biker bar at one in the morning," I confirmed.

"Good you're pretty, babe," he stated, leaning toward the table, putting his strapping forearms to it, making the breathing I'd managed to begin doing again start to be difficult. "'Cause that shit's whacked."

This was insulting.

It was kind of true, in a way, for someone who didn't get it. For someone who didn't have the curse.

But saying it out loud was not cool.

I was totally unoffended.

"I'm not your average girl," I shared the god's honest truth.

His eyes roamed my face and hair as his mouth muttered, "Already got that."

My insides melted.

Oh God.

"Um…"That came out, but even if I'd had no qualms flirting with any player, rocker, club rat, cowboy, jock, biker or businessman that intrigued me who threw out a line, with this guy I couldn't think what else to say.

He didn't lift away from the table even as he brought his beer to his lips, tipped his head and threw back a pull.

I watched and had another reason why no thoughts were coming into my head.

When he righted, I latched on to what to say.

"Thanks for the drink."

"I'd say you're welcome if you were drinkin' it."

I closed my pencil into my notebook and reached for my drink.

But even as I curled my fingers around it, I didn't lift it, but instead looked to him.

"What is it?"

"Jack and Coke."

This surprised me.

"How did you know what I drink?"

"Told the bartender I wanted to buy a drink for the girl with all the hair, all the leg and all the ass. He started makin' it before I got to the part about you bein' the only girl in this joint not into the scene. So, that's sayin' your hair, those legs and that ass made an impression and not just on me."

There it was again. Not an insult this time. But if he was trying to pick me up (and a man did not buy a woman a drink if he wasn't trying that), his pick-up conversation was unusual.

He was him. Take him as he came. He wasn't putting on airs for anybody.

Not even a girl with lots of hair, leg and ass.

A thought occurred to me and that thought made me even more melty.

"Just…you know, asking. I'm sitting in a corner. How'd you see my—?"

"Caught you walkin' to that table. Vision a' that might just be burned into my brain."

He hadn't looked at me when I was looking at him, that I knew for certain.

But he'd caught me on the short trek from deep freeze at the sight of him to hitting the table.

And it moved him to go buy me a drink.

Lord, I was in danger of a *Spinal Tap* drummer incident of spontaneous combustion where there'd be nothing left of me but a puddle of goo on my seat.

"Well...thanks," I said haltingly, shaking my cup a little to indicate that's what I meant even if it wasn't all I meant.

"Again, I'd say you're welcome but you're still not drinking."

I lifted the cup an inch off the table but common sense made me stop.

"Babe."

My gaze shot to his.

He was leaning deeper into his forearms and I noted at that moment that he'd never looked anything but serious. Like he was discussing something important, not picking up some chick at a bar.

Now he looked more serious.

"Motherfuckers do that kinda shit to women, they're motherfuckers," he stated, and I stared, not only not following where he was going but also a little surprised at his coarse language, regardless of the biker bar. "I'm no motherfucker. Wouldn't slip you shit. Not only because I'm not a motherfucker and it'd never fuckin' cross my mind to do that to a woman, but because I get a woman, not interested in her bein' under me passed out. Interested in her bein' under me and bein' seriously fuckin' interested in bein' under me. You with me?"

"I'm with you," I said, all breathy because in all I'd seen and all I'd done and all I'd met, there wasn't a single experience like him.

Not one.

Not to mention the fact that I was *so totally* interested in being under him.

"Name," he grunted, edging away a couple of inches.

I recognized this as a demand to provide my name so I said, "Justice."

That heavy brow knitted again. "Say what?"

"Justice," I repeated and shook my head. "My dad is a little..." How to explain all that was my dad? "Out there. He convinced my mom to be out there too. But just to say, it's arguable but she might be more out there than he is. She just loves Linda Ronstadt with a love that's more than a love so she wanted to call me Linda."

This was true. My mom Joss loved Linda. But, according to the story, the minute Dad suggested Justice, she'd jumped right on that train.

He stared into my eyes for long beats before he again took in my face and hair then back to my eyes.

"Suits you. Actually fuckin' cool. Justice," he murmured.

My nipples started tingling.

"You are?" I asked.

"Deke," he answered.

Finally, I lifted my drink, motioned his way with it, and said, "Thanks for the drink, Deke." Then I took a sip.

When I finished, he asked, "You here alone," he looked down to my notebook and back up, "sittin' in a corner, writin' poetry?"

He still looked serious but I had the strange impression he was teasing.

"No, I'm with a couple of girlfriends."

"They ditch you?"

"Well, they're hooking up but we never ditch each other. They're around."

Though, maybe Bianca wasn't. But Lacey wouldn't take off without letting me know she was going and letting me see who she was taking off with so I could look him over, cast my judgment and decide if I would allow her to go.

"They know you're in a corner writing poetry while they're hooking up?" he asked.

I drew in a quick breath at his words.

Maybe he wasn't serious.

Maybe he was ticked.

Ticked I was alone in a corner, forced to fall into my notebook while my girlfriends flirted and danced and had fun, basking in attention from the guys they'd wrangled, leaving me alone in that corner with my notebook.

"It's all good, Deke," I promised him.

He studied me and didn't say anything before, suddenly, he turned his head to look toward the bar. He turned it again to look outside to the patio and then again to me.

When I had his attention, he still didn't say anything.

I was about to when he finally did.

"Fuck, never seen such pretty hair."

Now *that* was a compliment and something in me knew he didn't give many. Not even to girls he bought drinks.

Not like that.

I felt the tears sting the backs of my eyes.

Wither to dust
Crumble like rust
Do it at your side

"You ride?" he asked abruptly.

"Uh...my own bike?" I asked back.

"On the back of one, babe."

Yes.

Yes, yes, *yes*.

"Yes," I answered immediately.

"Here on a ride with my bro. We're takin' off now 'cause we gotta meet someone. You open tomorrow to go for a ride?"

"Absolutely," I again answered immediately.

He nodded again, his serious hazel gaze starting to fire.

He wanted me on his bike.

I wanted to be on his bike but I wanted more, oh so much *more* to be the woman he wanted with him on his bike.

"You want me to pick you up wherever you are or you wanna meet me here at the bar?" he asked.

"Lacey and Bianca and me are at the dude ranch."

His lips quirked.

I felt like throwing my head back and screaming my victory at that minor show of amusement that *I* gave him.

"Eleven. I'll pick you up at that ranch," he declared.

I nodded but asked, "You know it?"

"See your point. No. Don't know jack about this place. Bein' where we are, though, there's the possibility of there bein' fifty dude ranches so sock it to me the name."

"Shooting Star," I told him.

He looked to the patio, jerked his chin up at somebody (undoubtedly his "bro") and back to me.

"Eleven, Shooting Star."

I nodded, heart racing, even in all the adventures I'd had, never, not once, not even back before the shine was beginning to tarnish, not *ever* looking forward to anything more in my life than seeing Deke at eleven the next morning at the Shooting Star Dude Ranch.

In a blink that was a shock to the system for a variety of reasons, I found my chin captured between the pad of his thumb and the side of his forefinger.

In another blink, his face was my whole world.

"Get back to your girls," he rumbled. "No woman, pretty or not, should have her face in a book writin' poetry and it's not about writin' poetry. It's about you bein' aware of where you are and what's happenin' around you. This ain't no coffee house, baby girl, have a care."

You, the only thing I need when I have everything
You, the breath I breathe I only get when you're laughing
Chain links
Worn jeans
Wither to dust
Crumble like rust
Do it at your side

"Okay, Deke," I replied quietly.

He did a slow nod as he released my chin but twisted his hand, forefinger extended, so he could slide the tip of it from the top of my throat along the soft skin under my jaw to the point of my chin.

I felt that light touch burn and when I lost it, I wanted to lean toward him to keep the connection, even if I only got another second.

"Eleven, Justice," he said.

"Eleven, Deke."

When I finished saying his name, he left his beer where it lay, turned and walked outside.

He disappeared around the side of the building.

He didn't look back.

* * *

BOUNTY

Ten hours later, I waited on the porch outside the reception area of the Shooting Star Dude Ranch.

I'd had not a wink of sleep.

I was not tired.

* * *

Eleven hours later, I was still waiting.

* * *

Twelve hours later, I went to find my girls to get a drink.

* * *

Deke never came.

CHAPTER ONE

I'd Take Them

Justice

Seven Years Later

"It comes with ten acres and we recently had the gentleman who owns an adjoining three come to us to say he's ready to sell that parcel of land. So it could be thirteen acres. And just to say, on the south side of the property, the man who owns that acreage is getting on in years. His children are gone and not coming back. Word is he's having trouble taking care of the place so it might not be hard to get him to let go of some of his land. He has fifty acres. He might be approachable to double your lot, say, in case you want horses."

I wanted horses.

I wanted the land.

But I stood in that shell of a house, immobile.

"As you can see," the real estate agent went on hurriedly, knowing exactly what I could see and what a mess it was, that being what made me immobile, "it's a little rough but when it's complete, it's going to be something amazing. And the couple who started it wanted to live in it while it was being finished so the master bed and bath are completely done and fully functional."

At this news, I didn't move a muscle. Not even to blink.

And I didn't say a word.

"And it's all here," the agent continued. "All the materials, even the appliances are in boxes out in the garage. Top of the line. Double door Sub-Zero. Six-burner Viking stove. Marble counters, though they need to be cut…"

She trailed off but it could be that I'd stopped listening because it wasn't only the marble counters that needed to be cut.

Everything needed to be done.

There were outer walls, windows set in, a roof over it all, and there was a fireplace in the middle of the room that looked mostly finished (but what did I know?).

That was it.

Inside, there were two-by-fours delineating rooms and cabinet-shaped, movers'-blanket-wrapped bundles sitting around the space, a kitchen waiting to be unearthed and constructed. There were also open steel boxes set high and low to the two-by-four-walls with wires poking out. Piles of what looked like hardwood floors waiting to be put in. Stacks of sheets of drywall waiting to be installed. More bags and boxes of this, that and the other, possibly powdered grout, tile, light switches (who knew?) to be unearthed and utilized.

That was it.

It needed walls. Flooring. Stairs to the upper level (even if the two sides of the levels already had a bridge that spanned the middle space to get from one side to the other, that bridge and the landings around it had makeshift railings).

Turning my head slowly from side to side, I could see copper pipes which meant at least the bones of some of the plumbing had been laid.

But there was nothing else. Except for a hallway that led off to the left where the garage was and where I was suspecting the completed master was, it was a shell.

I moved deeper into the space from where I stood at the front door, doing this cautiously, feeling my way with my feet as my attention moved from what was around me to what was beyond me.

"When done, there'll be this great room, complete with kitchen, of course," the agent persevered. "A study at the front of the house. Dining room at the back, off the kitchen, with semi-panoramic views. A playroom or informal family room between study and dining room. A guest suite with sitting room and its own full bath upstairs to the left. Two bedrooms with Jack-and-Jill upstairs to the right. There's the balcony off to that side. A covered deck blocked out to go in along the back, the roof over it already complete. A private deck off the master that's also already complete. A very big utility room with five plus cubic foot front-load appliances ready to be installed, big sink, storage, drying racks. This space we're in is designed to be warm and cozy but as you saw in the specs, the house is actually over three thousand square feet with four bedrooms and three and a half baths."

As she droned on, I kept moving, drawn to the huge windows opposite that went from counter height two stories up (and then some) to reach the peak that ran down the center of the house.

I stopped at the windows and looked out.

As the agent said, poles embedded in the dirt that blocked out a deck, a roof over it, the columns holding it up beautifully laid with stone, but no deck.

Then there were trees, more trees, and some more trees.

Last, not far from the house, down a rather steep slope the deck would jut over, there was a small river gushing along smooth gray rock.

"The couple who had this place designed and started the build had a, well... uh, we'll call it a marital meltdown," the agent carried on. "But the contractor who began the job for them is willing to finish it. In fact, he's eager to see the job done, and not because he needs the business. Holden Maxwell is a busy man in these parts. Just that he, like I, think once this is done, it's going to be incredible. A quiet, forest oasis. Hidden away. Private. A masterpiece, really. And if you want more space, stables, other outbuildings, Max, that's what Holden is known as, can surely accommodate you."

"Please, no offense," I said softly, "but can you be quiet a second?"

She did as I asked.

I stared at the view.

Nothing but trees, dirt, leaves and water.

No other houses. No other sounds. No cars. No roads.

Nothing.

Nothing but quiet nature as far as I could see, which wasn't far as the cool shade of the green trees swallowed up any space, even most of the sky, making me feel, as I stood there at that huge window, like this was the only house on the planet.

Dad would have loved it here. He'd have been here all the time. Taking up the guest suite. Sitting on that deck. Wandering through those trees, on foot, on horseback. He'd build a studio there so he could work, close to all that, close to me.

Dana would love it here too. Maybe enough they'd have built somewhere on that land. To be there. To be together.

To be with me.

It was less than I was used to.

But so much more.

Just what I needed.

And it had a space in that house. It had a space where I could keep both Dad and Granddad with me.

"I'll take it," I told the window.

"*Excellent*," the agent breathed excitedly.

I turned to her.

"Offer one hundred K lower than asking," I demanded.

Her face paled and her eyes got big.

"I want the three additional acres," I went on, ignoring her reaction. "I also want a friendly approach made to the neighbor. If he's not actually ready to sell, he's going to be my neighbor, so I don't want to start that relationship in a bad place. I can wait for that to happen, or not. But if he's willing to let five to fifteen acres go, I want it. And I'll need this Maxwell guy's contact details."

"One hundred K off?" she asked. "The owners have already come down twenty K."

"And the property has been on the market for ten months, they're in the midst of a messy divorce and they need to unload it. Offer one hundred K lower than asking, but be nice about that too. We'll jump off from there."

She wasn't far away but she shifted closer.

"With due respect, Justice, it'll be hard to be nice about offering that far under asking price. They'll be offended and shut us down. And they've had other offers so they know that there's interest. But if you want to settle around these parts, there *isn't* much that's available to you with the specifications you're searching for, including land on which to build."

"I don't know what these other offers were," I returned, "but beyond that three acres that's for sale is a ranch with twice this much acreage with a fully-functional house on it that's only fifty square feet less than this *and* it has a stable. It sold for what I'm going to offer to start. It's not a slap in the face. It's a healthy comp."

"That house was built in the seventies and needs an entire upgrade."

"That house is livable," I countered. "This one is not."

"You haven't seen the master and it's amazing."

I was certain it was. I saw everything this house could be.

Everything.

"Joni, with that comp's acreage and stable, it's a healthy comp," I returned firmly. "Communicated appropriately, it won't be insulting. And by that I'm saying keep the door open."

"Perhaps we should start with a more substantial offer so that…"

"Joni," I said low and she shut her mouth.

I stared into her eyes.

"You know who I am," I stated.

"I—"

She knew. I knew she knew. With my name, even if she didn't know because of who I was and what I'd done, she'd still know.

So I didn't let her continue.

"You do and you think I'm a whale. But I know I'm not a whale so I know how to guard against being taken advantage of. You're my agent, not theirs. I want this property and I'm willing to negotiate something fair with the current owners. It's over-priced and we both know that. Their agent also knows that. If they have a solid offer, cash, closing in two weeks, they will not shut you down. That's our starting point. This means you communicate that so we can *start* at that point and we'll move on from there. But the deal you negotiate will be the best deal for me. Not them. Not you. Me."

"Of course," she returned, clearly annoyed and not good at hiding it.

Not offended.

Annoyed.

I knew her kind. I could smell it a mile away. I'd learned that at age six.

However, she was the fifth real estate agent in that area I talked to and the only one where the stench wasn't overwhelming.

Precisely why I needed that forest oasis away from everything.

"Thank you," I said politely. "Now, I'll take a look at the rest of the space and wander the property."

"At your leisure, Justice," she mumbled, throwing out a hand.

At my leisure, I did just that.

* * *

Two Weeks, Three Days Later

I sat in my beat-up, red Ford pickup that I'd backed into a spot opposite the building and I stared across the space at said building, which was a bar.

Across the top, BUBBA'S, in neon.

Parked to my left, eight bikes—seven Harleys, one Indian slightly removed.

Parked to my right, a truck more beat-up than mine, a shiny black Escalade, a shinier red Camaro and black Dyna Glide Harley.

Other vehicles dotted here and there, all pickups and SUVs, except one silver Camry that had seen better days.

It was late day, but still hours before normal work time was over, and the bar had a good crowd.

This was the life of a number of bars.

Especially biker bars, which this one was. I could have sensed that even without the line of bikes sharing that intel and even with practice turned rusty.

It had been years since I'd been to a biker bar. Lacey getting on with her career. Bianca's journey taking an alarming turn. Me following in Dad's footsteps only to feel the quicksand of that life slurping at my feet, sucking me under, terrifying me to such an extreme I jumped right off that path and never went back.

Now I was here in a town called Carnal where I'd just bought a house.

I looked down at the seat beside me and saw the bulky, legal-sized, white plastic folder with the real estate agent's logo on the front.

My paperwork. The ink was barely dry.

As of about an hour ago, I owned a shell of a house in the middle of a forest that had a *killer* master suite and not much else.

And I was on Holden "Max" Maxwell's schedule to start up again.

The problem was, that schedule was busy so he couldn't even start for six weeks, and that was if his other jobs finished on time, something he told me happened, but also didn't.

In order not to think of this inconvenience, I dug my phone out of my purse as it had been ringing on my way to find somewhere to celebrate the news I just bought a home. My first home that was mine.

My oasis.

Alas, at this current juncture of my life, there weren't a lot of calls I wanted to take, and as I tugged my phone out of my purse and saw who had called and left a voicemail, I noted this was one of those calls.

But who it was, I had no choice.

I sat in my truck and engaged my phone, going to voicemail, seeing Mr. T listed at the top, the same name also listed under that (and under that), with Dana being under that, then Joni, then Joss, but Mr. T again under my mom's name.

I sighed, took the new voicemail and put it on speaker.

"Justice. I've had another communication from your brother and his mother. It likely won't surprise you it was another unpleasant one. I think I've been thorough in explaining to you the consequences if your brother continues on this path he seems bent on taking. It's become such a nuisance, the only reason I'm persevering in trying to find some way to get through to him is that I know how deeply distressed your father would be if he knew this was happening. I'm aware you're also trying to get through to him but I'm strongly suggesting you try harder."

His voice changed, became less cross and more threatening.

"I'm ready to let this go to court, Justice. Speak to your brother. Get him away from that woman and find some way to get through to him. I don't have to tell you the consequences will be dire if you and I don't succeed."

I pressed my lips together, rolled them and engaged my texts, pulling up Mr. T's string.

I then tapped in: *I received your voicemail and I'm still doing what I can. I closed today, Mr. T, so I'm having a celebration drink. I'll take a sip for you. More as soon as I can. Peace and love...*

I hit send and stared at the "Mr. T" fighting a smile.

My dad's balding, stooped, seventy-three-year-old sergeant major (literally, he was a former Marine) manager did not look at all like the famous Mr. T. I called him Mr. T for short (and this was adopted by everyone), not as a joke (he wouldn't get it anyway, he likely had no earthly clue who the famous Mr. T was) but because his name was William Thurston and calling him Mr. Thurston was a mouthful.

And no way was I going to call him William, Will or Bill (what my granddad had called him). He wasn't that kind of guy.

He was a guy who expected a Mister.

Even from my father, who gave it to him.

Though he was not like the other Mr. T, my Mr. T was ballsy, tough-as-nails, impatient, curt, had the bullshit detector to end all bullshit detectors and had never demonstrated he could be soft, or even pretend to be, even when he personally handed me my birthday presents.

But he was loyal to the extreme.

Dad, in part, was what he was because of Mr. Thurston.

So (in part) was Granddad.

So (in part) was I.

And it was no surprise even now Mr. Thurston was a dog with a bone with the shit my brother Maverick was pulling.

Not because I wanted to, but because Mr. T was right, Dad would want me to, I went to my contacts and phoned my half-brother.

It rang half a dozen times before I got, "This is Mav. If I like you, leave a message. If you're my bitch of a sister calling to hand me more shit, go fuck yourself. And if you're that greedy, gold-digging cunt who tricked my father into marrying her, eat shit and die."

This was new.

And a new, much deeper descent into assholery.

In order not to lose my fucking mind, I took in a very deep breath as I waited for the beep.

I was still close to losing my mind but had it enough in check to say, "Mav, dude, seriously low. You're better than that and I know it. Dad knew it. Not sure why you're hell-bent to prove us wrong. But that doesn't matter. What matters is you getting your head out of your ass because this shit has gone south and you don't want it to go any more south. It does, you'll be so deep in Antarctica, you'll freeze to death. I hope you take my meaning because Dad made things clear and ironclad. Don't fuck up, brother. I don't want that for you. And Dana doesn't either, by the way, so stop being such a douche about her."

I hit the button to disconnect, thinking I could have probably worded that better but, like Mr. T, beginning not to care.

When I'd arrived at that bar, it was time for a drink.

After all that, *it was time for a drink.*

My door screamed in protest as I pushed it open and it did the same after I jumped down and shut it. It was so loud, I jotted a trip to somewhere in this little burg to find some WD-40 in order to fix that. And it was also so loud I nearly didn't hear my phone beep with a text.

As I walked to the front door of the bar, I looked down at it to see it was from Mr. T.

Enjoy your drink but be safe and be smart. Congratulations on your new home.

I wonder if his fingers were burning having to type out the word "congratulations."

Thus I had a small smile on my face as I pushed open the door to the bar and walked in.

It didn't have a lot of windows and it didn't have a lot of light. It was sunny outside so it took me a couple of beats to let my eyes adjust.

And when they did, I went completely still.

This was because, at the end of the bar that was dead ahead of the door, standing next to an older guy in a ball cap who was sitting on a stool was Deke.

Deke.

Deke of the biker bar in the middle of nowhere in Wyoming who invited me for a ride and never showed. Deke who was now in a biker bar in the middle of nowhere in Colorado, looking no less larger-than-life, vital and amazing, chatting with an older guy in a ball cap who was sitting on a stool.

Deke who made me think during a conversation that might have lasted about ten minutes (if that) that in all I had, I could have more. Get to the important part. Finally find the reason I was put on that planet. Something that had, now for thirty-four years, eluded me.

Deke who didn't even know who I was and all that meant, but he still turned his back, walked away and never came back for more.

Seven years, ten minutes, and I knew him at a glance.

Seven years, ten minutes, I was right then drawn to him so deeply, it was taking physical effort to stop my body swaying his way, my feet from moving to him.

Deke, now leaning into a forearm in the bar, torso turned sideways, feet in motorcycle boots crossed at the ankles, profile expressionless (from what I could see), clearly not moved even to show interest at whatever random person just walked into the bar. Definitely not sensing that random person was his soulmate, lost in Wyoming, found in Colorado seven years later, turning to me and rushing me, sweeping me off my feet, begging forgiveness and then handing me a new world.

The world where I was meant to be.

"Yo! Free People! We got a show-at-the-bar, set-your-ass-down, buy-a-fuckin'-drink policy. Not a stand-inside-the-doors-and-stare-at-fine-male-ass policy."

I felt my body jerk as did my eyes to a petite woman behind the bar who had ebony hair, long, the ends flipped in a style that screamed 70's jack-off poster, the tips of the flips flaming red.

She was also glaring at me.

Unbelievably (because I couldn't remember the last time it happened), I fought the heat in my cheeks. At the same time I fought the desire to turn on my sandal and flee (and not just because I was embarrassed but also because it was clear the bartenders in this joint were cool with being unbelievably rude) as I forced myself to make my way to her. And as I did, I forced myself to look left first, to see bikers and other patrons hanging at tables and playing pool, before I looked right.

The right sweep included seeing Deke had turned toward me. His eyes were making a descent of my body, and as I walked, they hit the bottom and came back up.

He looked at my face.

Then he turned to the guy with the ball cap.

My stomach sank, and not for the first time I cursed the poet's soul my father gave to me because this didn't feel like that guy who you were attracted to not being attracted to you.

For a poet, something like that happening with a man like that was the end of the world.

I looked different, it was true. It wasn't just that seven years had passed (though they had). In that time, I'd embraced a variety of fashion options before I settled on the one I liked (or, I should say, my mom and I settled on it, since Joss was my stylist and this not just because she was my mom who would naturally have input into that kind of thing, but because she was my *stylist*).

Now my look was one that was not like the miniskirt, tank top, teased-out hair, rocker/biker vixen version of me Deke had met.

This meant I was in a long, flowing slip dress embellished with matte gold sequins in zigzags and diamonds, back gone completely to my waist, held up by double straps on each side that crisscrossed. The back of the dress was hot, though, but the front gave awesome cleavage.

My dark brown hair was mostly down, some of its thick curls loose and hanging to my waist, some hanging in braids, the top front twisted back in a messy way from my forehead.

I had on lots of jewelry, mostly necklaces, bangles at my wrist, earrings in the five holes I had curving up the shell of each ear, and also a jingling ankle bracelet.

Last, on my feet, flat gladiator sandals.

70's pinup was right.

I looked like an advertisement for Free People clothing.

Which was how I liked it.

So I looked different seven years down the road.

But it still hurt he didn't remember me.

I got to the middle of the bar, the only place with stools available that was far from Deke, and I slid up on one. I dropped my phone and fringed suede bag on the bar in front of me.

When I did, I was surprised to see petite 70's pinup with the loud, foul mouth was standing in front of me wearing her tight Harley tank over large breasts and a big pregnant belly.

"Yeah, I'm pregnant," she announced tetchily and my gaze shot from her stomach to her eyes. "Lexie poppin' out kids here, there and everywhere. Faye doin' it. Emme knocked up, though I got there before her. Bubba caught the bug. What am I supposed to do?" she asked belligerently—seriously and visibly pissed at me even though I hadn't said a word. "I love the guy and he melts like a pussy the instant he's in an infant's presence. Forget about it with a toddler he can actually play with. He's *gone*. Always volunteering our asses to babysit. Up in my face, '*Please*, my cloud. I'm *beggin'* you, Krys. Let's make a baby.' So tell me. I love him, what do I do?" she demanded to know.

"You get pregnant," I guessed hesitantly.

"Yup," she snapped, leaning in. "Knocked up. Too fuckin' old to be luggin' this around." She circled her belly with a hand in a way that was vastly different than the bewilderingly honest, deep and pissed-off ranting she was aiming at me. "Barfin' mornin', noon and night. My tits hurt. My head hurts. My feet are swollen. Gotta pee all the time and that includes gettin' up from the toilet after just peein'. Hadta get an entire new wardrobe I'm *never* wearin' *again* 'cause once this kid slides outta me, they're goin' right back up there and tyin' my tubes."

Having taken in the Harley tank, I was wondering what her old wardrobe consisted of when another voice sounded.

"Krys, no. Baby, what you talkin' about?"

My startled gaze slid up to a man who was suddenly there. He was as big as Deke, not as solid, a little bit older, light-brown hair, good-ole-boy eyes, thus a lot more jovial looking.

He was rounding the petite "Krys" with both arms from the back and curving his body at his height to disastrous levels in order to shove his face in her neck, his hands spanning the sides of her protruding belly.

Even with his face in her neck, I still heard him say, "We can't have just one kid. She's gotta have a brother or sister. Least one."

"Bubba, I'm thirty-nine years old," the pregnant woman snapped.

Bubba pulled his face out of her neck, tipped his head back, and with twinkling eyes and carefully pressed together lips, he winked at me.

She was not thirty-nine.

I gave him a stretched down mouth "your-woman-is-freaking-me-out" face.

He lifted up, didn't let his woman go, and burst out laughing.

At this point, extremely belatedly, I noticed the main entertainment behind the bar were not the only entertainment behind the bar.

Another man was there, tall, dark-haired, bearded, standing closer to where Deke and the guy with the ball cap were, leaning his narrow, jeans-clad hips against the back of the bar, grinning at the couple before me with an expression on his face like he was watching two kittens wrestling.

He was vaguely familiar.

He was also smoking *hot*.

"What you drinkin', gypsy?" I heard asked, and I tore my gaze off the hot guy down the way to look at the man who was clearly Bubba of Bubba's.

"Champagne," I answered, and to this, the woman called Krys bafflingly threw up her hands.

"Champagne?" she asked and took a step toward me, taking her out of her man's arms. She flicked only one hand high that time before she dropped it and asked, "Girl, what's this place look like to you? Unless I didn't feel it and the entire bar was picked up and transported to Manhattan, Sarah Jessica Parker has done left the building because the bitch never stepped one of her high heels *in* the building and never would."

"Krys, we have champagne," a rough, deep voice said from down the bar.

I glanced that way.

Tall, dark, hot guy was entering the conversation.

"Yeah, but we don't got glasses," she shot back to hot guy and looked to me. "And I'm not openin' a bottle of champagne only for you to drink one glass, no one touches it for the next night or three or three hundred and seven so I gotta dump that shit down the drain and lose money. I don't lose money. You want champagne, you drink it in a regular glass and buy the whole damned bottle."

"Deal," I stated.

"I'll get it," Bubba said instantly.

The woman named Krys narrowed her eyes at me, did a sweep of my head, hair and upper body, then her eyes got squinty.

"Your look don't say champagne."

"That's because it normally says beer or bourbon but I have something to celebrate."

"Babe, the troops been out of Vietnam for entire *decades*," she sniped.

I decided not to explain that her hair might be a different facet of that decade, but she shared something with me.

"She gets touchy when she's on her feet for a while," that rough, deep voice came back and I looked toward it to see he was close and tossing a beer mat in front of me. He then turned and grabbed a milky-glassed, oft-washed, possibly purchased in Krys and my fashion inspiration decade wineglass from the back of the bar, turned back and set it on the mat.

"Tate, do not speak about me like I'm not even here," Krys bit out.

He looked down at her. "Krys, you're makin' Twyla look downright friendly."

Her lips thinned.

I braced at the same time wondering who Twyla was and hoping I didn't ever meet her.

The champagne cork popped.

And with that distraction, I gave up the struggle, looked all the way right and saw that Deke was still at his place at the end of the bar, back now to me, attention not on the guy with the cap but across the space.

I looked where his attention was aimed and saw a mini-skirted biker babe leaned over the pool table, ready to take a shot, ass aimed Deke's way with a purpose.

God, he didn't only not remember me, he had no interest in me.

God.

"You're usually beer and bourbon," Bubba started and I jerked my gaze back to him.

I noticed he was pouring my champagne.

Krys was looking toward Deke.

The man called Tate was studying me.

I swallowed.

"Then what's with the champagne?" Bubba finished.

"About an hour ago, I closed on a house," I shared.

Krys turned her glare back to me. Bubba smiled huge. Tate kept studying me.

"Well, shit, woman, that's a celebration. Welcome to the neighborhood!" Bubba cried, lifting the bottle of champagne in a salute before he set it down by my now-filled glass.

"If you want, you can all share it with me," I offered, tipping my head to the bottle.

"Do I look like I can suck back a glass of champagne?" Krys clipped.

"No. Though you act like you need one," I retorted to Bubba's choked-back guffaw and Tate's lips twitching. "But I wasn't offering it to you. I was offering it to the guys."

"On-duty, darlin'. But thanks for the offer," Bubba said.

"Sweet, but I'm not a champagne kinda guy," Tate put in. "And I second what Bubba said. Welcome to the neighborhood."

I nodded to him.

With one last look at me, he wandered away.

I looked back to Bubba and Krys who were now attached with Bubba's arm around her shoulders.

"So, just sayin', good news," Bubba noted. "Not a lotta folk been movin' here past few years. Lotta folks been movin' *out*, not a lot movin' in. Nice to have a fresh face around."

"And a new ass to sit on a stool," Krys put in. "That crazy lumber guy in Gnaw Bone, hirin' hits, kidnappin' people and shootin' folk. Dalton, our own personal serial killer. Fuller and his pig cops keepin' everyone under their thumbs, framin' Ty for murder, extraditing his ass to LA to rot in prison for five years."

I was blinking rapidly at all her words, but Krys didn't notice.

She was still talking.

"Thought we hit enough extreme to last a lifetime, then we had those lunatics who lost their shit thinkin' it'd be exposed and buryin' Faye alive. Bigger lunatic church lady holdin' those two poor kids hostage in her basement for years. And if that wasn't bad enough, then came those fuckin' crazy teachers brainwashing kids into robbin' houses. All a' that goin' down, no one wants near Carnal, Gnaw Bone or Chantelle. It's the fuckin' Bermuda Triangle of the Rockies."

I'd thankfully stopped blinking but I knew I had my mouth hanging open, I just didn't have it in me to close it.

Real estate agent Joni hadn't shared *any* of that with me.

That house didn't sell for ten months because it was over-priced and incomplete.

Serial killers? Hired hits? Brainwashed kids?

A woman *buried alive?*

What the fuck?

At least it brought to mind how I knew that Tate guy. He'd been on the news about that serial killer.

I just didn't recall that all happened in Carnal.

Until now.

"Don't worry, girl," Bubba said, leaning himself and Krys toward me. "Been least a year since any of that kinda shit's gone down."

It would need to be two years. Better, three. Even better, twenty.

"I'm Bubba," he stated, jerking a beefy mitt my way.

I took it and shook it and let go.

"This here's Krystal, regulars call her Krys," Bubba went on.

"And you'll be a regular 'cause unless you wanna drive twenty miles to Gnaw Bone, only place to get beer and bourbon is Bubba's. You with me?" Krys shared her invitation in a way that was more a command that I be a customer.

I nodded since that was the only thing I thought prudent to do.

"Man gave you the glass, he's Tate Jackson." Bubba jerked his head Tate's (and Deke's) way. "End of the bar, you'll always find company with Jim-Billy. Spirit moves him, you'll also find it with Deke."

I suppressed my intake of breath.

"Happy to introduce you around," Bubba offered.

I didn't want him to introduce me around seeing as that round of introductions would include Deke.

"I'll take you up on that offer," I said, wrapping my hand around my glass and lifting it. "After I get a little of this in me."

"You got it, darlin'," Bubba replied on a smile, gave Krystal a squeeze and then moved down the bar.

Krystal kept staring at me.

"Didn't say your name," she noted.

I wondered if she'd figured out who I was with the way she was now staring at me. Some people did. Most people, luckily, didn't.

"Jus—" I cut myself off.

"Jus?" she asked when I didn't continue.

I nodded since that was true. Lots of folks shortened my name to Jus and friends and family called me Jussy.

"Jus," she stated like she wanted it confirmed.

"It's short for something, nickname. Prefer it." That last was a lie.

But new house, new town, new bar, new life.

And if they knew my real name, they'd put two and two together a lot faster. There'd be time enough for that to come out.

Now was just not that time.

Now was the time for me to just be *Jus*.

And anyway, if they mentioned me to Deke, he might remember me (maybe).

I didn't want that anymore. I wanted to go my way and do my best not to see Deke at all.

I did want to know older guy with a ball cap. And Krystal and Bubba were seriously crazy, but I'd known crazier and at least they weren't boring and Bubba was very friendly. Not to mention, he didn't hang around long, but Tate seemed to be a good guy. Strangely watchful, but when you'd run down a serial killer that worked at your bar, I figured that shit happened.

And I'd closed on my house. It was time to find my peace, my privacy, my place, my less that's more than I needed.

But in that less is more, I'd need people. Everyone needed at least *some* people and I was part of that everyone.

And these people resided in my peace, my place, my less that's more.

So I'd take them.

CHAPTER TWO

No Big Deal

Justice

MY PHONE RINGING woke me, and blurry-eyed and clumsy, I reached out to grab it from the nightstand, bring it to my face and stare at the display.

No name, so not programmed in, but the number was local.

I looked at the time on my phone.

Quarter past eight.

Jesus, who called this early?

Since the number was local, and therefore not someone I was avoiding, I took the call.

"'Lo," I answered in a mumble.

"Justice?" a gravelly-voiced man asked.

The voice was familiar, and if I was more awake, I could call it up.

Unfortunately, it was way too early so I couldn't call it up.

"Yes, sorry, you are?" I asked, pushing up to a forearm in the bed.

"Max. Holden Maxwell. You've got a deposit down on some construction work with me," he answered.

Shit. Max. Holden Maxwell. Hot guy number one I'd met in these Colorado mountains.

And that number was quickly growing. It was like there was something in the water or a local secret where, if you journeyed out, you had to vow not to share their bounty and sign that contract in blood or they could hunt you down and kill you. Even with serial killers, kidnappers and people being buried alive, the hot guy quotient would negate that and women would be flocking to those tall, rocky hills.

"Yes, Max, sorry, of course," I said, and went on to explain my rudeness, "I'm not a morning person."

When he replied, he sounded like he had a smile in his voice (and I'd noted in our meeting where I engaged him to finish the work that he was a pretty happy dude on the whole, in a tall, dark and hot way, of course), "Sorry, Justice. But I've got some news that may be good for you and thought you'd wanna know right away to see if you wanna run with it."

Oh God, I hoped one of his clients backed out or delayed or ran out of money.

This wasn't nice to hope but I had a mini-fridge in the garage, one working sink, no on-site laundry, a furnace installed that didn't work (and the nights were getting straight-up chilly) and not much livable space.

I'd been in my house for three days and I was already wondering if I should try to find a local VRBO to rent for a couple of months because I needed space. I needed a washing machine. I needed silverware that wasn't plastic that I got with my takeout that I'd eat sitting in my bed.

What I didn't need was to die of exposure *inside* my newfound oasis because there was no way to turn on my furnace.

But then I'd make coffee in the coffeemaker that sat on top of the mini-fridge in the garage and sit out on my personal deck outside my bedroom and I'd lose all thought of VRBOs.

"I'd love to hear this news, Max," I told him.

"Got a guy who's a temp for me. He's back in town, looking for work," Max replied. "Since he's told me he's in town for a while and he's not scheduled out on any of my other contracts, I could send him to you."

I pushed up to sitting, exclaiming, "Oh my God! That'd be great!"

"He's just one guy, Justice," Max warned. "The progress would be slow, but there'd be progress."

I could be happy with progress. I could make coffee in the garage and clean the pot out in the bathroom sink for a month if I had a working furnace (not to mention a washing machine).

Before I could share that I wanted this dude to start in the utility room (after hooking up my furnace, of course), Max kept talking.

"More good news, this guy does it all. Electrical. Plumbing. Carpentry. I'd have him as a foreman if he wasn't a travelin' man."

This just got better and better.

"Awesome," I said.

The goodness kept coming from Max.

"He's also down with doing overtime. So that progress will definitely progress."

"Hallelujah, God's answered my prayers," I praised the heavens in reply to Max.

Another smile in Max's rocky voice. "Overtime for just a few hours a day, two, three. Hard labor, don't like asking more from my men and they get beat, don't want the work to suffer."

"I'll take it," I accepted instantly.

"Gotta pay that overtime, Justice. And it's you that has to approve it since it's your money I'll be payin' him."

"Consider it approved."

"Great," Max said. "I've got some time late this morning, so does he. Wanna meet him there, show him around. He wasn't on the build when we started it so I gotta give him the lay of the land. Also gotta tell you, there's gonna be roadblocks he's gonna hit because he can do a lot but there's stuff at your place that'll be multiple-guy jobs. That said, he comes up to hitting that, he knows the job well enough he can give me a heads up and I can see if I can adjust some schedules to get guys out to your site so they can do what they gotta do to keep him moving."

"I'd be so appreciative," I gushed. "Really, Max. This is awesome."

"You good with us being there around ten, ten thirty?"

"Absolutely."

"Right, we're set. See you then."

"See you then, Max. And thanks again."

"Not a problem, Justice. Later."

"Later."

I dropped my phone to my lap and smiled at the blank wall across the vast space from my bed.

Finally, things were looking up.

On that thought, earlier than I'd done since I'd had to do it for press tours, I threw back the covers and shot out of bed in order to go make coffee in my garage and get a shower.

* * *

I was out on the deck, wearing my beat-up, too big but super-comfy overalls. I'd paired these with a tight, army-green tank. And my hair I'd decided not to wash was up in a massive messier-than-usual messy bun at the top of my head (meaning lots of long tendrils were hanging down and I didn't bother to secure them).

I was enjoying cup of coffee number three, the quiet and the view, when my phone sitting on the arm of my Adirondack chair rang (the chair I was in, painted a distressed sedate yellow, the one opposite, a mellow, deep purple—the first furniture purchase in my life and I'd done it before I'd even closed because I'd fallen in love, they rocked!).

I looked at the screen and hesitated not even a second before taking the call.

"Lacey!" I cried.

"Yo, babe," Lacey replied. "What's shaking?"

"Absolutely nothing," I answered, finding myself in that moment weirdly (or perhaps not so weirdly) glad this was true.

"So Bumfuck, Colorado is working for you," she noted.

"So far, mostly. Just got news the construction to finish the house will start six weeks sooner so now that mostly is even more mostly," I shared.

"Awesome, Jussy."

"How's the tour?" I asked.

"Insane. But good. We rocked LA last night and it was a blast. We got four days off in a few weeks, thought I'd fly out to Bumfuck and spend it with you."

"Oh…my…God! My great day just got better!" I yelled.

There was happiness in her voice when she said, "Love to hear that." Pause, then she went on and the happiness was muted. "Which makes it suck that I gotta tell you that Mav was backstage at my show last night."

Shit.

"Oh, Lace," I muttered, knowing this would not be good.

"Yeah. He was a jackass. Then he became a loud jackass. Then Jiggy had to get security to eject him. This he did after I begged him to go that route, rather than having Mav's ass arrested."

"Shit." I was still muttering, surprised Lacey's manager Jiggy allowed her to talk him into that. Jiggy didn't take a lot of shit and he allowed Lacey to take less (this being *zero*, if he could help it). "What was Mav on about?" I asked, not really wanting to know because I had a feeling I already knew.

"Wanted me to get you off his ass, mostly. But totally whacked, Jussy, if you can believe this, he also wanted me to corroborate that Dana is what him and his demon-from-hell mom think she is. After your dad's money. Told me he was gonna hunt down Bianca and get that shit from her too. Considering Dana is a fuckin' angel compared to the demon-from-hell Luna and the Satan's spawn she produced, I told him that shit was not happening. Jus, babe, I hate to tell you this but I figure you already know. Luna's got Mav totally brainwashed. He could be an asshole but this was off the charts. There was none of that okay Mav he could sometimes be in him. It was all her. That's all that's left of him."

She said the words and I automatically shoved them aside because I couldn't even think of this possibility. Outside my mom, he was the only blood family I had that I was even marginally close to.

This was because Joss's family disapproved of her path way before I was born and never jumped on board, even if it made her (for the most part, when she hadn't locked horns with Dad) happy.

Because of this, Joss wasn't super-hot on letting me in their lives when she and Dad had me, so she didn't. I'd never really gotten to know them and the only times I did, when I was older and they saw the merits of having a relationship with me (these not being because they wanted to get to know their grandchild or niece), it had been me who'd made the decision not to get to know them.

As for Dad's family, they were Dad's family. The way they were, the way they'd been for three generations, they were gypsies scattered to the wind.

It wasn't easy keeping in touch with a gypsy.

Luna was nothing to me, except Mav's mom, my dad's second wife, and the woman who taught me the important, but difficult lessons of precisely how *not* to be.

"They're being dicks to Mr. T too," I shared with Lacey. "And he's *this close* to letting Mav fuck up his life."

Lace didn't even hesitate before she advised, "Jus, you should just let Mav fuck up his life too. He's never been cool with you. Not really. Luna's been a downright bitch since before Mav was even born. We know people like that and they aren't worth the effort."

"He's my brother, Lace."

"I know that, Justice, but the terms of your father's will were not a secret. He shared them with you a long time ago. He shared them with Mav too. Your brother is an asshole but he understands the English language."

I felt the slash through my heart at the reminder Dad was gone, something else I was knowingly (and unhealthily) doing my damnedest to set aside.

Dad, gone from this earth. Ash settling into the rich Kentucky dirt where Dana and I had scattered him.

Four months and it felt like yesterday I'd sat with him, laughing and being goofy.

Four months and it felt like an eternity he'd been gone.

And I felt that eternity settle in my bones. If I allowed myself to think about it, it weighed me down.

So I didn't think about it.

I thought about the laughing and being goofy part.

"This is true, but when he shared that with us, Dana was not part of that picture," I pointed out. "And Mav was a little kid."

"Not *that* little. And Dana had been dating him for three years and married him not long after. She was married to him longer than your mom, even, and we both know Joss was the love of his life. Dana knew it too but she gave him good that came from deep in her heart. Your dad was Dana's Joss, and I don't give a shit she's only five years older than you. She treated him that way without all the fighting and bullshit and star-crossed lovers crap your parents never grew up enough to sort out."

I stared at the river rushing past and said nothing.

Even so, I felt a lot.

"Sorry, Jussy," Lacey said softly in my ear, knowing better than even my mom and dad how much I was feeling. "I love you and I'm about you and I always have been. I have zero tolerance for Mav's bullshit because he's not my brother and I've had to watch for years as he shoved it down you and your dad's throats. Your father split his estate three ways, you, Mav and Dana, and as far as I'm concerned, that's more generosity than Mav *ever* earned. But that's what your dad wanted. He was of sound mind when he decided that and everyone knows it, even Mav and Luna. He was also of sound mind when he knew Luna would go after it so he made it that, if any one of you contested his wishes, they'd be blocked out, disinherited, get nothing and their third would be split between the other two."

I drew in breath but just to stay calm. Not because I had anything to say.

It didn't matter, really. Lace wasn't done talking.

"Honestly, with that brother of yours the way he was, I would have considered entering the mindfuck that was trying to get his head straight about two seconds before he made his bed and jumped in. Another fourteen million to keep me flush until I died, that brother of yours, no skin off my nose. You're a saint getting this far. You did what you could do. Let it go."

"First, Lace, I love him. He can be a douche, I know that. But he could also be cool, if he was around Dad or me long enough for the stench of Luna to drift away. So I don't want him to make this huge a fuckup and screw up his life. And second, if I just let it go, it might be construed that I'm after half of his third."

"Jus, damn, girl, nearly thirty mil from your dad's estate on top of the royalties you got coming in and that continuing in perpetuity from Johnny's royalties, even if it's only a third? And this isn't even getting into what your granddad left you, which set you up for life. You don't need another fourteen million and everybody knows it. And, sister, I'll tell you something *else* you already know, you already *were* and that's off your own fucking back, not Johnny's, not Grandpa Jerry's."

It was safe to say I couldn't talk about this anymore.

"Okay, I love you. I miss you. I'm sorry my brother fucked what I'm sure was a show that you *killed*, drop the mic, top *that*. I'm glad you're calling because I love hearing your voice. But can that voice not be talking about this for now?"

"Jus—"

"Gonna try him again, Lace. He's not taking my calls. He won't. He keeps up with what he's doing, it's not like I'm going to leave what I found here and hunt him down. Did that four times in LA before I left to come out here and each of those four times was more unpleasant than the last. Try again, then I'm done and the courts can take care of him," I promised.

She hesitated a moment before she gave in.

"Okay, then I'll let it go."

"Thanks."

"Now we gotta talk about Bianca."

"Shit," I again muttered.

"You hear from her?"

"No. I can't say I've called much either."

This made me uncomfortable. I should have called. But with all that was going down with Dad dying, Dana's grief, mine, buying the house, Mav and Luna's antics, Joss going into a dark space because Dad was gone and she'd lost her adulthood-long partner in constantly messing up the best thing that ever happened to them, I hadn't had time for my girl.

I needed to make time for my girl.

"Concentrated effort," Lace declared. "We don't hear from her, we ask around. We don't hear from that, when I'm out seeing your forest oasis in a few weeks, we'll sort a plan to straighten out her shit."

The upcoming visit from Lace, love.

Straightening out Bianca's shit, not-so-love.

"We might have to sleep in the same bed," I warned.

"Slept with you more nights than any man I've had, won't be a problem," she declared.

The memories that came from that made me smile.

Lacey switched subjects.

"Love for you to be on my tour."

"Maybe closer to the end," I told her because that would be early next year, after Christmas in Colorado in my new (hopefully by then, fully-completed) house. "I'll join you, hit a couple of stops."

Something to look forward to.

A change of scenery at a time that was much more time than I usually gave it that I'd take it.

"What I'm saying, babe, is love for you to be *on my tour*."

I closed my eyes.

"Lace," I whispered.

"All I'm gonna say. You don't do my thing. Not sure you could put on even a single sequin and bust a move with ten dancers behind you. But you'd still kill. You always did. And it's safe to say, lotta folks would love to have you back."

"Mm-hmm," I mumbled.

"Think about it," she urged.

"Mm-hmm," I mumbled.

"Pain in my ass," she mumbled back.

"Lace?" I called.

"Yep?" she answered.

"Love you to the sole of my boots."

"Love you to the tip of my stiletto, Jussy. Let you go now. I'll be in touch about dates."

"Can't wait."

"Me either, babe. 'Bye."

"Later, Lacey."

We disconnected and I put the phone down to lift my cooling coffee mug up (one of two I owned, both costing $3.99 on sale at the local grocery store, both having been chipped already as they were super-sized and being washed in a bathroom sink, not my most logical purchase).

I sipped and stared at the river, feeling the nip in the air.

Summer was closing, it was the end of August. The leaves would change. It'd get wet. Then it'd get snowy. Then it's get wet again. Then it'd get warm.

Change of scenery in one place.

God, how had I not seen that was how life could be? Always chasing the horizon. Never realizing, if I stood still, the sun actually came right to me.

On this thought, I heard someone's vehicle approach and I engaged the screen on my phone to see it was ten eighteen.

Max and his man.

Right on!

I pushed up from my chair, grabbed my mug and phone, and walked through the French doors that led to the private deck that jutted off the side of the house. I moved through my bedroom, in which I'd only put a big four-poster bed, two nightstands, a couple of lamps and a dresser. All new, picked for me, approved by me, ordered and arranged to be sent by the interior designer Dana used in Kentucky.

Before I found my forest oasis, I had no furniture because I was me.

I was a Lonesome.

I was a gypsy.

Until now.

I moved out of the finished space into the skeleton of the house, a hall that led to what would be a powder room, the utility room and the garage.

I exited this and hit the main room, thinking how strange it was that I was beginning to long for walls.

It would never have occurred to me that I'd find myself in a place in my life where I'd yearn to be closed in.

Yet I was.

My step in my crocheted flat sandals (you didn't go barefoot in my house, except if you were going to remain in the bedroom) faltered when I looked to the door.

The door had been an early sign this space was going to be mine, it was that magnificent.

The house was made of stone, wood and windows, but mostly windows and stone. The front door was recessed from a graceful stone arch set in another stone arch in which was set a kickass wooded arch and even the door was arched. The wood of the door was painted a distressed, fired-earth green.

The entryway gave an impression you were about to arrive someplace cozy, snug and mountainy. Not over three thousand square feet of house but somewhere you'd sit fireside with a glass of wine or eventually be handed a stick on which to put a marshmallow so you could make a s'more.

The door also had an arched window with what looked like antique glass, the waves distorting what lay beyond, even as you could see it.

And what I saw was not Holden Maxwell.

It was a wall of chest in a white T-shirt that at a glance, without having clairvoyance ever in my life (except when I was six, met Luna, saw through her fawning over me and knew she was going to be a bitch), I still somehow knew was Deke.

I kept moving, thinking my God or no god could be so mischievous as to play with me like this, making Deke the "travelin' man" temp that Max would make a foreman at his company if he just stuck around.

Bubba was a big guy too. Tate was no slouch, same with Max.

Maybe in the mountains they made them huge.

So maybe it was another guy.

But as I opened the door and looked up, I saw that my God was feeling just that frisky.

It was Deke.

Fuck.

He looked at me and his head twitched slightly.

I looked at him wondering if I should have found a forest oasis in Oregon.

"Yo," he greeted.

"Hey," I pushed out.

"Max not here yet?" he asked.

"No," I answered.

He looked beyond me, his head twitched again, then he looked again to me. "You're the woman who came into Bubba's."

I was also the woman he'd stood up at a dude ranch.

I didn't remind him of this fact.

"Yeah, uh…Jus," I introduced myself. Juggling phone and mug, I stuck out a hand.

He stared at it like he'd never been offered a handshake before he finally took my hand in his, gave a firm squeeze and let it go.

"You're Max's guy," I stated.

"Deke," he replied.

I nodded, my mind in a jumble.

I lived there but I knew no one.

Sure, days ago at Bubba's, after Deke had left his position at the end of the bar to make a successful approach to the biker babe (I knew it was successful because they left together fifteen minutes later, not something that put an added shine on my celebration, like, *at all*), Bubba had introduced me to Jim-Billy. He'd also introduced me to Nadine, another regular at the bar. And last, a woman named Lauren came in and I'd found she was Tate's wife when I was introduced to her as well.

All nice people, but in our time, even if this time was hours and included alcohol consumption, they had not become BFFs.

Deke, fortunately by that time, was gone.

But at that moment in my life, I had that shell of a house and not much else. I didn't have friends to hang with, things to go out and do. I'd bought my house but I hadn't really started my new life.

And now it would seem that Deke would be in that house, day in, day out, for weeks, working on it.

With me there.

Yeah, God was feeling frisky and the blank way Deke was staring at me, I knew this was *very* frisky.

I stared back, thinking, in Wyoming, he only gave me a minimal spark. The drink, our brief discussion and him asking me out for a ride were the only ways I knew he was into me.

Now there was nothing. Not even words.

Finally, he gave me words.

"Max is gonna show me around but could take a look before he gets here, you let me in."

God, I was staring up at him mute and barring the door. And he'd been staring back, mute, waiting for me to get out of the way.

Shit.

"Right, of course," I murmured, stepping back and to the side.

He moved in, ducking his head slightly to do so.

The door wasn't small, it was normal height.

Deke just wasn't.

He moved in to about the place I'd stopped dead to look at the space when I'd first entered it and he did just that.

Stopped dead.

Then he muttered, "Jesus."

I left the door open and headed his way, coming to a stop not very close, and agreed, "I know."

He didn't look at me but approached the stack of drywall, inspected it, glanced around and finally gave me his attention.

"Gonna need at least ten times this for this job," he stated.

"There's more in the garage."

Though, that being so, I didn't think there was ten times more. As far as I could see, there was another stack about that height.

He didn't nod or anything, just moved to the pile of wood flooring. He studied it briefly before heading to a blanketed cabinet.

He pulled back the blanket to expose a few inches of the wood and mumbled, "Custom-build."

I said nothing because he knew it was and so did I.

He wandered to boxes of grout, tile, and I watched, trying to figure out a way to get out of this.

I couldn't tell Max I didn't want Deke doing the work because I had no reason to do that. I could ask that he switch Deke out for another guy on one of his other jobs but I had no reason to do that either. And Max and I both knew I needed the work done so I couldn't back out and say I'd wait for the full team.

I was stuck.

Stuck with days in, days out of a man who moved me with one meeting then stood me up and didn't remember me working in my house.

"Hey."

The voice came from my front door and I turned to see Max walking in, hand wrapped around a travel mug, smile on his handsome face, and I was not surprised I was so deep in my thoughts I didn't even hear his truck approach.

"You got here before me," he said to Deke.

"Yep," Deke agreed to the obvious.

Max looked at me. "Hey, Jus—"

"Jus!"

It was not loud but not normal level either, it was quick and it sounded desperate.

It was all this because, in front of Deke, I couldn't have Max calling me Justice and maybe reminding Deke we'd met, something I had not done.

I pulled it together and said, "Jus. Or Jussy. Sorry, that's what friends call me."

Max gave me a funny look before he shook it off and replied, "Right. Cool. Jus. Good to see you again."

"You too."

I shoved my phone in my overalls pocket as Max approached to shake my hand.

I shook his and he noted, "So you've met Deke."

"Yeah." It was my turn to agree to the obvious.

"Great," Max said and looked to Deke. "Told you it was a big job, man."

Deke didn't agree to this assessment.

He stated, "Weather's gonna turn. She needs insulation. She got a furnace?"

Max nodded, heading toward Deke. "She's got one, AC too, ducts in. Been months, Deke, think they're good but need you to go over them and install the thermostats."

"Insulation first," Deke returned.

Max shook his head. "Got that equipment working at the Porter place next couple of days. It'll be free on Thursday."

"Can't drywall without it, Max. And she needs the walls up," Deke retorted.

Max looked to me. "Got a choice, Ju...uh, Jus," he started. "We recommend that you blow foam insulation in and that's what's on your job spec. Lasts longer, works better, keeps utility bills down, doesn't settle or need replacement as quickly, keeps rodents and bugs out, doesn't hold water. Deke's right, we were ready to spray the foam in before this build came to a halt. Deke can sort out your furnace but not much more he can do until the insulation is in. You want him to start, we can get cellulose or fiberglass but it's not recommended."

"Work on the deck."

Both Max and I turned to see Deke had moved to stand at the big window where the kitchen would someday be.

When he had our attention, he kept his on Max and declared, "Not a priority but she's got the lumber somewhere, can get that going. Spend today inventorying what she's got here, make sure it's what she wants and it's enough. We need more, you get on that. Something she doesn't like, she works with Mindy to order it so we got it when we get to it. Spend the rest of the time after I get heat sorted out until the equipment is free on the deck. Weather turning and if we have a rough winter, that deck might not get done until spring."

Max moved his way, speaking. "On the plans, there's an outside fire pit meant to be built in stone, up the middle of the deck. Got a gas line laid to it, but plan has it multi-functional, gas and wood burning. Stone's under a tarp outside. So is the lumber, if a miracle happened and no one got to it while this house was sitting, waiting to be sold."

That miracle happened. I'd seen those stacks outside.

Thank God.

"Got the plans?" Deke asked.

"In my truck," Max answered.

"Right, won't be a problem. Show me the rest?" Deke prompted.

"Let's move," Max replied.

I stood there feeling like I wasn't there until Max caught my eyes and grinned at me when they were going to move by me.

Deke didn't even look at me.

"Uh, can I just say…?" I called when they'd almost hit the doorframe to the hall.

Both men stopped and looked at me.

"I'm happy for anything getting done but when work starts inside the house, can I get my utility room first?" I requested.

Another grin from Max. "Women and laundry."

I gave a slight shrug. "What can I say? We can't recycle clothes like dudes can, turning them inside out and wearing them again."

Max chuckled.

Deke stared at me, expressionless.

"Once the insulation is in and we got your furnace running, Deke'll give you a utility room," Max agreed.

"Awesome," I said on a bright smile I hoped didn't look *too* forced.

Max lifted his chin, turned away and disappeared through the doorframe.

Deke just looked away and disappeared through the doorframe.

As for me, I stood there and stared at the empty doorframe.

Right, this was happening.

I met a guy who asked me out and stood me up and now I'd met him again and he didn't remember me.

Whatever.

It was not a big deal.

Sure, I'd written a song for him. I'd recorded it. I'd released an album with that song on it. It and the whole album had been critically acclaimed, sold relatively well and nominated for awards.

So what?

He didn't know that.

He didn't know me, the me he asked out or the me I turned out to be.

Now he was going to install my deck, inventory the stuff in my house, blow insulation in my walls, make my furnace work and give me a utility room.

No big deal.

I had bigger things happening in my life.

Deke Whoever-He-Was and the fact he was totally immune to me was not one of them.

I'd learned one thing in my life really well.

How to move on.

My dad was dead and I'd made the decision to move on.

So I was moving on.

* * *

Two hours later, I stood in one of the minimal open spaces left in my packed-full garage and watched Deke set a box on top of an alarmingly large stack of boxes he'd shifted aside as we'd gone through the stuff that was there.

Prior to putting in the offer on the house, I'd had a look, but not knowing what was what or where it would go, I obviously didn't look closely.

Now that I'd lived in the house and we'd gone through things thoroughly, that large stack of boxes was fixtures and fittings I'd nixed.

This was because the stuff chosen for the Jack-and-Jill bathroom was dire. The guest suite bathroom stuff was uninspired. And I had an entirely different vision that was far more dramatic for what I wanted for backsplashes and countertops in the kitchen.

Deke turned to me.

"Didn't use it. They'll take it back, 'specially since you'll be gettin' more and buyin' more," he announced.

I would assuredly be getting more and *buying* more. The assertion that all that was needed was included with the property because it was housed within the property was not true.

This I knew beforehand as Max had already warned me more materials would be needed prior to me signing the papers not only with him to do the job, but to buy the house (one of the reasons I got the price I wanted on the house).

Just how much more I needed was a surprise, even though Max had called what was needed "significant."

"You know Mindy?" Deke asked, taking me out of my thoughts.

"The lady that works in Max's office?" I asked back, for I did know that Mindy since I'd met her when I'd gone in to talk to Max about finishing the job.

"Yeah, part-time and not normal. She's got another job but Max's regular woman is out on maternity. Instead of getting a temp who don't know dick and messes everything up, since Mindy worked there before gettin' her degree, she's helpin' out."

His sharing this with me was surprising, considering for the last two hours since Max left his conversation was minimal as he studied plans, opened boxes, counted stuff, measured stuff, got a ladder from the garage, brought it in and wandered around upstairs, told me where the materials were meant to be used, this last being the extent of his conversation.

It hit me that this was his way of saying that it wasn't normal operating procedure at Max's office, so I could not assume someone would be at my beck and call and thus I'd need to deal.

He was looking out for his employer who was also, obviously with the way I'd noted they interacted, a friend.

This said good things about him.

"You call her, she's got brochures," he continued. "You can go in, look at 'em, decide what you want and she'll do the orders. She also knows the places you can go to look at tile, stone, slabs, whatever. Make your choices, tell her, she'll get it in. Yeah?"

I nodded my acceptance of this.

"I'll let Max know he's gotta deal with these returns," he stated and jerked his head to the stack of rejections.

"That'd be great," I replied.

He said nothing to that. He simply grunted, "Furnace."

Apparently, it was time for him to get to his next order of business.

"Right, yeah. Furnace. Good," I mumbled. "Nights are getting a bit chilly."

As mentioned, this was the truth. I was glad Dana's interior designer had sent a down comforter with all the bedclothes I'd chosen. It kept me cozy. But I was still thinking about hitting the local mall Lauren had told me about to get an electric blanket. It had to drop twenty, thirty degrees at night and I was feeling that.

Deke again had no comment, just moved my way.

"Do you want me to make a pot of coffee for you?" I indicated the mini-fridge I was standing in front of, on top of which was a small, four-cup Mr. Coffee. "I also have bottled water in the fridge," I went on to share. "Yogurt, fruit, not much else. You're welcome to any of it."

"Need caffeine, take a break, go into town, get it from Shambles," he muttered as he moved by me, through the door and into the house.

He didn't hold the door for me and so it closed behind him.

I stood where I was, looking at the closed door, wondering if perhaps it had been a good thing he'd stood me up seven years ago.

He wasn't full of conversation. He was brusque when he actually did say something. And he was kind of rude.

However, he was still the man who'd rocked me, closed off in a way I wanted to put in the effort to open him, and I liked the way he moved. His hair was a lot longer so now he didn't wear it in a ponytail but an unkempt man-bun at the back of his head. And his cheeks and jaw weren't covered in stubble but a full beard.

It didn't matter, none of it did.

I was a job to him, nothing else, he'd made that clear.

Whatever drew him to me seven years ago was long gone.

I had a feeling I knew what it was, no longer mini-skirted and nursing a drink at a biker bar.

He was of his people. I was not his people. Then, he didn't know that. Now, it was clear he did.

So be it.

It wasn't like I hadn't been around hot guys I was attracted to who were either taken or weren't taken with me.

I'd been wrong. He wasn't the only man who mattered in my personal universe.

He was just Deke, the guy who was now going to make progress on my house so when the team could come and finish the job, they had less to finish.

That was it.

I walked to the door, opened it and moved through, these being my thoughts.

These and the fact I was doing my best to tamp down the feeling that, ridiculously and way-too-keenly to be comprehensible or even logical, those thoughts hurt.

* * *

Deke

Deke Hightower sat in the low, folding deck chair in the grass, his long legs stretched out, his hand wrapped around a bottle of beer, his eyes on the glassy surface of the small lake in front of him that looked now like a mirror but would soon color with oranges and yellows. Then pinks and purples. Then blues.

Until there was dark cut only by shards of silver.

And he sat there thinking that he had no idea how any woman who had a body like the woman who called herself Jus would wear bulky overalls, the only thing making them worthwhile being that tight tank and the glimpse of skin you could see inside at the hip, which also included a glimpse of her panties.

Right, so there was that, the glimpse of skin. Smooth. Tan. Nice.

"Fuck," he muttered to the lake, lifting his beer and taking a sip.

Then again, down all hippie and messy and parts braided, or up in a jumble with bits of it hanging, the woman had a serious shit ton of hair and hair like that meant she could wear anything and a man's thoughts still would be consumed with what he could do with that hair.

Deke took another sip, not letting those thoughts consume him, and repeated, "Fuck," as he lowered his beer.

He had to work on her house. He just had to hope she had a lot more ridiculous clothes to put on that would put him off while he was doing it.

Didn't matter. The bitch was loaded. Her bullshit beat-up truck that was sitting outside her fucked-up house—a truck she bought because it was cool and she thought it augmented her style, not because she couldn't afford anything else—couldn't hide the fact that she was rolling in it.

Her crazy-ass clothes didn't hide it either.

He knew what a house like that cost, especially on the land it was on, even if it wasn't finished.

He also saw the plans and knew how much more she was pouring in it.

After getting her furnace sorted and taking a look at the deck, deciding how to tackle it the next day, he'd left and she hadn't given him a key or told him she'd be out to work the next day so they'd have to figure out how he could gain access to her place in the morning.

She'd just said, "See you tomorrow, Deke."

He'd watched her say that as she was closing the door on him to close herself in the fucked-up house she'd bought, and not for the first time he'd been unable to shake the feeling he'd looked into those big brown eyes before.

That didn't matter either.

Out of his league. Even if he wanted to go there (and being essentially his boss, he wasn't going to go there, he'd learned that lesson all too well), he wouldn't go there.

He didn't need her shit. Didn't need to feel less when it was obvious she could give herself more.

What he needed was a job. His resources were running low. It didn't take him a lot to get by but it was coming time when weather could not be assured he could jump on his bike whenever he felt the need to take off. This meant it had come to the time where he settled in Carnal, got a job and made some cash so when the weather turned, he could jump on his bike whenever he felt the need to take off.

It would not suck, shoving his hand down those overalls to trace with his fingers the lace he saw of her panties. This being before he took those fucking ugly things off.

But that wasn't going to happen.

Deke knew her kind and he'd learned a long time ago not to go there.

He set her out of his thoughts and stared at the lake, thinking about her deck and the fire pit, which, once done, were going to be dead cool, just like the rest of the house.

A house Deke knew was not a place he'd ever belong.

And he watched the mirror of the lake turn yellow and orange, pink and purple and then blue.

When it was blue, he got up, walked to his Airstream, climbed in, closed the screen behind him and started dinner.

CHAPTER THREE

Bounty

Justice

LOUD BANGING ON my door made me open my eyes.

I blinked, rolled, reached out, missed the nightstand, shoved forward, tagged my phone and engaged the screen.

The banging continued.

I stared at my phone.

It was ten to seven.

In the morning.

What the fuck?

The banging stopped only to start again.

"Goddammit," I muttered angrily, tossing back the covers, feeling the violent hit of the chill of the early morning and ignoring it to throw my legs off the side of the bed.

I reached down to the floor to grab the wool socks I'd worn to bed (because the down didn't kick in for a while and last night it had gotten super-chilly, then the comforter kicked in and I'd had to take them off). I yanked them on and nabbed the big, bulky, loose-knit cardigan at the end of the bed that I'd thrown on last night when it started to get cold.

I pulled it on as I stomped out, the banging stopping. But I kept motoring toward the front door even if I was in my PJs under the sweater, which meant a cropped tank top and pair of baggy but clingy silk short-shorts that had flowered embroidery up the hips.

I tore my hand through my hair as I saw a white T-shirt at the door and suddenly I was not one with the idea that Deke Whoever-He-Was was not the only man in the universe for me.

Suddenly, I was *ticked off* that Deke Whoever-He-Was had not felt the same as me yonks ago in Wyoming, which meant we'd spent the ensuing time together and he knew I stayed up until earliest midnight and never got out of bed before nine.

Which was what I'd done last night, reading in my cold as fuck bedroom until two in the morning.

I unlocked and yanked open the door just as the pounding started again.

"Okay, okay," I snapped, looking up at hot, man-bunned, colossal, alert Deke, a Deke who was so hot, the man bun worked so well on him, was so big and so… *Deke*, I didn't notice his eyes take a quick journey south upon my opening the door. I just declared, "I'm up. What the hell?"

His brows shot together and his attention cut to my face. "What the hell?"

"Yes, what the hell?" I asked.

"Woman, I'm here to work on your house," he informed me.

"I know that, Deke," I returned. "But it's not even seven in the morning."

"Hours seven to four," he stated shortly, something I vaguely remembered Max mentioning to me during our meeting. "For you, since you want overtime, seven to six. It's seven."

"It's *ten* to seven," I shared.

"It's as good as seven," he shot back. "You want me to show right at seven, whatever. I'll do that tomorrow. Now I'm here."

"Yes, and the here you're here for, it's my understanding, requires work *outside* the house. Not you banging on the door and dragging me out of my bed."

"Can't start work on a property without letting the owner know I'm around."

"Is that a rule?"

"You want me to get on with it without disturbing your beauty rest, I'll do that too. But just sayin', construction ain't quiet."

He had me there.

And I was acting crazy, something I was wont to do on the rare occasion I was dragged out of bed before nine.

But Deke hadn't spent the last seven years learning that about me so I reined it in.

"Point taken," I granted. "Now I know you're here. Go for it. I'll keep the door open if you need anything. Do you want coffee?"

He did a slow blink.

It was hotter than him just standing there which in and of itself was hot enough.

"You bite my head off and ten seconds later offer me coffee?"

A new tone from Deke.

Incredulous.

"I'll be making some, and if you drink it, I can make you some too," I pointed out.

"Had some already."

It was my turn to blink.

"You've been up long enough to make and drink coffee?" I asked.

"There are some of us who live in the real world, gypsy princess," he struck out, his aim true, and I felt the sting of the bite. "Get up. Get juiced up. Go to work. That's what real people do."

"I didn't mean—" I started, my tone conciliatory.

Deke didn't feel like being consoled.

"We done here?" he asked.

"You haven't answered about the coffee."

"Thanks," he clipped, not sounding grateful at all. "I'm good."

He then turned on his work boot and tramped out of the arched entryway, shifted left and I lost sight of him.

As I seemed to do a lot around Deke, I stood in the door where I noticed belatedly the chill from outside was no more chilly than the chill inside and I stared at the place I last saw him.

Okay, so I'd sorted my brain about Deke yesterday, which was good.

Today, it was barely dawn (right, so actually it was past dawn but it seemed barely dawn to me), and I'd already created a situation where I needed to sort different things out with Deke.

"Shit," I muttered as I closed the door.

I moved through the house to get to the garage to start coffee, wondering if I should have turned on the furnace that now had nice, shiny thermostats in three places.

Since I had no insulation, and even rich as sin, I didn't feel like warming the Colorado night around my house along with warming my house, I hadn't.

I'd be glad for insulation.

Which meant I needed to be glad I had Deke because I'd be screwed if I didn't.

Which meant I had to sort things out with Deke.

Shit.

* * *

An hour and a half later, hair wet and hanging down, wearing a dress made of pretty much nothing but cream lace (over a cream shift, of course) that had short sleeves and a shorter hem (this hitting me at mid-thigh) as well as a pair of sky-blue wellies with ladybugs on them, I made my approach to Deke. I was carrying a mug of hot coffee in one hand, a carton of milk in the other, a bag of sugar held against my chest with my arm.

He heard me coming, turned, gave me a once-over, and his usually expressionless face formed an expression.

Irritability.

I'd earned that, being a bitch, so I ignored it.

"Hey," I called as I got close.

He did not return my greeting.

I finished getting close, which was to say stopping four feet from him, doing this a little surprised that the large rectangular fire pit that would eventually be the focal point in the middle of the deck was already constructed to three feet up, rising from the moist earth.

He worked fast.

And it looked good.

I turned my gaze to him.

"I brought you coffee," I shared unnecessarily.

He didn't even glance at my hands.

He also didn't say anything.

"Okay, dude," I started quietly. "Just to say, I'm not a morning person."

"Got that," he grunted.

"Doesn't give me a right to be a shrew," I went on. "I'm sorry about that."

He shifted but only to cross his arms on his chest.

This brought my attention to his chest which was not a healthy place for it to be if I didn't want to blurt out I'd met him years ago, that meeting meant something to me, doing this just moments before I jumped his bones (something

I didn't want to do, because I *did* but he *didn't*), so I looked to his face and that wasn't much better.

I persevered.

"I'll set an alarm from now on."

"Don't tax yourself."

Now, wait.

I'd apologized. I'd brought coffee. I'd been a bitch but I'd explained and now I was being cool.

He needed to meet me halfway.

So I didn't give up.

"Or I can give you a key and you can just," I swung out the mug, "get on with things."

"Whatever way you want it. You're the boss," he returned.

Deke was stubborn.

Damn.

I kept trying.

"I'd like you to be comfortable here."

"Comfortable enough when I'm workin'," he replied.

Which meant he'd be good if I just left him alone.

He wanted it that way, fine. I'd been uncool, apologized for that, he wasn't going to let it go, that wasn't my problem.

He was there to work. He was not there to become my best friend.

"Right," I murmured, turned, saw the stack of wood tarped and bound with thick wires that was sitting up against the side of the house, and I moved there. I put the mug on top, the milk, the sugar, and turned back to him. "There's a spoon in the sugar, you need it. I'll come out and get the stuff later. I won't bother you when I do."

"Obliged," he muttered and turned back to his stone.

I didn't linger.

I got out of there.

An hour later, I went back and the pit was up five feet.

It was going to be awesome.

I grabbed the milk, the sugar and the (I was weirdly pleased to see) empty mug and took it back to the house.

* * *

I listened to my brother's ugly voicemail message again and waited for the beep.

Then I sat at the edge of the seat of my Adirondack chair, leaned over, staring at the toes of my wellies, and left my message.

"You'll be glad to know, but I hope you know how sad I am to say it, that this is the last message you'll get from me. I really want you to do the right thing, Mav. I'm still holding out hope you'll figure out what that is and do it. And I hope that you've got it in you to realize that if Dad was still here, how this would cut him. Straight down to the bone, baby brother. He'd die another death, a more painful one this time, knowing his boy was acting this way to the two women in his life that he loved the most. Please, please, *please*, Maverick, the only person you're hurting is you. I hate that for you. Dad would have hated it for you. So don't do it."

I hit the button to disconnect but I didn't wait that first beat as my thumb moved on the screen to find Bianca's number.

Get all the shit out of the way and move on.

Dad hadn't taught me that, Mr. T had (though, he didn't use the word "shit" since he never cursed).

I hit go and there was no ringing.

Bianca's phone was obviously off. It went right to voicemail.

So I went right to leaving the message.

"Right, so I was freaked, I couldn't get hold of you. Then I got more freaked. Then worried. Now, I'm panicked, Anca. Lace is coming out in a few weeks and I'd love for you to come out too so we can be together and you can fill us in on what's going down with you. Thick and thin. Three Musketeers. You know that, baby, *always*." I even heard the edge of alarm in my voice when I finished, "Let me in, Anc. You know you can give anything to me. *Anything*. I'm here. Always here for you, my beautiful sister. Know it. Anything and *always*."

I hit the disconnect and a second later heard the gruff noise of a throat clearing.

My head shot up and I looked to my right to see Deke standing at the side of the deck, at the top of the steps that led down from there, one hand to the railing, eyes to me.

"Sorry," he muttered. "Thought you heard me comin'."

I gave a short shake of my head and replied, "Not a problem. Everything okay?"

"Pit's as done as it needs to get at this juncture, I'm gonna start on the decking. This means I'm gonna be cutting wood and things are gonna get noisy."

I pushed up to standing. "That's okay. I'm headed to Gnaw Bone to meet with Mindy anyway."

He nodded shortly. "Right."

"Anything I can bring you back?" I asked.

"No," he answered.

I wanted to push it. Offer to bring him a sandwich. Go to whoever Shambles was and get him a coffee. Maybe tell him I'd bring back a pizza we'd both share while he took a break.

Nothing about him invited anything friendly from me and it wasn't just that I'd been a bitch earlier, nothing about him had invited that yesterday either.

So I said, "Okay, then. You want my number in case you need to phone me?"

"I need somethin', I'll call Max."

Definitely didn't want friendly.

"Fine," I said and it came out more curt (or hurt) than I wanted it to.

He didn't miss it. Oh no, he didn't. I knew this with the way his chin jerked slightly to the side and something slid over his features only to vanish before I could read it.

He didn't want friendly, that was okay. If the ticked-off morning bear I could become didn't raise her ugly head, he could not want whatever he didn't want.

I was still going to be friendly.

"You change your mind, I'll be back in a few hours and happy to pick you up a sandwich or get a pizza," I offered. "Just call Max and ask for my number."

He said nothing.

I decided not to roll my eyes or give him a glare.

I just turned on my wellie and walked into my bedroom, calling behind me, "Later, Deke."

I shut the French door behind me seeing he'd already disappeared.

* * *

I sat on my Adirondack chair, bottle of beer resting on the arm, brochures Mindy had given me scattered around, all of them now having Post-it notes sticking out of the tops and sides, but I was scrolling through images on my phone that Dana's interior designer had sent to me.

Reception out there was spotty, which sucked and made anything loading take forever.

I needed cable and Wi-Fi.

Then again, I needed a lot of things.

"Yo." I heard and looked right to see Deke standing at the bottom of the stairs.

I was not thrilled to see that after work, sweat making his shirt cling to his chest, flecks of wood sticking to his tee, he looked better than he did fresh and alert and recently caffeinated in the morning.

"Hey," I greeted.

"Done for the day," he declared.

Still not friendly.

His call.

"Okay, great, thanks."

"Be back at seven," he stated.

"Yes," I replied.

"Gonna be doin' the insulation. You might not wanna be around," he warned.

"Noisy?" I asked.

"That and other things," he kind of answered.

I nodded. "I'll make myself scarce. I'll do whatever for insulation. Nights are getting nippy."

Deke had no comment.

"Enjoy your evening," I bid.

He lifted his chin, turned and walked away.

I wondered about my poet's soul. I was thinking, as I watched him walk away, that it might be faulty, seeing as it was what picked that guy for me.

I gave it some time before I set my phone aside, got up and wandered down the stairs and around the house only to stop and stare.

Except for some minimal decking around the edges, the railing and the finishing touches at the top of the fire pit, the deck was done.

And it looked *amazing*.

It was huge and it was perfect and I loved it.

I also wished I'd seen it before Deke had left so I could tell him that.

I hadn't so I'd have to tell him tomorrow.

Right then, it was time to send an email to Dana's designer.

That deck needed furniture.

I'd also have to talk to Max. I'd be willing to wait another day to be able to do laundry to have that deck done and available to me.

Totally.

* * *

Deke

Deke sat in his chair outside, watching the lake turn orange, his mind not on the lake but on the fact that he wouldn't have to dip too low to find the bottom of Jus's short, lace dress and slide it up over her ass.

These thoughts shifted uncomfortably to her saying, *He'd die another death, a more painful one this time, knowing his boy was acting this way to the two women in his life that he loved the most.*

She had trouble with her brother, some that sounded really not good.

And her dad was dead.

Jus didn't look to be much older than thirty. Either the man had babies late or he'd died young.

Deke's mind barely wrapped around that fact when he heard her voice say, *I'm here. Always here for you, my beautiful sister.*

Something was going down with a sister as well.

Neither of those calls sounded good.

Still, she made them then looked at him, pulled it together and offered to bring him back a pizza.

He thought for certain the way she opened the door to him she was what he thought she was, a fake gypsy princess slumming in the Colorado mountains on millions of dollars' worth of land.

Her offering him a sandwich, wearing that cute-as-fuck dress and stomping around in those ridiculous boots that she looked comfortable in, not like she was missing her high heels, he was wondering if he was right.

"Christ," he bit out, pushed up, went into his trailer and made a bologna and cheese sandwich.

He ate it and went right back out to head to Bubba's.

He did this hoping Jus wasn't there.

At the same time denying he hoped she was.

* * *

Justice

I was in the garage the next morning, staring impatiently at Mr. Coffee as it dribbled brown elixir, when I heard the muted banging.

Deke was there.

I moved into the house, through it and to the front door.

No PJs that morning. I was barely dressed and had had no shower. But I was dressed, awake, and determined not to be a bitch.

I opened the door and looked up.

"Hey," I greeted.

"Hey," he greeted back.

"I'm making coffee," I stated, shifting out of the door to let him in, and he came in while I was still talking. "I'll bring you a mug when it's done. Then I'll hit the shower and get out of here while you get on with things. You want me to come back around noon with food or something?"

He'd stopped inside and was studying me as I spoke.

It took him a couple of beats before he said, "Thanks. No."

"Sure?" I asked.

"I'm good," he answered.

"Okeydoke," I replied, turned and moved back through the house, asking, "How do you take your coffee?"

When he didn't reply by the time I hit the frame of the door to go into the hall, I stopped and turned back.

He hadn't moved except to shift in a way that he was facing me.

"Deke," I prompted.

"Milk, not much, one spoon of sugar."

I grinned at him, said, "Right," and took off.

I brought him his coffee while he was hauling some things in from outside.

As I was setting it down on a blanketed cabinet, he spoke.

"Get as much done as I can, Jus."

My gaze shot to him when he used my name.

"Do my best to get it all," he continued. "Shouldn't be a problem, though can't get the rafters without another man here. Even so, means at night you can fire up the furnace. I tested it earlier. You're not home by the time I take off, I'll set it before I go."

"That would be...that'd be..." Why couldn't I handle him being a decent human being? "That'd be great, Deke. Thanks," I finally got out.

"You got one, leave me a key and your number," he ordered. "I'll lock up before I go, you're not back. Call you if there's anything needs reporting."

I nodded.

He watched me nod then walked right back out the door, presumably to get more stuff.

I smiled to myself as I went to my bedroom, got one of the extra keys Joni had given me on closing, wrote my number on a Post-it and took them back out to set them by his coffee.

"Have fun insulating," I called to him as he walked back in with more stuff and I was walking back to my bedroom.

Apparently reaching the end of his ability to be a decent human being, Deke said nothing.

* * *

I stood in one of the two convenience stores that somehow the small town of Carnal seemed to be able to keep alive and stared, grinning at the cover of *Twang* magazine.

Lacey was on the front. Just Lacey against a gray background, though standing at her right foot was a male peacock, its tail fanned out behind Lace in full glory.

Her stance was wide. Her short but shapely legs oiled. A tiny dress made entirely of a peacock array of sequins barely covering her petite body. Her hair teased high just at the top, falling stick straight down the back. Her hands on her hips like she was Wonder Woman.

At the bottom, next to her silver-sandal-stiletto, it declared,

Lacey Town

Paints Her Tour Peacock

Oh yeah, I was sure she was, seeing as *Peacock*, the title to her latest album as well as her current tour, went platinum the day it released, the tour sold out in ten countries.

I yanked the magazine out of its rack and flipped through until I saw the article.

More pictures of Lacey, posed as well as mid-dance move, mouth open, mic curled around her cheek onstage.

Also one of her with her dad, Terrence Town, drummer and half of the decades-long partnership of songwriters of the still-touring (except in its fifth incarnation), multi-platinum R&B group, Heaven's Gate.

I flipped the page and drew in a sharp breath.

And another photo, with me, after one of my shows five years earlier, our arms around each other, smiling big at the camera, my dad standing close and looking proud, the caption reading, *With longtime friend, acclaimed rock balladeer, Justice Lonesome, and her father, the recently sadly passed legend, Johnny Lonesome, two of the strong line of Lonesomes spawned by the late, great, mythical rock god, Jerry Lonesome.*

I remembered that show. It'd been in Louisville. A smallish venue but a hometown crowd. One of two sold-out, back-to-back nights. The best vibe I'd felt in my life, and there had been some good ones, before and after. But none better.

On top of the world yet sinking down in the mire.

I stared at my father, looking so proud.

Uncle Jimmy and Aunt Tammy both had careers. They were good, still toured, cut records, put themselves out there, made beautiful music that was appreciated by many, ticket sales strong, venues not arenas but nothing to sneeze at.

Neither were as good as Dad. Dad's career rivaled Grandpa Jerry's. Everyone said that. Even Grandpa Jerry before he died, and when he did, he said it with pride.

To the end, Dad was the closing act at festivals, teeming crowds as far as the eye could see shouting the words to his songs back at him. He rocked football stadiums, not arenas, never anything less after he hit with his first album.

Dad did nothing but soar.

Uncle Jimmy and Aunt Tammy also both had kids, but none of them had inherited what they needed to carry on the legacy. My cousin Rudy had tried, and failed, and let it make him bitter which led him off the deep end, so even Aunt Tammy didn't see her son anymore. But he'd expected the name Lonesome (which he'd taken on, his father's name was actually Smith—he was still a Lonesome though), would pave his way.

It hadn't.

That life didn't accept imposters or anyone riding coattails. You might ride for a while, but you had to demonstrate you were the genuine article and had staying power or it'd cut you out so fast, you'd wonder if it was a dream you ever got in.

Dad had been beside himself with happiness I'd entered the life.

He'd been devastated I'd decided to leave it behind.

But he'd let me leave. He'd seen the life chew people up and spit them out, his nephew not being the first, or the last, and after all that had gone down on my tour, he didn't want to see that happen to me.

I had it, though. That's what he said. What the critics said. What the folks who bought my album said. What Grandad said, and that was the good thing.

Granddad got to see me do it before he died.

And I didn't end it until after he was gone.

I closed the magazine, grabbed the rest of them and went up to the cashier with them, my can of WD-40 and my bag of bite-size Baby Ruth bars (the latter the real reason I'd come in, perfect for nighttime munching while reading in bed and not requiring fridge, stove or microwave).

The cashier gave me a look when she saw the magazines.

"Lacey Town fan?" she asked.

"Big time," I answered.

Her next look took in my clothes. It registered surprise, for Lacey was not rock or folk or alternative, she was R&B, like her dad, but the cashier said no more and stuffed my purchases in a plastic bag.

I headed out of the store, hit my truck, dumped the bag and then made the rounds. I had time to kill before I went home and now I had a mission that would kill some of it.

Small grocery store in the middle of the town that did have a magazine rack, but that rack didn't carry *Twang*. All the way down to the other end of town, doing this window shopping, getting used to my new place, I hit that convenience store and went through almost the same conversation with the male cashier as I bought out their *Twang*.

I did this even knowing people would eventually know who I was.

So why I was doing this, I didn't know. It wasn't like I'd window shop every day, hang out in Carnal, become a fixture like Jim-Billy clearly was at Bubba's and have my identity discovered (perhaps) within moments.

But I'd be around. They'd see. And someone would remember me. The cat would get out of the bag, I knew it. And in getting to know the people around me, forming relationships eventually (I hoped), I'd have to come clean.

I just didn't want to be Justice Lonesome for a while.

Just a while.

It'd be soon enough when I had no choice but again to be me.

I was walking back with my plastic bag filled with *Twang* when I noticed the red Camaro I saw parked outside of Bubba's was sitting in a parking spot not outside of Bubba's but outside what looked to be a tailor that specialized in sewing patches on leather (if the plethora of announcements sharing that fact that were taped to the windows all around the door were anything to go by).

I would have ignored the Camaro except it wasn't parked and empty.

A pregnant 70's pinup was sitting behind the wheel, hands wrapped around it, the car not on, her eyes staring vacantly out the windshield.

I passed the front of the car, holding my bag close to my chest with one arm, waving at Krystal with the other hand.

Krystal didn't move. Didn't blink. Even though I walked right in front of her, it was like she didn't see me.

This made me stop and slowly approach, still waving.

Only then did she move, but not because she saw me. Because her head dropped down in a disturbing manner to rest on the wheel between her hands.

Damn, something was wrong.

I thought quick, made a decision, moved to the passenger side and rapped on the window.

"Hey, Krys!" I called.

Her head shot up and she turned it to me.

Mascara running, just beginning, not yet a mess but on its way—she'd dropped her head to start crying.

Shit.

I'd been around her once and you would blow me over with a feather if you'd told me she was a crier.

This did not say good things.

She did not call back a greeting. Instead, her hand went to the ignition.

Shit, *shit*.

I pulled open the door.

She again jerked her head my way.

"What're you doin'?" she demanded to know as I angled my ass into the seat.

I slammed the door and turned to her.

"You okay?" I asked.

"Yeah, I'm okay," she totally lied.

She'd done a quick swipe as I got in, this I knew because she had mascara wings at the sides of her eyes.

"You're crying," I pointed out.

"I don't cry," she retorted.

I looked to her temples and said softly, "I saw you, Krys."

Her lips thinned, probably in order not to confirm or lie again.

I shrugged one shoulder. "You want me to go, I'll go. I get needing your space when something is up. You don't know me very well and I get you wouldn't want to lay anything on me if something is going on that's deep or heavy. But you're also pregnant, upset, you're a sister and I don't want you driving until you're together. So you can take this time to get it together and then I'll leave you alone so you can go where you're going. Or you can take this time to lay it on me and I'll listen and *then* leave you alone."

She stared at me.

I stared back.

Eventually, she snapped, "I'm pregnant."

"I know," I replied.

"Pregnant bitches do stupid shit, like cryin' for no reason."

"I've never been pregnant," I told her. "But I've heard that. Let's just not let you do more stupid shit when you don't have it together and you're behind a wheel."

"I can drive my own ass home," she declared crabbily.

"I've never been in a car with you so I don't know that for certain, but I'm guessing it to be true. Still, I think I need about another two minutes of you being nasty for me to know you're all good so I can let you drive home."

She glared at me until all of a sudden the glare melted and a tear washed a black streak halfway down her cheek.

"Krys," I whispered.

"I'm pregnant," she whispered back.

"I know," I repeated what I'd said before, but this time did it gently.

"Got no call to have a baby," she shared, her voice unravelling.

Where did that come from?

I leaned forward a bit and asked, "Why on earth would you say that?"

"My momma was a bitch. Fucked-up, crazy-ass, selfish bitch. Treated me like shit, total shit, you would not believe. I didn't even fuckin' believe it, until I had no choice. That is, she treated me like shit when she remembered I was breathin'."

I nodded, said nothing but felt a lot, pissed and sad that Krystal had gone through that.

"That's what she taught me," she declared.

Ah.

There we go.

"You're not your mother," I replied.

"I'm fucked-up, crazy-ass and selfish and there are few in these parts who would shy away from using the b-word when it comes to me too."

This, I did not doubt.

I also didn't confirm it.

What I did was think of Tate Jackson watching Bubba and Krystal while they played their roles of local good ole boy and hard-ass bitch and doing that watching with obvious affection.

"You babysit?" I asked.

"What?" she snapped.

"You said your man volunteers you two to babysit your friends' kids all the time. Do you do it?"

"Of course," she answered immediately.

And still, she did not see.

"You a fucked-up, crazy-ass bitch to your friends' kids?" I pushed.

"They aren't mine twenty-four-fuckin'-seven," she informed me.

"Babe," I said quietly, leaning closer. "Just the fact that you're a good enough friend to babysit your friends' kids says everything about you. Hell, the fact you have friends says everything about you and that isn't getting into the fact that they want *you* to babysit. Your mother do anything like that?"

She looked to the windshield.

I didn't know her as far as I could throw her.

But I still guessed that meant no.

"You acted like a fucked-up, crazy-ass bitch when I met you," I shared and her eyes shot back to me, squinty, but she was in a vulnerable place and couldn't quite hide the hurt even if she had to know I spoke truth. "But, girl, when you touched your belly, it was like you were stroking the miracle you know that's growing inside you. You give it good, I'll give you that," I told her, nodding my head. "That wall you got around you is built tall and edged in razor wire, keeping anyone out that might cause you harm. Thing is, you built that wall, let your man live back there with you, and you're gonna have your baby behind it with the two of you. I think you've made a good start."

She dropped a hand to her belly, looking down at it, and saying, "What if I fuck this up?"

"You sitting alone in your car, my guess, tough as nails, yet worried to the point of tears, I'm not thinking that's gonna be a problem."

She looked again to me but didn't move her hand from her belly.

"Shit like that can rear up, you don't even know it."

"Don't let it," I returned.

The impatient snap was back. "Simple as that, you think?"

"I don't think anything about parenthood is simple and, I don't want to fuck with your head, girl, but even if you get beyond thinking stupid shit like this, you're still gonna have other stuff rear up."

The snap was now angry. "This shit isn't stupid."

I leaned close and hissed, "Yes it is. Because, Krystal, if you can build that wall to protect yourself, what are you gonna do for your child? Whatever happened with your mom did not break you. You're still standing. You got a bar. You got friends. You got a man. You got a baby on the way. You're hot. You're crazy, but you're funny. You don't take any shit and got the balls to give it. Not sure a baby doctor would list all those things in the pro column of how to be a good mother and live your life in a way you teach your child valuable lessons of how to be a survivor. But the way this world runs and all the fucked-up, crazy-ass shit in it a parent has to shield their kid from the best they can, especially in this burg, which seems like a magnet for it, I'd say that doctor didn't know shit from Shinola."

She'd tucked her chin in her neck as I spoke but when I was done, it came out and she declared, "Jesus, girlfriend, don't beat around the bush."

"I don't like to see women crying in their cars and being down on themselves. And for future reference, even though you won't need it, just so you know, I can be sensitive. It's that I'm just as good, swinging both ways."

"Well, if you'd swing your ass out of my car, I could get home before the ice cream melts and ruins my trunk."

I grinned.

It was all good now.

She lifted her eyebrows as a prompt to exit said vehicle.

I grinned bigger and opened the door.

I'd swung out but hadn't cleared the door before I heard her call, "Jus."

I bent down to look at her.

"Thanks," she muttered, but she did it looking me right in the eye.

"Don't mention it, Krys, but do put me on your babysitting list. I love babies."

She rolled her eyes, turned forward and kept muttering as she said, "Whatever."

I grinned again but only because I saw her lips were quirked up.

Then I moved out of the door, shut it and made my way to the sidewalk.

I didn't watch her pull out and drive away but I saw her go as I made my way back to my truck.

I threw my plastic bag in and then wondered how to kill more time while Deke blew insulation into the walls of my house.

I got in my truck and wondered why I wondered how to kill time.

There were two always ready answers, just one that required the right time of the day.

That being booze.

The other was food.

So I got right back out of my truck and headed to the diner.

* * *

It was dark by the time I got home since I moved from food to booze and spent the afternoon and early evening shooting the breeze in Bubba's with Jim-Billy, meeting Izzy, another bartender, and the female-mullet-haired Twyla—who *did* make Krys look like a friendly Girl Scout selling cookies—and eventually talking Jim-Billy into going to dinner at the Italian place with me (my treat, which meant talking him into it took two seconds).

BOUNTY

The afternoon and dinner with Jim-Billy was awesome. He was a hoot, a sweet-as-heck guy, and I learned quickly why everyone looked at him and talked about him with such affection.

Now, I was home and I couldn't see much because I didn't have any light in the main space because I had no working outlets in there.

What I had was moonlight dimmed by tall pine.

And warmth.

I could see the creamy white foam in the walls.

And as I carefully made my way to the thermostat (that still had, plastic wrapped around it), once I smoothed it over the screen, I saw Deke left my furnace set at seventy degrees so I'd come home to a warm, snug house.

I was grateful for thermostats and a new deck and creamy foam in my walls.

I was grateful for Jim-Billy.

I was grateful for fate setting my feet on that sidewalk so I could be there for a woman I barely knew, but she was a woman that needed me.

I was just grateful that the life I'd been born into already giving me so much, continued to offer me bounty.

I went back to my bedroom with my *Twang* magazines, my Baby Ruth bite-sized and jumped on top of the bed in my cozy, snug, gorgeous four-poster so I could munch chocolate and read an article that sang the praises of my bestest bestie.

Bounty.

CHAPTER FOUR

Prime Rib Sandwich

Justice

UPON DEKE'S BANGING the next morning, I threw open the door, and in lieu of a greeting, I jerked a pointed finger to my nose and demanded, "See this?"

His gaze narrowed and he clipped in return, "Got eyes, don't I?"

"Well, thanks to *you*," I turned my finger and jabbed it his way, "it's still where it's supposed to be and didn't freeze off last night." I gave him a big grin I didn't even know I had in me to give that early in the morning and cried, "I love insulation!"

For a second, he stared at me, blank.

Then something lit in his hazel eyes I knew I could bask in its warmth for eternity (so I pretended I didn't see it, though did this poorly, but just enough to fight my desire to lean in, say, with my mouth touching his, to see it in close proximity).

And he gave me more.

"You're a little crazy, gypsy."

He said it like he thought it wasn't a bad thing, a lovely nuance coating the rumble in his voice that I also could bask in for eternity.

I pretended I didn't hear that as well, moved back, allowing him entry, and kept moving toward the hall to the garage, doing this speaking. "Coffee's on, I'll bring yours out."

"Jus," he called, and I stopped walking and turned back to him. "Max says you want the deck finished?"

"Yeah, do you mind?" I asked. "It's looking awesome. I'm not going to be hanging in the utility room so it'll be nice to have another change of space to hang."

He nodded. "I'll get on that."

"Appreciated, Deke."

He moved toward the glass door set in the wall of glass that led now, thanks to Deke, to the back deck.

I went to the garage to get him coffee.

* * *

An hour and a half later, showered, dressed and ready to hit town, this being finding somewhere with Wi-Fi so I could deal with emails coming in (specifically the ones from my interior designer), I opened the door to the back deck.

And Deke.

I again admired the herringbone way the boards were set in, making it just that much more interesting, and I did this so as not to admire the man working on the railing.

I didn't have to call to him. The minute I opened the door, he'd stopped what he was doing to look at me.

"Hey," I greeted, stepping out.

He jerked up his chin.

"Going into town," I told him, stopping a few feet outside the door. "Need anything?"

"Nope," he answered.

This made me curious.

"Do you bring lunch in your truck or something?" I asked.

"Yep," he answered.

Wow. Deke packed a lunch.

Now I was surprised and curious.

"Water?" I went on.

"Yep," he repeated.

"Cold water?" I pushed.

"Cold enough."

Yeesh. He didn't need to bring water.

I crossed my arms on my chest. "Dude, you can help yourself to the water in the fridge."

"I'm good, Jus."

"What's for lunch today?" I asked.

"Bologna."

"Yum," I said.

He stared.

Then he asked, "You like bologna?"

"Well, cold, I can take it or leave it. Fry that up until it's *just a bit burnt* with a slap of American cheese and put it on toast with loads of yellow mustard, dee-*lish*."

He stared again, this time without speaking.

"What was for lunch yesterday?" I asked, still filled with curiosity, as, unfortunately, I probably always would be when it came to Deke.

"Bologna," he repeated.

"Deke, you need variety."

"Not sure about your eyesight, Jus, but I ain't exactly wastin' away."

This was very true.

I grinned at him.

This made him look weirdly annoyed.

I decided to ignore that and get on with my morning.

I did just that, turning but saying loudly, "I'll bring you a sandwich from the deli."

"Don't bring me a sandwich," he said loudly back.

I stood in the open door and looked over my shoulder at him. "And chips. Maybe a cookie."

"Jus—"

I slipped in, closed the door and walked across the creamy-white-foam-coated space to grab my laptop, head out the door and to my truck.

* * *

The only business I'd noted that had a notice that said free Wi-Fi (and theirs didn't say free Wi-Fi, it said ♥♥♥Free Wi-Fi!!!! ☺☺☺) was Carnal's coffee house, La-La Land Coffee.

So I hit there because I could use a latte as well as Wi-Fi.

I walked in and knew why Krys had called me Free People.

She knew the difference between boho and hippie.

This was because the dude and chick behind the counter were so hippie, I wondered if they had a time machine.

"Hey," I called as I walked up to them, noting the girl was doing something at the cash register but the dude with his bandana wrapped around his forehead and round specs with blue lenses was staring at me.

She looked up and caught sight of me.

Neither of them moved, including their mouths to use to greet me.

I stopped in front of the counter, clocking their looks and knowing the jig was up.

It was actually nice it lasted as long as it did.

"Hey," I said more quietly.

"You're Justice Lonesome," the girl stated breathily.

"I am, honey," I confirmed.

"Groovintude," the guy whispered reverently.

"I…I…I…" the girl stammered, then shut up.

After that, they both remained silent.

I got closer, and to break the awkward, said, "It'd be super-cool if I could use your Wi-Fi and do it drinking a butterscotch latte with one of those butterscotch caramel muffins."

I tipped my head to the case that looked filled with selections from Heaven's bakery.

"Butterscotch is my theme today, baby," the dude said, as if he was a robot.

I smiled. "That's cool, since I love it. Now, you know I'm Jus. How about you tell me who you guys are?"

"Shambala, Shambles," the guy said. He shifted closer to the chick. "This is my girl, Sunray Goddess, Sunny."

Total hippies.

I dug them immediately.

And this was the source of Deke's coffee.

"You…you…'Chain Link' is Shambles and me."

This came from Sunny and I looked at her, trying to stay loose and cool, rather than get tight and freaked out.

Chain Link.

Deke's song.

"Wither to dust, crumble like rust, he's the only thing in life that's right," she continued.

"I love that," I said gently.

Suddenly, a startling amount of tears filled her eyes indicating she was a bit unhinged in her like of Justice Lonesome music, or indicating something else.

"Thank you for saying what I couldn't say to him." It came out in a garble before she took off running down the counter, disappearing behind a door to the back.

I watched her do this but looked back alertly, ready to take off if need be, when Shambles filled her spot at the cash register.

"Okay, all right, that was weird but I hope you stay because I gotta go after her and I *really* wanna make you a latte when I come back." He started to move but turned back to me and shared on a hushed rush, his face twisted in a way that made my heart lurch, his next words explaining that look. "She was attacked. Hurt real bad. It messed her up. She didn't treat me real good through it. Your music helped. Thank you."

Then he took off.

I stood where I was, experiencing one of the many things that didn't feel like quicksand about that life I'd left behind.

Experiencing something so beautiful, I could fiddle with the lyrics of a song forever, and not get it right.

Experiencing connecting with someone in a way so meaningful, it shared just how connected all we beings were through a variety of sources. Music. Books. Art. Movies.

The tragedy was, most didn't recognize it and there were some of us with hate in their hearts about things they didn't understand who would refuse to acknowledge it.

I let that glide through me before I chose a table, sat down, opened up my laptop and tapped in the password Shambles and Sunny had kindly tacked to the back of the counter under the menu.

Ten minutes later, they came back.

Sunny let me give her a hug.

Shambles made me the best latte I'd tasted in my life, which I used to wash down the best muffin I'd ever consumed.

I got to my email, though I didn't answer any.

I was too busy gabbing with two totally awesome hippies.

* * *

Two hours later, I walked to the back deck, saw a finished railing and a Deke who was working on completing the edge of the rectangular fire pit.

He looked up at me as I moved through the door.

Then he looked down at the hefty white paper bag I had dangling from my fingertips.

After that, he looked to my other hand which had a huge bottle of chilled Fiji water.

I held out the bag to him when I got close.

"Roast beef and Swiss. I had them heat it up. French roll. Regular potato chips, Big Grab. If you tell me what flavors you like, next time, I'll get saucy. Also in there are two of Shambles's butterscotch cookies with chocolate chips." I then offered the water. "This needs no explanation."

"Woman, you don't need to buy me food," Deke rumbled, straightening to his full height which meant I had to tip my head back to look at him.

"Dude, you pass out from dehydration or malnutrition, no way in hell I can carry your carcass to my truck to race you to emergency. I couldn't even drag it. You need sustenance."

I jiggled the bag.

"I'm not gonna pass out," he clipped.

"And I'm not gonna have someone at my house who eats bologna day in, day out. Yes, it's yummy, but you need variety. So today, roast beef."

I jiggled the bag again.

"Jus—"

"I have a deck," I said softly. "It's an awesome deck and I don't give a fuck you're being paid to give it to me. I love it and it means something to me to have it so take the damned sandwich, Deke. If you don't wanna be nice, okay. But be cool enough to let me be nice because that's who I am and that's what I do and I'd really appreciate it if you'd let me."

He studied me a long time before he finally reached out and took the bag and water, doing this with no words.

"Just sayin', a non-frozen nose means more sandwiches next week," I warned.

"If I told you you were a pain in the ass, would you report that to Max and get me fired?" he asked.

I felt my lips curve.

"No," I answered.

"Then you're a pain in my ass."

"So noted. I'm still buying you sandwiches."

"Whatever," he muttered, bending to put the water on the stone and opening up the bag.

"*Bon appetite!*" I cried, still grinning, and I walked away.

* * *

I sat in my Adirondack chair, scrolling through stuff on my laptop the designer sent me that I'd downloaded at La-La Land that I'd go back to La-La Land to feedback on when I saw Deke come up the side steps.

"Yo," I called.

He shook his head for some reason and announced, "Fire pit's done. You wanna see how it works?"

"Hell yes!" I exclaimed, jumping up, putting my laptop down on the seat I vacated and rushing past him. I then dashed across the pine-needle-ly grass, dodging the standing pines left close when they'd built the house (which were the obvious source of the pine needles in the grass), to race up the steps to the main deck.

I stood next to the fire pit that now had a beautiful rim of flagstone and did this with hands clasped in front of me.

Deke came slower, eyes to my hands at my chest, before they rose to my face.

"You regress to a six-year-old?" he asked.

"Do I have a new toy?" I asked back.

His lips curled up slightly. "Reckon you do."

"Then yes," I answered.

He got close, bent deep in a squat and said, "See this key?"

I looked down to the key sticking out of the side of the fire pit that he was pointing to with a long finger.

"Yes."

"Turn it, you'll hear the gas come on. Light it, do that carefully, holding your body away. Adjust it however you want. When you turn it off, it'll take a minute for the gas to burn off and the flames to die down."

He then pulled a lighter out of his jeans pocket and demonstrated this.

As I watched and saw the flames dance happily, I fought against girlie-clapping at my chest.

"See those handles?" he asked.

I nodded. I saw a handle inside the pit, one on each side.

"Lift that out, lifts out the lava rock. There's a grate to burn wood to switch out to in your garage. Use it one way or the other, not both. Only switch out when it's not recently been used. And do not use the gas if you're burning wood. Yeah?"

I nodded again.

"Be good with cleaning out everything, ash and all, when you switch back to the rock."

I nodded gain.

"You want me to leave this on?" he asked.

I kept nodding seeing as I *so totally* was hanging at my fire pit that night.

He shook his head.

Then he kept questioning, "How bad you want a utility room?"

"Really bad," I answered. "Like, I might bring you a prime rib sandwich, bad."

He kept shaking his head. "I'll work tomorrow, get it started. Not Sunday. Be back Monday but at least I'll have a start on it."

"That'd be great, Deke."

This time, he nodded. "Right, done for the day, Jus. See you tomorrow. Seven."

"Right, Deke."

He started moving away.

I waited until he was just about around the corner before I yelled, "Fire pit says prime rib sandwich too!"

In return, not surprisingly, I got nothing.

* * *

Deke

That night, Deke took a bite of the fried bologna, American cheese, yellow mustard on toast sandwich.

It was a fuckuva lot better than cold.

But not as good as prime rib.

* * *

Justice

I grabbed the white bag, jumped from my truck, and strolled into the house.

I went directly to the laundry room.

It had three walls and a ceiling, the sheetrock not taped, but totally fitted, and Deke was starting on wall four.

He looked to me, the bag, then back to me.

"Plans say tile floor in here," he declared. "You rejected that tile. I'd recommend concrete. Easy to clean. Grout won't get fucked up. And you glaze it, shit looks awesome."

"Can you do that?" I asked.

"Yep," he answered.

"Concrete it is," I told him.

"You'll need to pick it, Jus."

"I don't think I got concrete brochures from Mindy, Deke."

"Best get on that, gypsy," he stated, moving from his wall, coming to me, bending low and snagging his bag.

But in sucking in breath at his proximity, I got a whiff of him.

He smelled clean, like soap.

It was amazing.

How could he smell good drywalling?

Gah!

He lifted the bag, tipped his head down, opened it and looked inside.

"What's today?" he asked.

"Warmed honey-roasted ham, melted provolone, Dijon-mayo on an onion bun with Fritos. I'm sorry to say, the deli doesn't do prime rib sandwiches. This means I'm on a mission. Someone in this county has to make them or I'm taking over someone's kitchen and doing it myself. That's the bad news. The good news is Shambles was in a marshmallow mood. I have absolutely no clue what that marshmallow thing is but I do know it has chocolate and cashews and I ate two and they fuckin' *rock*."

He lifted his head. "You buy me two?"

"I have a fire pit, Deke. I bought you four. You don't have a stomach big enough to consume them all for lunch, you can take them home."

"Future reference, Jus, Fritos, affirmative. Chips, sour cream and chive. Barbeque. Cheddar cheese. Anything. Just not plain," he shared.

Why did I feel like I cracked the Da Vinci Code?

"Monday, I'll get saucy," I promised.

He shook his head and I was realizing he did that when he thought I was being an idiot.

I just hoped he thought I was being a cute, amusing idiot.

"You gonna get out of the door so I can plant my ass somewhere and eat?" he asked.

I vacated the door.

He shifted out of it, down the hall and I went to the garage to grab a bottle of water before I went in search of him, finding him sitting on the stack of drywall in the living room.

I handed him the water.

He took it but didn't express gratitude.

"Eat hearty," I bid as I moved away, wishing I could sit next to him, hang with him, shoot the shit with him. If he wasn't into me, at least be his friend.

I exited the space and moved into my bedroom.

He did not call me back.

* * *

Deke

The next afternoon, Deke sat in his deck chair close to the shore, his line in the lake, a cooler of beer in between him and his bud, Wood, the only guy Deke knew in Carnal who liked to fish.

Luckily, he was a decent guy, was good with being quiet and being in the sun by the lake with a rod and a beer, but when he talked, it wasn't about bullshit or the man could be funny.

"Hear Max's got you workin'," Wood noted.

"Place on Ponderosa Road," Deke answered.

"Flash?" Wood asked, being a lifetime Carnal resident, knowing that area and knowing most of it now, with new builds and renos, was flash.

"Yeah and no. Gonna be the shit when it's done, but not in-your-face the shit."

"Who's the client?"

"Woman named Jus. Loaded. Crazy."

"Crazy-loaded or loaded and crazy?"

"Both."

"Pain in your ass?"

"She brings me sandwiches."

Deke felt Wood's eyes so he looked to him.

"That's crazy?" Wood asked, grinning.

"Don't want her bein' nice to me, don't need her charity."

Wood quit grinning and started looking watchful but puzzled. "Charity?"

"Rich bitches like that, gotta stay alert. They give with one hand, take a lot more with the other."

"Seems you got experience," Wood muttered, still watchful.

Deke absolutely fucking did.

"Dad got dead when I was two," he told Wood. "Ma did what she could, which meant bein' a maid. Live-in 'cause she needed a roof over our heads. Ate shit for as long as I could remember. Watched her do it. Folks she worked for had three daughters. Little cunts, all of 'em. Treated Ma like dirt, same with me. They had friends, not a one of them better than the three. Wife of the man who paid my mom was no better. She had friends too. Different colored hair, cut from the same cloth. So yeah, Wood, I got experience."

"This Jus woman like that?" Wood asked.

"They don't come off like that when they need somethin' from you, so no. All that kind got it in 'em, though."

Wood looked to the lake. "Didn't think you had it in you, paint everyone with the same brush."

"You watch your mother clean up vomit splashes every fucking day, 'cause two of those bitches were bulimic and one was the mom. Watch them shout at her like the world was about to end when she didn't set a table like they wanted, that bein' not buyin' *coral* roses for a centerpiece instead of *peach*, whatever the fuckin' difference is. I could go on for days, brother. Fuckin' *days*, and it gets worse. So Jus seems cool. But I don't open wide for women like that. No fuckin' way. You don't keep your shit, you get burned."

"Not bein' funny, just pointing out, known you years, first I heard of this so you don't open wide for anyone, Deke. That bein' said, you the last man standin' in our posse who doesn't have a chain you don't mind dangling from your ankle, it's especially with women," Wood remarked.

"Got reason," Deke grunted.

"One of those bitches burn you?" Wood asked quietly.

Clearly sun, beer and a rod in his hand put Deke in the mood to share. Share shit only a few people knew and the only two of those in town were Tate and Jim-Billy.

Or maybe it was being around Jus, day in, day out, the temptation of her, that meaning he needed to get this shit out and remind himself who he was and how that came about.

"One of the daughters played me. Went from nasty to sweet. She did this because she wanted my dick, panted after it. I was fifteen and the only thing on my brain was pussy, so I gave it to her," Deke stated. "When I didn't want more, she told Daddy. He canned Ma's ass then blackballed her and Ma and me ended up in a homeless shelter six months later, this was after livin' most of those months on the street. All that Ma endured and all that was on me. So yeah, one of those bitches burned me, Wood."

While he was talking, Wood looked his way. "Jesus, Deke. Had no clue."

"Ma eventually got a job, I was old enough, so did I. We got out. Took two months, but we got out. Worked and didn't go back to school to keep us out of that fuckin' place."

"That sucks, brother," Wood said quietly.

It fucking did.

It was the worst.

He could hack it. Deke could hack anything. He didn't need much. Learned not to need it so his mother could live with not being able to give it to him.

But he'd fucking hated watching his mother suffer like that. Worry so bad, she never slept (and Deke knew she hadn't because he didn't and he heard her toss and turn in her cot in that fucking shelter). Kick her own ass she couldn't give her boy better. Beg child protective services to let her keep him as she pulled her shit together.

He hated all that because there was a lot to hate.

And most of that hate was about him putting his dick where it didn't belong and making it so his ma went through that.

Since there was no reason to reply to Wood, Deke didn't.

"I get what you're sayin', man, but Emme's family's got money and she's not like that," Wood noted.

"Yeah, and Emme's got Decker's ring on her finger," Deke returned.

"What I'm sayin' is, your story sucks and you're a brother, we're tight, I hate knowing that happened to you and your ma. But still, not all kinds are the same as their kind. Emme's proof of that."

Deke looked to the lake.

"This Jus young? Old? Pretty? Married?" Wood asked.

"Young. Not pretty, fuckin' pretty. No ring, no man I can see."

"And she's bringin' you sandwiches."

Deke returned his attention to Wood. "She likes the fire pit I built."

Wood burst out laughing.

Deke looked back to the lake.

Wood was still laughing when he asked, "You that clueless?"

Deke turned eyes back to Wood.

"She's into me," he said quietly. "She tries to hide it but she gives it away a lot. I am not gonna go there, Wood. Even if she isn't a cunt like most of her kind are, she's not Emme. Shit, pregnant and Emme's fightin' Deck about letting her do some drywalling or whatever the fuck in that fuckin' wreck of a house of theirs. Emme's not like a lot of women."

"This is true," Wood muttered.

"Jus doesn't work," Deke kept at him. "I don't even know what she does, except talk on the phone and spend money. Bangin' the woman who's payin' my wages is fuckin' stupid. It's not gonna happen. Been there, learned that lesson the hard fuckin' way."

"Yeah you did," Wood replied quietly.

Deke heard his words, didn't acknowledge them because he didn't need to and kept going.

"Job's done, going there, unless the promise of her is a total lie, it'd be fuckin' great. But I'd go in knowin' there was nothin' but a lot of fucking to get our fill and nothin' on the other end for either of us. Got enough experience to know most women don't like that shit. Women like her would like it less. So it's not gonna happen."

"Why would there be nothing?"

"Lot her place is on cost more than I've made, maybe in my life, Wood. Wherever she came from to get here, she doesn't need to work, and trust me, she did not just win the lottery. Kinda money she's got, you can smell it from a mile, sunk down deep in her bones. Would you be down with that?"

"Fucks me to say, I see your point," Wood replied.

Deke's gaze went to the lake.

"I see your point, Deke, but the woman's bringing you sandwiches," Wood said. "She might not be what those bitches treated you to. And if she's into you, be cool."

"Not bein' a dick," Deke told the lake, though he was, just enough of one to put her off.

He could be a bigger dick but she didn't deserve it. He knew that even if he had no idea about her and the little he knew he wished he didn't.

He also wasn't being a bigger dick because when she was being cute, he didn't have it in him. No one could be a dick to Jus when she was being cute, and if you didn't wake her up, she was cute all the fucking time.

He didn't share this with Wood. He also didn't share that he still could not shake the fact that there was something familiar about her.

But Deke knew he couldn't have met Jus before, and not just because she was so damned friendly, if he had, she'd be all over that.

Because he'd remember her, no way he'd forget meeting a woman like Jus, those eyes, that hair, those legs, that ass, all that fucking cute. No way in hell.

Even knowing that, something in his gut told him he'd seen those eyes, that ass, those legs and definitely that fucking amazing hair.

He had to get through this job and get paid.

That was it.

"More to all this too, I reckon," Wood noted. "Seein' as she's settlin' in up there and not a lotta women are good to leave it all behind, jump on the back of their man's bike and take off to nowhere whenever the winds change."

"There's that too," Deke agreed.

He agreed but he hadn't thought of that.

It was good Wood threw that out there. As gypsy princess as her clothes and truck were, no way a woman like Jus would close down a house like she was going to have and take to the open road with no destination, no purpose, just riding until the breath you were breathing felt right again.

"Have you noticed nothing's biting?" Wood asked, ending the conversation because there was nothing left to say, he knew it and he knew not to push Deke if he didn't agree there wasn't.

Yeah, Wood was a good friend.

"Have you noticed we're sittin' on our asses on the shore, not in a boat, so odds are, anything bites, it'll be an inch long?"

"Not feelin' rowing out to the middle of that fucker," Wood remarked, leaning to his left and pulling out a cold one.

"That's good 'cause I got no boat."

Wood burst out laughing again.

This time, Deke joined him.

* * *

Justice

Sunday afternoon, I swung up on the barstool next to Jim-Billy.

He turned his baseball-capped head my way as I did and grinned his broken grin, one tooth missing.

I didn't figure he was going to get it fixed but I hoped he didn't. As I'd noted thus far in my journey through life, there were some imperfections that were perfect. Jim-Billy's missing tooth was one of them.

"What's shakin'?" I asked.

"Nothin'," he answered.

"I don't know whether to be happy or sad about that," I remarked.

"I do. Simple life, simple pleasures." Jim-Billy lifted up his draft. "Means you always avoid disappointment."

I stared at him a beat, rocked by this wisdom, before I asked, "What are you, a mountain man maharishi?"

"Yup," he muttered and looked away, chugging back a big gulp of his beer.

I burst out laughing.

I finished laughing with Jim-Billy again looking my way and grinning.

Krystal appeared, throwing a beer mat on the bar in front of me.

"What you drinkin'?" she asked.

"Beer. Cold. I don't care what kind but none of that fancy shit or you'll make me testy," I answered.

She looked from me to Jim-Billy. "I know this is goin' against all I am, but I already like her," she declared, jerking her head my way.

That felt great.

"Pregnancy is softening you up," Jim-Billy commented.

Uh-oh.

Wrong thing to say.

"Take that back," she snapped, proving my assessment right.

"Not a bad thing, darlin'," Jim-Billy pointed out.

She leaned in to him. "Take that back."

"Krys—"

"My name is Justice Lonesome," I blurted the reason I was there (outside to hang, have a beer and get to know my Carnal neighbors some more).

Both Krystal and Jim-Billy looked to me.

I'd started it, it was time. Shambles and Sunny knew. Although I'd asked them to keep it quiet until I was ready to let it loose, and they'd promised to do that, the more I got to know these folks, the longer I left it unsaid, the bigger the chance of me courting the possibility of hurting people's feelings. Because anything important left unsaid eventually became a lie if you let it get to that.

"My father is Johnny Lonesome. Aunt and uncle Tammy and Jimmy. Granddad was Jerry."

I sallied forth even though both of them were staring at me, silent.

"I cut a record six years ago. It did well. I toured with it. I did well. Then my drummer overdosed. He was a good guy. A good friend. He'd been with my dad before he went on the road with me so I'd known him years. He was part of the family. It tore me up. On tour, I hooked up with another guy in my band. He was into that shit and us losing someone didn't make him stop. He wanted me on that trip with him. I wanted nothing to do with it. The pressure was heavy because the life is extreme and there's a lot of times when you just need *something* to keep going. We weren't serious but it was an ugly break. That tore me up too. A lot of the shit I did and saw and had to eat to live that life tore me up. So I left it."

Jim-Billy and Krystal kept staring.

I kept blathering.

"Dad died of an aneurysm four months ago. No warning except he ate anything he liked and drank all he wanted and didn't take care of himself, but he ran around onstage like he was still twenty-one, so the doctors said if it wasn't that, he'd have a stroke or a heart attack and not later, but sooner. He was Johnny Lonesome but to me he was just my dad. I loved him. He loved me. A lot. And I miss him."

"Jus," Jim-Billy whispered.

I knew why. I felt the tears brimming in my eyes.

I focused on him because Krystal looked pissed.

"I didn't tell you because I wanted peace," I whispered back to Jim-Billy. "Just some time where I was Jus. Not Justice Lonesome, not Johnny Lonesome's daughter, Jerry's granddaughter. I wanted you to get to know *me*. And lots of stuff is happening since Dad's died and it's a pain in my ass. So I wanted that peace. I'm sorry I didn't share right off the bat. But can you understand why I wouldn't?"

"Of course, sweetheart," Jim-Billy said immediately.

"Justice Lonesome," Krystal said over him.

I looked to her and braced.

"Heard Johnny's daughter cut a record. Heard a song. It was slow and sappy. So, hope you don't mind, but I gave my cake to your old man. Bought every album he put out seein' as he was a goddamned rock 'n' roll genius," she declared.

"I don't mind," I told her quietly, warmth stealing around my heart at her words about Dad, still braced because she wasn't sending warm vibes to me.

"Saw him in concert twice. Two best concerts of my life," she stated.

"Yeah. He was great live," I agreed.

All of a sudden, her hand came out, palm flat on the bar in front of me.

She didn't touch me, not even close.

What she did was look me in the eye and say in a tone in my not-very-long acquaintance with Krys I'd never heard or suspected she could take, "His loss was a great one."

And there was the warmth.

I couldn't hack it.

Grief was a tricky thing. When we lost Granddad, I'd learned that, for me, it wasn't those who gave you sorrowful looks, gazing on you with understanding, keeping their mouths shut.

It was the folks who offered sympathy.

It meant the world and it was necessary to have to file away and take out at a time when the loss was less raw and those words could be soothing.

But when the loss was raw, it tore the wound wider.

"Thanks," I replied shakily.

Krystal knew my kind. She saw exactly where I was at.

"You need a beer," she decreed, pulling her hand away.

I cleared my throat. "Yeah."

Jim-Billy moved and he didn't stop short of touching me. He took my hand on the bar and gave it a lovely squeeze before letting it go.

I gave him a lame smile.

I'd done right, picking that crazy house in this crazy town with these crazy people.

So right.

Krys came back with my beer.

I kept on mission.

"If you guys could, you know, not lie but not spread it around. I'll share and all. If you know Shambles and Sunny from La-La Land, well, they listened to my stuff so they already knew me, obviously, before we met the other day. But, you know, a little bit more of that peace would work for me."

"Babe, you're gonna get peace. Any motherfucker fucks with your peace, they got my buckshot in their ass," Krystal declared.

My eyes got wide.

"Not to scare you or anything," Jim-Billy leaned toward me and stage-whispered. "But she ain't jokin'."

"Damn straight," Krystal said and indicated my draft with a quick movement of her ebony-flame-tipped-haired head. "Holler, you need a refill."

She wandered off.

"Bubba shoulda knocked her up years ago," Jim-Billy noted, watching her go.

I shook off the emotion their kindness left with me and gave him a grin.

It wasn't the pregnancy.

It was and it wasn't.

It was just that Krystal, as hard as she was on the outside, was not stupid.

She, too, recognized bounty.

And it felt fucking *awesome* she saw it in me.

CHAPTER FIVE

Bad Timing

Justice

MY PHONE RINGING Monday morning woke me.

I reached out blindly, knocked it off the nightstand, mumbled, "Damn, shit, fuck," as I pushed to hang off the edge of the bed and grab it.

I remained hanging over the edge of the bed as I looked at the screen telling me it was just after six and the number calling was local but not programmed in.

Damn these mountain folk. With all that quiet and nature and peace, why did they get up so fucking early?

I'd programmed in Max's number. Jim-Billy's. Krystal's.

This one…whoever it was, I didn't know.

I took the call and put the phone to my ear.

"'Lo," I muttered.

"Jus. Deke," his deep voice reverberated in my ear.

Sleepily, and agreeably, I felt that reverberation in my pussy.

I was enjoying that as Deke's alert, attractive morning voice kept coming at me.

"Max got your text about the glaze you want. He's got shit on today…"

Deke continued speaking about picking up materials, the fact I needed to select a color for the paint for the utility room, how Max couldn't get the supplies to the house until Tuesday afternoon, and other stuff about Deke having more than enough to do in the meantime but my utility room was going to have to be delayed. This information coming at me included the option of Deke going that morning to pick up the stuff, which would mean he'd be late getting to my place.

There was also something about Bubba coming to help him on Wednesday when he was going to blow insulation into the rafters so my heat didn't escape out the roof, something he stated was priority.

It was a lot of words, especially from Deke. And I liked listening to them, especially the way his voice sounded and the fact it was sounding over the phone in the morning after he'd called me.

But unfortunately he stopped talking.

Though I'd find he didn't stop talking.

I'd just let his voice lull me back to semi-sleep, hanging over the side of the bed.

"Yo! *Jus*! You there?" I heard him bark.

My body jerked, I blinked and put a hand to the floor to push myself up into the bed.

"Yeah, I'm here. I'm listening."

Nothing from Deke and I thought I'd lost him right before I heard him mutter, "Jesus, the gypsy princess fell asleep fuckin' talkin' to me."

"I only fell *semi*-asleep," I corrected. "I'm fully awake now," I shared (partial lie, I was only mostly awake).

Another mutter of, "Jesus." Then, "I'll let you get your beauty rest and go pick up the shit."

"No," I said, this part groggy, part desperate. "I like progress. You're so fast and so good, four hours of lost progress could mean anything. You could have the kitchen done in four hours." That was an exaggeration, but whatever. Slightly groggy thoughts of a kitchen were dancing merrily in my head as I finished, "So no way I wanna lose four hours."

"Be at your place at eleven, eleven thirty and you'll get progress," Deke replied, obliterating my merry kitchen thoughts.

"How about you be at my place at the normal hour, tell me where to go to get the shit and then I'll go pick it up so Max doesn't have to waste his time to see to that errand."

"So she did hear me," Deke replied, though he did it like he wasn't actually talking to me.

"Like I said, dude, *semi*-asleep."

"Whatever."

I lounged on my side on my bed but I did it feeling the amusement laced in his one word not only in my pussy, but also several elsewheres and those elsewheres were not (all) erogenous zones.

"Deal?" I asked, doing my best to pay no attention to those elsewheres.

"Deal," he replied then, not surprising with Deke, he offered no words of farewell.

He just hung up.

Me being me and way too into Deke, I grinned at my phone thinking that was hot.

*   *   *

I stood outside my truck on the side of the road, the wind picking up, so much of it that it was blowing even my heavy hair in my face as I put the phone to my ear.

"Yo," Deke answered.

"Houston, we have a problem," I shared.

"You got lost," he guessed.

"I can read directions, Deke, even in your handwriting, which, by the way, is a little scary," I told him.

Deke ignored my assessment of his handwriting.

"Then what's the problem?" he asked.

"I have a flat. I also don't have a spare. And I further don't have AAA. Though I do have a bunch of stuff in my truck and some of it's back in the bed." I looked to the heavens. "Last, I'm no meteorologist but I think in about five point two seconds, it's gonna start raining."

"Where are you?"

"You know that road off the main road into town that you turn off to before you turn off on the road that you then turn off on to finally turn onto Ponderosa?" I asked stupidly, not having memorized the road names (some of them being county road numbers) that led to my house.

Deke did not confirm he knew that road.

He just stated, "I'll find you," and hung up.

As I stood there waiting for Deke to find me, I tried to enjoy the lovely feel of the wind whipping against my skin. I didn't often get opportunities to stand outside and have the wind glide through my hair, shape my clothes to my body.

However, I wasn't able to fully enjoy this lovely feeling. I was too busy glancing at the back of my truck where bags of cement that didn't look waterproof were laying.

Fortunately, Deke's arrival in his bronze Ram with patterned steel tool cabinet in the back growled up like the monster it was, the sound of the engine beating back the soft wafting of the wind.

Deke was behind the wheel, phone to his ear, and I watched with some marvel as he drove past me, executed a three-point turn then drove past me again to park at the side of the road in front of my truck, all with his phone still to his ear.

He angled out of his truck, yes, with his phone at his ear.

"Yeah, County Road 18. 'Bout a mile off of Main Street." I heard him say as he sauntered toward me and my vehicle.

He glanced at me as he passed me and stopped beside the bed of my truck.

"Tow it. Fix it. I'll text you Jus's number so you can deal with her on it," he kept speaking. "Right. Cool. Later."

He disconnected and shoved his phone in his back pocket, his gaze coming to me.

"Wood, man who owns the local garage, is sending a tow."

"That's cool you did that. Thanks," I replied just as a gust of wind blew a hank of hair across my face.

I pulled it away, flicking it back over my shoulder and finding when I'd accomplished this, Deke's eyes were at my shoulder.

"Paint's in the cab. The rest in the back," I shared.

His head twitched like his mind was elsewhere and I'd alerted him to the present then his chin lifted and he turned to the bed.

I moved around the hood to get the paint that was on the passenger side, which included cans of primer, as Deke instructed I buy.

I moved all the paint to his truck. Deke moved all the cement and grabbed the glaze.

I started to go to his passenger side when he said, "Leave the keys under the floor mat, you got one in that heap."

I lifted my gaze to his.

"Say what?" I asked.

"Leave the keys under the floor mat. Wood'll need 'em."

"Like, leave the keys to my truck under the floor mat with my truck abandoned on the side of the road?" I asked incredulously.

"Yeah, like leave the keys to your truck under the floor mat with your truck which has got a flat and can't go nowhere so it's on the side of the road so whoever Wood sends out with the tow, someone who'll be here in probably ten minutes, can get your truck and they'll have the keys."

"Why do they need the keys?"

"So they can deal with your flat and not have to roll that old-ass fucker out of a bay to park it while they wait for you to come pick it up."

"Deke, I'm not leaving the keys to my truck right here."

"Jus, no one's gonna steal that wreck and not just because they can't without changing the spare themselves, a spare that doesn't exit. But because they won't have enough time *and* no one would want that wreck in the first place."

He was ticking me off.

"It's not a wreck," I snapped.

He looked to my truck and back at me.

"Jus."

That was it.

Just *Jus*.

Like that said it all.

Sure, my faded red old Ford pickup *looked* like a wreck.

But it was no wreck to me.

"Maybe I'll wait until they get here," I suggested.

"You wanna hang at the garage while they find time to fix your tire?"

This did not sound fun and I had things to do that day.

"Deke—"

"Keys. Truck. Now, Jus. It's gonna start comin' down and soon and we want that cement in your house, not in my truck turnin' into concrete while we argue about somethin' stupid."

Shit.

With no other choice, I stomped to the driver side and put my keys under the front seat (for he was correct, I had no floor mats).

I then stomped to the passenger side of Deke's truck. He was already at his side.

We climbed in.

Deke started up his behemoth and we took off.

"Need to get a new ride, Jus," he advised me.

"I do not. My truck's perfect."

"Perfect for that gig you got goin' on. Not perfect for a woman who lives alone in a remote location like this with an unpredictable climate like the one we got in Carnal."

"It's fine."

"Unless you take serious good care of it, you're lucky you only got a flat."

"I take serious good care of it," I assured. Then asked, "The gig I got going on?"

"The whole gypsy princess thing."

I looked from the road to him. "It's not a part of my gypsy princess thing. My gypsy princess thing isn't even a gypsy princess thing. It's boho."

"Whatever," he muttered.

But I was still put out.

"Not whatever, Deke."

He glanced at me before looking back to the road and ordering, "Calm, Jus. Not bein' a dick. Just looking out for you and that truck is thirty years old, it's a day."

"You're correct. It's also the truck my granddad owned when I was two and my family was visiting him and we took our *first* special just-grandfather-granddaughter trip to go get ice cream. That first being the first of many. Something that was special to me for years, but started off special, if the story my folks and Granddad often told that, when I was three and he said he was getting a new truck, I demanded he give the old one to me. I guess I was pretty adamant about it and made an impression. No matter how many trucks came later, we never went for ice cream in anything but that truck. He kept it for decades. The last time we went to get ice cream, I was twenty-nine, and it was in that truck. And he left me a lot when he died, most of that really good memories. Part of that was that truck."

When I was done telling my story, Deke had no reply and the interior of the cab felt strange. Not good. Not bad. Just strange.

And I guessed I wasn't done laying it out because I continued to do so just as I'd been doing, sharply with unhidden temper.

"On the sad day that truck dies, I'm parking it in my front yard, filling the bed with dirt, and planting flowers in it. In other words, I'm keeping that truck forever, Deke. Forever. And ever. And *ever*."

"Baby, calm," he urged softly, not taking his eyes from the road.

I sucked my lips between teeth and felt the sting of tears hit the backs of my eyes so I turned my head immediately to look out my side window.

Baby, calm.

And with just that, I was calm.

About what he said about Granddad's truck.

Everything else that was Deke, I was *not*.

God, *why didn't he remember me?*

Why could he not be mine?

Why couldn't I have his voice in my bed in the morning, feeling that in my cunt when he could do something about it?

Why did I have a life that gave me so much, so *fucking* much, all of it meaningful, all of it amazing, and yet the one thing I ever saw that called to my poet's soul in a way that I knew only it could feed it, nurture it, give it peace, I could not have?

Baby, calm.

"Shouldn't've said dick about your truck, Jus. Wasn't cool," Deke said quietly.

I drew in a deep breath and replied, "It's okay. You didn't know."

"And sorry you lost your granddad."

God, seriously, he just had to stop.

"Thanks," I murmured.

Deke said no more.

We got home. I brought in the paint. Deke brought in the other stuff, doing it while the skies sprinkled water.

It wasn't until five minutes later, when I was behind closed door in my bedroom, when the heavens opened.

I sat on my bed sideways, staring out the two-story slanted wall of windows into the storm, thinking the visual I had was sheer beauty and hoping I never got used to it at the same time counting my blessings, the only two I could come up with at that moment was that I had that view and that I had a roof.

Then I got my shit together, opened my nightstand, and took out my leather-bound notebook. A different one than the one Deke saw me scribbling in when I wrote a gold record song about him seven years ago.

I'd filled that one up. This one was new.

I flicked the band from around it, opened it to where the pencil was wedged into the page and I stayed cross-legged on the bed, head bent, letting some of what I'd just felt pour onto the page.

It was past time. My agent had phoned weeks ago saying Stella Mason (her stage name was her maiden name, Stella Gunn) of the Blue Moon Gypsies wanted another song.

She and the Gypsies had turned three of mine multi-platinum in the last four years.

They'd always only recorded their own stuff along with a number of kickass covers. It was an honor they'd branched out to me.

But Stella was also a friend. She was killer talented, so amazing onstage, it was hard to believe. She'd loved my album. *Loved* it. Got her hands on it and reached out to me before it was even released to connect about how much it had moved her.

And she was that one shining beacon in the life that didn't let that life in any way consume her, chew her up, take pieces out of her.

She had her shit together. She also had a man who hung the moon for her. Not to mention, they made two babies who they doted on.

It was like that life didn't touch her, even as entrenched in it as she was, as crazy as her band was (and they were all nutcases, lovable ones, but extreme ones).

She had the love of a good man, of her family, of good friends (some of whom I'd met) to keep her safe.

So she stayed that way.

I finished the lyrics, had set the notebook aside and was tapping them into a text to Stella when I heard a knock on the door.

I looked up to my wall of window to see it was still raining, not hard but coming down.

I threw my phone with my unfinished text on the bed, crawled off, walked to the door and opened it.

Deke stood there.

No.

Deke carrying a white deli bag stood there.

Lord, he'd gone out to get lunch.

Apparently, *for me*.

He held it out, (yep, for me).

"Tuna melt," he announced. "Sourdough. Cheddar cheese chips. Shambles is all about caramel today, so it's one of those cookie-lookin' brownies, not chocolate, but with caramel."

I took the bag, my poet's soul keening, my lips muttering, "Thanks."

"Wood says they'll be done with your truck around four. Just needs you to phone in with a credit card. He's good with a couple of his boys bringing it up."

"I'll call him."

"Also said, your truck is so kickass, he wants to buy it. I told him not to go there."

He told him not to go there.

Looking out for me.

I could do nothing but say, "Thanks again."

He nodded and shifted as if to move away so I continued on a blurt.

"My dad died not very long ago. We were tight. It's fresh but I'm…I…" I shook my head, "I'll never be over it. Brings up other stuff. Like Granddad dying even though losing him was a while ago. I overreacted then sulked. I'm sorry."

Deke nodded briskly. "Lost my dad when I was two so I don't know what you're feelin' since I don't remember the man. Still know it sucks not to have a dad and I get where you're at so you don't have to apologize for me puttin' my foot in it."

Damn, he'd lost his dad when he was two.

Two.

That keening turned to longing, to touch him, soothe him, something.

Anything.

I could do nothing except defend him against himself.

"You didn't know."

"That don't mean I didn't put my foot in it."

This was true.

I let that go and said softly, "Sorry you lost your dad, Deke."

"Long time ago," he noted.

"I'm still sorry," I pushed.

"I am too." After he said that matter-of-factly, he put an end to that part of the discussion with, "We good?"

I nodded, preposterously overwhelmed that he bought me lunch, unhealthily overwhelmed he wanted us to be "good."

With me having nothing more I was willing to give him on a blurt or in any way, I had nothing more to detain him when he turned and walked away.

* * *

At around eleven thirty the next day, I wandered from my deck, through my room, down the hall and to the utility room.

Yesterday, Deke had primed it and painted it the soft blue I'd chosen.

Right then, smooth, wet, concrete floors were drying.

I moved down the hall, all of which was now drywalled (but not taped), what Deke had done when I was picking up the stuff and between paint and cement drying. Following the noises, I found him in the powder room which it was clear upon stopping in the doorframe he'd just begun to start with the sheetrock.

Our communications yesterday afternoon and this morning were subdued.

I needed subdued with Deke. I needed a giant step back.

But I was learning something new about myself.

Apparently, I had an iron will when it came to saying no to snorting coke, dropping acid, throwing back a variety of pills to speed me up, slow me down or make me unconscious, drowning myself in bourbon.

But I had no willpower whatsoever when it came to Deke.

In other words, I was done with subdued.

"Pizza today," I declared into the powder room and his attention came to me.

"Again, you do not have to feed me," Deke stated.

"I think it's been made pretty clear my hearing is functioning so this has been noted. I just don't care." I allowed my lips to quirk. "And you might not have had the briefing, but gypsy princesses tend to get their way. They do this by being stubborn and adorably annoying."

He rested the sheet of drywall he was wrassling against the wall so he could turn fully to me and plant his hands on his hips.

I couldn't tell if he was amused or annoyed.

Or relieved.

Though I was fascinated to note he looked all of those.

However, he said nothing.

"What do you like on your pizza, or you can answer the alternate question of what *don't* you like?" I asked.

"You goin' all out on pizza, you gonna skip La-La Land?" he asked back.

"Hell no," I gave him the obvious answer.

"No pineapple or peppers and I don't mind anchovies."

"I do," I told him.

"So don't get 'em," he returned.

I lifted my hand up to my forehead in a salute and executed my take of a precise military turn on my leopard-print-strapped, flat sandals that had feathers dangling.

Deke was no longer in my vision so I couldn't see the expression on his face when I heard his audible grunt that also sounded both amused and annoyed.

On my way out to my truck that two of "Wood's" men did, indeed, return to me last night at four thirty, I engaged my phone, hit the number to the pizza place in town I'd Safari'ed and ordered it on my way down.

I hit up Sunny and Shambles. We had a short gab. I then grabbed the pizza and a six-pack of Coke and headed back.

I'd thrown one of the mover's blankets over the stack of drywall in the great room, the pizza down on it, put the Coke in the fridge with one out for Deke and a bottle of water for me, before I shouted on my way down the hall back to the pile of drywall, "Soup's on!"

I was cross-legged on the floor with another blanket under me, throwing open the pizza box when Deke strolled in.

Yes, I was maneuvering having lunch with him, not just bringing lunch to him.

Yes, I was fucked because he'd demonstrated that he could be a nice guy, somewhat forthcoming and definitely cool after he'd fucked up. This meant not only was he too attractive by half, cracking that nut that was him was something I was enjoying, even knowing I would never really be able to dig into that shell and get to the meat.

He didn't even hesitate to plant his ass on the drywall by the pizza I'd torn a wedge from and was now munching.

He also didn't hesitate to grab his own wedge.

"Pepperoni, sausage, Canadian bacon with mushrooms thrown in for vitamin D," I declared through a half-full mouth.

"I approve," he returned on a full mouth after taking a big bite.

"Bubba tomorrow?" I asked.

"Yeah," he answered.

"I thought Bubba worked at Bubba's," I remarked.

"Bubba works for Max. He's only at Bubba's to help out and be with his woman."

Interesting.

"You guys do your thing, should I take off?" I went on.

"Yep," he replied.

I munched.

Before I could lock on something that would crack deeper into Deke, my phone rang.

I did a stretch, yanking up the lacy weave of my long sweater that hung over my battered khaki short-shorts to pull my phone out of my back pocket.

I looked at the screen.

It said, Joss.

Mom had bad timing.

But I hadn't heard from her in a while, she'd been suffering from Dad's loss too, and if she needed to connect, I needed to let her.

I shifted to a hip in order to find my feet while muttering, "Gotta take this."

Deke just gave me one nod.

I took the call. "Hey, Joss."

Side note, I'd never called my mom "Mom." This was not because she was not a mom person. She was. She'd been a great mom.

She was just a cool mom.

And she also left her home to be a groupie at age seventeen. She further raised me to be grown-up enough to start the switch from mom to friend at age seventeen.

So, since she'd been living for the day when she could set the mom part aside and go to concerts with me, she'd always been Joss.

"You need to talk to your stepfather."

Right.

I'll provide added detail.

She'd always been Joss until my stepfather did something stupid and then she became my mother only so she could order me to deal with her shit.

"What's going on?" I asked and did it not hiding the fact I didn't want to know.

I also did it lamentably leaving Deke behind so I could take my phone call and pizza slice out to the back deck in order that he not hear my conversation.

"He wants to do a reality program," she informed me.

My blood heated.

"And he wants me to sign to be on it with him," she continued.

That heat intensified.

"And he wants me to talk to you to see if you'll come to town and do a few walk-ons on the show," she finished.

I was on the deck, the door closed behind me, swiftly and angrily making my way to the railing, doing it asking loudly, "Is he high?"

"He's pissed I'm reacting to Johnny's death so he's pushing my buttons. But his tour didn't sell great last year and he's also taking advice from that shit-for-brains manager of his on how to increase his profile and get on the radar of younger fans."

My mother was not only a groupie who caught the eye of an up-and-coming legacy rock star who would eventually make it huge.

She also was not only Johnny Lonesome's first wife.

She was a personality in her own right and *this* was not simply because, between Dad and Joss's current husband, Roddy Rembrandt (a ridiculous name his handlers made Rod change to, also a name Rod couldn't ditch later because it had become part of him to his legions of fans), she was girlfriend and muse to a number of big name rockers.

She was a stylist. A rock stylist. A good one. She styled bands and singers for tours (hell, she styled *tours*). She styled bands and singers to attend events. Photo shoots. Anything and everything. And everyone wanted her.

This was because she was good at it. And it helped she lived the life, walked the walk, talked the talk, but best, rocked the look herself.

If Joss wasn't so well known as my mother, someone could mistake her for my sister.

These were all some of the reasons why she'd caught the eye and married Roddy Rembrandt, lead singer, lead guitar and just plain leader of the hair metal band The Chokers. A guy who was only nine years older than me, ten years younger than Joss, right in the very weird middle.

The Chokers had been cool because they had an edge of alternative and punk that both dulled and amped the metal in a good way, their lyrics having more meaning, their songs more like short (but sometimes epic) stories, their vibe angrier than metal, less angry than punk, gliding the line of call-the-shit-of-life-as-you-see-it grunge. They were kind of a morph between Bon Jovi, Guns 'n' Roses, Nirvana and Green Day.

They just didn't hold that edge. Booze, bitches, dope and success just straight up dulled the good right out of their music so now everything seemed a retread. But mostly, they didn't often record anymore. Just toured and fed off the love and loyalty of their fans.

This was not a bad thing.

I just could not imagine doing it, not making music. Challenging myself to keep making it better. Even if I didn't record my own stuff or perform anymore,

I sold songs all the time which meant I wrote them all the time. Sometimes, for people I liked, I even went in to produce.

I could never just coast.

And it sounded like Rod was done coasting too.

But it sounded more like Rod was done watching his wife grieve another man.

"I am not going to be on a reality show," I bit out.

"I'm not either," she told me. "But he's up in my shit about it constantly, Jussy. He will *not* let it go."

"He can dog-with-a-bone it all he wants, Joss. It doesn't matter. You don't sign to be on camera, he can't do anything about it. And I'm sure as hell not going to sign."

"I need you to call him and tell him to back off."

It was safe to say I was done with this. And this wasn't about Dad dying.

This was about Joss dealing.

"He's your husband," I pointed out.

"He listens to you," she retorted.

"Which is weird and it makes me uncomfortable. I'm not your marriage guru."

"He adores you. He knows you adore him. He respects your craft. He knows you dig his music in a way that's meaningful. You guys have that connection and it's a connection, Jussy, baby, you know I can't have, no matter how much I dig the music. You can get through to him."

"You know, he died for me too."

It was out of left field at that juncture in our conversation, blunt and not nice.

But I couldn't take on her shit with all the rest.

And it pissed me off she called to ask me to.

Joss said nothing.

I did not return that favor.

"You need a break from Roddy. You need to get your shit together because *Rod* is your *husband* and as much as he's not Dad, will never be Dad, you love him and he's important to you. So you have got to get your head wrapped around the fact that this *hurts*. Rod's a dude but he's got feelings and watching his wife grieve the love of her life has *got* to *suck*. You either have more patience with him, Joss, or you take a break from him and get sorted then come back and give him back his wife."

"That isn't cool, laying it out like that, Justice," she said quietly, the hurt evident in her tone.

I felt guilt.

And I also didn't.

"Mav is contesting the will," I shared.

"Not a surprise," she retorted. "And you know that. That fuckin' cunt stole my husband. She tried to take Johnny to the cleaners when he got shot of her. And she's been giving him and Dana shit for years. Her playing puppet master with that pissant of a son of hers is no shock."

This was all true, including the fact that Luna was a homewrecker.

Of course, this meant Dad cheated, something unforgivable that Joss never forgave him for, no matter he paid the price in a lot of ways, including losing the only woman he ever truly, deep down to his own poet's soul loved. A fact he was well aware of. Marrying Luna because she was knocked up with Maverick, dumping her not long after Mav was born because he could take no more, he tried to get Joss back.

Joss was just so certain they were the only ones for each other and they were forever, Dad cheating had broken something in her and she just couldn't trust him again.

So she never went back.

"Bianca's disappeared and no one knows where she is or has heard from her, not even her mom and dad," I declared.

"Fuck," Joss whispered. "Perry and Nova never did take good care of that girl."

She was right.

Perry and Nova, Bianca's lead guitar of a heavy metal band dad and B-movie bombshell mom, loved their daughter, to be certain.

They'd just never taken good care of her.

But the time wasn't right to talk about that either. Not that there was anything to talk about. Joss and me had often lamented the fact Bianca's folks were so into their dysfunction, they never really were about looking after their daughter.

"And the man I met who inspired 'Chain Link' is working on my house."

Total silence. A void so deep, it felt like it'd suck me, my house and all the nature around me into it.

Then, a loud, shrill, "*What?*"

Suffice it to say, when your mom turns into your friend, with the kind of history you two share, she becomes your best friend.

Lacey and Bianca knew everything about me.

Joss did too.

"Yep. Right now sitting on a stack of drywall in my house, eating the pizza I bought."

"Oh girl, you go. I cannot *believe* you found him again. That is *so cool*."

"Joss, he doesn't remember me."

More silence before, "You're shitting me."

"I wish I was."

And I totally did.

"How could he not remember you?"

"I don't know, because it was seven years ago, we met in the wee hours of the morning, talked for ten minutes and I was rocking my biker vixen look. My hair wasn't as long. I had on an inch of makeup. And it was seven years ago for ten minutes."

"Girl, man's any man at all, he'd *never* forget your hair. *Ever*."

Mom wasn't being conceited.

I had my dad's hair.

And Deke had said back then I'd had pretty hair.

And it wasn't like he didn't notice I was female. He did. I saw it when he did, like when we were standing in the wind and he was looking at my hair over my shoulder.

It just didn't do anything for him.

"Well, all evidence suggests he has," I told Joss. "He's been working on my house for nearly a week and there's nothing."

"Shit, baby. I'm so sorry. Totally sucks when the fates are feeling sassy and they've got you in their sights."

"You are not wrong about that."

"Maybe while he works on your house, you can come visit me and Rod. And before you say it," she said the last swiftly, "this is not me trying to get you to come here and deal with Rod and my shit. I'll tell him to back off, I'm not signing to be on any reality program and we got more problems if he or that shit-for-brains manager of his breathe a word of it to you. It's me wanting to look after my girl."

I loved being with Joss. I also loved being with Roddy.

But I didn't want to leave. I liked it there. And that wasn't all about Deke.

"I'll survive, Joss. It's not that big of a deal. He's just not into me."

"Jussy, darlin', 'Chain Link?' Who you talkin' to?"

I drew in breath. Then I munched pizza.

Joss let me.

I swallowed pizza.

"It sucks," I whispered. "And I'm still loving every minute of getting to know him."

"Shit," she muttered.

"It'll be okay."

"Only reason it will is that it'll spawn a thousand songs, one of which will be sure to get you onstage, accepting a statue, which should have happened for 'Chain Link,' any other song on that vinyl or any song you've had recorded since."

That was the mom in Joss. Blind devotion, blind loyalty, no one was better than her kid.

I decided to move us out of this, not the blind devotion and loyalty part, the talking about Deke part.

"Was a bitch with a purpose, laying it out for you earlier, Joss. I was still a bitch. I'm sorry I got nasty."

"Sometimes you know you gotta smack me out of it, Jus. You didn't say anything that wasn't true. I'll deal with my own crap and Rod's. And you and me'll plan some time together soon. No Roddy. Just us girls."

"I'd like that."

"Okay, baby. Now go back to the torture that'll feed the Lonesome curse and make beautiful music."

I rolled my eyes but grinned, even if all she said was the damned truth.

"Later, Joss."

"Love you, babe."

"You too."

She disconnected.

I munched pizza on my way back to the door.

I walked through to see Deke also walking through…his walking being the room to get back to the hall.

"Good pizza, Jus. Thanks," he said before he disappeared.

I looked to the pizza to see it was half gone.

Joss.

Hell and damn.

Bad timing.

* * *

That evening, I got a text from Krystal.

Deke know about you?

It was a good question that brought to mind he didn't, she did, and Bubba was coming the next day. Bubba being her husband and baby daddy so no doubt she'd told him about me.

No. And if you don't mind, I'd rather keep with the peace, I texted back.

Deke won't care, she informed me.

He might.

He might not.

My stepfather wants to do a reality program. He wants me on it. He comes to town, I might ask you to load your buckshot.

I didn't get a return text for a few minutes.

Give you more peace.

That meant Bubba would be cool.

Grateful, I replied.

And I was.

* * *

Bubba came with Deke the next day and he was friendly, but he was cool, calling me only Jus.

I left so they could blow insulation. I hung with Sunny and Shambles and their Wi-Fi, dealing with business and interior design suggestions and doing online browsing, logging a bunch of favorites for the time when I had bathrooms, walls and a kitchen and could therefore indulge in some serious shopping, all the while gabbling with my new friends.

Late afternoon, Deke texted, *Done*.

It was monosyllabic but thoughtful and I didn't need further proof Deke could be thoughtful.

I still gave him the whole day, driving to and dinking around the mall to do it.

I returned and he was gone.

Thursday, Friday and more overtime Saturday, Deke and I had minimal banter, I often acted like an idiot, I brought him sandwiches and he made progress on my house.

Sunday he kept sacred, clearly, as his day off. So he told me he wasn't going to show.

He didn't.

I wanted to feel relief.

I missed him.

* * *

Deke

Late Sunday night, in the dark, in his bed, Deke lay on his back, one hand wrapped around his dick and pumping, the other hand over his head, fisted in the pillow.

His eyes were closed, his mind filled with visions of Jus riding his face, her head thrown back, all that long hair falling down, gliding against his chest.

It did not take long for him to blow a huge load on his stomach.

Still stroking, he opened his eyes and didn't see pussy.

But, fuck him, he could taste her in his mouth.

Flowers.

She'd worn perfume the day before. Not the first time but she didn't always wear it.

And she smelled like flowers.

He bent his knees and kept stroking his cock, his thoughts turning from Jus riding his face to memories of Jus reacting to the blue concrete glaze with silver and pearl whirls *she* had picked, he'd just done. She'd lost her mind, clapping and smiling and laughing, telling him he was a genius.

His thoughts went from that to her hugging the wall in the hallway after he'd finished the taping, her arms both outstretched, her cheek pressed to the sheet-rock, her mouth crying out, "I love walls!"

He didn't even allow himself to think of how she'd reacted after he'd finished the counters and cabinetry, installed the sink, put in the light fixtures, mounted the drying racks and finally fitted the washer and dryer.

Fuck, the look on her face when he found her and showed her he got her utility room done, he thought she would kiss him.

And he'd wanted that, right to the gut, straight to his dick.

"Fuck," he whispered, rolling out of bed, going to the bathroom, cleaning up and hitting the sack again.

He lay on his back thinking he should tell Max he wanted him to switch out the man for Jus's job, sending someone else in, taking him out.

Not only did his mind violently reject that idea the minute he had it, Deke had no reason to give Max why he wanted that.

And Max would likely wonder about why he'd ask, doing that for about a second before he'd figure it out. Wood would just know. If Tate heard, he'd wonder half the time Max would before he called it.

Then people would talk.

Deke didn't need that shit.

He turned to his side, closed his eyes and tried to find sleep.

All he could think was how Jus would fit in the curve of his body after he'd turned into her to get some shuteye when he was done fucking her, how it would feel to bury his face in all that hair.

Not able to get those thoughts out of his head, his dick started getting hard.

So he had to jack off again just so he could get some sleep.

CHAPTER SIX

And Left It at That

Justice

"THIS PART, I don't know, just wondering since the plans say double doors here, if it could be something else. Something that opens totally. Not double doors like on the plan. This whole space so I can close it off but also open it completely. Do you get me?"

It was the next Wednesday.

I was standing in the main space talking to Deke while dudes were unloading a delivery of more drywall. The two stacks Deke had for use were gone. Now there were two new stacks that were twice as high as the old one in the garage, and they were erecting their second much taller stack in that space.

Deke was not paying attention to the delivery guys.

He was looking at the framing behind me.

Since he returned to work on Monday, we'd carried on as normal, banter, sandwiches, me being an idiot, Deke leaving at six o'clock and doing it not looking back longingly at me.

However, in that time, I'd had one glorious moment.

This was when he'd finished drywalling the hall and the powder room yesterday, ceilings, tape and all.

He'd then asked me if I wanted him to completely finish that space before he moved on to the main part of the house.

I told him I wanted a kitchen.

His reply included a softening of his eyes I'd never seen but liked a great deal which I'd find was a precursor to him sharing something he didn't want to share, this being that he didn't think it wise to give me what I wanted.

A special gift.

It also included another special gift.

This being him saying, "Babe, drywalling is dusty. You can cut off that space you're living in when I install the door so you don't gotta cope with the dust. I do the kitchen for you before finishing the..."

He went on but I heard nothing but his *babe*. And once he gave it to me, I didn't care that as a general rule, contractors put up all the drywalling and did all the taping and painting before they started to get to the good stuff, like installing floors and fitting kitchens.

I'd give up anything for that *babe*.

So I'd agreed.

But since, he didn't give me another *babe*.

He definitely didn't give me another *baby*.

That was beginning to be my lot.

Now we were in the main space which had seemed cavernous due to it being empty and wall-less, but was seeming even more cavernous as I'd noted how much longer it was taking Deke to make progress. He'd put up a sheet and it felt like an inch was achieved since there still was *so much more* left to do.

And now, before he got around to giving me actual walls on that side of the house, I was talking to him about the extra room to the south side that had a special purpose.

Deke looked from behind me to me. "Weight of the roof held up by joists, load bearing for your second story not around those doors, so sure. We can figure something out."

"You do know I heard nothing but blah, blah, blah, so sure. We can figure something out."

His lips tipped up and his hazel eyes lit.

I did a mental, *Yee ha!*

"Bro, sorry to interrupt," the delivery guy interrupted and Deke looked to him. "We're done. Gotta check this and sign off."

"Right," Deke replied and moved his way as my phone rang.

I pulled it out of my pocket, saw the display said Mr. T was calling and I sighed before taking it, ticked even more Mav and Luna were making me dread calls from Mr. T. They weren't always the delight of my day, but he'd been a staple in my life since I started it. I cared for him deeply, in the only way he'd allow me to do that. So I'd never dreaded his calls.

Now I did because now there was never anything but bad news perpetrated by my brother and his shrew of a mother.

Regardless of this, I took that call how I usually took all of them, with a, "Hey, Mr. T."

"Justice, how are you?" he asked.

"Hanging in there, you?" I asked back, beginning to move to the door to the back deck.

"Unfortunately, I'm calling to inform you we've had official communication that Maverick is contesting your father's will."

"That sucks," I muttered, thinking this would be it so the call wouldn't be long and glancing at Deke to see he was in the middle of counting sheets of drywall with the delivery guy standing close so not paying a lick of attention to me and my call.

Therefore, instead of going outside and leaving his presence (I'd been fucked and was getting more fucked, not even wanting to walk out of a room Deke was in—he was like a goddamned drug), I leaned a shoulder against the doorjamb and stared out at the calming view.

"This means those assets are frozen, Justice. I know they've already been distributed but you can no longer use them until this has played out."

"Awesome." I was still muttering but now I was doing it sarcastically.

"This means your brother also can't use his," Mr. T pointed out.

I thought about how Luna had used her son to keep her living the good life, using him by flying through the divorce settlement in a couple of years, not getting a job and consistently threatening to take my father back to court in order to increase already substantial child support for a son they shared custody of so she could live off her kid's back.

Dad didn't make her take him back to court. To make things easier on Mav, he just increased the money.

That legal agreement had ended when Mav turned eighteen and didn't go to college.

The situation didn't end, however. Mav used his share of Granddad's royalties as well the trust fund Dad set up for him to keep not only himself but his mom living the life they'd become accustomed to, but mostly, I figured, the life *she'd* become accustomed to.

To my knowledge, that trust fund was quickly dwindling, which was why Dad augmented Mav's funds frequently, something Dana let slip one night before

Dad died when she'd gotten a bit tipsy. Something Mr. T allowed to happen and followed through on because Dad said it would be so. Not like what had happened with Aunt Tammy and Rudy when they'd not only cut off Rudy's access to his trust fund when he'd started pissing it away, they'd used a caveat in Granddad's will to cut off his access to his share of Granddad's royalties.

This, I suspected, was one of the reasons Luna and Mav were making the foolish play to try to get half of Dad's estate.

The other reason was that Luna was just a greedy bitch.

"Hope someone's paying attention because that's not gonna happen," I noted.

"We'll do our best to pay attention," Mr. T confirmed and went on, "Now, you won't feel that pinch but I'm sorry to say that, although your father provided a healthy stipend to Dana when he was still with us, and she didn't use it indiscriminately so she has some resources, cases like these can drag out and those resources are not limitless. It may cause financial strain if we can't get a judge to throw this out expeditiously."

This, likely, being Luna's plan. She hated Joss. She hated Dana. She hated Dad. She hated everybody except herself, and on occasion, she could show affection to Maverick, but only when she could use him to get something she wanted.

"I'll cover Dana," I said on a sigh.

"I suspected you would. I'll share that with her and we'll keep an accounting of that should it occur so you can be reimbursed when this sorry business is concluded."

"Thanks, Mr. T."

"I'm afraid I have more bad news."

I kept my eyes on my view, the rays of the sun shafting through the trees, twinkling on the water of the river.

I still braced.

"And that is?" I prompted when Mr. T unusually did not dive right in. No procrastination for him, he got the bad stuff out of the way or *any* stuff he had to do and he did it with no delay.

"The documents we received have made special note that your brother is laying claim to the entirety of your father's collection."

My mind seized, every nerve ending screamed, I straightened away from the door with utterly no thought to where I was and who was with me as I shrieked, "*You have got to be joking!*"

"I'm sorry, Justice," Mr. T said quietly, a careful edge to his tone which was almost soft with understanding. "I'm not joking."

"That…is…*fucking insane!*" I shouted.

"Justice—"

I cut him off. "That's not his. He *knows* that. He fucking *knows!*" I yelled, took a pace, found movement too difficult while my mind was gripped with agony at the very thought Mav would get hold of Dad's collection, and I came to a juddering halt.

If Mav got Dad's collection, that meant Luna would get hold of it and it was her that wanted it.

So she could sell it.

That collection being my father's guitars. He had many. All of them used to create and make amazing music. Most of them used by him and then by me to teach me how to do the same.

And some of them were Granddad Jerry's that Dad had inherited so he could have them, with the caveat he'd then leave them to me.

They were worth a fortune not only because they were awesome guitars but because they were Johnny or Jerry Lonesome's guitars.

And now they were *mine*.

Dad tried to teach Mav how to play but my brother didn't have *it*, that became apparent to them both quickly, but Dad didn't give up on Mav. Dad felt (rightly) that his son didn't have to have a gift to enjoy making music.

However, instead of sharing he just wasn't into it, something that would make Dad back off, it aggravated Maverick. So he'd act out and storm off, being a little shit doing it. He'd even once thrown one, damaging it beyond repair.

And those guitars were what I was going to put in that space I wanted to be able to open so I could see them. So, when I had a mind to spend some time with my dad and my grandfather, I could open up that room and have them both with me.

Always they'd be there but whenever I wanted, I could spend some time with them.

"Justice, you must know that this is an exercise in futility for Maverick. He'll never break that will," Mr. T assured me.

I was not assured.

"I do not give that…first…*shit*," I snapped. "He knows this is beyond the pale. He knows this is an asshole move that redefines asshole moves. He *fucking* knows."

"Justice, please calm down," Mr. T urged.

"I'm not gonna calm down," I bit out. "The time for me to lose my calm was months ago when all this bullshit started. But, like always, I'm my father's daughter and I wanted to hope for the best from my little brother. Dad died before Mav showed him what Dad believed he had in him all along. A decent bone in his entire body. I'm done waiting."

"Justice, it's important you allow me and your father's attorneys to deal with this," Mr. T told me.

"And I will, after I call that piece of shit and tell him I think he's a piece of shit. Then I'm done with him. *Done*. For good and *forever*."

"Justice—"

"Good-bye, Mr. T."

"Jus—"

I hung up.

Then I engaged my contacts and listened to it ring through to Mav as my phone signaled. It signaling, I was sure, because Mr. T was calling me back.

I listened to my brother's sick, twisted, fucked-up voicemail and when I got the beep, I launched in.

"Four months ago, you lost a father. That had nothing to do with your behavior. Today, you lost a sister. And that's *all on you*," I spat into my phone, eyes now not to the calming view but my feet. "I know you're going after Dad's collection and *you know* that's not right. You know that, Mav. *You know.* Since you've been born you've treated Dad like shit and didn't give me much better. Thinking you're entitled to what, I do *not* get. You had his love. He believed in you. He gave you that *all the time* and you threw it in his face. You did the same to me. And today, I'm done. Thanks. Thanks so much, Mav. I'm grieving Dad and now I'm grieving you. All this goes down and you and your mother go down with it, do not ever try to contact me again. Today, I lost a brother. Today, you cease to exist."

With that, I tore the phone from my ear, looked down at it while I stabbed at the screen to disconnect and I stayed there, frozen, staring at my phone, seeing I was shaking and doing it violently.

Shit happened. People twisted things. Other people believed them.

Mr. T said that Dad's will was ironclad. Maverick and Luna would not get what they wanted and Luna had laid a trail of vicious greed for years that any attorney could pick up and any judge would see through.

But *shit happened*.

I didn't care about the money.

I cared about Dana and her being safe and comfortable because Dad would have wanted it that way.

But I didn't care about the money.

I cared about those guitars.

They were Dad. They were Granddad. They were hundreds of concerts. Hundreds of sessions. Thousands of hours held in strong, capable, talented hands making beauty.

And now, Dana keeping them safe for me until my house was done, they were *mine*.

The very thought of Luna getting her grasping, bitchy hands on them and selling them to the highest bidder made bile race up my throat.

"Jus."

Deke's voice carved into the perverse, bitter sick my brother and his mother stirred up in me and I lifted my gaze, twisted my neck and looked to his face.

He was not close.

But he was concerned.

And that concern undid me.

I turned fully to him, dropped my head and fell forward.

He was not near and then he was, right there for me to collide with as everything pressed into me. So much, I couldn't hold it back, and the tears came.

He wrapped his arms around me as he stepped farther into me so he could hold me close.

That was when I started sobbing. My body shaking with it, automatically burrowing into his heat, his solidity, his bulk, all Deke.

His arms tightened.

"I miss him," I whispered into Deke's chest through a hitch.

The words with that hitch barely sounded before I felt Deke's hand glide up my spine and tangle in my hair.

"Get it out, Jussy," he murmured, his words stirring the strands at the top of my head so I knew he was bent to me.

Deke.

Fuck me, *Deke*.

"My brother's a p-p-piece of shit," I pushed out through the tears.

Deke's arm around me got tighter and the tips of fingers started stroking the side of my ribs.

Even this did not make me feel better. In fact this—all that was Deke enveloping all that was me—made it better at the same time so much worse.

"He's contesting the...the will," I shared.

Deke said nothing.

I kept crying.

It came to me slowly that I was pressed hard to him and had my hands clenched into his tee at the back. I felt the damp material against my cheek and knew how many tears had leaked and that Deke took them from me.

I also knew he was being cool, a nice guy, because that was who he was.

But I couldn't let this go on.

So I pulled my shit together, unclenched my hands and smoothed the shirt before I dropped them to his waist and tipped my head back.

"Sorry."

Lamentably, he took my cue and let me go.

Incredibly, he didn't do this completely.

He put his hands on either side of my neck and bent close so his face was a couple of inches from mine.

"Think, from what you've told me, you get that times get bad. Hope, Jussy, you also get that those times pass. Whatever's happening, this will pass."

Jussy.

Shit.

I nodded because that was all I could do.

"Sorry, I...well, your shirt's all wet," I said, taking one hand from him to wipe my face.

"It'll dry."

I nodded again.

His fingers curled around my neck gave me a gentle squeeze.

"You good?"

I was not.

I gave him another nod anyway.

His eyes moved over my face and I knew he knew that nod was an inaudible lie but he didn't call me on it.

He just said quietly, "Good," gave me another squeeze and dropped his left hand.

But with his right, he lifted it up and I held my breath because I thought he was going to touch my face, dry a tear, something.

Instead, he raised it to the top of my head and tousled my hair before he gave me another close look, turned and walked away.

Shit, Deke comforted me then tousled my hair like I was his little sister.

Shit.

I didn't like that.

But it was kind and it was sweet and it came from Deke.

So as was becoming my lot, I'd take it.

* * *

Deke

He had a screw loose, he knew it and fuck him, he couldn't stop himself.

This was why, the evening the day after Jus got that call that set her off (and he kept a close eye on her yesterday afternoon and all that day, saw she'd pulled it together enough to fake it, but she couldn't hide something haunted her eyes), Deke was in his truck on his way to her place.

He'd left work there, gone home, showered, changed, hit the grocery store, and as night was quickly falling, he was heading back.

It was whacked. It was stupid.

And it was dangerous.

With all of that, the fact remained she wasn't sharing and she also wasn't hiding that shit in her life was clearly extreme. She'd lost her dad. Her brother was being a dick. And something was going on with a woman she called Joss. Deke had no idea what it was but he heard Jus's voice raise on the deck even if he didn't hear what she said and then he'd watched her through the windows, knowing by the line of her body she was agitated.

Fuck, every phone call she got set something off in her or sounded fucked.

But Jus, she pulled it together and faked it as best she could.

She was new in Carnal. As far as he could tell, she had no one close. And the one she should have should not be him.

He still had a brown paper bag filled with hot dogs, buns, condiments, a tub of macaroni salad, a big bag of chips and the makings of s'mores. Next to that bag he had a six-pack of cold beer. He'd also tagged a bunch of wire hangers from his closet. And he'd brought his wire cutters.

Now he was heading to her place because he was a dumbfuck.

It wasn't early. It was getting late.

Maybe she wouldn't be there.

This would be good.

Maybe if she was there, she'd eaten.

If she had, he'd eat, he'd listen if she talked and she could drink beer while he gave her someone to be with, such a fucking moron, not able to cope with thinking of her in that fucked-up house all alone with shit bearing down on her that was extreme.

Oh yeah, fuck yeah, he had a screw loose.

"Shit," he muttered, rolling up to her house and seeing her granddad's truck there.

She was home.

"Fuck," he sighed.

But he didn't turn around. He didn't leave. He parked, got out, moved around the truck and got the shit.

She'd heard his approach and he knew this because the door was open and she was standing in it by the time he started walking to it.

"Is everything…uh, what's going on?" she called.

He didn't answer and stopped in front of her, feeling his mouth tighten.

Sun almost gone, the space behind her was dark.

The next day, he needed to finish some outlets. Get her some light in that area. It was dangerous, her moving around that space in the dark.

And Max had told him that she'd contracted with some man the name of Callahan, a hotshot in the security business, probably the kind of guy only people like Jus could afford. This he knew because Max told him she was flying Callahan in in a couple of weeks to install her security system.

He was going to talk to Max to talk to Callahan to speed that up. Callahan wouldn't need walls and floors set in to give her security.

"Deke?"

His eyes dropped to hers.

"You eat?" he asked as greeting.

"Generally, yes, as you know since you've seen me do it and likely are aware all beings need some form of sustenance to survive," she sassed. "Tonight, not yet. I was about to go out because I'd heard there was a Mexican place in Chantelle that can't be beat."

"Rosalinda's. Hit that, hit jalapeño heaven."

Even that deep into dusk, he saw her pretty face light with a smile.

Total dumbfuck.

"Tonight, though, we're breaking in your fire pit," he told her.

At that, she beamed.

"Please say hot dogs," she begged through the rays.

He shoved the six-pack her way and gave her what she wanted.

"Hot dogs."

"Far out!" she cried, too fucking cute for any man's peace of mind, especially his, grabbing the beer from him, turning and moving into the dark space.

"Light the pit, Jus. I'll go get the chairs."

"You got it," she said, hustling to the back door.

He followed her, dropped the bag by where she'd put the beer on the decking and left her lighting the pit. He came back with one of the chairs that sat on her other deck to see the pit dancing but she was gone. He took off to go get the other chair and when he returned, she was back.

"Napkins," she declared, waving some in the air. "No plates, dude. Sorry. And only plastic cutlery. So sorry again."

"I look like a man who gives a shit about plastic forks?" he asked.

"Not really," she answered.

"That's 'cause I'm not."

"That's good, Deke, but I have no plates either."

"You got some flesh-eating virus I'll get from sharin' a bag of chips and a tub of macaroni salad with you?" he asked.

"Not that I know of," she answered.

"Then we're good."

She said nothing and he didn't look at her face because he could actually fucking *feel* she was smiling.

He squatted and reached into the bag. "Open a beer for me, yeah?"

"I live to serve."

Deke wanted to test that but do it when they were both naked.

Fuck him.

Total dumbfuck.

She got him a beer while he clipped the hooks off the hangers and straightened them out. In no time, they were both opposite each other at the pit. Jus sitting on her chair but leaned in with her dog on her wire roasting in the flames. Deke had sat back, feet up on the edge of the pit, soles of his boots warmed by the fire, his dog also in the flames.

He was thinking there was probably one place on earth he'd like to settle in for a time that wasn't his place by the lake.

It was here.

Total *dumbfuck*.

She started it.

"So, Max called tonight. Says scaffolding is being delivered."

"Need it to drywall the upper areas and get started on laying the wood ceiling."

"And we get Bubba a couple of days," she went on.

"Yep," Deke confirmed. "Not smart to work alone on scaffolding."

"I could spot you."

Deke amended.

"Not smart to work alone two and half stories up laying a ceiling on scaffolding with a five foot five woman in baggy overalls spotting your ass."

He heard her soft giggle.

He liked it.

"I'm five six," she corrected.

A foot shorter than him.

She seemed smaller.

He said nothing.

She didn't either.

They roasted dogs.

Finally, she ended the silence.

"I've got a friend coming to town end of next week."

He looked through the flames to her and said quietly, "That's good news."

And it was. When times were bad, she needed someone close who meant something to her.

She caught his eyes also through the flames and he saw her expression change, the feisty went out, nothing but sweet left.

He could not do this.

And he couldn't *not* do it.

He was totally screwed.

"We'll be trying jalapeño heaven," she shared.

"You can thank me when you do."

"I hope so."

"You will," he affirmed, taking his dog from the flames and reaching out for the bag to get the buns.

"I know you're a manly mountain man, Deke," she suddenly stated and that weird statement made him look from the buns to her. "So I'll get this out of the way so you can be done with it. But this means a lot." She indicated him, the fire and the night by circling her dog. "You're right. The crap Mav is pulling will get sorted and life will go on. But right now, life sucks a little bit. And it feels nice you give a shit enough to bring some dogs, beer and marshmallows to make it better."

Wood had been right. Nothing about Jus suggested she was a rich bitch of the variety he knew.

She wasn't Emme either.

She was all Jus and aside from not liking mornings, there wasn't much to her that wasn't good.

He still was not going to go there. She had cabbage and a lot of it and he was not that man who could be down with that when he'd not only never earn as much as she had, he didn't want to.

He was also not that man who was down with settling. He'd lived a life with significantly limited options up until he was twenty and his mother was solid enough he could take off. He needed endless options now and not many women were good to go on the back of the bike whenever he was ready to roll. Jus, he was certain, considering she was laying roots in Carnal in that house, being one of that many who wouldn't be good to go.

But he knew a lot of people in a lot of places that meant something to him. Some of them were women, taken and not.

So they couldn't go there.

That didn't mean they couldn't have something.

So as much of a dumbfuck as it made him, wanting her, knowing he wasn't going to let himself have her, knowing she wanted him and he wasn't going to let her have that either, he also knew she gave every sign she'd take what she could get.

So he was going to give her that.

To that end, he asked, "You wanna talk about it?"

"Buns," she muttered.

He tossed them to her. She dug for one, they prepared their dogs and she opened up.

"Suffice it to say, my brother is a douche."

"Got that."

"My dad cheated on my mom with his mom when I was around six."

"Christ," Deke murmured.

"Mm-hmm," she agreed and kept on, "She got pregnant. My mom was *way* not down with the cheating thing, the pregnancy thing was just salt in the wound, so she ended things. Dad did right by his unwanted baby mama which I think was more an effort to do right by my unborn brother. It didn't work out and by that I mean it spectacularly didn't work out. She was terrible to Dad. To me. To everyone. And unfortunately, although there were brief moments of glorious respite, time passed and she kept finding ways to be terrible. It's her that's steering Mav into doing stupid shit. My dad…he had some, uh…money."

Deke took a bite of hot dog and just nodded to her through the flames.

That had not been lost on him and she had to know it.

She nodded back. "Luna wants her share of it."

"How long they been divorced?" he asked.

"Think now it's about twenty-six years," she answered.

Deke's chin jerked back. "Serious?"

She nodded again. "Dad remarried…yeah, again." Her last words sounded on a sigh. "Good woman this time. I like her. Luna wants Dad's last wife's share. Dana was a lot younger than Dad but she wasn't a gold digger. She really did love him and they were together for over a decade."

"Not seein' she's got call to get your dad's wife's money," he noted.

"She doesn't and Dad wasn't stupid so his wishes, I'm told, will eventually be carried out. But Mav is going for it for himself, not Luna going for it. It's just that he'll give it to her."

"So what you're sayin' is, this is a headache you just gotta wait out." Deke lifted his hand when she opened her mouth. "Not sayin', Jussy, that that headache doesn't cause pain, 'specially now when it's not long after you lost your old man and shit's obviously still raw. Just sayin', you can find it in you to put that in its place, you can move out from under the emotion it's making weigh on you."

"I know that logically, Deke, I just don't know how to get to that place."

"Over beer, dogs and eventually s'mores," he replied.

Her head tilted, making the shadow of her hair sway over her shoulder. He felt his groin tighten just at that and tighten more when she grinned at him and took a huge bite of her dog.

Through a not-anything-like-a-petty-rich-dainty-princess, her mouth being full, she said, "Good idea."

"Slide the dogs over to me, Jus," he ordered.

She slid the opened package across the flagstone.

He ate his last bite and loaded up another dog.

She finished hers and did the same.

They drank beer. They ate the food Deke bought. They made s'mores. Eventually, she cleared everything up, taking it undoubtedly through that dark to her utility room, which was now her makeshift kitchen, and came out with another two brews for them, where they sat, both their feet up on the ledge, chairs turned to the night.

And through this they talked about Krystal and Bubba and their baby.

Deke told her the whole story about Dalton, Carnal's now incarcerated-for-life serial killer, including the fact that Jim-Billy helped saved Lauren's life when she was taken. News at getting, Jus informed him she wasn't surprised about, making it clear she'd gotten to know Jim-Billy and the good soul he carried.

He also told her he had a bike and Max's "travelin' man" comment she'd mentioned meant he didn't stay put for very long and would probably be on his bike again by April, heading out and only coming back for short stays before he took off again.

Jus told him she played guitar. She further shared she was born in Kentucky, "...but my dad was kind of a travelin' man too, and he liked his family with him, so he almost always took us along." News Deke did not like to hear because she said it not like she missed having roots while growing up but like she liked being a tumbleweed as long as she was tumbling close to someone she loved.

She also told him her friend's name was Lacey, they were tight and she was looking forward to the visit because they used to spend a lot of time together, but didn't get much of that anymore.

Deke had no problem giving to her what he gave.

Jus seemed hesitant, careful and sometimes even uncomfortable sharing all of hers, doing it all like she was protecting herself.

He got why.

She wanted to give more. It was just that Deke was making it clear that wasn't where this was going.

It cut, way deeper than he expected, and he wondered at the wisdom of his play.

But when the time had come for him to go home, she walked him to the door and purposefully fell into him sideways, her arm hitting his. A show of friendly gratitude. An indication she dug the closeness. A communication she was still good with taking what he could give.

"'Night, Jus," he said at the door.

"'Night, Deke. And thanks again. Beer, dogs and s'mores work wonders. Good company, though…"

She let that hang and Deke did what he was making her do.

He took what she could give and left it at that.

* * *

Justice

On my belly in the dark in my warm, snug bedroom, on my bed, one vibrator in me, my hips hitched up slightly, my other vibrator in my hand aimed hard and twirling at my clit, I was going for the gusto. My mind filled with Deke's voice, his face, his hands, and all the rest of him. My imagination soaring with all he could do with them, doing all of it to me.

I came hard, gasping against the sheet, grinding into the toy until I could take no more.

I turned it off and shifted it away, letting the one inside me keep going until I was fully sated. I reached down, twisted it to off and rolled to my back.

I stared at the dark ceiling.

Then I slid it out in the close confines since I was still wearing my panties. I got off the bed, went to the bathroom, cleaned the toys and took them back to my nightstand.

I got in bed, pulled the covers over me—and filled with beer, dogs, chips, macaroni salad, s'mores, good company, satisfied with the orgasm Deke gave me (but didn't)—alone in the dark Colorado night, I fell asleep.

CHAPTER SEVEN

Pleasure and Pain

Justice

"You did not," I declared, staring at Bubba who'd just taken a huge bite of the turkey sandwich I'd bought him (and I'd bought another for me and another for Deke).

"Hurts to say it, I did," Bubba confirmed, not looking like it hurt to say it at all.

I turned my attention to Deke.

"Can't confirm. I wasn't there," he stated. "And I'm glad."

He would be.

I looked back to Bubba.

"I'm uncertain, I have not had the opportunity to ask him, perhaps I'm wrong and he rolls whatever way anyone wants to roll with it. But it also could be the master rock storyteller, Bob Seger, is not fond of men all over stripping down to their tighty-whiteys and dancing around to 'Old Time Rock and Roll.'"

"On the whole, Tom Cruise has a lot to answer for," Deke muttered and I turned laughing eyes and smiling lips to him.

He looked at my mouth, his jaw got visibly tight before he looked away and loosened it to take another bite of his sandwich.

"Lost a game of pool," Bubba reminded me of that part of his story before I could come to some internal understanding of why Deke's jaw got tight while looking at me.

Probably a good thing.

"Why on earth would you bet stripping down to your skivvies and dancing to Seger in a bar on a game of pool?" I asked Bubba.

Bubba grinned at me. "'Cause I didn't think I'd lose and the woman I was playin' looked a fuckuva lot better in her skivvies and I know this 'cause it was Krys."

I burst out laughing.

"Those crazy times are over," Bubba continued when my laughter died down, doing this with his eyes sparkling. "Don't miss 'em. Just glad I got some good stories to tell my babies and then the grandbabies they give me when that time comes."

"Always best to have a stock of those, the more embarrassing the better," I replied.

"Reckon that means Bubba's gonna be the best daddy and granddaddy there is," Deke noted.

"Bet your ass," Bubba agreed proudly.

I started laughing again. Bubba laughed with me. Deke just allowed his lips to quirk.

Since his lip quirk caused a clit spasm, this was both delicious and frustrating.

We kept eating. Bubba told more stories. Each one was wilder than the last, indicating he'd embarrass the hell out of his children when the time came, at the same time providing fodder they should do as their daddy had done.

Suck the most out of life as you could while you had it.

Then we were finished with sandwiches, chips and Shambles's daily contribution to our lunch (Reese's Pieces peanut butter cookies, peanut butter being the day's theme). The guys got down to starting back up with work and I got down to the limited business of cleaning up lunch.

It was Thursday, a week after hot dogs and s'mores with Deke.

We had Bubba for that day and the next in order to drywall the higher areas of the walls and start on the ceilings.

The men didn't figure they'd get the whole thing done in those two days but they weren't messing around.

As for Deke, the Friday after we had our cookout, the first thing he'd done when he came back to my house to work was give me a few outlets in the main area, and after doing this, he brought in three rickety (but working) standing lamps which he'd plugged in.

He'd then ordered me, "Keep this on at night, Jus. You don't need to break your ankle if you gotta move through this space and folks out there who might be around need to see this house's got someone in it. Yeah?"

I had noted that outlets and light in that area were kind of a priority, but I hadn't mentioned it since everything was and I didn't want to mess with his mojo and ask for something that was not in the contractor rota.

But he gave it to me anyway.

Deke looking out for me.

Pleasure and pain.

That was what my days were made up of.

The pleasure part being, after giving me outlets, Deke spending the time in between then and now actually making serious progress on giving me walls. The whole downstairs was done. And he was taping because he needed an extra man to help him get the sheets of drywall upstairs so he could begin on that.

The pain part came the day he told me, when we had him, Bubba would be helping with that too. To which I'd told Deke I could help him get the drywall upstairs.

He'd then asked me to help him lift one bundle, which was two sheets.

He was a powerhouse and lifted his end like he could also hurtle the double sheet through the air onto the upstairs landing. But even so, we barely got it up before I set my end down and announced that I'd like to enjoy my house when it was done and do it without a hernia.

The pain was in the gift he gave me after I'd said that. That gift was him bursting out laughing, filling my crazy space with the deep, abiding beauty of his mirth in a way it seemed to tunnel through the drywall he'd put up, the foam insulation he'd blown in, to settle there for eternity. All I had to do to call it up was walk to a wall he'd given me, press my ear to it, and Deke's rich laughter would sound in my ear like the waves in a seashell.

Not done with the Deke-style generosity he had no clue he was sharing with me, he'd then walked to me, cupped the back of my neck in his big hand and swayed my whole body with it for a few beats, saying, "You're damn funny, gypsy."

See?

Pleasure and pain.

That hadn't been it.

No.

More pain (and pleasure) came when Max called on the Monday telling me he was arranging for Joe Callahan to come earlier to put in my security system.

Max had shared this by saying, "Deke's not a big fan of you up there all alone with not a lot of light, no animal and no security. So I'll arrange things with Cal and get that sorted."

Deke's not a big fan…

I agreed to Cal coming earlier. Joe "Cal" Callahan did all my family's security. As well as Lacey's. And Lacey's dad's. And so on. He was the best in the business and in our business, which included some crazies, the best was what you got no matter the cost (and Cal cost a load, but he was worth it).

It was a good plan and I should have actually asked Cal there before I'd moved in, to be honest.

And I felt the warmth of friendliness Deke was giving by looking out for me.

I just wished that warmth was of another variety.

Needless to say, the boundary that Deke had swept away over hot dogs and s'mores he intended to keep swept away.

But there was still another boundary.

That said, he liked me. He showed it. The banter remained.

He also asked once to check in if I'd heard from my brother and made it clear with his expression after I'd said no that he was there to listen if I did.

And I'd straight up told him over sandwiches about how my girl Bianca had disappeared and how I was making calls to everyone she knew, I knew she knew but I didn't know (if I could get their numbers), and anyone else that might tell me something.

And coming up with zilch.

Through this I'd shared that I was concerned with her partaking of certain substances, her increased imbibing of certain liquids and the fact that she had quickly dwindling resources (this I didn't share being the trust fund her mother and father gave her, something with her behavior the last few years her dad had been staunch about not augmenting).

And last, that even before this descent, she'd begun to seem aimless and lost so even if I was to get her to think about tackling the dope and the drinking, these, as ever, were seated in deeper issues that I did not have the tools to tackle.

I'd obviously not shared that all this began with Bianca around the time Lacey and I started to follow in our parents' footsteps, gain our own attention, acclaim and fame, and Bianca had gotten herself an agent in order to go out on auditions for television shows and movies.

She'd been asked to do some commercials and had been offered some movies of the straight-to-video variety that had a lot of sex scenes. All of these she'd turned down, declaring no way she was going to do shit like that. She was no model or spokeswoman. And she wasn't going to be her mother and be all about tits, ass and hair (even though, being all about this, her mother made a ton of money, earning a lot of fame along the way, and she made no bones about how she did it).

Bianca, she'd proclaimed, was a serious actress.

The problem was, she had the lush, big-blonde-haired, big-blue-eyed, big-chested, slim-bodied, fuck-me beauty her mom had with a lot of attitude and rock 'n' roll her dad had thrown in.

But she wasn't a good actress. Lace and I had seen her in a couple of plays that didn't do so well, the reason was partially her, partially the plays sucking, but that well had dried up due to the it being partially her part.

So I felt a strange sense of guilt I rationally knew I shouldn't feel (and I knew, since we'd talked about it, that Lacey felt the same) that I was part of the reason she started to turn to the dark side.

I hadn't shared this with Deke either.

He'd had no advice, just listened and commiserated, his face intent and sharing open concern, but not for Bianca.

For me and my state of mind that I had too much shit on my plate and he didn't like that for me.

More pleasure and pain.

And last, I'd been showing him stuff my interior designer sent me, as well as other stuff I'd clocked as possibilities to buy to make my house a home (once I had walls, floors and the rest).

I did this as a joke at first.

But Deke shocked the crap out of me by not only being interested, but opinionated.

About everything.

"No one needs a white couch," he'd shared about one of the pieces the designer was suggesting.

"It's cream," I corrected him, looking from my laptop to him.

"No one needs a cream couch," he'd amended. "Not only are you fucked, you slop ketchup on it, you get a dog, the hair'll show and bottom line, it's butt-ugly."

He'd been funny.

He'd also been right.

So out went the cream couch.

There was further from Deke.

"Don't get nonstick pans. Coating always gets scraped off. Get the stainless steel stuff."

And…

"You paint the guest bath pink, I'm taking away your cool card."

Also…

"Why women buy kitchen towels I do not get. Why d'you think paper towel was invented? Use it, toss it, don't gotta throw it in the wash, done."

I was going stainless steel (or actually thinking more along the lines of Le Creuset). I also threw out the misguided whim of painting the guest bath pink (the hue I'd showed him was more of a rose, but I didn't correct him about that).

But I was buying dish towels. They were more environmentally friendly, but it wasn't that.

Lots of dish towels were pretty and you could switch them out for holidays and everything.

Something I'd never done. Items I'd never owned.

But I was looking forward to it.

These were my lovely, yet dismal thoughts as I took our trash from lunch to the garage and was moving back through the hall when I saw Deke come through the door that led to the great room.

He looked at me, jerked his head toward my bedroom, and before I could ask what was up, he walked into the hall and turned right, going directly into my bedroom.

Deke had never been in my bedroom.

Standing at the door had been bad enough.

Him in it?

Catastrophe.

Fuck, my bed was unmade and I hoped like hell I'd closed my nightstand drawers, or that there weren't cords leading into them doing any special charging, because my vibrators were getting a workout, what with Deke around six days out of seven. And no girl wanted anyone, man or woman, but especially a man-bunned hot guy she was pining for to see her sex toys.

Unless she was handing them over for him to use on her.

Fuck.

I walked in with Deke already in but standing at the edge of the opened door.

A quick look while he closed the door behind me and I saw the nightstand drawers were all the way closed and no cords.

Thank God.

Deke led with, "He won't ask, Jussy, so I'm askin'."

I turned to him and tipped my head back to catch his gaze.

"Who won't ask what?"

He jerked his head to the door. "Bub. He won't ask."

"Won't ask what?" I queried when Deke said no more.

"Preface this by sayin', you say no, he won't know I asked and it's all good. I get it. Even if he knew I was askin', he'd get it. It's a lot. But I'm still askin'."

I took a step toward him, matching my voice to his that was low, and demanded, "Dude, spit it out. Ask *what?*"

"You know Max pays time and a half on weekday overtime. He pays double time on weekends."

"Yes, I know this, Deke," I confirmed.

"Get shit done faster got another man workin' with me on Saturdays. And the bar does a good turnover. They ain't hurtin' but they ain't rollin' in it and both Krys and Bubba wanna give good to their kid when she comes. Bub especially."

He shifted even closer to me and I had to tip my head way back and modulate my breathing, especially when his hand came out and his fingers lightly touched the back of mine.

Pleasure.

And pain.

"Those stories he was tellin'," Deke continued, "they're funny but if he said some of that shit in front of Krys, she would not laugh. This is 'cause he used to be known as Bender Bubba. Took off on her to tie one on, have a good time, gone more than he was home. When he was gone, did shit no way he's gonna tell his babies and grandbabies because it wasn't right by any stretch of the imagination, the way he stepped out on Krys and did it constantly."

"Oh my God," I whispered, not quite able to believe that Bubba, who obviously doted on Krystal, also had stepped out on her.

Constantly.

Deke nodded and kept talking.

"They nearly didn't make it. She bounced him. He dried out, doesn't drink a drop, not anymore, and he pulled out all the stops to get her back. Haven't seen him look at a woman unless he's helpin' at the bar and askin' her what she wants to drink. Lives for Krys. Lives for them. But I still get he's got the drive to prove she made the right decision by takin' him back. Been years but he put her through the wringer and it's penance that needs to be paid. If he could bring a little extra in, anytime he could, lighten their load, give her more, help set up their life so they're ready for their kid, he'll wanna do it. So you took him on on Saturdays, even that little'd mean a lot."

What that little would mean was that on Saturdays, I wouldn't have Deke to myself.

And even if this wasn't what I wanted, I recognized it as a good thing.

Further, I hated knowing this history because I liked Bubba but I knew the effects of cheating.

I didn't want that for Krystal and I wondered if that was part of her tears and fear in her car, something that was too intimate and maybe embarrassing to share with someone she barely knew. This not only being fear of the unknown of what she'd be like as a mother, but also if that huge change in their life might cause Bubba to go back to his old ways, including straying.

What I did want for Krys was for that little to mean a lot.

Bonus, stuff would get done faster at my house.

"You want me to ask him or do you wanna tell him I'm down with it?" I said by way of answer.

Deke smiled at me.

I let that feed my poet's soul the only way it could and smiled back.

"I'll ask him if he's up for it, tellin' him you're wantin' as much progress as you can get so you're down with it. But I know he'll be here on Saturday."

"Cool," I replied.

Another brush of his fingers on the back of my hand before he said, "Awesome of you, Jus."

"I want as much progress as I can get, Deke. So this is not a big sacrifice."

Right then he gave another gift.

More pleasure.

More pain.

Deke winked at me.

Then he muttered, "Gettin' back to work," turned and walked out my bedroom door.

I stared at the door thinking "Pleasure and Pain" would be a great name for a song.

So I grabbed my notebook, my guitar from its stand in the corner of my room, and I went out to my deck.

* * *

I was strumming, and alternately jotting, when I heard a deep, "Yo."

I turned in my Adirondack chair and saw Deke standing there, a few steps outside my opened French door.

"Yo," I returned. "Time to knock off?"

He said nothing. He just stood there staring.

Not at me. Not at me with my guitar.

At the notebook balanced on the arm of my chair.

"Deke," I called when the nothing he said stretched.

His body gave a weird jerk and his eyes came to mine.

"Yeah, time to knock off," he grunted, sounding just as weird as his body jerk had been.

"Right," I said, standing and resting my guitar on the chair, feeling funny for a lot of reasons.

I'd definitely worked when he was around but he'd never seen me do it.

I'd also been writing out lyrics to a song the first time he'd met me.

So there was a lot of evidence there of a number of things he might figure out that could be uncomfortable because I hadn't shared them with him.

I didn't know what to do because he just stood there, his gaze moving from me, to my guitar, to my notebook.

"Deke," I said softly.

His attention sliced back to me.

"Back with Bub tomorrow at seven, Jussy."

Jussy.

That indicated it was all good, even if he still seemed removed in a way he hadn't since the beginning.

And I knew looking at him the time for my peace that came with being just Jus was over.

Deke and I had become friends. And friends didn't keep important things from friends. Such as the fact their father was a famous, alas now-dead rock star. Their grandfather was the same. And they'd followed in those footsteps, however short that path had been.

This bringing on giving him my first name and coming clean we'd met before.

It was ten minutes seven years ago, but if he remembered the name Justice, that would have to happen.

"Krys says Bubba's has a band coming in tomorrow night," I told him. "Feel like meeting there, throwing a few back?" *And me sharing a bunch of shit that might piss you off but you need to know and my best bet is to tell you in a public place so if you lose your mind, our location might help contain it so I'll have the chance to explain*, I didn't say.

"Got plans."

Arrow through the heart.

Plans on a Friday night for a man who looked like Deke.

I didn't want to know, and there were other options, but if the one I figured it was actually was…

I didn't want to know.

"Okay, Deke," I replied but kept trying. Sooner rather than later. Don't procrastinate. I'd done enough of that already. "Wanna come over tonight?" I shot him a forced grin. "Go into town, get takeout from the Italian place. I'll drink wine out of a red Solo cup, doing it with guilt heavy at what that cup will mean to the environment. You can have beer. And we can toast to my addition of kitchen utensils, that being after I buy a wine opener."

"Wiped, Jus. Thanks but work like today takes it out of you. But just so you know, talked to Bubba. He's on for Saturdays as long as that lasts."

He wasn't being an ass and he wasn't being closed off.

Yet he was for that last.

With no other choice, I nodded. "Sounds good."

I said that but I did not like this. Bubba coming tomorrow through Saturday, I wouldn't have alone time with Deke until Monday.

Maybe I could get Krystal or Jim-Billy to tell me where he lived and pop by on Sunday.

Though, if there was a woman, a woman who, say, packed bologna sandwiches for Deke's lunches, I didn't want to hit his place on Sunday (not a circumstance I'd considered after he'd picked up the chick at Bubba's that day I'd closed on the house—then again, that chick might have had staying power, another reason he held us at friendly).

But what woman would let her guy go for hot dogs and s'mores with another woman, alone, even if they were friends, especially if her guy was Deke?

Maybe they were new and she didn't pack his bologna sandwiches for lunch every day. Just the mornings after the nights she stayed after he fucked her.

Shit.

"Jus?"

It was me who gave a weird jerk when I focused on him.

"You good?" he asked.

I was not.

"Yep," I told him.

"Good. See you tomorrow."

"Okay, Deke. See you tomorrow."

He did a farewell head tilt and off he went through my door, into my bedroom, sauntering through it like it was his bedroom, and he disappeared into the shadows of the house.

"Okay," I whispered to the windows. "That was weird and it was a bad weird and it could be a *very* bad weird."

It might have just been me, but it seemed the windows agreed.

* * *

"We don't do this that often," Lauren, Tate's wife, shouted at me over the band playing at Bubba's the next night. She was sitting on a stool in between Jim-Billy and me at the end of the bar. "Krys introduced it a while ago. Hit big." She grinned. "As you can see."

I looked from her gorgeous face to the bar, which was heaving.

An aside, to say she suited Tate was an understatement. They were like Barbie and Ken in their forties, with Barbie having a killer ass and Ken not being Ken but GI Joe except with longer hair, a beard and a lot more badass.

"Couple of bars in Gnaw Bone have live music," Lauren kept shouting to me. "They rake it in. We've got some friends, Zara and Ham, live in GB. Ham runs one of the bars there. It's the competition," she said, still grinning, like it actually wasn't, or if it was that competition was friendly. "It gave Krys the idea."

I nodded, shouting back, "It was a good one!"

She returned my nod and twisted back to the band that was also good. Obviously, I'd heard better and this was in my dad's living room, but they didn't suck.

I'd done my best to slink in unseen because the peace of being just Jus might be done for me with Krys, Jim-Billy, Bubba, Tate, Lauren, Sunny, Shambles and soon Deke, but it was still there for everybody else.

And with musicians around, I knew better than to waltz in as Justice Lonesome.

I was no Johnny and I was no Lacey but I was a singer, songwriter, producer, guitar player and many in the biz, precisely those who'd play a biker bar, no matter how removed from the glitz (and perhaps precisely those) had no interest in Lacey Town, who didn't write her own music or play an instrument.

But they'd know the likes of Jerry, Johnny, Jimmy, Tammy, the Blue Moon Gypsies…and me.

It seemed I'd pulled it off, doing it enjoying a few brews and getting to know Lauren better.

Now the band had begun playing, they were loud and there was no getting to know anyone better without shouting.

And I had a strict philosophy. If someone was on any stage and I was in the same room with them, my attention was on them. They deserved that respect. Lauren shouting a few words to me was one thing. But I was not one of those douchebags who sat while a band was playing their heart out or a singer was belting it out and held a full-blown conversation. If I needed to do that, I walked out of the room.

So I was trying to get into it.

But my mind was on other things.

That day Deke had again not been closed off, even if he had, but he could pull this off with Bubba around because Bubba was what I'd clocked him as when I first met him. A good ole boy filled with jokes and stories and a never-ending supply of camaraderie.

They'd be back the next day so I couldn't sit down with Deke. I'd have to get through more weird and after that wait until I had him on Monday.

And that was a lot of time to be stuck in your head thinking over all the possible reactions, coming up with none good and letting that devour you so you were a nervous wreck and fucked it all up by the time you actually had your shot to set things right.

I'd already fucked up. I should have told him early—about all of it.

Mr. T would be disappointed with me.

I looked to the front of the bar where they'd pushed back and scrunched together the tables so they could lay the makeshift stage. And I watched and listened to the band, remembering Granddad telling me the stories of the road. The dive bars. The honkytonks. Playing for cash handed over at the end of the gig, cash barely enough to gas up the car and buy the band an end-of-gig meal at a late-night diner. Sometimes the cash was short so things would get dicey. So as they got bigger, more well-known, which meant more asses in seats and even traveling groupies, they'd actually had to employ a manager who was mostly an enforcer so no one would fuck them over.

Dad had had a little of that. He'd had to pave part of his own way. Prove his salt. Show he had what it took and could give all he had to give.

I hadn't had that.

I'd had three record labels gagging for it and my choice of producers.

I looked around the bar, seeing folks chair dancing, others off to the sides on their feet just plain dancing.

And I looked around, a funny feeling in my stomach—the bad kind of nostalgia.

But also the kind of feeling I sometimes got around Deke. Having something so close that I wanted so badly. Something that I had a taste of, a piece of. But I'd never taste it fully, have it be *mine*.

I was feeling all of this thinking I could have killed the road if it had been like this for me.

People out on a Friday night for a good time, a few drinks and that vibe. Just the love of the notes through the amp, the lyrics through the mic, so close to your audience you could see it move over them. Their heads bobbing. Their lips moving. Their bodies swaying. Loud or quiet, the moment of connection lasted as long as the set. And then the next one. In between and after the gig was through, you drank at the bar amongst your people. You weren't whisked to a dressing room.

You were always right in the thick of it, creating it, building it, that connection. Music, one of the few things that did nothing but make life good, you *were* it, down to every note for that night in a bar in the middle of nowhere.

The song ended and I stopped bobbing my head, looking to the lead singer as the band didn't go right into another song.

He started talking.

"No possible way to believe that we'd hit this joint and be in the presence of greatness."

My scalp started tingling.

Uh-oh.

Lauren and Jim-Billy's heads turned my way.

Maybe I hadn't slunk in under radar.

Shit.

"But we are and *damn*," the lead went on, "I know you know it'd be more than cool if we could talk the beautiful, the talented, the kickass Justice Lonesome into comin' up on the stage and joining us in a couple of songs."

Nope.

Not under radar.

"Shit, crap, shit, crap, shit," I chanted, doing that trying not to allow my lips to move, staring at the stage where the lead singer was now giving me a broad, in-the-zone rock 'n' roll smile.

You could not say no to this.

No one could say no to this without looking like a douche.

Hell, I'd been out with my father on more times than I could count, in a dark corner, thinking we were incognito, just wanting to take in a local band, and he got called out.

He never refused to take the stage.

Not once.

"Shit, crap, shit, crap, shit," I chanted again.

"What do you say, Justice?" the lead singer prompted, his smile faltering, and I felt but did not look to see folks peering around to find out who he was talking about, spurred to curiosity not only at the man's words, but at the mention of the name Lonesome.

Or who knew me and were just looking to find *me*.

"Don't worry, sister, got my shotgun in the back." I heard Krys decree and turned my head to see her moving out from behind the back of the bar.

I looked at her, shocked to shit that Jim-Billy had not lied.

She was heading for her shotgun.

"No!" I whispered loudly.

Shit, crap, shit, crap, *shit*.

Krys scowled at me.

"It's good," I decided verbally. "It's time. It has to come out. It's a great vibe. Might as well be now. I'll do it."

She kept giving me a glare that was also an inspection. "You sure?"

I was not.

"Sure," I replied.

Krys's eyes went beyond me to Lauren. "She ain't sure."

"Whatever, shut up, I'm going," I said.

"Don't tell me to shut up," she snapped.

I could not do this with Krystal now.

So I didn't.

I looked through Lauren, saw Jim-Billy watching me and felt his hand grab mine and give it a squeeze as I walked past him and heard the stilted clapping that got less and less stilted, stronger and stronger, until there were a couple of hoots and a couple more hollers as I took my first step on stage.

I smiled my stage smile, giving handshakes to the band, getting their names, feeling them move close in a huddle and one of them handed me a guitar.

Then he handed me a pick.

"Extra," he said. "Amped you up. You're good."

Fabulous.

"'Chain Link,'" the lead singer declared. "Vibe's for rompin' stompin' but it would be fuckin' amazing, Justice, doing 'Chain Link' with you."

He was jazzed. I saw it. He was beside himself he was standing onstage with a Lonesome.

But no way in hell I was doing "Chain Link." I didn't want to let the guy down, not any of them, but that was just not happening.

"This vibe, this bar, boys, I got a better idea," I told them.

They huddled and they must have more than known me because they were all fired up to give up "Chain Link" to do what I always did at my own gigs.

An homage to my mom.

I pulled the guitar strap over my head, settled it on my shoulder.

I moved to the mic stand, adjusted it for my height.

The boys moved to their places.

I looked out at the crowd and put my mouth to the mic.

"Hi. I'm Justice."

Everyone shot to their feet, cheering and shouting, even if they didn't know me, the word had gotten around from those who did.

Or they just felt it.

Onstage, Jerry, Johnny, Justice, it just seeped out of us.

No holding it in.

Shit, crap, shit, crap, *shit*.

"Gonna give you a little bit of what my dad Johnny gave to me and do it through some songs my mom loved," I told them.

More cheers.

I looked down to the guitar, took the pick to a few strings.

Standing on that stage in front of that crowd, the nothing notes flowed out of the amp.

And right through me, filling me, *saturating* me, adding something to my system as integral as water, calories, oxygen.

When I felt that—a feeling that was like a lost limb had grown back, or four of them—without hesitation and with a need I'd denied for half a decade, I shot a glance over my shoulder at the band, turned back to the mic, put my fingers to the frets, played two notes and sang three words into the mic…

Then those two notes again and two more words…

And it happened.

A broad smile spread on my face and the Lonesome shot right out of me as I played and sang Linda Rondstadt's "When Will I Be Loved."

The crowd went crazy.

And with a band of boys whose names I didn't remember, to a group of locals I'd have to live among, smiling no stage smile but feeling the rapture of rock 'n' roll shine right through, we gave them Linda's country rock anthem.

Two minutes of pure brilliance.

And dancing, clapping along and shouting the words, the crowd gave it back.

Everyone was out of their seat when we finished so I could offer what anyone onstage feeling what I was feeling, giving what I was giving, getting what I was getting, the two words that said it all but never near enough.

"Thank you."

More cheers.

One of the boys threw out the beginning of "It's So Easy" and I went right back to the mic, drawn to it in a way I didn't even try to resist.

We hadn't cleared the first verse when I looked out the sides of my eyes to take in the audience to my right and I saw him.

Deke head and shoulders above the back of the standing crowd pressed close to the tables.

No.

Shit, *no*.

The show went on. It had to.

No matter what.

So I kept singing, turning my head and staring at his blank face.

His expression showed nothing but his eyes were glued to me.

It was a great song. I loved that song. My mother loved, then hated (due to Dad and what that song turned into), then loved again that song.

But right then, staring into Deke's eyes, it said way too much.

I kept singing it right to him. I couldn't stop. Music was moving from me, communicating through me (this time right at Deke), and I was a Lonesome. That was in my DNA. If I could use it to say what I had to say, I would do it and my brain couldn't stop it.

You'd have to rip the guitar from my hands and gag me.

And "It's So Easy" didn't have a lot of different words.

But for Deke, it still said it all.

I managed to tear my gaze away during the twanging guitar solo.

But during the harmony at the end and my final notes, my hair flew everywhere as I yanked the guitar strap over my head, holding the guitar out to no one, saying into the mic when the song was done, "Thank you. Thanks for listening. Now keep enjoying this awesome band."

I did this because Deke was prowling out.

One of the guys in the band took the guitar. I quickly mumbled my thanks and other musician brethren stuff and ran off the stage, jumped down, pushed through the applauding, shouting crowd and hit the door to hit the chilly night and see nothing but a full parking lot.

I looked left. I looked right. And lucky for me (or not, as the case I would have to find out would be), he was a man who was easy to see, even at a distance.

"Deke!" I shouted, dashing that way, my long, spangled gypsy skirt flowing back, my cowboy boots hitting the pavement not drowned out even if the music inside was leaking through the concrete walls of Bubba's. "Deke!" I shouted again as I saw him throw a long leg over a bike. I was no longer dashing, now I was sprinting.

He looked at me and watched me make it the last fifteen feet, stopping on a near-skid at his side and taking in a huge breath.

I peered into his impassive face.

"Deke," I whispered.

"Shouldn't've cut the set short," he replied.

"I—"

"Get it, Jus," he stated, his words clipped. "You bein' Jus. Just Jus. That bein' important to you, 'specially at a time like this. Get it. Probably not easy bein' you. Dad like that. People wantin' a piece of you."

I moved closer, not sure whether to lift a hand and touch him, watching his face intently.

"I was gonna—"

He jerked his head to the bar. "You got what your dad had. You should do something with it."

My mouth snapped shut.

He didn't know me.

Or at least the Justice Lonesome part of me.

Then he proved me wrong.

Partially.

"Gettin' this out there, we met," he announced.

"What?" I was again whispering.

"Years back. Night my ma had her first heart attack. We met at a bar up in Wyoming."

He *remembered?*

Wait.

The night his mother had a *heart attack?*

Again.

Wait.

Her *first one?*

His eyes went to my hair then back to me. "Bad night, heard word, took off, nearly lost her," he stated emotionlessly. "It'd be her third heart attack few years later that finally did her in but that first one shook me. Your hair. Those eyes. Knew I knew you from somewhere, musta blocked it because that night and the next however many fuckin' sucked. Saw you today with your notebook. Came to me. Met you that night and you had a notebook almost like that. You were at a dude ranch. You don't remember but we met."

"I do," I told him quietly. "I just thought you didn't."

He nodded, sussing it out immediately.

Maybe.

"So no Justice."

No, dammit.

I didn't give him Justice.

I got closer. "Deke—"

"I get it. Must be hard, bein' you."

"There's more to tell."

"Not really. Got a famous dad. Shit ton of money. Even more talent. He's gone, don't pay attention to that shit but still know the media feeds off anything just as long as it's shitty. Go into a frenzy they got the shot to feed off your grief. Your brother bein' an asshole, more fuel to that fire. You disappear in the mountains. I get it."

Actually, thankfully, the media had not yet locked onto what Mav was doing.

I didn't share that with Deke at that juncture.

"It's that and it's other stuff, Deke," I told him. "Can we go somewhere? Talk?"

"'Bout what, Jus?" he asked. "I get it."

"The other stuff," I repeated.

"You don't gotta give me what you don't wanna give me. Got no call to own it. Don't want that call. Made that clear so you know that."

At his words, I took a step back.

He looked down at my feet then up at me.

It was late. Dark. But Krystal and Tate didn't mess around with lights in their parking lot.

I saw his flinch before he hid it.

He knew the barb he'd thrown stung and did that in a big way.

We'd been dancing around the fact that I was at one place, he was in another and we both knew what one wanted and the other didn't.

That being me wanting him and Deke not wanting me back that same way.

He'd pushed the boundaries back, gave me the friendly.

But he'd done it never being a dick about establishing precisely what those boundaries were we'd never cross.

Until now.

"Jus—"

"You look like you're rarin' to get home so I'll let you do that," I muttered, shifting to move away.

Deke caught my forearm.

I turned my eyes to his.

"Jus," he said softly, his hand putting on pressure like he wanted to bring me closer.

I put pressure on the other way, slipping it out of his grip.

"See you tomorrow, Deke."

I started to walk away.

"Jus—"

I turned back to him.

"Sorry about your mom," I said. "Hate that happened. I'm really sorry. Both parents gone, that sucks for you and I get that's in a big way. But I hope you don't take it wrong when I say it's good to finally know why you stood me up."

Another flinch before, "Jussy—"

I didn't want to run. I didn't want to make a bigger drama of it than it already was.

So I just lifted a hand behind me in a wave good-bye, not looking at him, but I did walk really fast back to the bar.

It took me a while, having to force smiles, stop and take a few photos, scribble my name on a few napkins, but I finally got to my purse at the bar.

I muttered shit I didn't remember to get out of talking to Krys, Lauren, Jim-Billy.

Then I left, going to my truck.

In all this, Deke did not come after me.

And I would realize that I was now becoming addicted to the pain that came with less and less pleasure because I gave into that pain as I walked to my truck.

This meaning I looked toward where Deke's bike had been.

Both the bike and Deke were gone.

* * *

Deke

Jussy's song "Chain Link" sounding out of his phone, Deke sat on the couch in his trailer and read online encyclopedia entries.

She was right. There was other stuff to talk about.

A lot of it.

"Chain Link" wasn't his normal thing. Shit like the Allman Brothers and the Foo Fighters were his normal thing.

And Johnny Lonesome.

But it was beautiful.

Jussy's voice singing her own song was better than her standing onstage in a biker bar belting out Linda Rondstadt, and she'd fucking *killed* that. Rondstadt had one of the best voices in the business. That sweet goodness that could pack a punch. Rise from that low right up the scale to hit high and not once lose its power.

Jus had that.

She had presence up there too. Her smile, Christ. It did a number on him sitting in her fucked-up house eating a sandwich.

Onstage it was spectacular.

Reading about her Deke saw he was not the only person who thought that.

One album of her own, nominated for awards. A tour where the critics raved about her live performances. She wrote for the Blue Moon Gypsies and had more than a couple dozen other credits, including as a producer. Fuck, he even knew each of her songs the Gypsies performed because he might not listen to songs like "Chain Link" (and even if he didn't, he still thought it was a fucking gorgeous song), he listened to the Gypsies, including their slower stuff, which was what Jussy did for them.

She was out of his reach.

He knew that the minute she'd walked into Bubba's. He had not known that with the biker babe slumming she'd been doing with her girlfriends years ago in Wyoming, stepping into that role so completely, he didn't get that first whiff she was what she was. But he knew from the first time he saw her in Carnal she was untouchable.

Now he knew she wasn't just untouchable, she was not even in his stratosphere.

Even if Deke could get past the working for her barrier (and he couldn't) then the money barrier (and he couldn't with that either) then the rootless life barrier (and that also wasn't going to happen), he couldn't get past this.

That said, that night he did it quiet, not outright ugly, but he still struck out, pissed for whatever reason he was, not wanting where those feelings came from to show, and he'd been a straight-up dick.

She didn't deserve that. She'd kept herself to herself, guarded for good reasons with the life she led, and he knew from the last couple of days she'd come to a place she was ready to share it with him.

But the reasons she kept it to herself were good reasons. It wasn't anyone's to have until Jus decided to give it to them.

He lifted his head from staring unseeing at his phone to staring unseeing at his trailer.

Fuck, he had to get them back there. He had to do what he could to heal that hurt because, as whacked as it was, he still figured it hurt him to hurt her more than the hurt he gave her and he figured this because he was right then feeling that pain.

But he gave her that hurt, he saw it, fucking hated it, so he had to do something about it.

She meant something to him and she didn't hide he was coming to mean something to her. He broke that so he had to mend it.

He stared down at the phone in his hand as "Chain Link" shifted to another song that was Jussy's.

There was a photo on her online encyclopedia entry. She was at a mic, chin down and twisted, like she was looking at her guitar.

And she was smiling in the way she always smiled. Big and out there and open. Like tonight onstage. Like sitting in her fucked-up house on drywall while they ate sandwiches.

Big and out there and open.

And so fucking gorgeous, it was almost hard to believe.

Deke'd never know how that smile would change after he made her come. After he made her breakfast. After she climbed off the back of his bike when they were done with a ride.

It's good to finally know why you stood me up.

These thoughts the only ones in his head, he didn't think it before he did it but he did it and his phone was slicing through the air, slamming against the narrow wall by the tiny kitchenette.

He worked construction and had that kind of life. He didn't need much and part of what he didn't need was to fuck up his phone so he had to buy a new one. This meant he had a protective case on it so it bounced right off the wall, the counter, to the floor without a scratch.

But the screen had been touched in a way the music died.

Jussy's voice blinked right out.

And right then, that worked for Deke.

CHAPTER EIGHT

Your Life, Your Choice

Justice

SINCE I HAD zero sleep the night before, I was up when the banging on the door came early.

Six thirty.

This did not bode good things.

I went from closet, where I was trying to figure out what to wear, to bedroom, hall, great room and saw Deke was wearing a blue T-shirt that day.

He didn't wear white every day but he switched it up only occasionally.

I hadn't yet seen blue.

But I had noted that army green did spectacular things to his hazel eyes.

I had on a droopy cardigan over my pajamas.

I did not care. They covered me up, mostly. Little floral print shorts with pompom edging. Flowy camisole that had some lace and another floral pattern that didn't match but didn't clash.

Fake gypsy princess.

Outed rock princess. Heiress to the kingdom, she'd abdicated her throne.

And Deke now knew it all.

Or most of it.

Whatever.

I opened the door, lifted my eyes to Deke only to cut a glance through him before I turned and started walking away but did it talking.

"Hey. You're early. Coffee isn't started yet. I'll hit that and then hit the shower."

"Jussy."

I carried on like he didn't speak. Definitely carried on like he didn't speak in that sweet, soft, remorseful tone that with one word, that word my name, did a number on me.

"Four cups, doesn't take it long to drip. But favor," I turned and looked toward him, my gaze hitting his neck, not his eyes, "if you and Bubba drain it, make some more for me. When I get out of the shower, gonna need it."

"Jus, I'm here early to talk."

He'd come in, hitting the center of the space, to his right side was the low, round, stone fireplace that Deke had told me was going to have a long, narrow copper hood that would look awesome without obstructing too much of the view when they got it in. A fireplace that was in line with the front door and in line with the fire pit on the deck.

Symmetry.

My life had never had symmetry. It was a zigzag line that led me to there, a place I'd wanted to end the zigging and zagging.

Now I suddenly wanted that back.

"You were right last night," I replied. "If you get it, and you said you did, there isn't anything left to say."

He opened his mouth but I wasn't done.

"Except, what I'd guess you'd guess is that wasn't the first time I hit a stage. I work in the business."

He nodded, doing it cautiously, and returned, "Know that, looked you up last night."

So very easy to find so very much on Justice Lonesome.

He could read every word and have no clue.

I nodded too, just once, not cautiously.

"Right, then the only other thing left to say is that I was...well, we were in a weird place last night since I'd kept things from you. It's cool you get it but just to explain, I knew you the minute I saw you." I gave a one shoulder shrug. "It was kinda embarrassing you didn't remember me, so I didn't bring that up. But also, partially, it was about you being right with this gig also being me needing to be just Jus. A time-out from all the shit festering out there. And it's also cool you're down with giving that to me even though you didn't know you were giving it to me. But all that said, last night I didn't have it together enough to say but a few words about it so I'll say now I'm really sorry for your loss. Your mom. I know what losing a parent feels like, not both, fortunately, but still. So I know there are no words to say except I'm sorry."

I stood my ground, continuing to talk even if I did it while he was moving toward me.

He stopped way too close and I had to tilt my head back way too far in a way that made me feel small and vulnerable which, in a different world, feeling these around Deke would have special meaning.

But in my world they didn't.

"Thank you, baby," he said gently.

I closed my eyes and when I opened them, I requested quietly and not ugly, "Please don't call me that, Deke. I'm not your baby. I'm not even Jussy to you. I know what I am and I think for both our sakes, especially mine, a good way to move on from here is that we both keep it just like that."

There was a lot in his face, so different from the Deke I'd met years ago and the same man that came back into my life weeks ago. This being that he was showing it all to me, all of it good which meant all of it was bad.

And worse, he lifted a hand and filtered it up in my hair from the neck, where he rested his palm.

"Jussy—" he began.

"Don't," I whispered. I felt the pads of his fingers press into my scalp so I whispered again, "Please don't, Deke."

"Known you only weeks, babe, still know you're one of the best women I've ever met so—"

I cut him off before he could say *I hope we can find a way to still be friends.*

That was what we'd do. I knew I couldn't live without at least having that from Deke.

But right now it hurt too much to be reminded, especially in his beautiful voice, that was all he wanted.

And anyway, I didn't need a reminder.

I lived that knowledge day in and day out and it was lacerating my poet's soul.

"Please," it came out trembling, and dammit, I felt my eyes get moist, "don't."

It looked like it caused him pain to slide his hand out of my hair.

I knew it caused me pain.

But I was getting used to it.

He stopped touching me but he bent his neck deep to get his face closer to mine even as he swayed in several inches so his big body was invading my space.

"Bein' that, Jussy, I want you to know it'd mean a lot to me if we can find a way to move on from here."

"We will," I assured him. "You're a good guy. Of course you get I think that so we'll find a way. It's just that right now I need some space."

"Not sure how to give you that, needin' to be in your space to get work done for you, Jus, but I can say I'll try."

"You don't need to worry. I'm beginning to have walls. I'll soon have floors. I need to look at paint chips and wooden spoons and shit. It's time I got busy. And so..." I made an instant decision. "I'm gonna go to Denver and do some shopping. You've got a key. You and Bubba just do your thing. I'll be back on Monday."

"That's a good idea."

He had no problem with me being away.

And I got it then. It hit me like a shot.

My situation with Deke.

My dad's with Joss.

In order to feed on what it needed, a poet's soul sought that which it'd never find, or in Dad's case (just a guess but I suspected a good one), sabotaged what it had in order to feed that need.

There had to be yearning. There had to be melancholy. There had to be pain mixed with pleasure, but the pain had to come stronger than the pleasure, knowing it never would get what it *really* needed.

No poet could be truly happy or their soul would waste away from starvation.

I nodded and made another instant decision.

"Right. I gotta get on that but I'll make you boys coffee before. Just help yourself."

Without letting him say anything, I moved back, got the hell out of his space and turned to do just that.

"Jus," he called.

Shit!

I turned back and forced my eyes to his.

"You onstage last night, went home, pulled down a few of your songs," he told me and I braced. "You got amazing talent and a beautiful voice, baby."

One of the songs he probably heard was "Chain Link."

And he had no idea.

And *that* was something he'd never know.

"Thanks," I muttered then quit fucking around and moved swiftly.

It didn't matter I was hasting a quick retreat, he didn't call out to me again.

So I succeeded in doing something I should have done from the beginning.

I escaped Deke.

* * *

Deke

"Not my business."

"Bub, don't."

"Not my business but I gotta—"

"Bub, I'm tellin' you, *don't*."

It was late morning. They'd been hauling drywall up to the second floor so Deke could get to work up there next week, but now they were on the scaffolding, laying the tongue-in-groove ceilings.

Bubba had let it be for three hours.

Being Bubba, it was a miracle it lasted that long.

"Was there last night, Deke. Everyone was," Bubba told him.

"You speak English?" Deke asked.

"Wood. Maggie. Tate. Laurie. Jim-Billy. And, dude," his voice had become a warning, "Krys."

That they could talk about.

"Then it's good you brought it up," Deke said. "'Cause I can tell you to tell your woman to keep out of it."

"What happened?" Bubba asked.

"None of your business."

"Was everyone's business the way she sang right to you. *Right* to you, man. And then after she was done, you took off and Jus took off after you." Bubba's head tipped to the side. "You two are tight. Easy to see. You've known Krys for years. Laurie. Lexie. Faye. Not tight with any of 'em the way you let Jus jabber at you and you actually listen. You got something goin' with her?"

She sang right to you.

Right *to you.*

Fuck him, he'd never forget Jussy looking right at him and singing about how easy it was to fall in love.

Yeah.

Fuck.

Him.

Deke buried that and shook his head. "Work for her, been with her every day for weeks. She's a good woman. Good soul. Good sense of humor. So she's a friend."

Bubba's eyes got big.

Fuck, he shouldn't have said anything.

But to shut down the shit he knew was ramping out there, he had to say something.

"You? A friend who looks like Jus who doesn't have one of your buds' rings on her finger?" Bubba asked doubtfully.

"She's my boss."

"Max is your boss," Bubba shot back. "She's the woman who pays Max to do the job. The hot woman with all that hair, Jesus." Now Bubba was shaking his head. "My baby's got a good head of hair and she switches it up constantly so I always got somethin' new and pretty to look at but Jus's hair—"

Deke felt an unhappy heat start spreading in his gut.

"Stop talkin' 'bout her hair," he clipped.

"Stop bein' such a narrow-minded, short-sighted fuckwad, open your eyes and *see*," Bubba clipped back, using a tone not only had Deke never heard from Bub, but also not one anyone who had eyes in their head and could see all the man Deke was had used on Deke. Not to mention Deke wouldn't have even guessed his friend had it in him. "She's into you, man. So fuckin' into you, she wasn't Jus, and that shit might come from her bein' a Lonesome, which I'm guessing you know now, bud, but it also comes from just bein' Jus. No matter what she does, she exudes cool. Any other woman was into you like that without you giving anything back, it'd be cute but it'd also be dorky and maybe even a little sad."

Fuck, it felt like the man had punched him in his throat.

"It's not sad," he forced through that throat. "We're good. We know what we are and it's all good."

"Not good the way it could be," Bub returned.

He had that right.

"So it's all good," Bubba kept at him, "why'd you take off and why'd she run after you?"

"Because I didn't know she was a Lonesome until last night, somethin'," Deke said with eyes narrowed on Bubba, not that he cared, just using that to deflect the shit Bubba was giving off Deke, "seems like you knew but you didn't share. And she thought I was pissed. It was a surprise but I wasn't pissed. We talked it out and it's all good."

"You talked it out and it's all good, why no sandwiches today, man? Why'd she get ready in her room, not findin' a dozen reasons like she usually does to come out and have a natter with you, which translates into coming out and just bein' *around* you, and instead she hauls ass outta here tellin' you she'll see you on Monday?"

"'Cause shit's getting done in her house," Deke explained logically, since it was true but it was also a lie. "She's only a couple of weeks away from a full crew gettin' in here and she's got you helpin' to keep that goin' and she doesn't have any furniture, brother. She lives her life like this," Deke threw out a hand to the space, "she gets a microwave, she's gonna be on that like white on rice. Can't be on that if the woman doesn't even have plates."

Bubba gave him a look and changed tactics.

"You should go for that, man."

"She's not my type."

Bubba's head twitched. "You got a type?"

"Yeah, and it isn't Jussy."

"Jussy," Bub whispered, looking now like he was trying not to smile.

"Yeah, Jussy," Deke bit out. "A Jussy who wants ceilings and walls, not two men standin' around on scaffolding gabbin' like women. So how 'bout we get on givin' her that?"

Another change came over Bubba and he said low, "She told Krys who she is 'cause her and Krys are getting close." A small smile hit his lips as he shook his head and went on, "Don't get that, how Krys makes everyone go through her twelve circles of hell to get in there but she let Jus in. Jus let her in in return. And Jus said she didn't want us sharing."

"I get that."

"Sorry, bro. But it was hers to give."

"I get that," Deke repeated. "Now can we get to work?"

"Yeah," Bubba replied. "After I go on record saying I think you're making a big mistake." He leaned toward Deke. "*Huge*." He leaned back. "I don't know what's holding you back but whatever it is, got a bad feeling you're throwin' away the best thing that ever dropped in your lap." He lifted a hand, palm up Deke's way when Deke opened his mouth. "Your life, your choice. Not gonna say another word but I'll have a word with my woman to get her and her posse to rein it in. But there it is. I'm on record. And I hope you think about it. But your life, your choice."

"Can I take it with that we're done?" Deke asked.

Bubba nodded. "We're done."

"Then let's get to work," Deke muttered.

Bubba gave him a long look but thank fuck, after giving it, he turned away.

Deke turned his thoughts from all Bubba had to say.

It's good to finally know why you stood me up.

Shit.

She sang right to you.

Right *to you*.

Fuck.

He turned his thoughts from Jussy too.

And he turned them to giving her the only thing he'd be able to give her that she couldn't give herself.

Something she actually could give herself since she was paying for it.

That being progress on the house she bought that she needed done and made safe so she could find her peace.

* * *

Justice

Sunday night, I stood in the great room where I'd come home to all three lamps lit because Deke had left them that way.

I put that thoughtfulness out of my mind and looked up.

I had a quarter of a fabulously stunning, wood ceiling laid in a herringbone pattern, the theme from the deck flowing through that space.

Symmetry.

I was finally getting it.

Right in time not to want it.

Zigs and zags were a lot better, I realized. You could cut and run on a zig, leave it all behind on a zag.

Now I was stuck.

I also saw the drywall upstairs ready for Deke to get started on giving me rooms the next day. And with the way he was going, it'd all be done, taped and primed by next week.

So it was good that that weekend I'd decided what color every room would be painted.

A flatbed truck was not the best vehicle to go crazy shopping in when you were shopping in a city a couple of hours away so you couldn't safely put much in the bed, but I'd bought myself so much stuff, on the way home the cab was stuffed full of it as well as my overnight bag.

In that stuff was kitchen towels and Deke would just have to deal.

He also wouldn't because he'd never be using them.

I sighed and moved to the front door to go out and haul in my stash.

I brought it in and made sure the front door was locked behind me.

I then moved to the other doors to make sure of the same.

I only kept one light on when I went to my bedroom.

Tuesday, Joe Callahan would be there to start work on my security system. On Saturday, Bubba would be there. And on Sunday, Lacey was showing.

Which meant, with Cal saying it would take a few days to do his gig, my hope was I'd only have one day alone with Deke next week.

But that day was the next day.

I had to find a way to get through it. Show him I could go back to sandwiches and banter.

I was going to do that but he'd have to deal with me pulling back.

He got why I'd been guarded before.

This time, I knew for sure he'd get me.

* * *

I heard glass breaking and my eyes shot open.

I lay still in the dark in my bed, listening.

Silence.

But the skin all over my body was tingling like it did when you had a bad dream, woke up and for those first seconds you were sure it was real.

I didn't remember dreaming but it could be a dream.

And anyway, I might not have a security system but I did kind of have one because the roads were a maze to get up there. They were well-tended but the closer you got to my house, the deeper in the mountains you were, there was not a single streetlight. Not to mention, my house was *way* off the beaten path, down a long lane so you couldn't even see it from Ponderosa Road. In the dark, you might not be able to see the lane. My mailbox was outside my house, the postman came all the way down the lane, so there wasn't even a postbox or number to share that up my narrow lane there was anything.

Not that anyone would know I owned that property. Mr. T made it so my LLC owned it and you'd have to dig deep even to find I owned the LLC.

So no one there.

But Deke would be there within hours and Cal would be there to set me up the next day.

I relaxed, rolled and started to reach for my phone to check what time it was when I heard my bedroom door opening.

Now moving automatically, adrenaline spiking through me, I didn't nab my phone.

I rolled the other way, jumped off the bed and ran like hell toward the French doors.

I was caught by my hair in a vicious grip and thrown back savagely, hitting the floor on my back with not even an elbow to cushion the fall, this knocking the wind right out of me.

Which meant he could get on top of me, straddling me.

I stared into his shadowed face, the ski mask hiding his features and I sucked in breath, twisted my hips and started to try to escape him when he hit me.

Shot to the left cheekbone first. Another direct hit nearly at the same place. A third one and I hadn't even turned my head to shake the second one off or had the chance to get my hands up to deflect the blows.

Stars exploded in my eyes the first and second but scary black started encroaching on the third before he took my hair in a brutal grip at the crown, slammed my head into the hardwood floors (fuck, I needed a rug in there) and then I felt the cold at my neck.

I quit breathing.

His ski mask got right in my face.

"Don't be any more stupid," he bit out.

A guy. From what I could see, white. No way to tell the color of his eyes.

All this I took in because I had the ability of sight. I wasn't being smart or thinking ahead.

I was barely breathing.

And all of my concentration was on the cold at my throat, cold I knew was a blade.

He got closer.

I wanted to swallow. *Needed* to swallow.

But I was scared shitless at swallowing and what that might do with what was pressed way too close to my throat.

"Now be good," he whispered.

The cold was gone but he used his grip in my hair to drag me across the floor.

I felt my eyes roll back in my head, my hands darting up to his wrists to hang on and draw myself up so there wasn't so much weight pulling on my hair, doing this because the pain of that was so immense, it was *insane*.

He dragged me up to my bed, and if I was coursing with adrenaline and panic before, him taking me to my bed, and what he might do to me there, it consumed me and I didn't think about any blade.

I just started struggling wildly, pushing, shoving, kicking out my legs, twisting, doing this all begging, "No, please, please, no."

He quelled my exertions with four more blows to the face, leaving me blinking and fighting to remain conscious before he got me on my back on the bed, straddled me, wrapped his hand around my throat…*and squeezed*.

Moving with reflexive desire to remain breathing, my legs kicked out behind him without me telling them to do it, my hips bucked, my nails tore at his wrist and forearm.

He just reached beyond me, nabbed something from the nightstand and I saw it illuminate his masked face when he engaged my phone.

"Password," he bit out.

I kept struggling and since he was choking me, gurgling.

He lifted me by my throat and slammed me into the bed, apparently totally unfazed by any of my thrashing.

He got in my face, released some pressure on my throat and barked, "*Password!*"

"Eight, seven, three, nine," I breathed then sucked back a harsh, desperate breath but only got half of it in.

He started choking me again.

And he did this making a call.

I didn't care if he called Geneva, just as long as I got out of this alive.

So I kept fighting.

He was bigger than me, leaner than me, fitter than me, obviously stronger than me and really fucking good at choking people.

He was going to kill me.

At this realization, my stomach dropped, thoughts exploded in my brain, feelings grazing through me leaving wounds. Fear. Panic. Regret. Disbelief. Pain.

Fuck, Deke was going to find me.

Fuck, Deke had a key and if this guy left me where I lay after he was done throttling me, it would be Deke that found me.

I bucked ferociously with my hips and scored deep with my nails in his flesh, feeling myself tearing through fabric and breaking skin.

It was like he was a rodeo rider, he held on without a flinch.

It was happening. Oxygen depletion. The fight going out of me. My vision getting fuzzy. The black seeping in from the outsides of my eyes. He was fading and nothing was in my brain. Not a thing.

Except focusing all my efforts on dragging in air that just wasn't coming.

I stopped flailing to concentrate everything I had on trying to breathe and the gruesome, useless noises I was making attempting to pull in oxygen filled the air.

"That's your girl, Justice," he said into the phone. "Listen," he ordered and my phone was to my face.

I feebly lifted an arm to shove it up his jaw in one final effort to push him off me, but it just glanced off, dropping to the side as I kept suffocating.

He took the phone from me and said in it, "You get me what you owe me. You fuckin' get it to me. You got a week. You don't get it to me, she goes down and that other one does too."

With that, he threw my phone on the bed and took his hand from my throat.

I twisted to the side under him, curling into myself, drawing in long, grating breaths, one after another, my hands to my throat.

"I will get to you. I don't get paid, you pay," he whispered in my ear. "You let her know that."

Hand to my throat, he turned me, and I thrashed in terror at his grip there again, rasping out, "No!"

But he just hit me.

And again.

And again.

Which was when it all went black.

* * *

I woke up on my bed, no idea how long I'd been out. But my face was on fire, my throat was on fire and I had only one thought.

Get the fuck out of there.

I scrambled to my hands and knees, awkward and clumsy in my fear, and fell off the side of the bed, landing all my weight on a wrist.

I didn't even feel the pain.

I grabbed the bed and nightstand, the lamp falling off as I hauled myself up.

I felt around on the nightstand for my keys, and in my agitated searching, they fell to the floor.

I dropped to my knees to find them, and in the dark actually hit them, sending them careening away from me.

I did this twice, frantically crawling after them, until I snatched them up in my hand and I held them so tight, the metal bit into my flesh.

I got to my feet and I *ran*.

Out the bedroom into the great room and to the front door.

I slammed into it.

It was locked.

With fumbling fingers, I unlocked it and tore out of my house, my bare feet going from the smooth flagstone walk to the biting gravel of my driveway, and I didn't care.

I threw an arm out, half hugging my granddad's truck, running my arm along its side, the hood as I rounded it to get to the driver's side.

I got there, whispered my chant of, "Together, keep it together. Get in the truck and go. Together, keep it together," in an effort to get the key in the hole to open my door without wasting another second dropping them from my violently shaking hands.

It worked.

The door made not a noise when I threw it open (WD-40 could not be beat).

I climbed in the seat, slammed the door, locked it and went to the ignition.

"Together, keep it together. Keep it together." I kept at it to focus on getting the key in, the truck started up and getting the fuck out of there.

It worked again and I threw the truck in drive, did a tight turn in the wide (but not that wide) circle of gravel that was the end of the drive at the front of my house. And I floored it when I hit the lane.

Through this, I did not look anywhere or think anything but where I was going.

And I continued to do this as I drove like a fucking lunatic down my lane, Ponderosa Road and all the rest until I hit Main Street.

I must have taken that street in the early morning dark going seventy.

I did not care.

I drove direct to the police station, screeched to a halt at an angle to the front doors, taking up both handicap spaces. I threw the truck in park, pushed open my door, shoved myself out of the truck and ran to the front door.

It was locked.

I looked through the glass door at the officer at the desk and started banging with open palm at the door.

"Let me in."

It came out as a scratch.

I cleared my throat, still banging, and shouted as loud as my damaged throat would let me. "Let me in!"

I heard a buzzer.

I yanked open the door, threw myself through it and raced to the desk where the officer was already standing and on the move, beginning to make his way around it, eyes locked to me.

I came to a rocking halt and declared, "Someone tried to strangle me."

That was when the tears started to flow and there was nothing for it.

I sank down to my knees and totally lost my shit inside the Carnal Police Department.

CHAPTER NINE

Christ Almighty

Deke

DEKE DROVE TO Jussy's house Monday morning knowing one thing.

If she didn't go out and get them sandwiches that day, he was doing it.

She'd had her space.

They could do this.

And they were fucking going to.

He was not losing her the only way he could have her.

Which meant he was just not losing her.

These were his thoughts as he turned into her lane but he had them knowing Jus would be in that place. That was who she was. If she could take all the shit that was fucking with her life—her brother acting like an asswipe, her friend descending into a world not a lot of people pulled themselves out of—then shake that off and do it with a smile and a wiseass crack, she could get into the right space with Deke.

These were his thoughts when he drove up the lane, and if he was honest with himself, he was not even close to content with them, but he was not giving himself another choice.

When he saw two police cruisers in the lane, these thoughts were history.

He had no thoughts.

His gut had clamped in on itself and the pain was pure agony.

That didn't mean he didn't shove his truck into park, throw open his door with such strength he had to kick out a boot so it didn't slam right back, and he angled out of the vehicle without even cutting the ignition.

He didn't close the door as he jogged toward Jussy's house.

An officer came out, looked to Deke, and Deke did not spend all his time in Carnal. Not to mention, they had a lot of new cops since the department was swept clean after Arnie Fuller's downfall. He did not know this guy.

He did not care.

"Sir—" the cop started, one hand going to rest on his gun, the other arm lifted toward the aggressively advancing Deke.

"Where's Jus?" Deke demanded.

"Sir, I need to know—"

"*Where's Jus?*" he roared but didn't wait for an answer.

He began running, right by the guy, right toward the house.

"Sir, that's a crime scene. You cannot go in there," the officer bit out quickly.

Crime scene.

Deke's gut twisted, the excruciating pain shooting straight down, to his balls, and straight up, to clog his throat, and he sprinted into her house.

"Goddammit! Sir! You cannot go in there!" the officer shouted after him.

"Jesus, Deke," Jon, one of the officers he did fucking know came out of the hallway that led to Jussy's bedroom.

"She in there?" Deke asked, his gut now in knots so goddamned tight it was a wonder the coffee he drank that morning didn't come up.

"No, man. She's down at the station with Chace," Jon answered.

She was down at the station.

With Chace.

Deke turned on his boot and sprinted the other way.

"You know her?" Jon asked his back as Deke nearly ran over the other cop who'd chased him in.

Deke didn't answer.

He raced to his truck, got in, did a three pointer and hauled ass to the station.

He saw Jussy's truck there like she'd glided it in the spot, all of her faculties firing.

He barely was able to do the same in one of the few open spaces before he put the truck in park, got out, slammed his door, didn't beep the locks and jogged up to the station.

When he got in, he noted the activity but he only had eyes for the woman in uniform behind the desk. A woman he'd met, forgotten her name and didn't give a fuck.

She was all about him too.

She didn't even speak and he didn't even get to the desk before he barked, "Where's Jus?"

"Sorry, Deke, uh—"

He stopped at the desk, leaned toward her and thundered, "*Where's Justice Lonesome?*"

Her face registered shock and alarm, her hand inching toward her sidearm, but he didn't give a fuck about that either.

He felt her and his eyes sliced that way.

She was racing out of the hall at the back wearing the most ridiculous pajamas he'd ever seen, top to bottom. Pants and camisole in a busy print that was mind-scrambling. She also had on a Carnal Police windbreaker. She had nothing on her feet. Her hair was down.

And the left side of her face was beat to shit and there were angry, ugly, purple bruises spanning her beautiful throat.

He saw it all but he checked it all as he moved her way and he didn't stop even when he heard the officer say, "Deke, I gotta ask—"

He kept moving and Jussy kept moving so when they hit, they slammed into each other.

He curled his arms around her and she wrapped hers around him, pushing… no, fucking *burrowing* into his body.

He lifted a hand and cupped her head, pressing her good cheek to his chest when she shoved out a fractured, "Deke."

"I'm here. Right here, baby."

He felt her body start trembling.

Fuck, all he'd lived through, all he'd done, all he'd seen, all that had been done to him, his ma.

He'd made it through all that with delivering just a few deserved ass-kickings in the process.

Now he was going to fucking *kill somebody*.

"Deke."

That was not Jussy.

He lifted his eyes from the top of her gorgeous hair to see Chace was there, not close, not far.

"What fucking happened?" he demanded to know.

He felt pressure on his hand as Jus's head went back and he looked down at her when she started, "I—"

"Not you, gypsy," he whispered gently and again lifted eyes to Chace Keaton, friend and Carnal detective. "You," he bit out.

Chace glanced from Deke to Justice and back to Deke.

"I take it you two are close," he remarked.

"*Talk to me!*" Deke boomed.

Jussy's body jerked in his arms.

Deke instantly curled into her, saying into the top of her hair. "It's good, baby. I'm good, Jussy. Just hang on."

"You stay good, we'll take this to a room," Chace said.

Deke turned his attention to Chace and jerked up his chin.

"You good?" Chace asked.

"Good," Deke grunted.

Chace took him and Jussy in another beat before he said, "Let's go."

And that was when Deke bent at the knees and gathered Jus in his arms like she was a wounded foal who was on her last two breaths.

She pressed into him when he had her up and she stayed pressed deep as he followed Chace into a hall and watched Chace throw open a door and stand outside it.

Deke prowled through, went right to a table in the middle of the room, turned his ass to it and hefted himself up on it.

He arranged Jussy in his lap so she was close and tight in his hold. She had her hands fisted in his tee, her good cheek to his chest and her eyes closed.

All he could see was the swollen, bruised, fucked-up side of her face.

He checked that too and looked to Keaton who'd entered the room behind them and closed the door.

"Now, talk to me," he ordered, his voice low and shaking with the fury he was restraining.

Chace talked.

"Someone broke into her house. Justice said she heard glass shattering. He got to her, assaulted her, held a knife to her throat, strangled her and—"

Chace said no more when each word lashed through Deke with the understanding she'd endured them all and Deke bent his lips to the top of Jussy's head and whispered, "Christ almighty. Christ almighty." His arms got tight. "Christ almighty, baby."

"Had emergency come 'round," Chace stated, voice now lower, calming. "Checked her out. They reckon she's good, physically. No lasting damage, Deke. She's got a sprained wrist she needs to be careful of and keep wrapped for a week or so. But mostly she'll just need rest and lots of aspirin and she'll heal."

Deke looked back to Keaton.

Keaton's body went on visible alert and his mouth said, "Keep your shit, Deke."

Deke kept his shit.

Barely.

"She give you a full statement?" he asked.

"We were finishing up. She needs to make some phone calls and I was about to call Krys or Lauren to come in and—"

"She's gonna be with me."

He felt Jussy's head tip back and her eyes on the underside of his jaw but he didn't take his from Keaton.

Chace gave him a long look and gave away nothing through it when he said, "Okay, then let's finish this up 'cause we've had ice on her face and she needs rest but before that she needs to make some calls. This guy who did this to her was using her to send a message to someone else. Boys are gonna bring down her phone since it was her phone he used to send that message." He paused and then went on warningly, "Now gonna say this and you need to keep keepin' your shit, Deke."

"I'm good, Keaton, just say it," Deke bit out his lie, bracing for the worst.

Chace gave him another look before he nodded and said, "It was while he was strangling her that he made the call. Put the phone to her while he was choking her so they could hear. Threatened her and someone else. Boys got her phone. She gave us her password and we know he called a female friend of hers that's had some trouble."

He looked down at Jussy. "Bianca?"

Her lips trembled and she nodded.

"Fuck," he grunted and turned his attention back to Keaton. "You know she's famous."

Jussy's body got tight in his arms.

He held her closer.

Chace nodded. "It's early but from what she's shared, this isn't about that. It's about this Bianca. We got guys up at her house and the crime unit is headin' up there now to see if he left us anything." His voice changed, went cautious and he said, "He used gloves so we reckon no prints but she tore through during the struggle and got some of his skin. We got that."

Tore through...got some of his skin.

Christ almighty.

Deke closed his eyes and hefted up Jussy so she was resting right against his heart, her head tucked under his chin.

He opened his eyes and ordered Chace, "Call Krys. She needs clothes and shit. Get your boys to let Krys do her thing at Jussy's place. She's comin' with me to my trailer."

Chace's body shifted. "Deke, man, this guy gave her girl a week to pay whatever he's owed and said he was comin' back. Not thinkin' the trailer is a good idea. It's remote and easy to breach."

"She won't be alone."

"She'll be a lot less alone and a lot safer she stays with Tate and Lauren or Lexie and Ty. They both got security systems."

Deke set his jaw and said, "She's gonna be with me."

"Deke—"

"Jonas ain't a kid anymore but they've had enough shit, it came right to their front door, they don't need more. So Tate and Laurie are out. You know the same with Ty and Lexie and they do got kids, little ones and a lot of those fuckers. So it's gonna be the trailer."

Jussy was still trembling and his words made her do it more so Deke started stroking her back.

"Deke, dammit—" Chace started.

Deke cut him off. "You got the resources, keep a unit at the trailer. I don't give a fuck. Won't matter, I'll talk to the crew and they'll take shifts, keeping an eye. But she barely knows Tate and Laurie and I don't think she's even met Ty and Lexie. She needs to be with me."

"I want to be with Deke."

That came from Jussy.

Her voice didn't sound right, scratchy and hoarse, and Deke checked it, hearing that too.

He made no response physically or verbally to Chace. He just stared at his friend to make his point.

Chace looked from Deke to Jussy and his face got soft. "Right, Justice. Whatever way you want it. We'll do our best to put Deke's trailer on patrol and if we can, keep units out there." He looked to Deke. "Need you on speed dial, man, and you get the crew set up. Haven't been to her house so I don't know what we're working with, professional or somethin' else. Glass shattering says something else. Professional would get in another way and that's the one bit of good news we got so far. But I gotta see. In the meantime, you don't take any chances and we'll have an unmarked follow you when you go, keep a look out to see if..."

He trailed off but Deke got him.

Whoever did this to her might have eyes on her. If they had an unmarked following them to Deke's trailer, they'd spot a tail.

"Tate won't get made," Deke told him.

"Then I'm callin' Krys and I'm callin' Tate," Chace replied and his gaze dropped to Jussy. "Justice, I'm gonna step out. Make a few calls. Sort a few things. Then we can let you go and you can get home with Deke. Once we process it, I'll give you your phone before you go and I need you to make your calls and give me anything you got. Right?"

"I remember the plan, Lieutenant Keaton," she said quietly.

Chace nodded.

"You keep a lid on this," Deke demanded and got Chace's attention back.

His words were firm when he replied, "We are."

Deke meant Jussy didn't need the media crawling all over this.

He figured Chace knew what he meant but Chace also knew they *really* didn't need the media to be crawling all over this. After Dalton the serial killer and Arnie Fuller's bullshit, Carnal had a definite reputation and that reputation was national. They were coming out of dark times and hitting the light. So Deke hoped like fuck not one cop in that building wanted to do anything that might threaten that.

He looked down at Jussy and she must have felt it because she tipped her head back and looked up at him.

Christ, the motherfucker did a number on her.

Deke beat that back and said, "Need you to sit in here two minutes while I talk to Chace."

More scratchy and Deke had to beat that back too when she replied, "You can talk in front of me."

"Need you to give that to me, Jussy."

She stared at him. She pressed closer into him.

Then she relaxed and nodded.

He slid off the table, took her to a chair and carefully put her in it.

He noticed the ice pack she'd been using was on the table probably where she dumped it to run out when she heard him bellowing.

He reached to it, tagged it and handed it to her.

"Back on your face," he ordered.

She nodded, took it, staring in his eyes the whole time, and put it to her face.

"Good, gypsy," he whispered. "Be right back."

"Right, Deke."

He straightened, looked to Keaton and walked to the door.

He waited until they were through it and just down the hall before he turned back, spoke low and did it still braced for the worst.

"She's in her pajamas, bare feet, but somethin' you're not tellin' me?"

Compassion hit Chace's features he didn't try to hide but his answer was, "She wasn't violated, Deke."

He felt his gut start to unknot, actually felt his shoulders slump as the tension slid out of them, and he continued, "She performed at Bubba's the other night."

"I heard. I also saw, but not from being there. From what I can tell, two dozen people took videos and pictures. All over social media. Everywhere. Heard word that Krys is not pleased even if it means a few more folk have come in to have a drink. Krys likes asses on stools so I didn't quite get that until I heard Justice talkin' about how she's tight with Krys. Tate's just pissed. They want customers but they don't wanna be on radar. Things have died down now that time's passed since one of their bartenders was tagged as a serial killer. They don't need memories refreshed about that."

He was right.

But right then that was not what was on Deke's mind.

"You sure this," he jerked his chin to the room Jussy was in, "isn't about Jussy takin' that stage?"

"What she reported, he said her name but he didn't make a single demand of her. He was all about the phone call and the message he was sending. That said, if he was looking for her, those pictures and video hitting the Internet helped him find her."

Great.

Deke gave a nod and shared, "This bitch, her friend, she's got problems."

"Justice spoke freely about that."

Deke heaved out a breath.

Chace got close. "You need to get in there with her. How she made it here was a miracle but she lost it when she got here and that's not surprising. Clear she likes Krys a lot, not sure how that came about, and Jim-Billy, that one's easier to call, but the only close person she has in town is you, apparently." Chace give him another look. "Though she mentioned Krys and Jim-Billy in her interview and she didn't say anything about you."

"You got eyes or do I have to explain all you saw the last ten minutes?" Deke asked.

Chace pressed his lips together, not pissed, trying not to smile.

That made Deke pissed.

"Is this the time to do this?" Deke asked.

"Just keep an eye," Chace returned, getting a lock on it. "We need to get Victims Assistance to her, give us a call. And make that call, Deke. She was attacked, beaten and from what she reports, strangled to the point that it was a seriously close call. And keep your shit about that too," he said the last quickly, a good cop, a smart man, not missing any of Deke's responses from the minute he saw him to that second in the hall. "She's here. She's gonna be fine. And you gotta help her be fine if she needs someone to lay it out for who she doesn't fear is gonna go out on a mission of vengeance and wreak havoc across the United States until he finds that for her."

Deke didn't think he was funny.

What he did do was grunt, "I hear you."

Chace stood aside and said, "Go."

Deke didn't hesitate.

He went.

* * *

"Right, Lieutenant Keaton." Pause. "Okay, thanks, uh...Chace." Pause. "Right. I'll let you know. Thanks again." Another pause. "Right, good-bye."

Jussy hung up, kept at her phone, thumb sliding over the screen and Deke knew she was checking texts since it seemed like a hundred of them came while she'd been talking to Chace.

She finished with that and lifted her big brown eyes to Deke.

She was sitting cross-legged on his couch. She'd left the station with the windbreaker but the minute he got her up in his trailer, he found a flannel shirt of his and made her switch it out.

The cops didn't fuck around processing her phone so they could give it to her before they left and she didn't fuck around making her calls while Deke made her instant coffee, gave her aspirin, made his own calls to his crew and changed the sheets on his bed.

Now she was on his couch and Deke was hips to his kitchen counter.

"Well, you heard most of it but don't know the texts so let me sum up," she announced then launched right in, "Lieutenant Keaton is now Chace to me and he's fully briefed. I've called Joss and Dana and they lost their minds. I got through to Lacey and she lost her mind. I think I talked Joss and Dana out of dropping everything and flying out here because my mom can be dramatic and I don't need that. And Dana is sensitive, she'd take one look at me and lose it and I don't need that either."

She drew in a huge breath, winced through it, and kept talking in that grainy voice that was getting better but still pissed him way the fuck off.

"I *thought* I talked Lacey out of canceling gigs, getting in her private jet and hauling ass out here. I also *thought* I'd talked her out of showing on Sunday. But Jiggy, her manager, just texted and said she's back on that rant. He also shared that they've not had any threats or seen anyone creepy or, I should say, anyone creepier than some of the usual creepy that follows Lacey around. But he's beefing up her security because I told him that I figure that asshole meant Lacey when he said 'the other one.' And I told Jig to keep her away because we don't need to make things easier for that guy with both Lacey and me right here."

She stopped talking and Deke gritted his teeth, holding himself back, giving her space until it looked like she'd crumble under the weight of her words taking her back where she was just a few hours earlier with that fucking guy.

If she started to crumble, he'd go to her.

Just like Jussy, she pulled it together so he stood where he was.

"Jiggy assured me he'd talk her out of showing here, even on Sunday," she continued. "Lacey's a bona fide spitfire so he might or might not be able to do that. Mr. T, however," she lifted her phone and shook it, "doesn't get talked out of anything he doesn't want to get talked out of. He's texted that he's already booked his flights and will be here early this evening in order to 'oversee the investigation'... his words. I gave Chace a heads up about that too."

It was awesome, though not surprising, she had people who cared so much about her.

And it would be interesting (read: funny) to watch Chace work under the thumb of whoever this Mr. T guy was.

Carefully, Deke noted, "You didn't call your brother."

"I don't have a brother," she shot back.

He only lifted his chin slightly and said softly, "Your call, gypsy."

She looked away, swallowed like it was painful, Deke again beat back what seeing that made him feel then she looked back to him.

"Mr. T has also activated my publicist," she shared. "I don't use her often but she's on retainer. She's going to be contacting Chace in order to coordinate anything that needs to be done in case any of this leaks."

"Chace promised me he'd keep a lid on it and the man's a friend, Jussy. Know him well, through good times and seriously bad. So I can tell you he's a damn fine man and a really good cop. He makes that promise, he'll put all he's got into keeping it," he assured her.

"Good to know," she mumbled.

Deke studied her, knowing from what he saw that Chace was pushy about the ice because her face was fucked up but the swelling wasn't as bad as it could have been so it could have looked a helluva lot worse.

He just hoped it could have felt a helluva lot worse and now didn't.

It was what was at her throat that made Deke's gut burn.

Her voice was softer, beginning to tremble, when she told him something else he heard.

"I called Bianca. She didn't pick up. Left a voicemail. Mr. T has taken over dealing with her parents. He doesn't want me more upset than I already am. So he's informing them about what happened."

"Got another friend, also a good man and smart as a whip," Deke said. "He's got skills. He's also got a business where he uses those skills and he's got a team. You want, I'll talk to Decker. He'll find her for you."

"Can you call him?" she asked, the good side of her face starting to dissolve, now that she had nothing to do opening it up for the weight of what had happened to come crushing down.

That was when Deke was done with leaning his hips into the counter.

He moved to her, wedged himself in beside her and pulled her into his arms.

That last, he didn't need to do. She came out of her cross-legged position. Shifting to her hip, she fell to his side, landing with her chest to his as well as the healthy part of her face, snaking an arm around his stomach, pressing into him.

Only then did he answer her request.

"I'll call him."

"Thanks, Deke."

He held her with one arm and carefully wound his other hand in her hair.

"You wanna tell me who this Mr. T guy is?" he asked.

"Mr. Thurston. Granddad's manager. Dad's manager. He was also my manager when I was more active, and still is, to tell the truth, even if he isn't managing tours and making sure no one fucks me over." He felt her let out a big breath before she continued, "He's a good guy. A member of the family now. Though he isn't demonstrative. All business, always has been. I still think he'd push me out from the front of a speeding train even if it meant he took that hit."

"Good you got that, Jussy. All that you got," he told her.

"I know," she replied, like she totally did.

He gave her next what he needed to give her so she could mull it over as shit calmed down and stuff started fucking with her head.

"Chace wants me to talk to you about Victims Assistance. Early for you, baby, but puttin' that in your head. You need it there to know, things start fuckin' with you, we make a call and we'll get you some help."

"Thanks again, Deke."

"Now, want you to quit talkin'," he said. "You need to rest your throat. Also gonna put you to bed because you just plain need some rest."

He felt her cheek slide on his chest and he tipped his chin down to catch her eyes.

"I couldn't sleep."

"Try."

"I just drank two cups of not the greatest but very strong coffee," she told him.

He shot her a grin. "I know my gypsy's feelin' better, she's givin' me shit about my coffee."

"I'm going to the mall first chance I get and getting you your own four-cup Mr. Coffee. No coffee drinker should drink instant."

"I like it."

"It's awful."

"It's coffee."

"It's awful coffee."

"It's an excuse for you to bust my chops so you're not layin' down and tryin' to get some shuteye."

"This is because there is no way I'll achieve the shuteye portion of that order."

"Then you can't sleep but you can rest."

"Deke."

"Justice."

They went into staredown, something Deke had a feeling he'd win but he didn't get the chance to bring that to fruition.

He heard vehicles approaching.

He looked to the door and felt her head lift from his chest to look that way too.

Carefully, he detached from her, got up and went to the side window.

Then he blew out a sigh.

Krys's Camaro, Lexie's Charger, and if it wasn't bad enough Krys was clearly bringing a posse rather than just a bag filled with Jussy's things, that posse included Twyla and Deke knew that because her pickup followed Lexie's Charger.

He turned his eyes to Jussy.

"The big-haired cavalry has arrived."

Her brows drew together, she flinched and again his gut burned.

"Stay here," he ordered.

She nodded.

Deke went out the door.

He was at the bottom of the steps in front of the closed door by the time they all got out of their cars and started tramping his way, the girl gang including Lauren, who was carrying a bag.

"You couldn't carpool?" he asked.

"Get out of my way, big man," Krys demanded.

She was pissed and not hiding it, a staple in Krys's emotional stratus.

Though now he could see she was a lot more pissed than normal.

"She's had a rough morning," Deke growled.

"No shit?" Krys asked, stopping in front of him.

"She doesn't need you losing your mind," Deke told her.

Krystal had no reply except to put two hands on him to shove him out of her way.

There was no chance Krys could shove Deke out of her way.

What there was a chance of was a heavily pregnant Krys wanting to get to her friend so Deke would let himself get shoved out of her way.

This he did.

She threw open his door and stomped in.

"Hey, Deke," Laurie greeted, walking past him, face a warring mixture of amusement and concern.

Deke lifted his chin.

"Deke," Lexie said, also walking past him with the same look on her face, except with Lexie, it was clear the amusement was winning out.

Deke didn't say anything and not only because they heard Krys shouting from inside, "*Motherfucker!*"

"Yo," Twyla gave her greeting, not breaking stride as she walked right by him.

He followed Twyla in.

He had a decent-sized Airstream.

Him, Jussy and four women was four women too much.

"I do not believe this shit!" Krys was still shouting.

"Calm down," Deke grunted.

Her eyes cut to him.

"*Calm down?*" she yelled.

"Hey, Jus," Lauren said softly and he took his eyes from Krys to watch Laurie push through and set the bag on the floor by the couch. "Krys and I went to your place. Got some of your stuff. Think you're covered but you need anything else, you give us a call and we'll take care of it for you."

"Hey, I'm Lexie," Lexie stated before Jussy could get in a word to Laurie. Lexie was sidling closer to Jussy, doing it with a friendly but cautious smile on her beautiful face. "I get that it's not a good time for us to meet but Krys was calling around, saying you were staying out here with Deke and we thought…you know…"

She did not share what she thought Jussy knew.

Krystal did.

"Jus's gotta stay here with you, we're doin' a once-over of this place and an inventory. Told Chace I wanted Jus's ass at Bubba and my place and he said Jus wanted to be here so she's here. But she's here and we're gonna scrub it down so a female can live in your lair without toxic spores taking root in her lungs, not to mention we're makin' sure you got some food to feed her."

She said all this to Deke, not Jussy, and she wasn't done.

"And if you give me lip, I'll be glad for it because I'm lookin' for a reason to lose my mind and someone to lose it on and you're a big guy. You'll be able to take it when I do."

"You women wanna clean my trailer, I'm down with that," Deke replied and watched three women blink at him in surprise.

Twyla did not. She was a sister to her sisters and she was a sister to the brotherhood and not because she was a lesbian but because she was a badass. She knew any man would not turn down a pack of women cleaning his house.

So she was grinning.

"But you can come back and do it," Deke went on. "Jussy's gotta lie down and get some rest and before you give me shit," he said the last, his voice lowering. "I already changed the sheets."

"Talked with Tate," Twyla said at this point, cutting off a Krys who had opened her mouth to speak, or maybe snap, though she could have also been set to do more yelling. "I'm not on tonight at Bubba's so I *am* on tonight to keep a lookout here. Tate thinks, days, when she's up for it," she jerked her head Jussy's way, "she's at the garage with Stella, at the bar with Krys or at the salon with Lexie. Never alone. Public. Lots of traffic. She'll be good."

Deke announced an alternate scenario which was actually the only scenario.

"She'll be here with me and when she's good to go back home, I'll be there with her."

"Brother, you got work," Twyla reminded him.

Which reminded him of something else, he not only had to call Decker to activate him to find this Bianca bitch, he also needed to call Max.

"And that work's at her place so I'll do that work once the cops free up Jussy's house, doin' it with Jussy there," Deke replied.

"Okay then, now we'll look at the food situation and then we'll go shopping. We'll come back in a few hours to clean," Laurie decided.

"He needs a coffeemaker," Jussy put in. "If anyone has an extra or if one of you could go back to my house and get mine out of the utility room, it'd be appreciated."

"I got a kettle," Deke said to her. "Don't need a coffeemaker."

"Deke, you need a coffeemaker," she returned.

"No I don't."

"Let me rephrase," Jussy fired back. "*I* need a coffeemaker."

Instantly, Deke looked to Lauren. "You got the time, bring her coffeemaker."

And he watched Lauren's eyes get so huge it looked like they'd pop out of her head, and she did this, he knew, because she was trying not to bust a gut laughing.

Deke ignored that.

It had not been lost on him in the last couple of hours what his response to Jussy's attack, and more, Jussy's response to his response, meant.

That was not for now.

They'd talk that through later.

He had his gypsy princess with a banged-up face, a fucked-up throat and a man out there who they didn't know dick about intending her harm.

He'd lived through the shit that went down with Lauren and Tate, it being Deke who carried Laurie to his truck after she'd been kidnapped and stabbed and then he drove like a crazy motherfucker to get her to the hospital. It'd been Deke who'd taken Lexie's back when the dirty, now-dead police chief Fuller had targeted Ty to plant shit in his house that'd get his ass back in prison. And he'd been one of the men helping dig Chace's now-wife Faye out of the ground.

Shit for Jussy was not going to get close to being that extreme.

What happened happened.

And now for her it was over.

That was what he had to focus on.

After that, they'd sort out the rest.

"You all do the inventory and ask Jus what she likes. Make a list. Me and Deke gotta have words," Krys bossed, shot him a glare then stomped out of his trailer.

"You better go," Lexie urged quietly.

"Yeah, you better go," Laurie agreed.

Deke looked to Jussy.

She was grinning at him, fucked-up face and all.

He didn't get it, but from experience, it was always the way.

Inject the sisterhood in any situation, no matter one of their own had her house broken into, a knife held to her throat, strangled near to death, she had her girls around her, she was sitting in crazy-ass pajamas on a couch in a trailer and grinning.

He sighed and followed Krys out.

She was standing by her Camaro.

He did not speak until he reached her and when he did, he did it subdued so it could not be heard in case someone was listening.

"We are not doin' this now and just to make it clear, we're not only not doin' this now, we're not doin' this ever."

"When I told Chace she was comin' to stay with us, he told me you wouldn't care I was pregnant, you'd take me down I tried to get her from you."

Deke said nothing.

Krystal didn't return that favor.

"Bub says you two got somethin', Jus's all for it, you got your head planted right up your ass."

Deke remained silent.

Krystal's face softened.

Slightly.

"Brother, she just got attacked. Gonna be a tough row to hoe feelin' safe after that. Takin' on that row, she does not need to deal with the kinda hurt you can lay on her she feels one way, but you're puttin' in this effort just 'cause you two are friends."

To that, Deke spoke.

"Not gonna lay any hurt on her."

"Think you won't. It happens no matter how cool you're trying to be."

"Not gonna lay any hurt on her," Deke repeated.

She got closer. "I know you're a good guy, Deke, but I'm not thinkin' you're getting me."

"No," he grunted. "You're not getting me. I. Am. Not. *Gonna lay any hurt on her.*"

Krystal stared up at him and she was wide-eyed now.

"Go in, find out what she needs, round up your posse," he ordered. "Got some calls to make and I'll be back in. You guys hang until I'm back. Don't want her alone."

"Okay, Deke," Krys agreed readily.

Krystal Briggs agreeable.

Deke blew out another sigh.

She gave him a shit-eating grin, kept on giving it and didn't move.

"I got calls to make," he reminded her.

"Right," she said, still grinning and doing it as she moved around him and headed back to the trailer.

Deke leaned against her car, eyes to the road leading up to his property, pulling out his phone.

Chace first, see if it was good Joe Callahan started the work tomorrow that he should have done three weeks ago and see if someone could have access to the house to board up the window.

Next up, Max to share what was going down and get him to share the same with Callahan. Not to mention tell him that Deke was not at work that day but if Chace opened up the house, he was taking Jussy back the next day and getting on with it. The longer it took for her to get back in the saddle, the more fear she could build up about being in the place where it all went down.

It was her home. Deke needed to help her sweep that away.

That said, she'd be with him while he worked and they'd be back in the trailer when he was done until Callahan was finished with his work.

Then they'd stay at her house.

Last, Jacob Decker.

He needed to find Bianca Constantine's ass.

For Jussy's peace of mind for her friend.

And to find a way to get this shit done.

* * *

The women took off when Deke returned to the trailer and when he returned he saw they'd gotten her into his bed.

Fuck, Jussy in his bed.

She was eyes aimed his way down the trailer, on her side, hands under her healthy cheek, those eyes open and on him.

He moved that way and made his decision when he did.

So when he got there, gentle with her like she was crystal, he adjusted her so he had his back to the wall at the head of the bed, ass to the mattress and her cheek on his thigh.

He slid his fingers through her hair.

It was soft, the curls tangling around his fingers, clinging like they didn't want him to let go.

"Called Chace," he started on a whisper and kept going that way. "They're finishing up what they need to do at your place. It'll be open tomorrow. Called Max too. He's sendin' Bubba over to board up your window and he's ordering another. It's custom. It'll take a while to get in but he's on that."

"Okay, Deke."

She was talking in a whisper too.

Deke went on the same way.

"With the cops done with what they gotta do with the house, we're goin' back tomorrow. Callahan is good to get started and I'm gettin' back to work. You'll be with me. Callahan can stay with you while I get us sandwiches."

He felt her snuggling her cheek in his thigh, he didn't know if that was for closeness or to hide discomfort, before she repeated, "Okay."

He decided to go with discomfort even if it wasn't just so he could make sure it wasn't but get her beyond it if it was.

"You need to get back there, Jussy. It's your home. Work's gettin' done for you to be safe in it. But you will not be alone there and tomorrow night until Callahan has your system done, you're stayin' here with me."

There was a pause and no movement before she said again, "Okay."

She didn't argue.

Good.

"Talked to Decker," Deke carried on. "He's a busy guy but he's clearing things, favor for a friend. Means he's on the job. He's good, Jussy. He'll find her."

She lifted a hand and curled it on his thigh under her nose and gave him a squeeze.

She gave him a squeeze but he could feel the tension all through her.

Deke kept sliding his hand in her hair as he asked, "How do I get you to relax, baby? Close your eyes. Sleep a little."

"Daddy," she whispered.

"Say again?"

"My phone, Deke. It's on your nightstand. Can you pull up my music? Play anything. Anything by my dad."

Deke reached out, got her phone and he knew what he'd play.

It was on Johnny Lonesome's album *Living Room*, one of his last, the album her dad and his band recorded in one go during an acoustic session in that same room in his house.

For years before they recorded one, these sessions had been legendary. Everyone knew that all through his career, his band, who never lost a member until Lonesome died (except the drummer who had left him but only to tour with Jussy when she'd done her thing), would jam in his living room just for the fun of it.

So they decided one day, to the gratitude of their fans, to record a session.

It had been brilliant.

And Lonesome had been performing a certain song for years but that was the first time that song was even close to studio recorded. Deke had never seen the man in concert but he'd heard that song, from that album and well before, on live ones.

And Deke learned from what he'd read a few nights ago that Lonesome played his song "Never Missin' Home" at every concert.

It had some lines Deke thought he got.

But he didn't.

Never wanna leave my Justice, my home.
So I bring her with me, my baby Lonesome.
Don't matter, Justice is always there,
Always right there, no matter where I go.
My baby Lonesome,
Makin' it so I'm never missin' home.

He queued up the song, hit play and slipped down into the bed, drawing Jussy up so she was resting on his chest, her face in his throat, Deke's arms curved around her.

Johnny Lonesome sang about his daughter as she curled deeper into Deke and rubbed her face in his throat.

"Perfect," she whispered over her father's voice.

It was. He knew it.

He knew it because in bed with Deke, held close, her father right there with them, it took only three songs and she was out.

CHAPTER TEN

Catch You

Justice

IT WAS AFTER my nap.

It was also after the girls coming back, cleaning the trailer and stocking the cupboards and fridge. They stayed. We gabbed. Then they left.

And last, it was after Deke and I camped out in front of his small television which was fed from a satellite dish and we watched *The Professional*.

One of my favorite movies.

And I'd found it was one of Deke's favorites too.

I also found that Deke's face got soft when he noticed me crying when Léon had to let Mathilda go down the exhaust chute. It got soft right before he pulled me out of my corner of the couch into him in his and he held me throughout the rest of the movie (so he didn't see when I started crying again later, though with the way he started tangling his fingers in my hair, I think he guessed).

It was dinnertime and I was sitting cross-legged on his couch, watching him in his tiny kitchen frying bologna and making toast.

Frying bologna and making toast.

The girls had brought huge amounts of food. So much of it, some of it was taking up what little counter space Deke had. They hadn't prepared us for a few nights hanging at Deke's trailer. They'd prepared us for a three-month-long siege.

And he was making me fried bologna on toast, the American cheese slices out and at the ready.

Just like I'd told him I liked it.

It was with that—not to mention every moment of that day since I heard Deke's bellow at the police station—that I knew.

I could do his boundaries.

No.

I could *so totally* do his boundaries.

Sure, those boundaries didn't include sex and a possible future that included me birthing big baby boys with hazel eyes.

But with all Deke gave me, the care, the cuddling, the protection, the cuddling (worth a second mention since Deke was so good at it), making me feel the impossible after what had happened—safe in his sphere and especially in his arms—I could take that.

I had a lot of friends and family who loved me. The closest of them would do all the same things.

Deke was a part of that now. As were Krystal, Lauren, Twyla and the new addition of Lexie.

The girls didn't offer cuddles (though, all but Krys and Twyla, I was sure they would if Deke wasn't already providing that). But them kicking in like they did was super-cool.

And even with my newfound acceptance of what Deke was willing to give me, I knew there'd be a day when he'd find someone, or I would, and that cuddle-type closeness would have to go.

But he'd been there in every way I could need someone, and then some, on a day which, outside the ones I lost people I cared about, was the worst of my life.

So yeah.

I could do his boundaries.

Especially if it came with fried bologna sandwiches in his kickass trailer.

This thought made me look around his space yet again.

I found I was not wrong on first, second, third (etc.) perusal.

I loved every inch of his trailer.

It had not been a surprise that he lived in a travel trailer in the middle of nowhere but right by a beautiful lake. I didn't even spy a single house built around that lake. It seemed it was just Deke and his trailer.

And all of this seemed just so *Deke*.

Deke living isolated and on wheels. He sets that trailer to his truck, he's good to go.

I loved that about him. I loved that he was a man like no man I'd ever met and all of it was interesting, a lot of it was sweet, some of it was funny, the entirety of it good.

I felt a smile play at my lips as I glanced around and noted he was not only good to go but good to do it in style.

The interior of the trailer was like a museum of the road and an inner guide to Deke's psyche.

There were posters of rallies, music festivals and concerts glued to the walls. And if these posters were any indication, he not only had really good taste in music, he'd traveled far and wide and back again about fifteen times.

Just like me.

There were also stickers tacked everywhere for everything from bike shops to bars to diners to coffee houses.

Further, there was a bevy of bumper stickers that ranged from the hilarious to the profound. Like one that had a *Star Wars* Storm Trooper face on it and next to that "I had friends on that Death Star." And another one that said, "The gene pool could use a little chlorine." And another that said, "Contrary to belief, no one owes you anything."

Then there were the random quotes, like Walt Whitman's "Resist much. Obey little." And Kurt Vonnegut's "I want to stand as close to the edge as I can without going over. Out on the edge you can see all kinds of things you can't see from the center."

I saw Clint Eastwood behind the long barrel of a gun. Bruce Lee in the zone. James Dean leaning against a car. A fake baseball card with Will Farrell in a Cub's uniform.

All this was intermingled with liberal Americana. Eagles. Flags. Stars. Uncle Sam. Rosie the Riveter. "Don't Tread on Me." "Liberty or Death." Not to mention, the every real biker's maxim, "Ride free or die."

And this was Deke's wallpaper, from living room space to bedroom space and even in the miniscule bathroom.

It.

Fucking.

Rocked.

"Your trailer fucking *rocks*," I told him and his gaze went from the frying pan to me.

"Come again?"

"Your trailer…fucking…*rocks*," I repeated, grinning at him. "I could say the Storm Trooper bumper sticker is my favorite but I could also say Coelho's 'Don't waste your time with explanations…' is my favorite because people *do* only hear what they want to hear."

Deke stared at me.

"But, just to say," I kept gabbing, "the fact you went for an Airstream already made it total cool."

My smile got bigger as I indicated the space with a sweep of my hand, at the same time biting back the flinch that motion gave me because after the nap, my body made it clear it was protesting against nearly being strangled to death.

It had survived, that was the good part.

But it was reminding me of the toll that took.

I ignored the pain and finished, "It's just that with all this, you made it infinitely *cooler*."

Deke made no comment to my compliments.

What he did was take the skillet off the burner, go to the fridge, grab a bottle of brew, uncap it and open a cupboard. His hand went up and came out of the cupboard with two white bottles.

He then moved to me, handed me the beer and ordered, "Give me your hand, palm up."

I lifted my hand palm up.

Deke opened the bottles and tapped out two aspirin and four ibuprofen.

I was not averse to the power of legal pharmaceuticals.

However.

"Deke, that's a lot of pills."

"Take 'em," he commanded.

"But—"

"Take 'em or I give you your sandwich then put your ass in my truck and take you to Carnal Hotel. They got tubs. You can't even wave your goddamned hand without wincing. You need ibuprofen or you need a soak. Your choice."

Okay, I had to admit that, after all the cuddling, I had a feeling sex with Deke would be freaking *astounding*.

Still, his brand of friendly that included looking out for me in his badass way, I'd definitely take, even without the sex (though that last was given up begrudgingly).

"Leave your kickass trailer before I've read all your stickers?" I asked, lifting my hand and popping the pills in my mouth. All of them. I sucked them back with a tug of beer, and after I swallowed, unnecessarily gave him my answer. "I pick Airstream. And just to say, if I have a choice of here or pretty much anywhere on earth, except the room at my dad's house where he keeps his guitar collection, I'd pick here."

Something slid over his face that I really wanted to decipher but at that moment, my phone rang.

I looked down at it on the couch beside me and saw it said MR. T CALLING.

I looked back up at Deke. "Mr. T."

His eyes went from the phone to me. "Yup."

He started moving back to the kitchen (this journey taking Deke all of two steps) and I hit my screen to engage the call and put it on speaker.

"Hey, Mr. T. You're on speaker," I greeted.

"And who all would I be speaking to?" Mr. T's voice came back at me.

"Me and Deke."

"Deke Hightower?" Mr. T asked and my gaze shot to Deke.

His last name was Hightower?

Of course it was.

It was a cool-as-shit name.

But how did Mr. T know that?

"Uh...yeah, uh..." I stammered.

"I'm right now on my way from the Carnal Police Department, heading to the Carnal Hotel," Mr. T broke into my thoughts to say. "I've spent the last half an hour getting briefed by the mercifully capable-sounding Lieutenant Keaton. And Lieutenant Keaton informed me that you're currently in a Mr. Deke Hightower's charge."

In a Mr. Deke Hightower's charge.

Mr. T was hilarious.

"That I am," I confirmed, trying not to giggle at the look on Deke's face as he stared with unhidden irritation mingled with equally unhidden surprise at my phone. These saying he was not a big fan of being called "Mr. Deke Hightower" and he was a little shocked (and appalled) Mr. T was so snooty. I then asked Mr. T something that was also unnecessary, "So you made it to town all right?"

"Indeed, Justice."

"Deke's making us dinner," I told him. "When we're done eating, we'll come into—"

"You'll do nothing of the sort," Mr. T interrupted me brusquely. "Fortunately, as you informed him I would be arriving and gave him leave to speak to me as a member of your family, Lieutenant Keaton was rather forthcoming about your ordeal. You need to stay put and rest. In fact, you should be quite careful with all activity for the next few days, giving your body time to heal as well as the energy to do so."

I tipped my head to the side, a silent question to Deke.

I hoped he got my silent question because he nodded back.

"Do you want directions to come out here?" I asked. "Dinner isn't lobster but it's yummy."

"No, thank you," Mr. T answered, and even though I wanted to see him, especially in a time like this when he was at his best, the competent and capable calm in a storm, I was kind of glad.

I had my calm in a storm.

Deke.

And anyway, Mr. T would definitely not want bologna sandwiches.

"I have calls to make and things to see to," Mr. T went on to explain. "We'll schedule a time for the morning after you've had some rest. However, I need to speak with you now about a few of those things I'm seeing to."

"Sock it to me, Mr. T," I invited.

"Right," he stated, all business. "I've been in touch with Kai Mason. He currently has no openings on his team to send bodyguards. He's suggested a firm in Denver that he highly recommends. I've done some research on them and I'm in agreement with Mason. And this could be a multi-tasking opportunity because, although this firm does provide security services, they mostly do investigations. They're very good. And although her parents informed me they'll be looking into securing their own investigators, I'd like your approval to engage them to find Bianca. They can coordinate efforts with Constantine's team or Constantine, as he should, can employ this Nightingale Investigations directly."

I thought of Stella Gunn's husband, Kai "Mace" Mason. He played double-duty as her bodyguard (though, if you talked to Mace about this, it wasn't a duty in his eyes except one that had the adjective "husbandly" before it). He also ran a company of bodyguards and they were highly sought after because they were seriously good at what they did.

Lacey used them.

Dad used to use them.

I would have thought of them but Deke had wasted no time setting up a posse of local badasses to watch over us, and since he had, I didn't need to.

And I'd met Mace's old employer, Lee Nightingale. I knew his wife better because she was a really good friend of Stella Gunn. But I'd met a number of Lee's friends too, these guys were also his crew, and they were arguably more badass than Deke and Tate were.

I thought of all this as I watched Deke stop squirting mustard on toast to look at me and give me a negative shake of his head.

"Well, Mr. T—" I started.

"One other thing, Justice, before we discuss."

"Okay," I replied.

"Lieutenant Keaton has shared that Mr. Hightower already has some locals providing such security services. I was at first opposed to this idea but Keaton said this crew is being led by a Tatum Jackson. From what I could discover in the short amount of time I've had to look, Jackson has a skillset that would make troubling the men at Nightingale Investigations with sending out bodyguards unnecessary. They can still search for Bianca. However, if you wish Mr. Jackson to lead this local crew, I'll need to contact him for billing purposes."

At that, Deke spoke.

"Tate won't want paid."

"Lonesomes do not offer markers," Mr. T informed him instantly. "No Lonesome owes anybody anything."

This was true.

This was Mr. T's way which was, according to him, the *only* way.

"Tate, nor any of the boys'll want markers either," Deke retorted. "They'll be doin' this for Jussy. She lives here. She's one of our own. We take care of our own. So don't contact Tate and ask him to bill you. It'll piss him off."

Although I liked the idea of being one of their own, I cut in at this juncture because I was obviously a Lonesome and Mr. T had taught me well.

Don't owe anybody anything.

"I can actually pay them all for helping me out."

Deke's annoyed gaze went from my phone to me.

"That's not the point," he returned. "You wanna do somethin', this gets done, buy 'em each a bottle of their favorite hooch. You offer anything else, straight-up insult, Jussy."

I grinned at him and watched with great interest as his attention dropped to my mouth, and for some reason, for the first time in a while, his expression didn't grow annoyed (or, at that point, *stay* annoyed) when he saw me smile.

His face softened and his eyes warmed when they returned to mine after I started talking.

"Apparently, I have things to learn about mountain man badasses."

"We'll get you there," he muttered.

My heart skipped a beat.

We'd get me there?

As in me…and him? That *we*?

We would get me to understanding mountain man badasses?

Why would I need to do that if I didn't have one of my own?

In other words, what the hell did that mean?

Deke turned back to his mustard and did this speaking.

Not to me.

To Mr. T.

"And got a friend on finding Bianca. Know the Nightingale crew. They're exceptional. Wouldn't know the outcome of a faceoff between Deck and Lee Nightingale or any of his men. Just know my boy Jacob Decker will not fuck around and he's already on the job."

Okay.

Uh.

How did Deke know Lee Nightingale?

I wasn't sure I wanted to know.

Then again, trouble made a permanent home in Carnal, taking residence most recently at my forest oasis. And from what I knew, Lee Nightingale was a fan of besting trouble.

So that might have been it.

"Then I'll need to speak to this Jacob Decker," Mr. T said to Deke.

"I'll get Jussy to text you his phone number," Deke replied, slapping cheese slices on the toast, still talking. "Want Jussy at her house tomorrow.

Work to do there. Joe Callahan needs to get started on his gig. And she needs to get back in that saddle. We'll be there from seven on. She's not leavin' my sight so she'll be there until I knock off at six. You want lunch or dinner with her, we sort somethin' but she does that not leavin' me and not in town. I want her in a contained area where she's low on visibility, not just because of this jackoff but because she doesn't need any type of attention while this shit is happening, which she'll get bein' Jussy. But mostly it's because of this jackoff. She has eyes on her I can't control, it'll be after this asshole is behind bars."

Through that, my heart skipped many beats.

Dozens.

"Agreed," Mr. T replied and I turned surprised eyes to the phone.

Not anyone ordered Mr. T around. Not Dad during an artist's tantrum, not Granddad during the same.

And no one took care of the Lonesomes but him.

No one.

"I'll be at Justice's house at eight o'clock tomorrow morning," Mr. T continued. "Justice has reported to me the state of her house and I can imagine she does not yet have a kitchen. Do you need me to bring breakfast?"

"Go to La-La Land," Deke ordered. Having put the bologna on the sandwich, he was adding the next layer of cheese. "Get us coffees and anything out of the case. That'll do us."

"La-La Land?"

"On Main Street. Only coffee house we got. You can't miss it."

"Excellent, Mr. Hightower. I'll see you and Justice tomorrow at eight."

"Deke," Deke grunted, having upended a chip bag, he was covering my sandwich and the entire plate with Bugles.

"Fine, Deke," Mr. T semi-grunted back. Then came, "Justice, you rest. And text me Mr. Decker's number."

"Right, Mr. T. I'll do that ASAP."

"Enjoy your evening," he bid.

"You too," I replied, seeing Mr. T disconnect the call before turning my head and taking the mounded plate from Deke.

I sat with plate in hand, eyes tipped up, staring at Deke as he walked back to the kitchen area.

"You just bossed Mr. T," I declared, my voice flimsy, not just due to my throat still hurting but my utter shock. "And he let you."

"Babe," Deke began, slapping more bologna in the skillet, "you don't got far to look, you wanna learn how the folk in Carnal look after each other."

With their rather dramatic history, this was true.

Once he was done with the bologna, he turned eyes to me.

"You look, you'll find Chace is all over that," he said quietly. "So is Tate. They're involved with lookin' after you, they're good with you bein' with me, clear your guy is not stupid. He gets that and what that means. Didn't boss him as much as told him the way it is. Smart men don't waste time tryin' to prove who's got a bigger dick by arguing over what time in the morning we meet. A decision's made that makes sense, smart men move on and ask if they can bring breakfast."

I was learning a lot about Deke that day.

Top of that list (for a variety of reasons) was that he was a great cuddler.

Near to the top of that list, when asked to put on a song of my dad's, he was the perfect DJ.

And high on the scale of honorable mentions, he did not waste time on stupid shit, like proving he had a bigger dick (or one at all) by getting into it when the girls wanted to clean his trailer or staking claim in a way that would raise the hackles of Mr. T. But instead he settled a man who cared about me into the knowledge that I was being looked after.

"Jussy?" Deke called.

I shook off these thoughts and the happy feeling I got learning all this about Deke, thus getting it all for me, and focused on him.

"Thank you for—" I started softly.

That was as far as I got.

"Don't say it," Deke ordered.

His terse response made my head give a small jerk.

"But today, Deke, you've been really—"

Off went the skillet from the burner and suddenly Deke was bent over me, his face in my face, both his hands curled around the sides of my neck.

"I said, don't say it," he repeated, this time gently.

"I have to," I told him.

"My honor," he told me.

I felt my brows draw together, but even so, my heart didn't skip a beat at that. It squeezed.

Deke kept looking me right in the eyes.

"My honor, Jussy, to be that man who's there for you."

Okay...

Now what did *that* mean?

I didn't ask and I didn't know why.

Maybe it was because I was scared of the answer.

"Now eat your dinner, gypsy." He was back to ordering but still speaking gently.

Before he could take his hands from me, because I *really* did not want him to take his hands from me, I asked, "Can I thank you for my fried bologna sandwich?"

I saw humor flare in his eyes as he replied, "Yep."

"And my massive mound of Bugles?"

"You can thank me for that too."

"Then thank you."

His fingers slid back and up into my hair before he used them to press in so I tilted my head forward. Once he had me in that position, he kissed the top of my hair.

After that, he let me go and went back to his skillet.

It was better than my hair being tousled, probably not as good as a touch on the lips, though I'd never know.

But it was from Deke. Being gentle with me. Taking care of me. Looking out for me.

So I'd take it.

* * *

I lay in Deke's bed, alone, staring at the ceiling.

In the shadows I could see there were blank spots there but he was covering them up. The last white to his life's canvas was that ceiling, ready to be filled.

It'd be cool to help him fill it. So fucking cool to have a part in that canvas, look up and not just see the roadmap of Deke's life, but also see memories.

Deke was on the couch.

It was dark, late.

It was also after we ate bologna sandwiches and I won the argument that I had to move or my entire body would lock in place, never to loosen again, so I made him let me help with the minimal cleanup. And last, it was after he'd won the argument after that cleanup that we were watching *The Fighter*.

He might have won it but I got the last laugh because I liked that movie too so I didn't mind losing (and I knew before I even suggested it (something I didn't hesitate to do anyway) that I wouldn't get Deke to watch Ben Stiller's version of *The Secret Life of Walter Mitty*, or at least not without more energy for the fight and some buildup of bargaining power).

Eventually, I started getting drowsy. Deke noticed it so I was now in his bed and he was on his couch. And I didn't know what he was doing because he didn't seem drowsy when he sent me to bed but he did turn off the TV and I suspected this was because, in that small space, it was impossible for it not to disturb my efforts of getting rest.

I was now seeing the drawbacks of accepting the friendship Deke could offer.

I was totally down with falling asleep lying on his chest, listening to my dad serenade me.

I was down with movie-watching and bologna-sandwich-eating and banter.

I was down with examining his space and discovering in a lot of ways that there were a myriad of things to discover about Deke Hightower (including his last name).

I was not down with being separated from him.

I could push it. I knew with the way he was with me that day, all I had to do was call his name and he'd be with me in a shot. He'd climb into bed with me. He'd hold me. Or he'd not hesitate if I wandered down the hall and cuddled with him on his couch (bed was definitely the better of those two options, his bed was a decent size, the couch, no).

"Deke," I called.

"Yeah, baby," he called back.

Baby.

God.

I drew in breath.

But as that oxygen came in, I knew I couldn't push it. He'd been so cool. *Honored* to look out for me.

God.

Deke.

I needed to look out for him too.

"We should switch," I told him.

"Switch what?" he asked.

"I can sleep on the couch, you take the bed."

"Entry's here, Jussy," he told me. "Twyla's out there but no way in fuck you're gonna be on this couch with you closer to the door than me."

I hadn't thought of that.

I told him what I had thought of. "You're a big guy."

"You think I haven't passed out on this couch and not been good?" he asked.

I had a feeling he'd done that more than once.

"Right," I said.

I grew quiet.

Deke didn't break the silence.

I stared at the ceiling some more.

Then I called, "Deke?"

"Right here, Jussy," he called back.

"How do you have electricity out here?" I asked.

"Generator," he answered.

Oh.

Interesting.

"Water?" I asked.

"Fill up the tanks, babe."

"Wouldn't it be easier to connect to a water source?"

"It would, but don't have one out here."

"In other words, no long showers," I quipped.

"Not hard to fill up the tanks, gypsy princess. You want a long shower, you take it."

God, it was like he'd give me anything, all of it beauty, which meant all of it exacerbated the yearning for the thing I most wanted that he wouldn't allow me to have.

But with what he gave me, that being beauty, I'd take it.

"Can the water company not lay anything?" I asked. "Or the electric company doing the same thing so you don't have to use a generator?"

"Own this land but it's protected. Not allowed to build on it. No water. No electricity. Nothin'."

That was surprising. I didn't even know you *could* own land you couldn't do whatever you wanted to do with it.

"Really?"

"Yep."

"Uh, maybe a stupid question," I started. "But why would you buy land that you can't build on?"

"You see my view?"

I smiled at the ceiling.

"So what you're saying is, it was a stupid question," I remarked, my smile in my voice.

"Nothin's stupid, Jussy. 'Specially with that. Just to say, me and my Airstream here, it's about my ma."

I felt my tight muscles tighten further at a mention of his mom before I forced them to relax, turned to the side and stared down the short, dark hallway toward the shadow of Deke on his couch at the end.

I tucked my hands under my cheek and called, "What's about your ma?"

No pushing, he gave it to me.

"Losin' Dad, she didn't have it good, raisin' me on her own. Things got tough a lot. A kid is a kid but they still feel things like that. Especially things like that. Much as she tried to protect me from it, she was my ma, it was just the two of us, so I felt it."

I hated that he felt that.

Hated it.

I didn't interject that sentiment and Deke kept going.

"When I was a kid, she used to tell me stories. About how we'd make it one day, build a big house on a lake. Have a boat. Go waterskiing. Go fishin'. Lots of shit like that."

He stopped talking and to prompt him to do it more, I said, "Yeah?"

"Yeah," he replied, his tone softer, reminiscent. Through it he gave me a hint of melancholy and a lot of beautiful. "I got older and knew we'd never have that, but she didn't quit dreamin'. She said she was gonna retire by a lake. Not a big house. Little cottage, she said. Not much to clean. Not much to take care of. That was gonna be the end of her days, her in a cottage by some lake. She wanted that for her and I wanted it for her. She worked hard her whole life. She deserved that."

My voice carried, but it still was soft when I noted, "She didn't get her cottage, did she, honey?"

"No, Jussy."

"I'm so sorry," I told him.

"What she did was give her boy that," he told me. "She had a life insurance policy. Not much in it but it was enough that, when she died, I took it and found the most beautiful lake I could find. Bought this land. Bought my Airstream. Set myself up here. Just like she would have wanted."

"So the shit with Mav dies down, I get Dad's collection, I have him and Granddad with me. But you, you have your mom with you every second you're here."

He didn't answer immediately but his deep voice was sweet when he did.

"Yeah, baby."

I drew in another breath, this one deep and it burned a little at my throat, down into my lungs.

Once I had it in, the air of his trailer, the air Deke breathed, I let it out saying, "You know how you told me I was one of the best women you've ever met?"

He again didn't answer immediately, then his deep voice sounded.

"Don't, Jussy."

I did.

"You're one of the best men I've ever met."

"Jussy."

"That's it, Deke. I'm a lucky girl. Blessed. Given so much bounty, it's almost embarrassing how much God likes me. But He really must like me because I have all I have and He also gave me you."

"You're gonna be shutting up now," Deke declared, I could hear the gruff in his voice, the buried emotion.

That was beautiful too.

I grinned down the hall.

"You're also gonna be shuttin' your eyes and goin' to sleep," he commanded.

"You and Mr. T might have had a taking-care-of-Justice-meeting-of-the-minds but this is plain bossing *me*, Deke."

"Yeah, it is. And you keep talkin', you'll be talkin' to nothin' 'cause I'll be putting my earphones in."

It was my turn to boss.

"You listen to Dad, I want to hear it."

"You're talking," Deke noted.

"No, seriously. I want to hear it."

"Don't got one of those speaker things. And sound is shit through the phone."

"First chance, mall for Deke Hightower. Coffeemaker and speaker dock."

"You buy me that shit, I'll tan your hide."

Shit.

Deke spanking me.

A quiver slithered down my spine, the small of my back, through the crease of my ass to settle in between my legs.

I rolled to my back and stared at the ceiling, knowing I should shut up.

Even knowing that, I still wasn't going to let it go.

"You'll have to catch me first. Though, that might happen as you'll be caffeinated by decent coffee."

I rolled back to my side as I heard and felt the movement of Deke making his way down the hall. I watched his big body hit the small space I was in, filling it up. I also watched as his phone illuminated that space and in a couple of seconds, I heard Dad singing.

He set the phone on the built-in nightstand next to his bed.

Then I watched as he bent deep and after that, all I could do was feel.

Feel his hand cupping the back of my head. Feel his lips touch my temple. Feel the rumble in his voice as he whispered in my ear.

"You're safe here, Jussy. Got me lookin' after you. Got Twyla outside lookin' out for both of us. Got your dad watchin' over you. So stop yammerin' to keep sleep away. Close your eyes, gypsy, and I swear to God, you'll be safe in your dreams."

God, he could also talk sexy, sweet and protective, like a verbal cuddle.

God.

"Okay, Deke," I whispered back.

I felt his fingers press into my scalp before I again felt his lips brush my temple.

"Night, Jussy. Catch you in the morning."

Yeah.

One thing I'd learned that day in a way I knew it was for certain.

And it was something that would forever feed my poet's soul having it in the way I did, which I treasured, and in the way I never would, which I longed for.

That being knowing without a doubt that no matter what...

Deke would catch me.

* * *

I heard glass shattering and woke with a start.

Panic assailed me, freezing every inch of my body in sheer terror.

A beat of silence slid by, two and then it hit me that I didn't know where the fuck I was.

Deke's trailer.

Deke.

Without thought, I threw back the covers and swung my legs over the side of the bed.

I ran down the short hall, but even with that little distance, when I hit Deke, he was already standing from the couch.

"Jussy," he murmured.

"Glass," I whispered after I ran right into him, feeling his arms close around me, pressing into him, my hands flat against warm skin over the muscled flesh of his chest that I was too much in a state to appreciate. "Shattering glass."

Deke said nothing. He just shuffled us to the side until he hit a window and I bent with him as he glanced out.

He shuffled us again and took us to the door. Opening it slightly with me out of the way and only his shoulder wedged in, I looked up at him to see his eyes aimed over his shoulder.

There was clearly silent communication between him and Twyla because he nodded and flicked out a hand.

He shuffled me out of the door, closed it, locked it and did all this saying, "It's all good, Jussy."

Before I could speak, Deke lifted me in his arms and he had to walk sideways to get the both of us back to his bed.

My voice was trembling when I started, "Deke—"

"Shush," he hushed me.

I shushed but only because he put a knee to his bed and he didn't put me in it.

He put *both* of us in it.

Thank you, God, for more bounty.

He flicked the covers over us and gathered me close.

This was when I realized I was shaking violently.

Suddenly, I was embarrassed.

"I'm a wuss," I muttered.

"Shut it," he muttered back, his arms tightening around me at the same time his big body shifted into me, tucking me slightly under him.

Yep.

I'd been right way back when.

Deke could be a teddy bear when he cuddled, making me feel small and safe and warm and protected just by wrapping his arms around me.

And I knew by the way he'd bellowed my name at the police station, the hold he'd held on his rage that was at the same time strong, because he'd succeeded in holding it, and fragile, because it seemed like he was going to fail at any second and it would burst forth, that he could also be a lion, annihilating anything that might threaten to harm me.

"I'll just...get a lock on it and then—" I began.

"Close your eyes. Relax. I'm here, Jussy. Not goin' anywhere. I got you."

Yes, he did.

I closed my eyes and pressed my face into his chest. I felt the tickle of hair there and was glad for it. Deke having hair on his chest was the only way I could imagine it. And it was also the way I liked it.

"I need to know your favorite hooch," I told his chest.

"You'll know you shut up, relax, and get some sleep. You do that, I'll tell you in the morning."

"Just an FYI, I'm buying you a case of it."

"You say that like a threat."

"You're not good at receiving gratitude."

"I will be, that gratitude comes in the form of a case of my favorite hooch."

I smiled against his skin.

His hand slid up my spine and started stroking the back of my neck under my hair.

"There's my Jussy," he whispered.

He felt the smile.

His Jussy.

I relaxed in his arms.

"That's it, gypsy," he encouraged, his body settling more weight and warmth on me, and I felt the tremors start to subside.

Moments slid by. Then more moments.

Until, trembling long gone, sleepily, I mumbled, "It'll get better."

"Yeah it will, baby," he murmured. "We'll get you there."

"Thanks, Deke."

"Sleep, Jussy."

I drew in a breath and halfway through the exhale, held in Deke's arms in Deke's bed, feeling small and safe and warm in my teddy bear's arms, protected by my own personal lion, I was out.

CHAPTER ELEVEN

I'm Justice's

Justice

THE NEXT MORNING, I sat next to Deke in Deke's behemoth of a truck, my hands wrapped around a travel mug of coffee that I made in my coffeemaker that the girls had brought to Deke's trailer.

We were on Ponderosa Road, closing in on my house.

And my mind was not overwhelmed with thoughts of returning to the scene of the crime, that crime being perpetrated against me.

My mind was consumed with thoughts of seeing Deke in a pair of loose-fitting, light gray, drawstring, fleece shorts, the jagged hems having been cut off just above his knees, the rest of him bare.

There was a lot of him, this I knew.

What I didn't know was that it would all be so...incredibly...*Deke*.

I knew that made no sense.

It was still true.

He had broad shoulders, bulging biceps, fantastic forearms, all this more of what I knew.

He also had something else I'd discovered in the dead of night.

A hairy chest.

I just didn't know how fabulous that was until the sense of sight was engaged.

It wasn't like he had an overabundance of hair that grew over his shoulders and down his back.

There still was a lot of it. All of it covering exceptional pecs and the most amazing stomach I'd ever seen.

Not abs.

A manly *stomach*.

I had to admit, I was over the cut leanness that was all the rage. In the beginning, it was hot. But now it seemed daunting, men being so developed they didn't have an inch of extra flesh on them, not like they were human beings but like they were diagrams of a body's muscularity.

Not Deke.

Sure, with his line of work, it probably was impossible that he not have a powerful physique (which he did) including a defined ridge outlining the outer abdominals. He also had faint contours marking the two upper boxes.

The rest was a fur-covered stomach that didn't protrude like a beer belly but instead declared him a man who lived his life, ate what he wanted, drank what he wanted, and if that gave him a hint of a gut, he didn't give a fuck.

So Deke.

His knees down to his feet weren't bad either.

But I loved his chest, his stomach. Just a glance at it made me want to straddle his narrow hips while I rode his cock, my nails dragging over the hair on that stomach, my thumbs rubbing hard against his delectable, quarter-sized nipples.

And if that wasn't enough to turn my mind from the intimidating aspect of confronting my house, my bedroom, a place where I'd been certain I was going to be strangled to death (and all of that was more than enough), the way Deke was in the morning added to that significantly.

Needless to say, broken sleep (though the end of it was really good, tucked close to Deke), we got up early and early sucked, even if I woke up in that early tucked close to Deke.

It sucked worse with my body again aching, my wrist twinging with every movement, my face throbbing and my throat still feeling abused.

When Deke woke us (apparently having an internal alarm clock), I knew I was on the verge of being out-and-out grouchy (okay, not so verge, I was there) so I set about making that go away the only way I knew how.

Shambling around silently, trying not to get caught staring at Deke's chest, stomach, arms, legs and his ass that was far more distinct (and delicious) in his fleece shorts, I prioritized getting my hands on the only tool I knew that worked against my grouchy.

Coffee.

Deke, on the other hand, threw teddy bear into overdrive. If he was anywhere near me, he was touching me or straight up turning me into one (or two, if he had them both handy) of his arms. He slid my hair out of my face. He curled a hand around my neck and stroked my jaw with his thumb. And when he handed me my cup of coffee, once I took it, he bent and touched his lips to my temple.

In other words, he treated me not like I was an unexpected guest in his small space but like a fragile and precious object that needed to be cosseted and cuddled at every opportunity so she didn't come flying apart.

None of this, incidentally, said *friend*.

None of it even said woman he'd banged who he liked well enough to look after when life threw her a nasty curveball (though I was obviously not a woman he'd banged).

No.

It all said a *whole lot more*.

That was one place that morning where I absolutely *didn't* go in my mind.

I just let it happen because I needed to be that fragile, precious object he kept from flying apart so I wouldn't focus on the fact that I'd nearly been strangled to death, one of my best friends was clearly in some seriously deep shit, and therefore I actually might come flying apart.

If someone didn't hold me together, that was.

And Deke was doing a bang-up job of holding me together.

So I held on to that.

He suggested I take a bath at my place to help with the aches but I insisted I take a shower at his. I didn't want to be naked and vulnerable at my place and not able to dash to Deke the instant something freaked me in the likely event that something might freak me.

He didn't push it. In fact, his voice barely rose above a gentle, rumbling murmur not only then but all morning.

Though he did insist I go first.

While he showered (and I struggled with obsessing over the rest of what his body might look like, especially in a shower), I made us more coffee and also made us oatmeal, enjoying the novelty of having a kitchen (such as it was). Mr. T was going to bring La-La Land treats but I needed something to take my mind off Deke in the shower and what I used to do that was oatmeal.

He came out in a towel, something that didn't help matters, and closed the door to his bed area to get dressed (I'd dressed in his bathroom).

That day he wore a white T-shirt as if he knew the familiarity of that was a balm to my cluttered mind.

He couldn't know that, of course.

It still was a balm and I appreciated it.

We left the trailer and I saw Twyla was gone. This Deke told me she did after Deke went out and spoke with her while I was in the shower.

I made a mental note: another case of hooch for Twyla hanging out in her pickup all night.

Now we were headed to my house. I had my second big cup of coffee in my hands, my belly full of oatmeal, the ibuprofen and aspirin that Deke gave me working their way through my system, dulling the aches along with the pains, and I was getting out of the grouchy.

Unfortunately I was doing it in a way that could make me even grouchier, after that morning, now only just *relatively* certain I could do this friend thing with Deke.

No girl without a man could have a friend with Deke's chest (and stomach… and ass, it should be added).

I mean, really.

It was torture.

We growled along in his behemoth, these thoughts in mind, me deciding that, once all was clear with Bianca's lunatic, I was going to hang with Lacey during her tour.

I was also going to get laid.

This thought made saliva fill my mouth like I was about to get sick, thinking of having any man, taking any man inside me who was not Deke.

So with this reaction, I decided not to focus on whatever the future needed to be.

Instead, I was going to focus on the next minute, the next after that, and just deal.

Deke turned into my lane with a murmured, "Good, baby?"

"Good, Deke," I whispered.

He reached out a hand and squeezed my thigh before he turned it, palm up.

I didn't know what that meant but instinctively I took one hand from my mug and placed it in his.

That was what it meant. His fingers curled warm around mine and he pulled both to his thigh and rested them against the hard muscle there while he drove us up my lane.

I closed my eyes.

God.

He was just *so fucking Deke*.

"Callahan," he said.

I opened my eyes.

And there he was, Joe Callahan, standing at the side of a black SUV, shoulders rested against it, wearing jeans, a black tee and motorcycle boots.

I had not been in his presence often, a few times, but every time I was, I'd noted this was Cal's uniform.

I'd also noted he was smokin' hot in the sense that he could totally move to these mountains and fit right in.

Deke stopped and let me go to put the truck in park and cut the ignition.

For some reason, I waited until he'd done this, watching his profile rather than opening my door.

He felt my gaze, looked at me, his face softened and he gave me one nod before he unbuckled his seatbelt and turned to his door.

I unbuckled too and turned to mine.

Once I got out and shut it, I looked to Cal to see he'd pushed away from the SUV and was heading our way.

But he got a look at me not through the windshield and his tall body came to an abrupt stop.

Then his handsome face got scary.

I just barely made it to the hood of Deke's truck when Deke was at my side, and before I knew it, he had a hand curled around my neck. His wrist was at the back, his fingers around the side pulling me close to him so I had no choice but to move toward Cal with my side brushing Deke's and do it lifting a hand and hooking my thumb in his back belt loop.

It was a strange hold that communicated protection and, oddly (though I might be reading it wrong, that wrong being hopefully) possession.

Cal took us in as we made our way to him and Deke stopped us a few feet away.

"You're Callahan," Deke stated and Cal tore his angry gaze from my throat and gave it to Deke.

"You're Hightower," he returned.

"Yup."

Cal looked him up and down, clearly after having seen my face, he hadn't taken in the fullness of all that was Deke (just to say, I didn't look much at myself when I was in Deke's bathroom—I saw it was not pretty in such a way that I wasn't quite ready to go there just yet with any type of close inspection).

He did take Deke in right then and I knew his eyesight wasn't failing when I saw the pissed-off tense line of his body relax a smidge.

Cal turned his attention to me. "You doin' okay, Jus?"

"Got a lot of good folks looking after me, Cal," I replied.

He nodded, glancing at Deke before looking at me.

He then looked back to Deke. "You wanna let her go, man, so I can give her a hug?"

This was Cal's wife's doing. I knew this because he put in Dad's security in Dad and Dana's house prior to finding that wife and back then, although not rude or an asshole, he was about as huggable as Charles Manson.

When he did Lacey's house in the Hollywood hills, well after he'd settled into life with his new wife, he was an entirely different man. Still slightly taciturn, the rest was a shock. He was far more mellow and he liberally demonstrated he had a wicked sense of humor. He talked on the phone frequently with his woman and the family he collected when he got her (she was a widowed mom) and the one the two of them were making (something they enjoyed doing because as far as I knew, they had five kids, two hers before Cal, five hers and Cal's with Cal's seed making three of those).

It was a beautiful thing to see, how the love of an unmistakably good woman (though I'd never met her, still, the miracle she wrought was proof of that in my eyes) could change a man. Make him so visibly happy, even folks who barely knew him saw the blessings he'd received because he wore them almost like badges of honor.

Another of life's bounties, seeing that for Cal.

As I thought all this, I realized that the answer to Cal's question was a negative because Deke didn't let me go.

It was then I noticed Cal make a slight movement, shifting his left hand, but doing it so the wide gold band on it was easy to see.

Only then did Deke let me go.

Uh…

Okay.

Now what was *that*?

I had no intention to ask or any chance.

Cal came forward and pulled me in his arms, giving me a careful hug.

He also didn't let me go immediately.

He kept me close as he said, "Gonna get you safe, Justice. No way this shit's gonna happen again. Yeah?"

I gave his trim waist a hug. "Yeah, Cal. Thanks."

He finally removed his arms, I dropped mine, but he didn't remove himself until after he wrapped one hand around my right biceps and gave me a reassuring squeeze.

Then he looked to Deke. "Let's get to work."

"Let you in and you can take a look around," Deke replied. "Know Max gave you the plans and sent you some pictures but figure you need to get the lay of the land. You do that, I gotta take Jussy to her room. You're gonna have to give us a few minutes, brother. After that, she's gonna be with us, not out of either of our sight, not even in her bedroom. You with me?"

Cal studied Deke a beat before he nodded.

Deke looked down at me. "You with me?"

Me not hanging out in the room where I got strangled without Deke there with me?

I was totally with him.

"I'm with you."

That was when Deke nodded, took hold of me again, this time with his arm around my shoulders, and he turned us to the house.

And that was when all thought of Deke's chest, his stomach, ass, legs, cutoff fleece shorts, gentle morning mood and Cal's miraculous change due to the love of a good woman went out of my head as I stared at my front door.

My house was beautiful on the outside. All those windows. All that stone. That arched doorway. The flagstone walk that led from the graveled drive to the front door set in wide but lazy and meandering, curving here and there randomly. The old pines and aspen undisturbed around the front, the selection of the ones left standing so perfect I would not need a lot of landscaping. All of this making it seem like the house had been there forever. Like it grew up among those trees, not as it was, having been carved into them.

I concentrated on that, not the sick curl of fear in my belly.

I was there with Deke and Cal. Cal was going to give me a kickass security system. I had people around me who I had not known long but even before crisis hit, they'd shown they were good people and were going to be great friends.

This was my place, my space, my sanctuary, my oasis. I'd chosen it out of pure instinct and I'd chosen well.

And no asshole fuckwad was going to take that away from me.

This thought I must have communicated with my body somehow because I felt Deke give my shoulders a squeeze before he muttered, "That's it, gypsy."

I drew in breath and Deke jiggled his keys in his hand to find mine.

We stopped at the front door. He let us in. I felt Cal move in behind us.

Straight away, Deke headed us toward my bedroom.

I noted the light was different because the big window that was in the space where my dad's collection was going to be was boarded up.

It was weird, the guy came through that window, making all that racket. Much easier, I would think, to bust through the windows at my front or back door.

Deke didn't give me a chance but to glance at it.

He moved me right to my bedroom, attached to him, his arm strong around my shoulders, my thumb back in his belt loop.

We made it to my bedroom, sidling in on a connected slant, and Deke stopped us a couple of feet inside.

I instantly felt a tingling in my scalp, a memory of being dragged by my hair to my bed.

The next second I took in the room.

Except for fingerprinting powder on the nightstand, the lamp still overturned, it just looked like I'd gotten out of bed and that was it.

On that thought, Deke let me go and moved directly to the lamp. He righted it and turned to the bed. In one sweep of his long arm, the heavy down comforter went sailing to the floor at the foot of the bed. He then grabbed a pillow and shook it out of its case.

"Deke," I whispered.

He tossed the naked pillow to the floor, the empty case to the bed and looked to me, reaching for another pillow.

"Got extra sheets?" he asked.

I nodded.

"Get 'em," he ordered. "Hurry, want you right back."

I swallowed and nodded again.

Then I went to the fabulous laundry room Deke gave me, set my travel mug aside and got the extra sheets.

By the time I got back, the pillows were all nude and on the floor and he was yanking the flat and fitted sheets off the mattress.

He gathered them up and headed my way, stopping for only a second to say gently, "Start making the bed, Jussy."

I nodded yet again.

He moved out of the room.

I went to the bed, dropped the folded sheets on top and just stood there, staring at it.

I understood why Deke left me in there alone but with the knowledge he'd come right back. I also understood why he wanted me back in my house sooner rather than later so I didn't build on the rational fear I had of a space that was mine, making it irrational and insurmountable.

But I wished he hadn't gone.

Because if I tried really hard, I could hear the gurgling noises I made while attempting to breathe with that asshole's hand around my throat.

And for some reason, I tried real hard and heard them.

I stopped hearing them practically before I started because Deke was back in a flash and he moved right into me, close, and grabbed a pillowcase.

I forced my mind off shit that would fuck with it and onto working with him and together we made my bed.

When we were done, I was on one side, the side closer to the windows, Deke on the other. He barely put the last pillow into place before he bent low, and using the hem, he wiped away the black fingerprinting dust with the inside of his white tee.

"Deke, that might stain," I told him.

"Then the shirt goes in the trash," he told me, straightening and doing it pulling out his phone.

He touched the screen and put it to his ear while I stood there watching him.

"Jim-Billy," he said, paused then went on, "I know what time it is. I'm at Jussy's. She's hangin' inside with me while I work and she doesn't have any furniture. Need you to make some calls, round up something comfortable, chair, couch, don't give a shit just as long as whoever donates it doesn't care it gets drywall dust and wood slivers on it. Bring it up soon's you can." Another pause then, "Right, man. Thanks."

He shoved his phone in his back pocket and I watched him round the bed and move to the French doors. I pivoted with him so I was in the position to continue watching as he went out to my deck, grabbed one of my Adirondack chairs and came right back in.

"Close the door, babe," he ordered as he hauled the chair through my bedroom.

I jerked my body out of its stupor and moved quickly to the door.

I closed it, locked it and the instant the lock clicked, Deke kept being bossy.

"Follow me."

I did as told, following him as he maneuvered the chair at an angle that would not only get it through my bedroom door but also through the doorway to the great room.

He set it down there and I only got the chance to glance at Cal, who was standing inside the closed front door zipping shut a measuring tape, doing this watching us, before Deke spoke again,

"'Til Jim-Billy sets you up, Jussy, this'll have to do."

I looked up to him. "Okay, honey."

He got close and put a hand to my neck, sliding it back and up into my hair as he dipped his face to mine.

"Sheets are in the wash. Washin' him away. Your bed's clean of him. It's all yours again. That room all yours. This house all yours. He didn't belong here when he was here, he doesn't belong here at all, including up here." He lifted his other hand and lightly tapped my forehead before he dropped that hand. "Gonna take some effort but start that now, Jussy. Wash him away."

I nodded, feeling his hand warm in my hair against my scalp, nothing in my space, my world, but his strong, beautiful, bearded face.

I didn't know if I could wash that guy away.

What I did know was that, for Deke, I'd try my damnedest to do anything he wanted.

I watched his eyes smile before his fingers slid out of my hair so he could wrap them around the back of my neck and pull me to him.

He kept that one hand there, curled his other arm around me and I curved both of mine around him.

He held me and he took his time doing it, no squeezes, just offering me the undeniable evidence of his solid sanctuary.

Finally, he bent his head so his lips were at the top of my hair and he said there, "Gonna get to work on givin' my gypsy some walls."

He kissed my hair and only then gave me a squeeze before he let me go.

I drew in breath, still smelling the clean soap aroma that was Deke in the morning, or Deke drywalling.

Actually, just Deke.

Deke moved to his tools that he kept along a wall in the great room.

I moved my eyes to Cal to see he was paying us no mind and instead was doing whatever he needed to do to get done what I needed him to do.

I went to my Adirondack chair, taking my phone out of my pocket when I did.

And I sat in my chair and texted Joss, Lacey, Dana and Mr. T, telling them I was good, I was healing, I was safe.

And I was home.

* * *

An hour later, it started happening.

That "it" being, even if Deke hadn't begun the process of washing away what had happened in that house, the town of Carnal was clearly intent on doing that same thing.

However, it began not with a Carnal citizen.

It began with Mr. T.

Playing butler along with security expert, Cal answered the door to him at eight o'clock sharp.

I watched Mr. T walk in carrying a cardboard holder with four coffees (of course Mr. T wouldn't forget Cal) and a white bag with a colorful flower hand-drawn in Sharpies on the outside.

La-La Land treats.

"Callahan," Mr. T greeted Cal.

"Thurston," Cal greeted Mr. T back.

But I was up and moving quickly across the space.

Cal took the coffees and bag so when I made it to the man who'd devoted his life to making life easy for my granddad, my dad and me, I could move right in for a hug.

He stiffened, as was his way, before he gave me a perfunctory hug back and pushed me gently away with his hands on my upper arms.

This was not done to get me out of his space. It was done so he had an unobstructed view of my face and I knew this because I knew Mr. T and also because he didn't let my arms go.

And if Deke's fury yesterday morning was crazy-scary, Cal's look that morning was just plain scary, Mr. T's look was downright terrifying.

I'd never seen that. He could get irritated. He could get frustrated. I'd seen him smile (though barely and they didn't last long).

But I'd never seen him angry.

And obviously not *that* angry.

Even so, that look, as perverse as it seemed, calmed something inside of me.

And this was because he so totally would push me out of the way of a train and take that hit.

I let him have his look, doing this feeling all he was giving me at the same time hearing Deke coming down the ladder.

Mr. T kept hold at both my arms until he was forced to let go, this done by Deke wrapping an arm around my chest from behind and pulling me back into his body.

Once he got me in this position, he also, incidentally, did not let me go.

Mr. T looked from me and up. Then he took his time and did it brazenly looking down. Once he did that, he looked back up and I knew by the angle of his head and the shrewdness in his eyes that he was equally brazenly measuring up Deke.

Then he shocked the absolute shit out of me.

He pushed forward a hand and grunted, "Bill."

I blinked.

Deke's hand came out and they shook while he returned a grunt of, "Deke."

They separated.

But I was stuck on "Bill."

Granddad called Mr. T "Bill." I did not. Dad did not. Joss did not and Joss didn't recognize any authority figure in all the world, even going so far as, when referring to her, calling the Queen of England "Liz" like they were best friends.

Except Mr. T.

Joss called Mr. T "Mr. T" just like everybody.

This being the case, obviously I'd never heard Mr. T introduce himself as "Bill."

I had no idea what to do with this but didn't get the chance to wrap my head around it before Cal declared, "Bet I could get a lot more done if I wasn't standing here holding a tray of coffee."

I grinned, quickly pulled out of Deke's hold and moved to Cal. I distributed coffee. I opened the bag and discovered just by the scent that Shambles was in a cinnamon mood that morning.

Perfection.

I loved cinnamon.

I gave out treats, left mine in the bag for later, and set it aside as I reclaimed my coffee from where I'd put it on a stack of drywall.

While doing this, Mr. T demanded, "Show me around your home, Justice."

"Okay, Mr. T," I agreed.

I started to move but stopped and looked back to see Deke had a hand on Mr. T's shoulder.

Except for the hug I just gave him, and a few hugs I made him endure after he gave me presents and such, as well as a number of handshakes, I'd seen nobody, not even his wife, touch Mr. T.

But he stood under Deke's hand, his neck twisted, head tipped back to lock eyes with Deke and he nodded after I heard Deke whisper, "Careful with her in her bedroom."

Deke dropped his hand, turned his head to send a small smile my way, and he went back to the ladder.

I showed Mr. T around, inside and out, sipping coffee while Mr. T ate what he told me was a slice of apple cinnamon bread. We finished at my private deck.

We stood at the railing and Mr. T stared at the rushing river.

I stared at Mr. T's jaw, which was only slightly jowly with age, and was now tensed hard.

"I should not have allowed you to move in here without Callahan doing his work first."

Oh shit.

I shifted closer, starting, "Mr. T—"

He turned penetrating blue eyes to me, eyes that had not faded even a little bit over the years, and I quit talking.

Then suddenly, delivering another shock, he lifted a hand, took my chin in his fingers and gently turned my head so he could examine the damage to my face, his gaze moving from there to my throat before he righted my head but kept his hand there.

"Your father would be beside himself," he whispered.

I felt tears gather in my eyes so strong, they stung my nostrils.

"Mr. T," I whispered back.

"I promised them both," he stated.

"Promised them both what?"

"You and your brother, I promised your grandfather and your father, as long as I was breathing, I would never let anything happen to you. I've failed them both. I've failed *you* both."

I lifted a hand and wrapped it around his wrist. "Mav's Mav and you know it. You can save him from a lot, but you can't save him from her. And I moved in here without a system in. So intent on finding some peace after we lost Dad, I didn't think. It wasn't you, it was me."

He released my chin and dropped his hand, disconnecting us.

"You forget, I also failed your cousin Rudy."

"You couldn't save Rudy from himself either," I reminded him. "We all tried, Mr. T. You can look at it as we all failed but we didn't. In the end, Rudy failed himself."

Mr. T shook his head. "You can say a thousand words, put them in a hundred songs, Justice, and you would not have enough words to convince me I'm wrong."

I studied a man I didn't know until that very moment that I loved down deep in my heart where my dad lived, where my grandfather lived, where all the good love that was pure and right in any body took residence.

"I might not be able to convince you that you're not to blame, the only person to blame is the man who did this to me. But I hope I can convince you that everything you've done for me, for Granddad, for Dad, even for Mav, all of it, culminating in you dropping everything to be here right now with me, I love you for it because I just love *you*."

"The Lonesome heart," he replied reflectively, "all of them so soft."

"Which means it was a blessing Granddad found you so you could protect them."

He nodded. "Yes." He kept nodding. "Yes, a blessing."

I had a feeling he wasn't talking about the same blessing I was but he cleared his throat, looked away and announced, "You need stables."

I grinned and turned, bumping him purposefully with my shoulder before I opened my mouth and told him all my plans. The ones that were currently being carried out by Deke and the other ones that would happen pending the sale of the extra land that my real estate agent was negotiating for me.

While I was doing this, we heard a vehicle approach and Mr. T turned to my house, extending his arm for me to precede him.

I did this and we went through my bedroom to the great room to see Cal at the door and two men walking through it.

I stopped dead on sight of them.

One was white, had a salt and pepper (predominately pepper, *black* pepper) head of hair and goatee, a face that was gorgeous in a rugged way, and a tall body made up of what I was assuming since I kept running into it was patented mountain man muscle.

The other was black, as huge as Deke (maybe even bigger), and so outlandishly handsome, I could swear I'd seen him before and that had to be in a movie.

They were carrying a beat-up couch.

Following them in was Jim-Billy.

Jim-Billy looked at me, started to grin, the grin faltered, died, he stood still and immobile and I started toward him, calling a gentle, "Hey, Jim-Billy."

He didn't greet me back.

He turned on his battered boot and walked out.

Deke was down the ladder and on the move to the front door, saying, "Wood, Ty, Jussy. Jussy, my buds, Wood and Ty."

Then he was through the door.

I looked to Wood and Ty. Ty, the black guy, I knew was Lexie's husband. Wood was the man I hadn't met who took care of Granddad's truck.

I waved.

They did not wave back.

They were staring at me with stony faces and their mountain man, badass, pissed-off vibe was choking the air.

Okay, so maybe I should have a look at my face and perhaps get creative with foundation.

I walked to my front windows.

And I stood there and stared as I saw Jim-Billy, his back to me, hands fisted and to his hips, the line of his body tight, Deke standing close to him, his head bent to the older man, his hand wrapped around the back of Jim-Billy's neck.

They were talking.

I watched Jim-Billy's back heave with what was apparently a large breath.

Then he nodded his ball-capped head.

Deke dropped his hand and they both turned to the house.

I scooted out of eyesight, not an easy task as the walls were windows that rose unobstructed for two and half stories.

I did this thinking that was at least one thing that was happening in my life that it was easy to know what to make of it.

Jim-Billy really liked me.

And more serenity settled inside me.

Ty and Wood headed back out. Deke and Jim-Billy came back in. Wood and Ty also came back in, this time with a ratty armchair.

Ty went back out to get an ottoman.

Jim-Billy sat his ass in the armchair, lifted his dusty boots to the ottoman practically before Ty had it on the floor, looked at me and asked, "You got any beer, sweetheart?"

"It's not even nine in the morning," Mr. T. stated tetchily, staring at Jim-Billy and doing it making it clear he wasn't making much of him.

Jim-Billy looked at him. "Who're you?"

"William Thurston. I'm Justice's," Mr. T replied.

I waited for him to say more but apparently he meant that to say it all (and it did, and the way it did gave me more solace).

"And you are?" Mr. T asked when Jim-Billy didn't offer that information up himself.

"I'm Jim-Billy. I'm Justice's too. And I'm hangin' with my girl here so she don't get bored outta her mind watchin' men hang drywall." He turned his attention to me. "Now, darlin', you got beer?"

I felt my lips twitch before I said, "Coming right up, Jim-Billy."

I moved out to the garage, got Jim-Billy a beer and headed back.

When I arrived I saw Mr. T was still sipping his coffee but now doing this perched on the arm of the couch.

Jim-Billy had his hand out for the beer, which meant I didn't waste time making it to him so I could give it to him.

Cal was doing his thing.

But Wood and Ty were upstairs.

And Deke was coming to me.

I tipped my head back when he stopped, not Deke close, which was close but also not the close I'd like.

It was a new close. A what I thought of as a fragile-Justice-in-his-trailer close, in other words *close*-close, as in the close I *liked*.

A close he didn't need to use when we weren't in his trailer but instead I was surrounded by awesome people in my huge house.

But he used it.

"Baby, Wood and Ty are workin' with me today. You down with that?"

My brows drew together. "I thought Wood owned the local garage."

"He does, which means he can take the day off whenever he wants. He's also a man. And when I say that, I mean *a man*. Not sure he's ever hung drywall. That said, think men like him instinctively get how to hang drywall."

I'd been in Wood's presence for maybe five minutes and he'd not said a word to me and I still had the feeling he was the kind of *man* who instinctively knew how to do a lot of things.

"Ty works for Wood and Wood's givin' him a day off to work here," Deke informed me. "He's worked construction so he just knows what he's doin'."

"Are they, uh…does Max need—?" I stammered but Deke cut me off.

"Max won't care. He's tight with Ty, they've worked together on jobs back in the day and if you're talkin' about payin' them dick, I think we had this discussion."

"So crates of hooch all around," I muttered.

Deke grinned, caught me at the back of my head, pulled me to him, bent in, kissed my forehead then let me go and strolled to the ladder and up it.

God, I was going to miss those bits of Deke he'd surely take away when he decided I was no longer fragile and needed his affection so I wouldn't come flying apart.

I turned to the improvised seating area and saw Jim-Billy belting back a slug of beer.

Mr. T had eyes to the upstairs.

Those eyes came to me.

Then he rearranged his position, pulling out his phone and not perching on the arm of the couch like he would rather not have his ass touching it. An ass that was in trousers that I figured had another half back at a hotel in town, this being the suit jacket of a suit of Italian origin that cost more than that couch he was sitting on when it was new. Instead he settled right in that couch, rested his coffee cup on the arm and started sliding his finger on the phone.

At this juncture, a vehicle could be heard.

"Jesus," was also heard right after, this being Cal who started heading to the door.

"I got it," I told him and his eyes cut to me.

"No, you don't."

At the firmness of his tone, I stopped moving.

So Cal wasn't playing butler.

Even though it was highly unlikely my attacker would show in broad daylight with my house filled with people, Cal was playing bodyguard.

So sweet.

Cal opened the door.

Half a minute later, Lexie sauntered through accompanied by two adorable little girls.

She glanced at Cal, looked to me, said, "Hey," and at my hey back, she said "Hey," to Jim-Billy," to which she got a, "Yo, gorgeous," then her eyes slid through Mr. T and swung around and up where she clearly spied her husband because she called out, "Hey, baby."

Ty called back, "Mama."

Yikes.

Ty's rumbling "mama" might be better than Deke's "baby."

Though, not better than his "gypsy."

"*Hey, Daddy!*" one of the little ones shrieked.

"Hey, baby,"Ty called back to his daughter.

Okay, that "baby" was even better than "mama."

Yeesh.

Mountain men.

Who knew?

Lexie drew her girls closer to me. "Lella, Vivie, this is Miss Justice. Say hi."

The older girl standing and holding Lexie's hand waved shyly.

The younger one Lexie was juggling in an arm at her hip, shouted, "Hey, Miz Justiz!"

"Hey, beautiful babies," I greeted them.

The one at Lexie's hip beamed.

The one holding Lexie's hand moved into her mother's leg and ducked her head.

I did the round of introductions.

Once released, Lella wasted no time sharing her wishes that she wanted to be upstairs with her father. Vivie wasted no time crawling all over Jim-Billy who tickled her and blew raspberries on her neck all of which required her to squeal loudly and with easily discernable glee. When denied access to her father, Lella then joined the crawling-all-over-Jim-Billy activities to which he put his beer to the floor so he had two hands to tickle and squeeze.

Lexie collapsed into the couch, declaring, "Jim-Billy's gonna look after the girls. You're coming into town with me for a massage, mani and pedi. Nic's got it all sorted on the schedule. But we have about half an hour before we have to leave."

"I'm gonna look after the girls?" Jim-Billy asked.

"*Yay! Jim-Billy!*" the younger girl screeched before collapsing on Jim-Billy's chest, making him give an audible grunt, and determinedly (with tongue sticking out and everything) trying to tickle his sides.

"Right, I'm gonna look after the girls," Jim-Billy muttered, doing it grinning.

"That's not happening."

This came from upstairs, it was unyielding, and it was Deke.

Lexie looked upstairs. "Tate's meeting us here. He's taking us down. And he's sticking with us while we do our thing and bringing us back."

Wood showed at the edge of the upstairs landing beside Deke, his handsome face a mask of incredulity, his goatee-surrounded lips asking, "Tate is gonna hang at a salon while you girls are doing massages and getting your nails done?"

"Yeah," Lexie answered.

Wood burst out laughing.

Ty burst out laughing.

Jim-Billy burst out laughing and Lella and Vivie both collapsed on his chest, probably not getting it but they burst out laughing too.

Deke did not burst out laughing.

He pulled out his phone and stepped away from the landing.

I heard a murmured conversation, glanced around, saw a lot of smiles (except Cal, who was shaking his head while pulling at a large spool of wire he'd brought in from his SUV).

Deke came back to the edge of the landing with no phone.

"Tate's gonna take you," he declared. "He's gonna stay with you. You do that, you come right back. No sandwiches. Nothin', Jussy. You get right back here."

"You got it, boss," I called.

He was not amused.

He stalked back to where he was drywalling.

I looked to Mr. T. "You wanna hang during a mani-pedi?"

He shook his head, pushing up from the couch. "I'll take that as my cue to leave. I have things to do at a location where I might find Wi-Fi and wish to stop by the station to speak with Lieutenant Keaton. I'll be back with sandwiches."

I glanced around and back to him. "Bring a lot."

He glanced around and back at me.

When he did, I knew I was not the only one who'd been given solace that day.

Mr. T had as well.

"I will, Justice."

I grinned at him.

He did not grin at me.

With formal farewells, he took his leave.

I then hung with my new posse until Tate came to take us to the salon.

During the mani-pedi portion of the excursion, I took a call from Shambles. His tone was hushed, which told me something he didn't say with words, this being the call was not overheard by Sunny.

What he did say was that he and Sunny had heard what had happened, I was in their thoughts and they were going to bring me dinner one night, "later...when you're feeling better."

I sussed this as Shambles protecting Sunny from anything that seeing me in my state might dredge up from her own attack.

And I was down with that, totally. Even more so considering, if Shambles could inject heaven into baked goods, a dinner from him might be an exercise in ecstasy.

Tate took us back to my place. Mr. T brought sandwiches, ate with us, all the guys taking a break, Lauren showing and bringing more beer (mostly for Jim-Billy, the guys didn't drink, Lexie didn't either, Lauren and I did).

Mr. T took off.

Lexie and the girls took off.

Released from babysitting duty and Justice-entertaining duty, not long after, Jim-Billy exchanged his armchair at my house for his stool at Bubba's.

Tate helped the dudes for a while while Laurie and I chatted, Lauren and my conversation broken occasionally by Joss checking in, Uncle Jimmy checking in and Aunt Tammy doing the same (the latter two had been informed by Mr. T what had happened).

Eventually Lauren and Tate took off as did Wood and Ty.

And Deke and I took off while Cal was still working.

Before leaving, I noticed that three (and for a while, four) men got a lot more done than one (or two). They not only made up for what Deke couldn't do on the day he lost looking out for me, they drywalled one entire side of my upstairs.

So sitting beside Deke in his behemoth, grumbling down my lane, I did it realizing with all that had happened that day, it felt weirdly, but mercifully, like being strangled on my bed was a blip of life.

It happened.

It was over.

With the help of people who cared, I was moving on.

I had turquoise fingernails and plum toenails. I had a massage from Lexie (who was a massage therapist) that made me feel loose and relaxed, the pain still a dull throb in my face, the aches of my body vanishing under her capable hands.

I had new acquaintances that I had a feeling would be friends. Not only Ty and Wood, but also Dominic (also known as Nic), the outrageously flaming owner and operator of the local salon who cooed and coddled me like Deke did, except in a gay way that was hilarious at the same time heartwarming.

And the work on my house wasn't just still on track, it was cooking with gas.

Thus Deke's truck grumbled down my lane with me in the passenger seat on our way back to his kickass trailer.

And I was smiling.

* * *

After changing into my pajamas, I opened the door to Deke's bedroom area and I did it nervously.

I had to ask what I needed to ask.

But I couldn't ask what I needed to ask.

I looked down the hall to see the trailer dark except for Deke illuminated by the television set he was standing in front of, his tall, man-bunned head nearly brushing the ceiling of the trailer.

He'd taken the opportunity of me behind closed door and he was back in his fleece shorts, bare chest, head turned, eyes to me.

Before I could open my mouth, the trailer went dark because Deke switched off the TV.

I watched his shadow lumber toward me.

I realized he wasn't stopping so I moved out of the doorway just in time for him to move through it and catch me with an arm hooked at my waist.

That way, he shifted us both to the side of the bed. And with little effort and no coaxing, we both were in it.

Deke flicked the covers over us and pulled me in his arms.

Of course.

Deke being Deke, I didn't even need to ask what I needed to ask.

"You're right," I told his bristly throat in the dark. "Rosalinda's is jalapeño heaven."

"Told you," he muttered.

I'd discovered this that night when Tate, who was our night watchman, showed with Lauren, and his teenaged son, Jonas (a younger version of Tate, the resemblance was uncanny in a variety of ways, including the kid was a good kid, funny and confident to the point of cute because he was openly cocky).

They brought Rosalinda's.

We'd eaten. We'd shot the shit. Lauren and Jonas left. Tate took watch.

Now it was bedtime.

I snuggled into Deke.

Deke cuddled me closer.

"So, is Jonas the most popular kid in school?" I asked.

"Don't know. Not in high school anymore, gypsy," Deke answered teasingly.

"I know that but you can still know."

"He's got a steady girl. She's young but she's pretty in that way you were probably pretty. That way you know she'll always be pretty just doin' it gettin' prettier."

I stared in stunned silence at his throat.

Deke didn't notice.

"Jonas is a good-lookin' kid. Smart. Good grades. Football player. Good at it, like his dad, and sayin' that, Tate was in the NFL so Jonas is seriously fuckin' good at it. And he landed that girl. So yeah, all that suggests he's popular. The most popular, don't know. Teenagers are fucked in the brain. Could be the most popular kid wears all black, has got more piercings in his nose than you got in your ears and wears eyeliner."

"Uh, Tate was in the NFL?" I forced through a throat still clogged with the velvety cotton candy sweetness of his compliment.

"Blew out his knee early in his career. Became a cop. Then a bounty hunter, bar owner."

"Interesting life path."

"Best anyone can hope for. Either the contentment of knowin' they're right where they need to be, doin' what they should be doin' among the folk they should be with or takin' a path that, least it could be is interesting, best it's a god-damned kick in the ass."

"That's quite profound, Deke," I told him the truth.

"It's just real."

"It should be a bumper sticker."

I felt his body shake with laughter as he tucked me deeper under him.

"You feel like gettin' up and writin' that shit down?" he asked.

"Absolutely not," I answered.

I felt his words stir the top of my hair when he murmured, "Me either."

Okay.

Wait.

I did not just wake up terrified and needing his arms around me to take away the shakes, him being close to make me feel safe.

Any friend would do that.

I just opened the door ready for bed and there we were, in bed together, cuddling and bantering.

Lacey would do that (including the cuddling). Bianca would too. Hell, we'd all three done that together on a variety of occasions when life got tough or we were just drunk and being crazy but doing it together.

A male friend who knew I had a thing for him?

No.

I felt at this point it was safe to say that Deke's boundaries were getting really fucking blurry.

And perhaps at this point I needed to get a firmer understanding of them before I inadvertently stepped over a line I didn't know was there.

"Deke?" I called.

"Quiet, gypsy, go to sleep."

"But, um..."

I didn't know how to broach it.

"Wood's back to work at your place tomorrow. Max has cleared his day so he can work with us too. Three men, two laying, one cutting, we can get more of your ceiling in."

I wanted a ceiling, like...*bad*. My ceiling was righteous, more of it would be enormously righteous.

But I wanted more to know what was happening with Deke.

"Honey," I whispered.

He pulled me up and closer so my face was in his throat.

"Sleep, Jussy," he whispered back. "You had a good day. Give you a good day tomorrow. Get a brief from Chace, from Decker. Get you a ceiling. That's tomorrow. After that, we'll worry about the next day."

I didn't know what he was saying.

But I still kinda knew what he was saying.

Or hoped I knew.

I also dreaded what else it could be.

The hope was that all this meant something had changed for Deke.

The dread was that he was just that guy who looked out for folks.

Heck, just that day Lauren told me it was him that took her to the hospital after her ordeal and she'd been told he hadn't left until Tate came out to tell everyone she'd woken up and she was all good.

And Lexie had told me over mani-pedis that it was Deke Ty called when the dirty police chief showed to do a random inspection of the then-parolee Ty's house in order to plant drugs and get his parole revoked. Deke had dropped everything so he could show, taking Lexie's back, taking Ty's.

It was clear he did that kind of thing.

That could be what he was doing for me.

Though, he could do it on the couch.

I knew he felt my tension when he asked gently, "Baby, what'd I say?"

"Sleep," I answered.

"Yeah."

"Can I say one thing?" I asked.

He hesitated and on a sigh allowed, "One thing."

I got one thing in that moment; I wasn't going to waste it.

So I didn't.

"Dad would have really, *really* liked you."

His arms tensed around me in a move that seemed involuntary, doing this so tight, I felt the breath squeezed out of me, before they loosened and he tilted his big body, giving me more of his weight and warmth.

But he said nothing.

I gave him that, the best gift I had to give, and I gave him more, deciding to take his advice.

Get through tomorrow.

Then worry about the next day.

So I said nothing as well and I was drifting, close to sleep when I heard him whisper, "And my ma would've fuckin' loved you."

My eyes shot open.

No longer close to sleep, I whispered back, "Deke."

"Sleep."

"Deke."

"Jussy," another powerful squeeze, "*sleep*."

"God, you're annoying," I snapped at his throat.

"Justice."

"Deke."

He said no more.

I glared at his shadowed throat.

He still said no more.

I kept glaring.

After a while, I stopped glaring and started drifting again.

But it was only when I took more of Deke's weight after his drifting took him where he needed to be, the same place I was going, did I finally get there with him and fall asleep.

CHAPTER TWELVE

Quick on the Uptake

Deke

DEKE HANDED JUSSY her mug of joe and felt his lips twitch when she lifted her hands, wrapped them around the mug and pushed out, "Guh."

He moved back to the coffeemaker, poured his own, turned his ass to the counter, leaned against it and looked to her in her preposterous PJs tucked in the corner of his couch, heels to the seat, knees to her chest.

It was Sunday morning and she was still in his trailer.

Deke felt no shame taking advantage of a bad situation as well as Jussy's feelings for him, doing both to keep her right there.

He studied her, pleased to see that the bruising around her neck had faded quickly. There were shadows there but nowhere near as angry and they would likely be gone in a day, two tops. There was no swelling and only minor purpling left around the outside and under her eye, the rest of the discoloration at temple and cheekbone had turned yellow and Deke figured it'd disappear altogether in just a few days. Her voice was back to normal and she'd long since lost the stiffness in her body, moving normally, not carefully.

That wasn't the only progress made that week.

Deke had made calls to anyone he thought might lend a hand, sharing that he wanted to give Jussy as much progress at her place as he could. He reckoned if he could transform it, make it more the home she was hankering to have, it would erase memories of it being violated and create a space that was hers where she felt safe.

His buds had jobs and businesses to run but they came and gave time as often as they could. Sometimes it was only a couple of hours. Sometimes entire mornings or afternoons. Wood came back. Ham, his friend who managed a bar in Gnaw Bone, was there most often, giving a few hours every afternoon, able to do this since he worked nights. Max carved out time himself and did the same with some of his crew, sending a man here and there, usually Bubba but also one of his foremen, a man Deke didn't know too well but he did know the guy was solid, his name, Deacon Gates.

This meant Jussy had a full ceiling, all the drywalling was done with the insulation blown in the panels and it was all taped. Wood, Tate and Ty, along with Bubba, had all shown and they'd primed all the walls the day before.

Deke would be on to painting and maybe even beginning to lay her floors the next week and Max would be sending a full crew of seven more guys the week after that.

Then shit would get done and fast and Jussy would have her home.

That all happened and Callahan was now gone.

He'd left behind a seriously comprehensive system.

Code panels at each door. Inconspicuous panic buttons in a variety of places where, if Jussy was breached, she wouldn't have to run far to flip open the latch, hit the switch and Carnal cops would buzz out. And Cal had put in unobtrusive motion-sensor lights at all the outside eaves, the sensors hugging the exterior walls close so the bright light would only activate and scare the shit out of someone if they were right up at the house doing things they shouldn't be doing, not critters that may get close and constantly set them off.

Cal had also nixed the door to the laundry room, torn out and adjusted the framing and ordered a steel-reinforced door Deke would put in when it was delivered. He put a landline phone in there, effectively making that space a safe room that it would take a bigger blast than a grenade to get through or they'd have to hack through walls. If Jussy's house was violated, she got there, there was a panic button and a landline so she could communicate, call for help and stay safe until that help arrived.

And last, he'd buried all wiring to the house. All of it had been laid from road to home underground but it came aboveground to provide utilities on the outside. Callahan had shifted this inside so if someone wanted to cut her electricity or knock out her phones, they'd have to either climb electrical or phone poles or do it from the inside through a wicked screaming racket that would be made if any door or window sensors were breached, racing against time because a call would go directly to the cops within seconds.

Outside of having a guard at a gate at the head of her lane or cameras everywhere monitored 24/7, it was the most comprehensive, thoughtful security system Deke had seen. It was there but discreet so Jussy didn't have to face its existence with every animal that came close or every time her eyes landed on a panic button.

Callahan had taken off after Jussy had insisted on giving him a dinner of Rosalinda's (this, Deke went to go get and they ate in her living room) as well as a tight hug before he got in his SUV and drove to Denver so he could get back to his family in Indiana.

But Jussy's Mr. T was still around, his command center being mobile, managing her situation, as well as the careers of her aunt and uncle, him either running it out of Justice's living room, La-La Land or Carnal Hotel.

In order for him to do this, he'd somehow pulled some strings to have the cable company turn Jussy's service on as a matter of urgency (this meaning it was done by Wednesday afternoon). And that day he'd brought all the equipment to establish a network with Wi-Fi, set it up in the room that'd be her study, all of it protected from the construction with heavy plastic tarps.

This allowed Jussy to go full steam ahead with her decorating and she was approving shit her designer sent left and right (shit, Deke did not miss, she only approved if she had his approval too).

Not to mention, she'd already given the go ahead for some dead-cool deck furniture, a lot of it, all of it looking like it was made out of logs or hefty branches with thick tan cushions. That had been delivered and set up on her back deck.

This came complete with decorations. Big kickass outdoor candleholders, large colorful pots, even a fucking outdoor rug.

She loved it and Deke approved since she could sit out there while he was working, Jussy not breathing any drywall dust, and he could still see her.

Every day he worked. Every night they came back to his trailer and it was not lost on him that she did not lie when she said, outside of being with her father's guitars, being in that trailer was the second best place she could be.

She visibly relaxed the minute she climbed in.

At first, Deke sensed it was being in a place he'd made safe after what had been done to her.

Then it became more like she was just coming home.

It was a huge fucking understatement to say he liked that.

Since her attack (and even before, if he'd been paying attention), it had become clear she was no fake gypsy princess. She was a straight-up gypsy, more at home in an Airstream with electricity running from a generator and not a single soul within miles than she was in her big house by a river.

And with that, as well as driving up to her house and seeing two police cruisers, a lot more had become clear to Deke because those cruisers extricated Deke's head right out of his ass.

And he started paying attention.

Jussy was Justice Lonesome, the girl who'd inherited a lot of money and even more talent from her father, the girl who made her own mark on that world.

But that was what it was and it was only a small part of who she was.

In reality, she was just Jussy, even if being just Jussy said a fuckuva lot.

Deke had no idea if he could work with that.

What he did know was that he was going to try.

He also had no idea where Jussy's head was at with that except she did not once balk at waking up with him, going to work with him, coming home with him and bedding down with him.

She gave him long looks occasionally and he knew it was on her mind to ask what the fuck was up with him...with *them*...because in the beginning, all the shit he was doing could be shit any friend would do.

It had long since gone past that.

But on Wednesday he'd noted she'd just settled into it. She dug him. They were tight. She needed him. Shit was extreme. She was taking what he had to give, all of it, because she wanted it that way.

He'd share later exactly all that entailed.

Right then, they had to get through that day.

And that night.

That day being the day Brendan Caswell said he was going to come back and finish the job he'd started a week before.

Decker had found out who Bianca Constantine owed a substantial amount of money, that motherfucker being a man named Brendan Caswell.

Deck had not found Bianca, but he'd found she was in deep shit with this Brendan guy, a dealer, low level, ambitious, wanting to make his mark and move up the ranks. But he'd gotten in heavy with Bianca, thinking with her pedigree of having a fading bombshell B-movie star of a mom and the lead guitar of a heavy metal band dad that she'd be good for it...or someone would.

Bianca was in the wind. Caswell was too.

Chace's hands were tied to local investigations and they got nothing. No prints. No tire tracks. No one in town had seen the guy. DNA tests took weeks, sometimes months, but although Caswell had a record, he did not have DNA on file. They'd have to catch him and test him to put him there with Jussy because she couldn't identify him since he'd been wearing a mask.

The only good news with this was that Decker had reported he had solid leads and felt he was closing in on Bianca, his priority (according to Jussy) if not Caswell.

"Wouldn't say this, man, if I didn't believe it but think we'll have our hands on her in twenty-four hours. She proves even more slippery than she's been, intel we got is still tight so the most it'll be is forty-eight. So hang in," Decker had told Deke the day before.

No one knew if Bianca had gotten her hands on the cake to pay Caswell and that was why he'd disappeared.

All they knew was that there was no sign of Caswell anywhere in the county and the BOLO on him hadn't brought them anything.

And they knew that Bianca had burned through the huge trust fund her folks had set up for her, burned through more with friends she'd asked for loans she didn't pay back, that had dried up and now she was broke. She was also not in contact with any friends or family, was addicted to partying in all its incarnations (booze and dope, however she could get them) and way the fuck out on a limb.

Decker reported directly to Deke and Thurston and they both made the decision together to give Jussy all this information.

She was not weak. She was the kind of woman who felt knowledge was power, not ignorance being bliss. The details on her friend were a hit that Deke delivered while they were on his couch and she was in his arms, but she did what he had come to know was the only thing Jussy knew how to do.

She absorbed them, felt the pain, sorted her shit and kept on going.

And today he had to help her keep on going.

He had a plan that would culminate in her behind the fortress of security Callahan gave her, Deke there with her, that night being the first night she spent back at her house.

It had to come and Deke felt it was not only prudent to put her behind Callahan's security, with the cruiser that Chace was setting on her house, but it was also a big fuck you to Brendan Caswell if the moron actually showed that he might have gotten to her and taken her down, but she didn't stay there.

And anyway, she had a king-size bed. His was a double. Good enough for sleeping. But he'd be wanting room to move when they'd had their conversation and were doing a fuckuva lot more than sleeping in a bed.

"I do not understand why, on a Sunday, when you aren't working, I sure as hell am not gonna be working, that we're up this early," Jussy stated and Deke pulled himself out of his thoughts and focused on her.

Christ, all that hair, even prettier when it was a mess after she slept on it.

It'd be good they had the conversation they were going to have so Deke could do all he wanted to do with that hair.

"See the caffeine kicked in and you can speak English again," he joked.

"Deke, it's seven thirty," she told him something he knew.

"Which means we did sleep in. Nearly an hour and a half."

She rolled her eyes.

"Suck more of that back, gypsy princess, so I can get my Jussy back."

That bought him a narrow look, one she took her time giving him, one he knew behind it she was wondering just what the fuck was going on between them.

She'd get that tomorrow.

He had to focus on getting her through today.

And tonight.

"Brunch at Krys's," he finally answered her question. "Remember?"

"I remember but we're not supposed to be there for three hours."

"We need to take the water tanks to Tate's to fill 'em, bring them back, then you need a shower and I need a shower and after that we need to get to Krys and Bubba's. For that I need you caffeinated and on the other side of your morning grump because Tate and Laurie like you but they won't if you hand them a dose of your morning sass."

"I've been really good keeping a lid on my morning sass, Deke. And you know it."

"I do. I also know it took effort and I further know today that lid has slipped."

She released her mug with one hand so she could toss it out, saying, "It's Sunday and seven thirty. Unless you're going to church, which we aren't, it's law not to be up this early on a weekend, especially Sunday."

Law.

Fuck, his gypsy was funny.

"We could shower at your place," he told her. "That way we won't need to fill the tanks before we do it."

"We can also fill the tanks at my place. Which would eradicate a bunch of time driving and in turn would mean we can go back to bed for an hour."

We can go back to bed.

No way in fuck he was getting back into bed with her. He was awake. He was not going to be able to go back to sleep and he was not going to have Justice, her hair, her ass, her legs and her tits all pressed into him the way she pressed into him when he was unconscious, getting all that fully conscious and knowing in detail all he wanted to do with it.

Fuck, he'd been forced to try to find sleep with a rock-solid hard-on he took pains not to let her feel for days.

No, they were not going back to bed.

"Baby, get dressed," he ordered.

She glared at him.

"Dress or I dress you," he threatened.

Right there and open, she gave him the knowledge that she would be down with him trying that before she hid it, pushed out of the couch and grumped as she trudged through his trailer, "Oh, all right."

Deke fought back the urge to slap her ass as she passed and sipped his coffee after she closed the door.

He did that sipping grinning.

The grin faded as he started thinking.

She did not have a desk job. She wrote music. She could do that anywhere. He even saw her doing it years ago, late night in a crowded biker bar.

She'd also lived a relatively rootless life and sustained no damage from it. The way she was, the things she said, the only roots she needed were bedded deep in the people she loved and that never went away even if they weren't close.

She had a big house by a river in the mountains that was going to be spectacular. But she was more at home in a trailer by a lake.

She also had a shit ton of money but did not live large. She might be able to order furniture on the fly and pay for that in cash but she didn't have a butler, she didn't wobble around in designer shoes and she didn't eat caviar for lunch.

She was famous but one of the most real, down-to-earth women he'd met.

And she could take life's knocks, some of them brutal, and keep on ticking. Fuck, she'd been strangled near to death and that very night she talked to him about all the blessings God gave her.

Yeah, Deke was finally paying attention.

He'd watched Tate go down to Lauren and Tate did not do that fighting. He went down and stayed down because he liked the peace and beauty Lauren brought to his and his son's lives.

And Deke had watched Ty fight it with Lexie, nearly lose her, and make adjustments to the man he thought he was just so that shit would not ever happen.

Chace had fought Faye too. She was shy, sweet, but she loved him so it didn't take her long to pull her man's head out of his ass.

And it was Emme who fought Deck, and even if the demons she was battling were fierce, he never gave up.

His buddy Ham, and his wife Zara, on the other hand, had history together. It wasn't all pretty but what was far uglier was the baggage life had given them. In the end, they both were smart enough to know, you got a shot at good and a possible life where you faced the bad with someone who meant everything to you, you didn't squander it. So they hadn't. And Ham just that week told him Zara was knocked up with baby number two.

Deke had garbage in his past he had to work through. He was aware of it. He knew he had to get past it to give Jussy what she wanted—giving them a go.

Deke also knew he was a simple man but he wasn't a stupid man.

He'd watched and he'd learned.

He might not have been quick on the uptake.

But after he got Jussy through that day, and that night, he sure as fuck would be in remedying that because one thing he'd learned from all the watching he'd done was a man's garbage got sorted a fuckuva lot faster when he was man enough to let a good woman help him rifle through it.

And set it aside.

* * *

"Is this normal?" Jussy asked.

He glanced her way then back to the road.

It was after their showers, the water tanks filled and in the bed in the back of his truck. They were heading to his trailer to dump them, pick up their contribution to brunch (a case of beer, a bottle of bourbon, and some casserole Jussy had thrown together last night, put in the fridge and would bake at Krys's place).

"Is what normal?"

"Brunch at Krys and Bubba's," she explained. "Krys doesn't strike me as a brunch-type person."

She wasn't.

What she was was a woman who knew a friend of hers had been attacked and left with the threat that the attacker would return in a week, that week had passed, and now Krys was doing what she could to keep her mind off the fact that day had come.

"Think she's tryin' her hand at domesticity," Deke noted, and maybe it wasn't a total lie.

"God, if brunch is domesticity, I want no part in it," she muttered.

Deke grinned at the windshield.

Anytime she said shit like that...

Hell, *every* time and there were a lot of them.

Fuck, it was beginning to feel like Justice Lonesome had been made for him.

"Not a quiche kinda person?" he asked.

"Quiche is to food what pet sweaters are to little dogs. An evil invented for unfathomable reasons."

"Hear some of them little dogs get cold," Deke noted, still grinning.

He knew she turned her head his way when she replied, "They have *fur*, Deke."

"Some of it's sparse, Jussy."

"Then don't force them out into the cold while you go shopping or wander the park or whatever these people do with accessory dogs. Little bugger gets his or her walk and does his or her business then goes home to camp out in front of the fireplace or the furnace register. They need exercise, throw a damn toy for them in the living room. Don't dress them in a ridiculous sweater and make them prance through snow that's taller than them. It's undignified and inhumane."

Little dog sweaters, inhumane.

Deke kept grinning as he teased, "Do you need more caffeine?"

"No, talking about this, I think I need a little dog, *without* the sweater."

He glanced at her again, no longer grinning. "Babe, you get a dog, that dog has a bark that'll scare the shit outta Ty. Not a dog that's yappy and wouldn't scare the shit out of Vivie."

"I'll get one of both," she decreed.

"That's acceptable," he muttered.

There was a beat of silence before she asked, "Is there a dog that'll scare the shit outta Ty?"

"Maybe, that dog is a wolf, but even then, not sure that'd do it," he answered through his phone ringing.

He leaned forward to go after it in his back pocket and as he did it was not lost on him he was having a ridiculous conversation about dog sweaters.

It further was not lost on him that he didn't care because on the other end of that conversation was Jussy.

He checked the display on his phone. It said TATE CALLING so he took it and put it to his ear.

"Yo, Tate."

"Yo. Where are you?"

"On the way to the trailer to dump the tanks then we're headin' to Krys and Bubba's. Why?"

"Brunch is cancelled, brother," Tate said in a tone that had Deke's shoulders straightening. Tate didn't keep him waiting. "Krys went into labor about an hour ago, water broke, everything. She and Bubba are at County now."

"Fuck," Deke murmured. "What is she—?"

"This happens now, five weeks preemie," Tate answered the question Deke didn't get out.

"Fuck," Deke repeated.

"Laurie and me are walking out the door, headed to County," Tate told him.

"We drop the tanks, so are me and Jussy."

"See you there," Tate said. "Later."

"Later, brother," Deke replied, lowered the phone and felt Jussy's vibe that was a response to Deke's vibe.

"What is it?" she asked.

"Krys went into labor, baby. We gotta drop these tanks and get to the hospital."

"Shit," she whispered.

"It's gonna be good," he assured her.

"She's not even in her eighth month."

"It's gonna be good, Jussy."

She shut up.

Deke drove.

But he did it reaching for her hand, clasping it firm in his and holding both to his thigh.

He'd had women in his life, some with minimal staying power.

But since he was a lot younger, he'd not once held one of their hands.

Jussy's little hand in his felt made to be there too.

That wasn't lost on Deke either.

And he didn't mind it at all.

* * *

Deke didn't walk into the hospital room.

Jussy didn't either.

They stood arms around each other at the door to give Bubba the knowledge they were there with the intent to leave and hit the waiting room.

Lauren was also there, in the room with Bub and Krys. They'd seen Tate out in the waiting room, phone to his ear, making the calls.

Krys didn't look good, hair wet from sweat, makeup-free face red and pinched with pain or worry.

What she did do was take one look at Jussy and snap, "Get over here."

Jussy didn't take her eyes off Krys as she let Deke go and got over there.

The second she got close on the opposite side of the bed from where Bubba was standing like he was a guard, not an expectant husband, Krys grabbed Justice's hand in a grip that even from his distance, Deke could see was fierce.

She reached up with her other hand, and as Jussy bent toward her, she clapped it at the back of Jussy's head and pulled her straight in Krys's face.

Deke tensed and through it, moved into the room.

Lauren gave him a look that said be cool. Bubba didn't look at him at all, his full attention was on his woman in that bed.

Deke stopped close behind Jussy, seeing her head go up and down in Krys's hold, an indication of an affirmative to something Krys was saying, her hand gripping Krystal's just as tight as Krys had hers.

"Yes." He heard Jussy say. "Nothing's changed from our time in the Camaro, sister. You got this, Krys. You got it, beautiful."

"I got it," Krys replied, her voice weaker than Deke had ever heard.

"You got it," Jussy said, her voice stronger than he'd ever heard.

Nothing came after that for some time before Jussy told her, "We're not going anywhere. We'll be right outside with Tate. You got this. Give your man a pretty baby."

This gave Krys her cue to let Jussy go, something she did.

When she did, Deke moved in to claim her, wrapping an arm around her belly and pulling her back into him, but not taking her from Krys's space.

Krys looked to him, to Jussy, to him and then to Bubba.

"We are not havin' another kid," Bubba said before she could open her mouth.

His anxiety was clear in voice, expression and posture.

"Need an ice chip, baby," Krys said quietly, some, not all of the weak out of her tone.

Bubba reached to a bowl of ice.

"See you soon," Jussy said softly.

Krys looked to her and nodded.

Deke moved Jussy out while Lauren moved to the side of the bed they vacated.

They nearly crashed into Jim-Billy who was running into the room as they left.

Deke took Jussy to Tate, left her with him, went out and bought a shit ton of donuts and coffees. He came back to Ty and Lexie there with their girls, Jim-Billy having been kicked out when the contractions kicked up, and Tate and Jussy on phone duty giving updates to Twyla and the crew at Bubba's, Chace and Faye, and the great number of folk that loved Krys no matter how skilled she was at throwing attitude.

As they waited, Deke didn't bother putting in the effort not to watch Justice goofing with Lella and Vivie. He also didn't bury how it made him feel, seeing she was just as good with kids, maybe even better, than she was with adults.

And he didn't bury the fact that she'd been in Carnal just over a month and she was one of the crew like she'd been there years.

Last, he didn't hit her up about what that was with her and Krys and the Camaro.

Something else he'd learned, women had shit with their sisters and if they wanted to share it, they did. If they didn't, you didn't push it.

Two hours later, Bubba came out looking a lot fucking happier when he told them Breanne Lauren Briggs had made it into the world, breathing good, all ten fingers, all ten toes, and looking like her momma.

And Krys had done it. Unintentionally, but she'd still excelled at what she'd done.

On a day her friend needed her mind off what might be to come, she gave her a helluva something to keep her mind on.

An hour later, when they were let in in shifts to see Krys was all right and have their time with Breanne, Jussy returned the favor.

While she was holding Bubba and Krys's tiny baby, smiling her big, happy, open smile, she dipped her face close, gently rocking Breanne like she'd given birth to a dozen baby girls, and in her sweet, low voice, quietly she sang Croce's "Time in a Bottle."

Deke couldn't tear his eyes away. But as she sang, he saw Tate get close, his phone up, videoing Jussy's gift to two new parents, something priceless, a baby's first lullaby delivered by Justice Lonesome.

When she was done singing, not only was Breanne asleep.

So was Krys.

The song ended and Justice kept humming and rocking, her attention riveted on the little, scrunched-up face which was all you could see through cap and swaddling. And as she hummed, Deke noticed that his gypsy's features were dominant.

Dark hair, brown eyes.

He had not lied, his ma would have loved Jussy.

Dark-haired, brown-eyed babies?

She'd have loved them a whole lot more.

He watched his gypsy humming to baby girl Breanne.

He did it with the realization he was sinking deep in all that was Justice Lonesome.

But for the life of him, he didn't care he was getting caught in that mire.

* * *

"Uh, I'm not liking that," Jussy proclaimed.

They were in his truck after leaving the hospital and they were on the way to the mall.

Deke had just told her their plans for that night and he knew her proclamation was not about the fact they were going to the electronics store to buy her a TV for her bedroom that they could watch while they ate pizza in her bed that night.

It was about the fact they were spending the night in that bed that night.

"It's safe, Jussy," he said gently. "And you gotta get back there."

"*Tonight?*"

That came out as a squeak.

Deke grabbed her hand and for the first time she resisted.

This didn't last long because he didn't give up. When she did, he held her as he kept talking.

"Your security system is tight and Chace is sending a cruiser. Men with badges, guns, radios and presence to keep watch all night. And I'll be there." He gave her hand a squeeze. "You gotta get back home, baby."

He felt more resistance at her hand. It surprised him, she'd never resisted. Not a single touch. But just as quick as she started it, she again gave in, letting her hand rest in his but she did all that without reply.

"He's not gonna get to you," he told her.

She didn't say anything and he glanced at her to see her looking out the side window.

"Jussy?" he called.

"I know," she said, her voice flat, something he'd gotten from her once, the morning they had their conversation after she performed at Bubba's. "I'm good. Cal's system. The cops. You. It'll be okay."

He didn't like her voice like that.

"Not gonna let anything harm you," he promised.

"Okay, Deke," she replied immediately, a verbal giving in he didn't like either.

She was unusually in her head and not giving him what was in it.

So he went for it.

"What's on your mind?" he asked.

"Oh, nothing, except that guy promising to come back and the first night I'm back in the bed he strangled me on and beat me unconscious on is the night he promised to come back," she answered, flat gone, sarcasm in its place.

"He slips by the cops, gets close to a single window, even the boarded one, babe, the whole forest lights up for ten yards and the cops'll be all over him. He keeps goin' and actually breaks in, that siren Callahan put in will be heard for a mile."

She again switched tactics. "You're right. All good. It'll be fine."

"Jussy—"

He knew she'd looked to him when she said, "If you want me out of the trailer, then tonight, at least, I'd feel better being at Carnal Hotel with Mr. T. Maybe they have adjoining rooms. We'll keep the doors open in between. He's not exactly young but he used to be a Marine."

Through this, getting what was on her mind, Deke's fingers around hers tightened.

"I don't want you out of the trailer," he shared that truth but did it carefully.

"You're being cool and I get it, Deke, that's how cool you've been. Way cool. Super cool. *Amazingly* cool. But you're right. I need to get on with it, take charge, get back to whatever is normal. But not tonight. Tonight I'm staying at the hotel with Mr. T."

Now he was losing that cool she said he was.

"You are not stayin' at a goddamn hotel with a man old enough to be your grandfather the only one lookin' out for you."

"We can tell Chace to park the cruiser outside my hotel door."

"We're not doin' that either seein' as you're gonna be at your place with me and that's also where the cruiser is gonna be."

"What I'm saying is, you've been cool. I appreciate it. You've done a lot. It's time to get on with things and I get that's what you're saying to me. So I'm getting on with things. You're off duty."

Oh no she didn't.

He might not have been forthcoming about where they were at but he wasn't stupid, she sure as fuck wasn't either.

He needed to lay it out and they needed to talk it out but she had to know why he was letting that slide after she got assaulted in her own home.

But she knew better than that.

And she just plain *was* better than this passive-aggressive bullshit.

"I ask to be off duty?" he bit out.

"Well…no," she returned hesitantly.

"That's because I'm not askin' to be off duty. I'm tellin' you, this guy is still around, and there is no evidence pointing to the fact he was stupid enough to make the play he made and stick around, he's actually even stupider if he makes an approach with a cruiser outside and me inside with you, knowin' from that his ass'll be in the can. You think you're gettin' what I'm sayin', Justice, but you're way the fuck off base."

"I…uh, well…okay," she stammered.

"And just to point more shit out you've probably had too much on your mind to figure out, the play this guy made was probably the only play he had and he knew it. Puttin' the fear of God in you by sayin' he'd be comin' back was just his way of being a bigger fuckwad than he already is. He did something to Justice Lonesome, to *anyone*, but specifically Justice Lonesome, something that had a permanent end, he's gotta know he'd have heat on him no way he could evade. He's tied to your girl, he can't erase that, made the damn call on *your* phone, cops would make that connection and he'd go down and he knows that. That's why he left it like it was rather than ending that shit he did to you in a different way."

"Okay, I hear you," she said softly.

She heard him but as harsh as he was giving it to her, she needed to hear more to make sure she got it so he kept going.

"He delivered the message he wanted delivered and now he's gotta know you got the resources to make any future plays a big fuckin' fail. You got those resources, you activated them and then some. He had his opportunity. He took it. He's got a brain in his head, he knows he shot that wad and he's gotta get to Bianca another way. He shows tonight or ever until he's caught, he's Darwinian. 'Cause breaking and entering, assault, criminal threatening and attempted murder are gonna buy him a long stretch and haven't heard a man bein' able to reproduce behind bars bein' the bitch to a brute who comes up his ass."

Her, "You're right, honey," came instantly.

But now her voice sounded choked and Deke cut a glance her way to see she was fighting back laughter.

"I say something funny?" he asked the road when he aimed his eyes to it again.

"I've actually never heard the adjective 'Darwinian' used that way."

"Right," he clipped. With her humor back, deciding to put a line under that bullshit, he asked, "Now we goin' to get you a TV, some beer, hittin' the trailer to get our shit, hittin' your house, settin' up that mother, ordering pizza and kicking back with a movie?"

"Yes, Deke, that's what we're doing."

"You're right, that's what we're doin'," he muttered irritably.

"I'm out of Baby Ruth bars," she shared.

"We'll get some of those too."

"What's your favorite candy bar?" she asked, now sounding just curious.

"That question is moot 'cause candy is candy and by definition it's all awesome. Unless it has coconut in it. Then it sucks."

"Right, no Mounds or Almond Joy, but I've got a taste for those new Butterfinger Cups. They're like Reese's Cups, just Butterfinger. And they're so good, I think they've redefined awesome. So much so, I'm thinking of starting a letter-writing campaign for all candy bars to be made into cups. Baby Ruth Cups. 100 Grand Cups. Snickers Cups. KitKat Cups."

"Gypsy, I already talked about little dogs and their sweaters with you today. I got a cap on how much ridiculous shit I can discuss in a week and that blew right past that cap. You want Butterfinger Cups, Baby Ruths, whatever, I'll get 'em for you. Until the time that cap's back on, we won't talk about them and that means we can continue a candy bar to cup discussion sometime next weekend."

"Okay, Deke."

She was now just out and out laughing.

He had them back where they always were, he did what he did with Jussy.

Took advantage.

"We're gettin' you an eighty inch TV," he declared.

Her hand jerked in his when she snapped. "We are not."

"Eighty inches, HD, movies will seem like we're watchin' them in a theater."

"We won't be in a theater, Deke. We'll be in my bedroom."

They fucking would.

And after that night, them being there would have a different meaning.

"You're loaded, Jussy. You get anything less than an eighty inch, they'll take away your membership in the Rich As Shit Club."

"I gave up that membership a long time ago. Most rich people are assholes," she muttered, and he knew she was again looking out the side window.

He also felt his ribs constrict.

Most rich people are assholes.

Christ, yeah.

Like she was made for him.

"Eighty inches, babe."

"Fifty, Deke."

He was screwing with her about the eighty.

But fifty?

Was she insane?

"No fuckin' way," he shot back. "Eighty."

"Okay," she gave in on a sigh then shared she wasn't giving in. "Sixty."

"Eighty."

"Deke!"

"Justice."

She shut up.

Two minutes later, they turned into the freestanding electronics store outside the mall.

In the end, they got her seventy inches.

Deke thought it was a good compromise.

Justice made it clear that for him, she was just giving in.

CHAPTER THIRTEEN

Made for Me

Justice

THE BED MOVED as Deke got out of it.

I didn't move.

This was because this was the fourth time this had happened.

The first time freaked me out, and when he got back, it took him a while to calm me down by explaining that he was just checking things out and it was all good.

The second time freaked me out too, but when he got back, it didn't take him as long to calm me down.

The third time, I woke, but fell asleep against him practically before he'd pulled the covers back over himself.

This time, enough was enough.

Shit, he was more freaked than I was about what might happen that night.

And if I didn't already have enough evidence to prove that things had changed (in a big way) between Deke and me, that would have done it.

In fact, after all the drama died down and he settled me back into the new version of life that he was giving me—work on my place, home to his trailer, togetherness every second of the day (except the rare times he let me out of his sight, but only when I was with men he trusted)—it became clear to me.

No friend showed at a police station and lost his mind, bellowing a woman's name, flipped out something had happened to her, and the instant he saw her, she was in his arms and held tight, versions of that closeness not ceasing for days that turned into a week.

This included sleeping with her every night. No couch for Deke unless I was in it with him, cuddled up and watching TV.

Nope.

No friend did all that.

Deke Hightower liked me.

He so totally *liked me*.

But I got why he didn't go there with me. It wasn't the time. All that had happened, my worry about Bianca, Mr. T in town, Cal around doing his thing, the threat of the bad guy's return, I didn't need more on my mind.

But still.

Deke definitely liked me and even if he hadn't said it straight out, unless I was letting hope cloud my judgment in reading the signs (and that was a possibility, though with the abundance of signs, it was unlikely) he still communicated it to me.

This would have made me smile if I wasn't so upset he was so edgy he couldn't sleep.

I should have known when he took a big gun out of the small bag where he'd packed his stuff to spend the night and set it on the nightstand before we settled into sleep (or me to sleep, Deke to not sleep).

But now after four times where he was so restless he had to get up and do a walkthrough of the house, I knew.

Deke was unsettled and he wasn't going to get himself settled.

I needed to settle him.

What he'd said that afternoon in his truck was true. I hadn't thought of it logically but the guy who did what he did to me had no intention of killing me. If he did, he would have done it.

It was a message. He didn't order me not to contact the police. He'd ordered me to tell Bianca he'd be back. Even if I wasn't Justice Lonesome, once reported, the cops would be all over protecting a citizen who'd had the same threat delivered like it was and he wouldn't get the opportunity to come back.

And it was clear that guy knew Bianca well enough to know that threat would work.

No one knew if he'd gotten paid.

But I knew that Bianca would never hear that message and not do what she could to get me out of the line of fire.

I knew it.

I just didn't let that penetrate until Deke had laid it out for me.

So the guy wasn't going to show. I felt that in my gut.

But even if he did, I had cops, Deke and Deke's gun.

So it was all good.

Deke, however, was not feeling this same peace.

I had to get him there.

I heard him come back and I stayed quiet and still until he was in bed and had the covers back over him.

Then I shifted into him, pressing close and drifting a hand up his chest to his neck where I wrapped my fingers around the side.

"You need to relax, honey," I whispered.

"I'm good," he totally lied. "Go back to sleep."

I pushed closer and tensed my fingers into the tight muscle of his neck.

"You're not good. You're on edge. You've been up four times, did four checks, came back four times because it was all fine because it's *all fine*. So you need to *relax*."

"I'm relaxed, Jussy. Now you relax and get back to sleep."

I dug the pads of my fingers deeper into the taut muscle of his neck, following it down to where it met his shoulder.

"You're wound tight, Deke. I can feel it. That is not relaxed."

"Right. Then I'll relax when this night is over," he finally admitted.

God, he freaking liked me.

I did let that give me a small smile, pushing closer, tipping my head back and gliding my hand back up his neck, sifting my fingers into his hair.

He had it tied up, like he always did. I'd never seen it down. Not in sleep, after sleep, even after a shower it was wet, twisted up and tied.

I wanted to see it down.

I put pressure on his head and tipped mine back. I knew unless he allowed it I couldn't force his down.

But he allowed it.

Because he was Deke. He'd give me anything.

So.

Totally.

Liked me.

"It's gonna be okay," I whispered. "You know that. You were the one who laid that out."

"I do know it. And in the morning when I'm proved right, I'll be good."

I stared at his shadowed face, something that was relatively easy to do in the moonlight filtering through the trees outside and my wall of windows.

I should just close my eyes and go to sleep. If he was on edge, nothing I could do would probably change that.

Except maybe one thing.

Taking his mind off it.

Something I was going to attempt to do in my bed with his big body, now in faded dark-blue fleece cut-off shorts and nothing else, pressed close to mine, (I couldn't know for sure about that "nothing else" but there was no indication, and I'd looked, that he also had on underwear).

I should wait, at least until tomorrow, when we were past this part of my situation and it was definitely time to talk about what had changed between us.

Smelling him, feeling his heat, knowing he was uneasy because of me, I didn't want to wait.

So I didn't.

I lifted up and, holding my breath, a knot that was part nerves, part something else in my belly, for the first time ever, I touched lips with Deke.

At that mere contact, I felt an electric charge tingle against my lips the likes I'd never felt in my life.

His body went completely still.

I didn't know what that reaction meant; it could be rejection or the opposite.

But in my head I heard that faraway roar of *Where's Justice Lonesome?* followed closely with the rumbled murmurings of *Christ almighty. Christ almighty, baby.*

He liked me.

And when two consenting adults liked each other, shit happened.

I went back in.

A lip brush then a whispered, "Relax, Deke."

His hand resting on my hip slid up to my waist and squeezed.

It did not push me away. It just squeezed.

"Jussy," he muttered. "Now's not—"

I went in for another lip brush, another whisper of, "Relax, honey," and then I went for it and slid my tongue out, gliding the tip along the crease of his lips.

God, he tasted yummy.

I had just enough time to have that thought before I drew in a soft breath when I suddenly found myself on my back, Deke's weight on me, all of his lower half pressing me into the bed.

"Jussy, don't," he growled, his words contradicting our new position. "Now's not the time."

Now was totally the time. If I didn't feel that "now was the time" gathering between my legs (which I did), I could feel that indication hardening on my thigh.

I moved both my hands to his neck, its back, fingers up in his hair and I used those hands and his stiffness to pull me up and I put my mouth back to his.

"Now's a great time," I said softly. "You've been taking care of me. It's my turn to take care of you."

"Jus—"

"Shush," I whispered.

"Jussy—"

I cut off whatever he was going to say by sliding my tongue in his mouth and touching it to his.

His head jerked back.

My body went solid.

He didn't move.

I held on to his neck and stared at him staring down at me.

Okay, maybe I shouldn't have pushed it. Maybe now *wasn't* the time.

Hell, maybe I was even wrong about the whole thing. Maybe Deke was that guy who went the extra mile to look out for his friends. And maybe the evidence that was growing hard against my thigh wasn't evidence of what I thought it was, but just that I was a girl, he was a guy, we were in bed in the dead of night and that was the natural order of things.

I started to feel weird, scared, embarrassment creeping in, and I was about to let him go when it happened.

Thunder rolled in my bedroom, feeling like it was emanating from his stomach, through his chest, his lips, swelling in the room, over my skin, straight between my legs.

Then he shifted one of his hands that were in the bed at my sides, his weight up on his forearms, so it was wrapped around the back of my neck and his mouth slammed down on mine.

I opened my lips and his tongue thrust inside.

Oh God, yes, fuck yes.

He tasted *yummy*.

Another fierce growl released from Deke, sinking down my throat as he slanted his head and took the kiss deeper.

Okay.

Yes.

Okay.

Damn.

The man could *kiss*.

I slid one arm around his shoulders, the other hand went up and into his hair. I yanked out the holder and it tumbled down, through my fingers, thick and sleek.

With the feel of that, the depth of his kiss, the taste of him, I whimpered into his mouth as my pussy quivered in a dangerous way that communicated I hadn't gotten myself any in a long time, I was being kissed by Deke, *Deke*, so things needed to progress fast and they needed to do that *immediately*.

I bucked my hips, and Deke, *so Deke*, rolled us to give me what I wanted.

Me being on top.

I broke the kiss, lifted up astride him and whipped my camisole off, tossing it aside.

I barely felt the material leave my fingers before he knifed up, his hand winding in my hair.

He pulled it back roughly, arching my spine, and I had a moment out of the moment as I remembered the last time someone pulled my hair.

I was instantly back in the moment when I felt Deke cup my left breast from the bottom, lift it, then latch on with his mouth and *pull*.

"Oh my God," I breathed, the electricity shooting from nipple to clit not a tingle. It was a full-on charge and it was not stopping.

I twined my fingers through his hair, holding him to me, feeling his beard graze the sensitive skin of my breast, all of that making me squirm against the hard cock I felt pressing through his shorts, my pajama shorts, right at the heat of me.

"Deke," I whispered.

He released my nipple but grunted, "Give me the other one, gypsy."

I moved faster than I'd ever done, taking one hand from his hair to cup my own breast, lift it.

He wrapped his lips around it and sucked deep.

"Yes," I exhaled.

He gave a soft yank at my hair and I arched further for him, shoving my nipple deeper into his mouth. Deke rewarded me by rolling his tongue around my nipple, then sending a reflexive buck through my whole body as he bit lightly, then he again pulled it in deep.

"Honey..." It was a plea but I didn't use more words.

I told him what I wanted by rubbing hard against his cock underneath me.

I was ready.

I needed him inside me.

He released my breast, cupped the back of my head and lifted his up, his mouth coming to mine where he again kissed me, hard and wet, deep and long, before he abruptly surged up, taking me with him.

He dropped me on my back perpendicular on the mattress and a slither of panic hit me when he backed off the bed, taking his feet at the side.

What was happening?

Was he going to do another walkthrough?

Now?

He bent over, gripping me behind my knee. I cried out softly as he dragged me so my ass was to the edge of the bed.

No walkthrough.

Thank *God*.

He shifted both hands to my shorts, and I gasped, feeling my pussy spasm as he tore them with my underwear down my legs.

Then I watched play out the sexiest five seconds of my life.

This being Deke dropping to his knees at the side of the bed, tossing one of my legs over one of his broad shoulders, clasping me behind my other knee and pushing it wide and high, and bending to me.

After that I saw nothing because his mouth was working me and my eyes closed, my head dug back into the bed, and I pushed with my heel into his back to lift my hips deeper into his mouth.

I should have known with the way he kissed he'd know how to do this.

And fucking hell, he knew how to do this.

I was panting, undulating my hips against his mouth, close and getting closer, when his hand behind my knee slid down the inside of my thigh, his other hand curled over my belly honing in from above. And then I felt him shove a finger inside me at the same time he worked my clit with his thumb and finally, I felt his tongue thrust into me.

He finger and tongue fucked me at the same time and I didn't even know you could *do* that.

But that was only a vague thought that flitted away almost before I had it.

No.

I had no thoughts.

I was nothing but cunt and clit and what Deke was doing to them.

"Honey," I panted.

God, I was going to get there. Deke taking me speeding there with terminal velocity.

I reached between my legs, skimming my fingers against his bearded cheek. "*Deke*."

I didn't know if it was a plea or a warning.

Deke took it as a warning because suddenly his mouth nor fingers were between my legs.

I opened my eyes, righted my head, was about to protest but looked up and saw him standing colossal like a mountain man god by the side of the bed.

And then I saw him pull his shorts down.

"*Yes*," I breathed.

"Got a condom, baby?" he asked, his voice thick, rough, his body moving.

Fuck!

"No," I told him, mind scattered, attention on his body, the shadow of his cock, his movements toward me and the hopes that my answer would not end things prematurely.

We'd get creative.

Hell, to get an orgasm from Deke, I'd kick the *shit* out of creative.

He bent to me. Shoving an arm between my waist and the bed, I was up against him. He put a knee in the bed and crawled into it, over it, dropping me to it and him to me, giving me substantial weight as he reached over the side.

Then his weight was gone from me. He was up on the bed on his knees, one on either side of my right thigh. He had his wallet. Then he tossed his wallet. Then I heard foil tearing.

And after that, I watched the second sexiest five seconds I'd ever seen.

Deke on his knees in my bed rolling a condom on his thick, long cock.

I was salivating and trembling and completely at a loss of what to do because I wanted my hand wrapped around his dick. I also wanted my finger at my clit. I further wanted his nipple against my tongue, his hair in my hands, his mouth on mine…it went on to infinity.

I didn't get the chance to decide. Again I had his arm around my waist and I was up, swung around, my legs automatically circling his hips as he twisted us so he was facing the headboard, I had my back pointed that way.

"Position me," he ordered.

I needed no explanation for his instruction.

My hand darted between us as I started falling back. I wrapped my fingers around his rock-hard cock, slid the head through my wet to where it needed to be, and he glided in, my hand shifting out, as he put me to my back in bed and covered me.

Connected to me.

God, he felt good deep inside.

God, so *fucking good*.

"Baby," I whispered.

He started moving, slow and sweet, dipping his head, trailing his tongue up a tendon of my neck to my ear.

"Like you were made for me," he whispered there on an inward glide, settling deep, so damned deep, and then gently grinding.

His words, the feel of him, everything about him, finally having Deke inside me, I felt tears sting my eyes as I wrapped him up, arms and legs, held him close, one hand drifting up and into his hair.

Deke was covering me.

Deke was inside me.

Deke was made for me.

"Need you to get ready, gypsy," he said in my ear. "That tight, wet heat, need it."

I turned my head and found his ear with my lips. "Take it."

He started stroking in and out with his cock.

It was slow, gentle, but his mouth warned, "I let go, might get rough. You say, baby. One word, I slow it down."

His voice was tighter, almost straining, his hips moving faster, but not rougher.

He needed to fuck me.

And I needed him to fuck me.

"Take what you want, Deke."

He shifted a leg, drawing up his knee, this pushing him even deeper on an inward slide and I gasped again, holding him tighter.

But he didn't let go and fuck me.

"Deke—"

"Brace, Jussy."

I held tighter.

"Deke—"

"One word, baby, I slow it down."

"Please, Deke." I dug my nails in where my hand was at the small of his back. "Just fuck me."

His body stilled, half in, half out.

He was making me crazy!

I opened my mouth before another, deeper, lower rumble of thunder rolled from him through me.

And Deke let go.

His thrusts were so powerful, his body so huge, taking me with them, I had to lift a hand to the headboard and push against it so he didn't drive me up into it.

This was not a bad thing because it meant I also drove down into him.

The base of his hard cock slamming against my sensitive clit, that cock belonging to Deke finally inside me, in only a few strokes, I turned my face into his neck.

I pressed it in, tensed against him with every inch of me, inside and out, heard his approving growl of, "Christ, yeah, baby," before my head flew back into the pillows and I cried out as I came.

Hard.

Hard and for what seemed like forever. Deke powering deep, grunting now, my body lurching with each thrust, I whimpered and gasped. Automatically lifting a hand to grip his hair tight in my fist, I shuddered through the best, longest and most intense orgasm by far I'd had in my life.

I was only just coming down, consciousness coming back to that bed, that room, my body loosening naturally in his hold as the climax drifted out when it tensed again because I felt his teeth sink hard into the soft flesh that was just down from where my shoulder met my neck. He buried himself inside me before his head jerked back and I watched in the moonlight as the muscles in his neck strained and he jerked as his hips ground into mine when he came.

His lasted a long time too.

And it topped both the other two sexiest things Deke had given me that I'd ever witnessed and not only because it lasted a whole lot longer than five seconds.

Finally, his big body sagged on mine, his neck bent deep, face in mine, and we both lay there, connected, both our labored breathing the only thing I could hear.

Yes, that was all I could hear and it might have been the sweetest music ever to hit my ears.

Okay, maybe my poet's soul knew what it was doing.

I felt his hand dig into the mattress along my back and up, fingers tangling in my hair as he lifted his head and immediately lowered it so he was kissing me, long, wet, and God, so damned Deke…*sweet*.

He ended the kiss and I shivered beneath him when he did it by scraping the edges of his top teeth against my lower lip at the same time he slowly slid out of me.

He dipped in and kissed the spot where he'd bitten me before he angled up and out of the bed, twitching the covers over my body.

I rolled to the side, curled into myself and laid there, watching another few seconds of sexy as he strolled through the dark into my bathroom.

Then I started smiling, slow at first until the smile felt so big on my face, it hurt.

Pain and pleasure.

This time it was the kind I liked.

I pushed up to my knees, turning to face the bathroom, sitting back on my calves and wrapping the sheet around me.

Deke didn't turn on the light but I heard the toilet flush, the faucet go on and off and then I watched a Deke with his blond hair down around his shoulders, his body silvered by moonlight, his heavy thighs delectable, the rounded ridges of muscles around his knees mouth-watering, his now semi-hard cock still impressive.

He was close to the bed when I pulled my eyes from his dick and looked at his face.

"You so totally like me," I declared.

I let out a shrill, girlie scream when he reached out a long arm and jerked the sheet away from me.

I emitted another girlie scream when I was again hooked at the waist with his arm and yanked up to slam into his body. He put a knee to the bed, twisted us, and I crashed into the mattress on my back with Deke on me, puffing out a breath at taking his weight and forcing focus on his face.

Not hard since it was right in mine.

His big hand cupped my jaw and he said, "Yeah, gypsy, I like you."

I knew I was smiling big and happy when I corrected, "No, you *so totally* like me."

Deke smiled back when he confirmed, "Yeah."

That smile.

God.

I wrapped my arms around his shoulders, lifted up my head and gave him a hard, closed-mouth kiss.

I dropped back to the pillows and whispered, "You relaxed now, honey?"

"First thing in the morning run for condoms," was his answer.

I kept smiling.

I had a feeling I could do that without being grumpy.

"Absolutely," I agreed.

Suddenly, he dropped his head and moved his hand from my jaw to the side of my neck so he could slide his lips surrounded by wiry whiskers from my chin to my ear, all this shooting tingles down my neck straight to my nipples. "Gonna get my shorts. Want you back in your PJs. Just because. Okay?"

Maybe he was relaxed, and he sounded it, no longer edgy.

But he wasn't taking any chances and he didn't want either of us naked on the off chance something happened.

I nodded. "Okay, Deke."

He pulled us both out of bed, on our feet and handed me camisole, panties and shorts before he bent to retrieve his.

We dressed.

Deke pulled me back into bed, flicked the covers over us, and tucked me under him in our normal sleeping position.

But this time he lifted my hips, twisting them so I got the hint he wanted me to hook a knee around his thigh, something I did.

This gave him access to shove his fingers up my camisole at the small of my back and down into my shorts and panties, where he cupped my ass. Not a cheek. Right at the center so his middle finger was resting just inside the crease.

I bit my lip and shivered again.

"Go back to sleep, Jussy," he ordered.

I pressed my hips against him. He pressed his hand deeper at my ass, his other arm pushing under me, curling around my back to hold me closer, and I shut my eyes.

"Just to make it official," I whispered into his throat. "I like you too."

I heard his soft chuckle and fell in love with that soft chuckle as I felt a warm squeeze at my back, an intimate one at my ass, and the stirring of my hair when he whispered back, "Good."

I settled in, smiling, warm, sated and happy.

Deke Hightower so totally liked me.

On that thought, still smiling, I fell asleep.

* * *

With his restlessness the night before, it wasn't a surprise that next morning, for the first time, I woke before Deke.

Nope, not a surprise.

What it was was more bounty.

Because this meant I could watch him sleeping.

His face lost years in sleep. Not boyish, exactly, but there were hard lines and edges I hadn't really noticed when he was awake that smoothed out in sleep. They were around his eyes and at the set of his cheekbones, which I realized on close inspection were very high, like he had Native American blood or something. Even at his jaw, which was hidden mostly with his beard, but I noted a definite lack of tension there in the peace of sleep.

He had stubby eyelashes, but a lot of them, and there was a vulnerable beauty to them as they rested against his cheeks.

It was a fascinating display that fascinated me so I allowed myself to take it in for a long time.

Then the knowledge that it was morning, we were in my bed, safe, no return of the bad guy, this meant I was probably free of that threat...

And Deke liked me.

Not to mention he was good with his mouth, fingers and cock.

So I wondered why I laid there staring at his face when I could have been doing other things.

Thus I decided to do those other things.

Tracing the tip of my finger over his hip, I lifted up and touched my lips to his.

His head shifted slightly on the pillow, his arm gave me a light, reflexive squeeze, and then his stomach tensed as I trailed three fingertips over it, *down* it, and touched my tongue to his lower lip.

His eyes opened.

I smiled at him and flattened my hand on his lower stomach, pushing down, my fingertips now inside his shorts and resting at the upper base of his cock.

"Morning," I whispered.

"No condoms," he growled, and I knew why because I felt something happening against my fingertips.

I also felt my smile change.

I pressed that smile to his mouth and whispered, "Hand job, honey," right before I wrapped his hardening cock with my fingers.

"Fuck," he grunted, a word I felt drive up into my womb.

I hooked him steady with my leg around his thigh and stroked.

"Fuck," he grunted again, his hips flexing.

I kept smiling.

And stroking.

"Hand job?" he asked, his morning voice rough with residual sleep and throaty with what I was doing to his cock.

Yes. That voice in the morning in my bed with me when he could do something about it (and so could I), just like I thought many weeks ago.

Heaven.

"Yes," I whispered.

His hand then slid from where it was resting inside my shorts at the base of my back, around, down and *in*.

I released a small gasp against his lips.

"Okay, baby," he agreed in a murmur.

We kept at each other, staring in each other's eyes.

This happened closer when Deke was fully hard and something magical he did between my legs meant I spontaneously gave a fierce tug at his dick and his grunt sounded, his neck bending so his forehead was resting against mine and our harsh breathing mixed.

I was eventually riding his hand, not paying much mind to what I was doing with his cock I was so focused on what he was doing to my clit and pussy. I'd snaked my other hand up into his hair, twisting my fingers in it as he kept at me, now thrusting his cock into my tight fist.

"Deke, I—" I began my warning.

"Do it," he ordered.

I shook my head, held his gaze and whispered, "I want you to come on me."

I barely got that out or accomplished the blink his next moves caused before his hand was gone, my fingers were no longer around his cock, his shorts were history, I was on my back, my shorts and panties down to my thighs, and he was straddling me, taking over.

As in *totally* taking over.

God, he was sensory overload, especially vision. Jacking his cock, that chest, those thighs, his stomach, his blond hair hanging down to his shoulders, his hazel eyes burning down at me, his other hand shoved between my legs, working, breathtaking, driving me there.

"Deke," I gasped.

"Top off," he growled.

I yanked my top off, my hair flying. When I could give him back my eyes, I saw his on my hair before they cut to my face.

"Get there, Jussy," he demanded.

I dug my nails into his thighs on either side and rode his fingers that were working me in the tight, drenched, hot space because he'd forced my legs together with him being astride me and my clothes hindering me.

It started coming.

"Oh God."

"Get there," he grunted.

"Oh my God," I breathed, my eyes traveling everywhere, his strong hand around his big dick, his chest, his thick thighs, my nails sinking deep in the hard muscle there. "Oh my God. Oh my God. *Deke*," I breathed, arching and coming.

Then doing it harder when I heard his groaned, "Yeah," and felt the warm splash of him across my belly and on my breast, the powerful jerk of his body through his orgasm, somewhere in the far recesses of my mind wishing I could watch, somewhere in the warm region of my heart knowing I'd have another chance.

I finished only moments before he finished, dropping his forehead to mine, his hands curved around either side of my neck.

I opened my eyes to find his still closed.

Those eyelashes, God, a thing of beauty.

He opened his eyes.

And then there was more.

He said nothing, his breath still coming heavy.

I said nothing, my breath doing the same. But I put my hands to his hips that were distant as he remained kneeling over me, sliding them up to his waist, stroking there lazily with my fingertips.

It took a while but it finally occurred to me we were no longer recovering from our orgasms.

We also weren't sharing a moment of connection. He was still up on his knees. The only parts of Deke touching me were the sides of those knees, his hands at my neck, his forehead on mine.

We were close.

Yet he was still far.

My fingers stilled on his skin.

Deke just kept staring in my eyes.

"Deke?"

I used his name as a question.

"Just came on you."

"I…yes," I answered hesitantly.

Didn't he like that? Was that too weird for him? It wasn't weird, but for some it could be.

He seemed pretty freaking into it when I'd asked for it.

"Fucked you hard last night, took it, fuckin' drove yourself into it, came for me while you did. It was you this morning wanted my cum on you," he reminded me of things I very well knew.

"Does that…are you…" I fought against clearing my throat to battle a sudden onslaught of anxiety and finished, "Does that turn you off?"

He lifted his head an inch but didn't take his hands from my neck.

"It seem to turn me off?" he asked.

"Uh…no," I answered.

One of his hands shifted, so did his eyes, and while he watched, I felt his thumb sweep where he'd sunk his teeth into me last night right before his climax.

His gaze came back to mine.

"Took my mark," he whispered, all three words were thick.

Thick with meaning.

Maybe even thick with emotion.

My fingers clutched his waist.

He slid his other hand down my chest, between my breasts, down, and my nails curled in when he slid his hand through his cum, smoothing it over my skin.

"Took my mark," he repeated.

I was thinking I was getting him.

Still, my, "Yes," was tentative.

His hand slid up and curled around my breast.

I bit my bottom lip.

Deke's eyes watched.

God, he was turning me on again.

He looked back to me. "You run this hot all the time, gypsy?"

"Uh...not so far, until, well...obviously...um..."

I trailed off.

He got me.

And I knew this because he smiled.

Slow.

So fucking slow.

Cocky.

Totally goddamned cocky.

Hot.

Unbelievably *smoking* hot.

He ran a thumb hard over my nipple, that rocketing straight to my clit, my fingernails digging into his flesh, all while he erased the inch he'd put between our faces as he whispered, "You like me."

It was not tentative that time when I whispered back, "Yeah."

Something passed through his eyes. I wanted to chase it for a variety of reasons, not the least of which it was amazing, but at that moment it made new wet surge between my legs.

"Made for me," he muttered, like I wasn't there, like he wasn't even a breath away from me, giving me those words and all they seemed to mean.

I lay unmoving under all that was Deke and stared in his eyes.

"Shower," he grunted suddenly. "Condoms," he went on. His mouth touched mine, "Lots of those fuckers."

Before I could agree, or what I was leaning more toward, kissing him, he was on his feet at the side of the bed. Then he was dragging me across the bed.

And finally, I was over his shoulder and he was stalking toward the shower.

Okay then.

We had our morning plan.

Shower.

And condoms.

Lots of them.

I had a feeling I was not going to get any progress done on my house that day.

And I did not give that first fuck.

CHAPTER FOURTEEN

Highly-Tuned Revenge Streak

Deke

DEKE DUMPED THE five packs of condoms on the counter at the convenience store in town.

He watched the cashier guy's face turn startled before he slowly lifted his gaze up to Deke's then turned it to Jussy who was standing close to his side, holding his hand.

The man's face stayed startled as his eyebrows flew up.

Deke dipped his chin and saw her smiling bright, bold, huge and unashamed right at the guy.

Christ, she was something.

Deke beat back the rush of laughter he was feeling and looked back at the cashier when he heard the beeping of their purchase.

"How's my face?" Jussy asked and his attention went back to her.

He took in her eye, saw the yellow was gone, almost all the purpling was gone at the side, but there was still some blue under her eye. His gaze dropped and he also saw he'd been right in his assessment the day before. Not even a shadow left at her throat.

They made it through last night.

They'd connected the way they both wanted to connect and it was fucking spectacular.

And that shit at her throat was gone.

A good day.

"Better," he answered.

"Good enough to go to La-La Land and not freak out Sunny?"

He stared at her, his lips moving. "We are not getting coffee."

She gave a cute pout. "I need coffee."

"Then make it after I take you home and fuck you again." Caught in Jussy's cute, the words came out of his mouth before it hit him he had an audience so he looked to the cashier and muttered, "Sorry, man."

The cashier was grinning. "Don't mind me. Just happy a brother is gettin' some a' the good stuff."

Oh, he was getting some of the good stuff.

Deke looked down to Jussy to see her again beaming at the cashier.

He tugged at her hand and she turned that beam to him.

Yeah, she was something.

"No coffee," he stated.

"Deke, we also need breakfast," she told him. "You ate all the pizza last night."

"Babe, you ate half that pie and I had to fight you for my last slice. That last slice being *my* slice."

"Okay, so *we* ate all the pizza last night and I can't breakfast on Baby Ruths and Butterfinger Cups and that's all we have left." She gave him a sassy smile. "And we're gonna need sustenance."

The way she fucked, this was undoubtedly true.

"Right, coffee," he gave in.

The sass went out of her smile and it got sweet as she turned into him and pressed her tits against his arm.

His cock jerked.

There it was, more indication of how things were going to be changing in a really good way now they both knew where they were at.

And Deke had a shit ton of indications that he'd be able to get beyond the fact she was rich as sin and famous to boot.

Christ, she took him hard last night, came through it and it was her that wanted his cum on her. Her eyes wild and hot, watching him jack off on her, her fingernails leaving red crescents in the skin of his thighs, she liked it so fucking much.

Biker bitches who knew how to live and long since lost any hang ups, drunk women who let the booze slide them to the place they needed to be would give that.

And then there was Jussy, sober as a judge, just drunk on him, and asking for it in a way he knew she'd give him anything he wanted. He could come on her again. She'd ride his face. She'd let him tie her up. She'd take his cock up her ass.

She fucked like she lived.

She wasn't just open and out there and together in life.

She was open and out there and together with sex. She knew what she wanted, asked for it or just went for it and got off on it.

Made for him, yeah.

Shit, yeah.

Straight up, one hundred percent made for him.

So she wanted coffee?

He'd give it to her.

He'd give her fucking anything.

And not just because he got off on her getting off on him jacking on her.

Because she stood in front of a convenience store cashier with her man, holding his hand and buying fifty condoms and she did it blatantly happy she was soon going to get herself fucked and good, but he knew she was more happy because she was standing right there with him, holding his hand.

His gaze dropped to the bruise under her left eye and he finished what he had to say about their imminent trip to La-La Land, "But you better hang outside until I know Sunny's not there."

"She's always there with Shambles. I should have worn sunglasses," she muttered.

"That'll be forty-three dollars," the cashier said.

Deke dug for his wallet, let her go to pull out the bills, gave them to the guy and took the change and the bag filled with what was going to make a day already really fucking good get a whole lot better.

"Thanks. Later," Deke muttered, using Jussy's hand to pull her to the door.

"Later," Jussy said to the cashier as they moved.

"Have fun you two," the cashier called to their backs.

"We will!" Jussy assured him as he tugged her out the door.

She was practically skipping at his side while they moved down the sidewalk toward La-La Land.

He looked down at her, feeling his lips curving. "Happy?"

Her head tilted back and she gave him another beam, open, out there, not hiding shit.

Fuck yeah, she was happy.

Happy to be with him.

Christ, he wanted that for her every breath she took. Wanted it in a way he knew he'd break his back for it, kill anyone who took it away.

Fuck. He hadn't felt like that for any woman, except his mother.

And he hadn't even given his ma the second half of that.

She adjusted her position so the side of her tit glanced against his arm as they walked and she kept smiling as she said quietly, "Yeah, Deke. Happy."

With a tug on her hand, he stopped them, turned into her and bent to her.

She got what he was offering, lifted up on her toes and he touched his mouth to hers.

Hers was still smiling.

He was pulling away when his phone started ringing.

"I'll take that," she said, reaching to the bag so he wouldn't let her hand go to get the call.

He gave her the bag, dug out his phone, saw it was Decker and took the call.

"Hey, brother, all good?"

"Yes, and maybe yes or also maybe no," Decker answered, sounding weird.

Deke turned eyes to Jussy. "Right, tell me the yes part."

"We found our target a couple hours ago, it just wasn't the primary target."

Deke felt his brows draw together. "Come again?"

"Place we were told Bianca Constantine was holing up was where she was holing up. It's also where we found the very dead body of Brendon Caswell."

Deke lost eye contact with Jussy as he cut his to his boots.

"Right…*come again*?" he growled.

Jussy moved into his space at the front, her fingers spasming around his, but he kept his gaze lowered, eyes now to her shoulder as Decker spoke.

"Caswell's dead, man. Shithole apartment building in LA. Women's clothes left behind, other shit too, nice shit. Designer. Expensive. Cosmetics. Some jewelry, though nothing worth a lot. Still, we found him, called the local authorities and a female detective at the scene says it's the good stuff. They're dusting, already ran prints. They got a lot of 'em and some of them are Bianca's."

"Two seconds, Deck," Deke said into the phone and looked at Jussy. "Go hit the truck, baby. Keys in my pocket. I'll get us coffees while I finish this call."

"No," she whispered, staring at his face, the happy gone from hers, and Deke felt heat hit his gut at the loss of it.

Fuck this Bianca bitch. He was that kind of man, he'd wring *her* goddamned neck.

He tightened his hold of her hand, drew in breath and focused on her throat.

"Back, Deck, you got more?"

"Well, if your first thought was my first thought, that Bianca heard Caswell strangling her best friend over voicemail and lost her shit during a meet and killed him, we're wrong. Unless she acquired a professional's skills while taking her walk on the very wild side, it was someone else. Guy was on his knees, took two slugs, bam, bam, right in the forehead. Have pictures of this girl. She's tall, got curves, but slim, not sure how she'd get this man to his knees. He was armed, gun in his back waistband, knife in his boot. She drew on him, he'd draw back and this would have an alternate ending. Someone put the fear of God into him. He didn't even go for his gun. Speculation but I'd say he knew who he was facing down, took direction to get on his knees, was probably hoping he could talk his way out of it, got proved wrong."

"Well, then that's good news and good news," Deke remarked.

"Maybe," Decker hedged and kept going. "Witnesses in this building say that Bianca has been around and not a week ago or days ago but a couple of folks saw her enter this apartment last night. They did not see her leave. They did see another man, well-dressed, good-looking, tall, lean, black, come in a while after Bianca. Neighbor down the hall was coming back from work, saw her open the door to him, smile at him, all friendly, *real* friendly, and let him in. They did not see Caswell enter and preliminary from the ME states Caswell bought it between midnight and three in the morning. No one saw either of the other two leave. No one heard gunshots."

"So, you're thinkin'…" Deke prompted.

But Deke knew what Deke was thinking.

She took care of her girl by finding whatever money she had to find to get a professional hitman to take care of the problem.

"Bianca Constantine either got her hands on some money or she made a very dangerous friend," Deck said.

"That's what I was thinking," Deke muttered and Jussy shifted into him. He looked into her eyes and mouthed, "Second, baby."

She pressed her lips together and nodded.

Decker said in his ear. "There's more, man."

"Give it to me," Deke grunted, his focus on Jussy blurring.

"Shithole apartment building, not a great part of town, but the furniture in here, Deke, it's not top of the line but it isn't crap either. Place is neat and clean. Neighbors say she has a service come in and clean it for her and this is not the kind of building that happens so that's been noticed. They also say a lot of other shit, loose mouths which is a surprise in this area, but not with what they're saying. She isn't one of them. They don't know this because they sense it. They know this because they see it. They aren't protecting one of their own. They're not big fans of having a hit carried out in a neighbor's pad, that neighbor not being one of them, so they're giving the cops everything."

"And what are they giving them?"

"She's always tricked out. She takes a ride, it's sliding into the back seat of a shiny town car with a driver. Nice clothes. Hair done. Heels. Jewelry."

"She's from money, Decker," Deke reminded him.

"She's clean, Deke," Decker returned. "Not a single witness says she looks strung out or acts in any way like a junkie or a good time girl. No parties. No callers. In early, not out on the town, stumbling home loaded or high. Quiet. Nice to folks in the halls, not in their business, clearly not wanting them in hers, but she isn't being an uppity bitch. She leaves at all, it's during the day, comes home early evening."

"Not sure how to take what you're sayin', Deck."

"What I'm saying is that it might be that Bianca Constantine got herself a sugar daddy who's into her at least in one healthy way. She was going down that rabbit hole, he pulled her out, cleaned her up and is keeping her. Apartment is rented under a corporation that's a shell we haven't been able to trace yet, but it's moneyed. Again, I've seen pictures of this girl and she's not hard to look at. She caught the right eye, I could see this happening."

"And this eye she caught, they're down with hiring that kind of thing to take care of a problem for her?" he asked.

"No. The way she greeted the guy who entered her apartment last night, this eye she caught is the kind of guy who knows how to execute a hit," Deck replied.

Deke blew out a hissed breath.

Jussy got closer.

Decker kept going.

"From all reports, these from your girl, Bianca's parents, Thurston…Justice and Bianca are tight. Seriously tight. Known each other years, best of friends. She heard her sister getting strangled on her voicemail, the man she might ask to pay her debt she wouldn't ask to pay her debt. She'd ask him to make the man who hurt her friend pay. And he's so into her, he did it."

"That's a lot of speculation, Decker," Deke told him.

"Her cupboards were bare, brother. Not a dime to her name. Credit card debt up to her ass. Her house foreclosed on six months ago. Car repo'ed. Not many of her friends have nice things to say about her because she screwed them over a variety of ways or she owes them money, some of that big money. No one has seen her for months but the last ones who did say, if she wasn't shitfaced or high, she was strung out. And now I'm standing in an apartment with clothes and furniture left behind she could hock easy for a fix or a payoff. Someone is keeping her. And that someone has means. Man who showed last night, witness who saw her open the door to him, that friendly he noted, man said she greeted him in a way you'd greet a lover. Took his hand, pulled him in. No one else seen coming or going. Man's dead ten feet away from me, Deke, is not dead for a payoff. He's dead for *payback*. And from what we got, he was done right in front of Bianca Constantine."

"You think it's too hot to try to find her?" Deke asked. "For you," he went on to explain and his voice went low. "Emme."

"Gonna ask around. Emmanuelle told me Krys and Bubba's good news, I wanna be home with my woman who's gonna be giving me that same good news in a few months. I'll report all this to Chace but told the cops that there's an investigation pending that I'd been hired to look into that involves Caswell so they're gonna give him a call too. And I know some folks out here who might know this tall, sharp-dressed black man. Won't go in hard or send one of my boys in until we know more about him and what Constantine got herself caught up in. But I'm just givin' it today. Gonna get back to my wife tomorrow. Leave a few boys behind to keep digging but do it careful. I'll let you know we find it's too hot or gut feeling tells us to back off."

"Sounds like a plan," Deke replied.

"Right. I'll let you go. But at least the good news is solid good. Your girl, she's safe from this asshole, and no matter how it's happening or who's behind it, it looks like her girl is getting her shit together, at least with the partying and dope. Company she's keeping, that's the question mark."

"Yeah," Deke muttered.

"Yeah," Decker said. "Later."

"Later, Deck. And thanks, brother." Deke disconnected and again focused on Jussy.

He didn't even lower his phone before she asked, "What?"

He looked into her brown eyes, knowing this was Jussy, his gypsy princess. She'd take it in, deal with it and move on.

"Okay, baby, good news," he started. "Brendon Caswell is no longer a threat and won't be because his dead body was found this morning in an apartment in LA."

"Holy crap," she whispered, those brown eyes getting huge.

"Now for the weird news," he warned her.

"Oh shit." She was still whispering.

"He was found in Bianca's apartment."

She closed her eyes.

"Look at me, gypsy," he ordered, shoving his phone in his pocket and lifting his hand to wrap it around the back of her neck under her hair.

She opened her eyes.

"Folks saw her, Jussy. Said she looks good, clean, healthy. Say she's at home at night, not out partying. Say she doesn't have folks coming by. She's nice to people when she sees them in the halls. Decker says the apartment building isn't the greatest, but her place was clean, good furniture."

She shook her head. "I don't get that, Deke."

Deke tried to explain it. "First, Decker, and my guess is the cops he called in, do not think Bianca killed Caswell. The hit appears professional."

Her eyes got huge again and her voice got loud when she shouted, "*What?*"

"Deck's speculating a lot but he's also still lookin' into things. He's coming back tomorrow and he'll let us know what he finds out. But in the meantime, it seems your girl cleaned herself up and seems to be gettin' on okay."

"Except some hitman killed someone in her apartment," Jussy stated.

"Yeah, except that," Deke grunted.

"Was she there?"

"They don't know but folks saw her go in, another guy go in too, that guy was a put-together, good-lookin' black man. She knew him. They seemed tight. No one saw either of them leave or Caswell go in. Decker found Caswell early this morning. Bianca and the other guy were gone."

"So what does all this mean? She had someone kill Caswell for her?" she asked.

"It means we don't know what it means until Decker finds out so we should just get on with what we're doin' and wait until we got solid information. Not make guesses and get tweaked about shit we don't know we should tweak about."

She moved and did it to pull her phone out of the fringed bag hanging from a strap that crossed her body over one of the few pieces of clothing she owned he really fucking liked.

It was like the dress she'd worn when he first saw her again, walking into Bubba's.

This one was long, down to her ankles, sleeves that went down to her mid-forearms that were flowy, the dress brown with a pattern of little cream flowers on it. The waist was belted under her tits with a narrow belt made of Native American beading.

That was all okay.

The part Deke liked a fuckuva lot was that the front was cut all the way down to that belt. The rest of her was covered, except her wrists, and that slash, exposing chest and the inside swells of her gorgeous tits that were not restrained with a bra.

Total gypsy princess.

With all that hair down, tangled and messy from sleep and sex, in that dress, she looked fucking amazing.

So amazing, he got caught in taking it in and almost didn't catch the fact she was making a call.

But he caught it and saw who she was calling on the screen.

He pulled her phone out of her hand and disengaged it.

Her head snapped back.

"What are you doing?" she rapped out.

"You aren't calling your girl," he told her.

She got close, up on her toes, and hissed, "Deke, the dude that strangled me was killed by an assassin in *my best friend's pad*." She rocked back. "Of course I'm gonna call her."

"Baby, the asshat that strangled you was killed in your best friend's apartment and you are *not* gonna make a call a few hours after a crime was committed that it's possible that best friend witnessed."

"The cops have got to know that this Caswell—"

"They know. Decker told them. That doesn't mean you're phoning Bianca," he returned. "Let Decker see if he can find out what's happening with her and—"

"She's my best friend, Deke, and I'm worried about her," she snapped.

"She's your best friend, gypsy," he said gently. "And it might be she's consorting with hitmen, it appears she's bein' kept and there is a lot of conjecture surrounding what went down in her apartment after what went down with you. Decker says this smacks of payback. What was bein' paid back was what happened to you. *You* were the one assaulted and *you* are a woman of means. Do *not* call your girl. You don't need ties to her at all except the ones you already got. Are you following me?"

She glared at him and took her time doing it.

Then she jerked her eyes angrily away and looked down the sidewalk, taking her time with that too.

Finally, her shoulders slumped, her head dropped, she muttered, "Fuck," and fell, the top of her head hitting his chest.

His hand still at the back of her neck squeezed.

Jussy.

She was following him.

"I need coffee," she told his chest.

Deke found her hand, gave her back her phone, dug out his keys and gave her those too. "Go get in my truck. Call Thurston with this news, set his mind at ease. I'll get you what you need."

She slid her head around until her cheek was pressed to his chest, whispering, "You always do."

Damn, that felt good.

She pressed close a second then pulled away.

Deke let her go.

Jussy looked up at him. "I need a double shot in whatever Shambles makes me," she announced. "I never tell him what I want. I let him rock my world. Though this time, he's gonna do it with a double shot."

"Gotcha," he replied.

"And a double dose of whatever he puts in a white bag."

Deke grinned at his gypsy. "Got that too."

She looked up into his eyes, hers melting warm. "Thanks, honey."

"Be back in a sec, Justice."

She nodded, turned and moved back up the sidewalk where Deke's truck was parked outside the convenience store.

He watched until she was safe inside his truck.

Only then did he turn and walk down to La-La Land to get his girl her coffee.

* * *

Jussy scored her nails down his stomach while he was shooting up inside her and that made his hips jerk, his cock throb, and he shot more like she'd cupped his balls and squeezed.

She collapsed on his chest when he just started coming down, her hair all over—his shoulders, in his face, down his arms—and he didn't shift any of it away.

He just folded his arms around her and worked to even his breath after watching and feeling her riding his dick to her own orgasm before she gave the same to him.

When he was almost there, he murmured, "Kiss, gypsy."

She pulled her face out of his neck, lifted and gave him her mouth.

He took it, long and wet, the taste of Justice sweet, then broke the kiss and twisted a hand in her hair, using it to shove her face back in his neck.

"Weird, life," she whispered there. "Asshole strangles me, I get you. Too bad he's dead. I'd thank him before I kicked him in the nuts."

Deke's fingers fisted in her hair as he blinked at her ceiling.

Shit, they needed to stop fucking and start chatting if she thought what happened was why he'd changed his mind about where they were at.

It was, in a way.

But it wasn't, because he'd been into her since the beginning.

The very beginning.

In other words, Wyoming.

And she needed to know that.

He gathered her hair at her neck and was about to suggest they clean up and have that chat when her phone rang.

She lifted up slightly, reached out still connected to him, and dragged her purse from the nightstand to the bed. He turned his head and watched her dig in, pull her phone out and look at it.

She then looked to him.

"Joss," she stated and took the fucking call.

Her mother was calling and she was taking that call while his dick was still hard inside her.

Fuck, his gypsy.

Deke felt his lips twitch.

"Yo, Joss," she greeted.

He watched her face turn confused, she ordered, "Hey, I'm not getting this. Talk slower," then he felt her whole body tense, her cunt included, and he stifled a grunt at how good that felt.

Her eyes cut to him and she lifted up still straddling him, hair hanging down more tangled than before, some of it over her chest, covering her tits, but he could see nipple peeking through.

Fuck, he had to get her off his cock or he'd be hard again and fucking her while she was talking to her mother.

Deke put his hands to her hips and gave them a squeeze. She looked at him, got the message and swung off to settle in a hip, legs curved beside her, hand in the bed holding her up, but her eyes stayed on him.

"Joss knows about Bianca," she mouthed.

Deke nodded, knifed up, moved in to touch his lips to the slight bite mark he'd made with his teeth the first time he came inside her and he did that with his lips curled.

That mark was not going to go away. He'd renew it every time he needed to renew it. She was taking him everywhere for as long as this was working between them.

On that decision, he rolled out of bed, dealt with the condom and strolled back.

She was staring at his dick, and as he climbed back into bed with her and she lost visual, she looked up to his eyes and smirked, indicating she liked what he saw.

He bent in and kissed her between her tits.

She slid her fingers in his hair but had trouble keeping them there when he pulled away, fell to his back and yanked her on him so she was resting on his chest.

One of his hands went to her ass, the other one reached for the covers, pulling them up to their waists.

"Yeah, Joss, you let me talk a sec," she said quickly, "I'd tell you *I know*. I hired an investigator after what happened and he reported all this to us this morning."

A pause then, "Us being me and Deke." Another pause, her attention came to him and she said, "We're not talking about that now."

He grinned.

She watched him do it, her eyes got lazy and totally fucking sexy.

Deke rolled into her, taking her to her back so he was on her.

She lifted a hand to his jaw and rubbed her thumb into his beard.

He'd never had a woman do that.

It felt nice, sweet, affectionate.

Jussy.

"Because he's here, right now, and I'd rather not share the Deke and me getting together story while Deke and me are *together*." Her eyes, dancing with humor, locked on his as she finished, "He might get embarrassed when I share how talented he is with…um, *everything*."

"I won't get embarrassed," he told her, still grinning.

She shifted her thumb to over his lips, saying into the phone, "Yes, Joss, I told you he's *right here*." A pause then, "Yeah, that'd be good." Another pause before, "I'm not watching. I don't want to know. But I need to call Mr. T." A few moments and then, "Right. Yeah. This is weird. Crazy and weird, but I can't deal with that right now. My investigator is still on it and we hope we'll have more information tomorrow." Silence and, "Joss, I don't know. I haven't talked to her in ages. I'm trying not to get freaked in the middle of a lot of pretty freaky shit. Help me with that, would you?"

She focused on Deke and shook her head slightly, listening, before she kept going.

"Yes, that help would be us not hashing this all out when we have no clue what's happening, all that hashing out doing nothing but totally flipping me out. And if this is happening, I need to call Mr. T. He needs to be briefed about this new shit. So I gotta go." Pause then, "Yeah, love you too. My love to Rod. I'll talk to you when I know more." Pause, "Right, later, 'bye."

She disconnected and tossed her phone to the bed.

Then she declared, "Apparently news leaked Bianca was involved in some way in a murder. Her folks are famous. It's all over the entertainment news and is hitting the real news too. That's how Joss found out."

Through this declaration, Deke's body went wired.

"They mentioning you?" he asked.

She shook her head and he relaxed. "Not according to Joss. But Mr. T has people monitoring that, like always, so he always knows what people are saying. So—"

She was cut off with her phone ringing.

Deke twisted, grabbed it, saw the display said it was her girl Lacey, and he gave it to her.

"Fun's over," she muttered as she took the phone from him.

"For now, Jussy. Take your calls. Make your calls. I'll be here when it's done."

She smiled at him, took the call and put the phone to her ear.

"Before you start, I know, and hang on," she said into it and put it face down on her chest. "Can I talk you into going to get sandwiches?"

She could talk him into anything.

He still didn't move.

"You good here on your own?" he asked quietly.

"Not sure ghosts can touch you and I think they have to be tethered to the place they died or their home or something so I think I'm all right."

She said that like she thought ghosts were real.

So he grinned at her.

Yeah, she'd be all right.

He dipped close, touched his mouth to hers then rolled off her.

He was reaching for his jeans when he heard, "I'm back."

Lacey also must have heard a few things because the start of her conversation was about Deke.

They'd moved on to Bianca after he was dressed.

He put a knee to the bed, bent to her and brushed his lips against hers, pulled away and looked into her eyes.

She nodded and his gaze fell to her mouth as she used it to tell him silently, "I'm good, honey. Go."

That was when Deke nodded, pushed away and walked out to his truck to get their sandwiches.

* * *

Deke let himself in Jussy's front door and heard her playing guitar, the sound drifting into the big space.

If you'd asked him two months ago if he could tell from someone playing a guitar if they had the gift or if they just knew the chords, he couldn't say he could tell the difference.

Listening to Jussy play, he could now tell the difference.

And it was good she was playing again. She hadn't touched her guitar in the last week even if she'd had time to do her thing, this because her wrist was wrapped.

That wrap was now gone.

More good.

He walked into the room, seeing her in a tank and panties cross-legged in her bed, her guitar in her lap, her notebook open beside her, pencil in it, and she still was strumming but her eyes were to the door, watching him enter the room.

Deke then watched those big brown eyes warm at the same time he felt that warm in his gut.

She sniffed and begged, "Please make that smell be the southwestern turkey grill."

Her favorite, turkey and jack with whole roasted green chiles grilled into a cheesy mess on white bread.

"Not gonna buy you ham the day after we found out that fuckface who strangled you bought it."

She hated ham.

Deke figured that wasn't the reason she grinned at him.

He walked to the nightstand as she swung her guitar out and set it on its back in the bed, walking on her knees to where he dumped their sandwiches and a grocery bag.

He pulled the two six-packs out, one of Coke for him, one of cherry Fresca for her. They were cold.

He popped a can from each, set them aside and muttered, "Be back."

He took the rest to her fridge, shoved them in and then he was back.

She was again on her ass, her hand wrapped around a pack of paper plates held up in the air.

"Dude," was all she said.

"What?" was his reply.

"Nothing says environmentally unfriendly more than a paper plate, except," she gave him a wicked grin, "a paper towel."

He sat on the edge of the bed and started pulling off his boots. "That's just plain not true."

"I'm a liberal artist. They find out I use paper plates, they won't ask me to play at concerts to save the whales and shit."

He looked to her. "You play those concerts?"

She was still grinning, though it was no longer wicked. "No."

"Then you're good."

"I am but only because I have stoneware on order and might get a kitchen in the next century, so soon we won't need to resort to paper plates," she muttered. "And just for the record, I do want the whales to be saved…in a big way."

He looked to her, smiling and twisting fully into the bed as she unwrapped sandwiches, putting them on paper plates.

"Speakin' to that, not the whales, the kitchen, called Max," he shared. "Told him progress on your house was suspended today due to celebratory circumstances."

She waggled her brows. "Did you tell him *all* the celebratory circumstances?"

"No, but I'm gettin' he gets 'em anyway seein' as he said his wife Nina wants us to pick a date to go to The Rooster. That's *us*, not you. They're payin'," he told her. "Client dinner. Max can write it off. Nina can look you over. And we can eat a fuckin' great steak."

"I'm in as soon as my black eye is totally gone."

"I'll let him know." Deke took the plate she gave him with the sandwich buried under an upended Big Grab of Chili Cheese Fritos. "Get your calls done?"

She'd taken a big bite, was nodding and chewing.

Once she swallowed, she said, "Lacey and Mr. T. Mr. T and my publicist are on it with the LA cops so they can put a lid on anything leaking about this having anything to do with me. Mr. T is good at that shit. I don't wanna know and he doesn't share his secrets, but I figure he's right now deep in the throes of palm greasing."

"Good news, gypsy," Deke replied.

"And Chace called too," she went on. "He says he heard word from your Decker friend as well as the cops in LA. During autopsy, they're gonna do a DNA test on Caswell so it can be compared to the DNA they got from me. That way Chace says all the T's are crossed and I can breathe easy. Though he said it's highly likely I can already breathe easy because I might not have seen the guy's face, but I gave a physical description of his body, and that all matches. Not to mention the other stuff," she mumbled her last sentence before taking another big bite of sandwich.

"That's good too."

Her phone beeped with a text, she looked at it, her brows drew together and she dropped her sandwich on her plate, quickly wiped her hands on a napkin and nabbed it.

"Fuck," she murmured.

"What?" he asked.

Her thumbs flew over the screen and she didn't answer him.

"What?" he clipped.

He heard her text go and she looked at him.

"Lacey," she stated.

"Doesn't answer my question," he informed her.

"And Anton Rojas."

She said no more, her phone beeped again, she looked down at it and immediately started replying to the text.

"Gypsy," he growled his warning.

"Two seconds, honey," she muttered, hit send and looked to him. "Anton Rojas. A black, sharp-dressed man."

Deke's shoulders went straight. "You think you know the guy with Bianca?"

She shook her head. "No, I didn't. But Lacey thinks she does."

Another beep came from her phone and he exercised patience with difficulty as she read and returned the text.

The second he heard hers go, he grunted, "Explain."

She again gave him her attention.

"Okay, Anton, Tony, he's...well, he's a good guy. We knew him years ago. Years and years. Like, we were in our early twenties when he was in our lives."

"And?" Deke pushed.

"And, he met Lacey first. Head over heels she went for him. He was totally her type. They'd been dating a few weeks before she introduced him to us and that is *not* her MO. We always got feedback from the posse before we went in deep with a guy. She did not do this. She was way in deep before Bianca or I ever laid eyes on him."

Christ, was he in for that in his future?

"I got why when we met him," Jussy continued through his thought. "Like I said, he was a good guy, her type. Handsome. Smooth. A gentleman. Really good with Lacey who can be a handful. The weird thing was that, although he was with

Lacey, the longer he was with her, the deeper she got, but as an outside observer, it seemed to me what was happening was that he was getting in deeper and deeper too. Just not with Lace. With Anca."

"Shit," Deke muttered.

"Yeah," she said, nodding, tossing a Frito in her mouth, chewing, swallowing and again talking. "Anc would in no way go there. Girl code. Not gonna happen. Especially with how into him Lacey was. But Tony, he wouldn't do that either. I got the impression he stayed with Lace for as long as he did just because he didn't know how to let her down easy. He knew he'd break her heart and he didn't want to do that. But I also got the impression he wasn't going to go there with Anca after he let Lacey down. They were just…well, both of them were that kind of people."

Another text beeped and Deke focused on eating while she read it and returned it.

Then she came back to him.

"How's this got anything to do with this shit now?" Deke asked. "This guy stick around?"

She shook her head. "No. It's been at least a decade since I've seen him."

"Bianca?"

"Far's I know, same thing with her. She started inching away from us well before Dad died but she was still in contact. And that's *totally* something she'd share. At least with me."

"She give you the heads up she was into this guy too while he was with your other girl?"

She was chewing sandwich and nodding.

When she could, she told him, "She confessed all. It was sad, honey. Because, honestly, love my Lacey girl, but Tony and Bianca suited each other. She has this…" she paused, "fragility. Lace and me, we could take on the world. Bianca was ballsy and she had attitude but under that, well, obviously since she sunk into the life she did, there was a disconnect. There was something missing. Something she needed. I was young and I obviously didn't know much about the world, I still sensed that something she needed was a man in her life like Tony. He was sweet but he was strong. And when it came to a woman in his life, it was all about her. I mean, he managed to do that being with Lacey at the same time falling in love with Anc."

She shrugged and finished.

"It's weird but true."

"Okay, babe, not gettin' why you two are on this bent about this guy," Deke told her.

She got another text. He clenched his jaw, ate more chips, waited for her to get through it, something she did nodding like she was agreeing with whatever her girl was saying, then she looked to him.

"Lacey knew," she declared. "She's not dumb. She felt it, saw it, what was happening with them. I think after it was all over, she kinda felt shit about it, not stepping aside for them. We never broached it. All of us or Lacey with just me. But things didn't end for her with Tony because of that. Things ended with Tony because Terrence put his foot down that Lacey needed shot of him."

"Terrence?"

"Terrence Town. Lacey's dad," she explained, ate another chip and told him through chewing it, "He was not a hardass. He was a lot like my dad. He and Dad and Perry, Bianca's dad, they were tight all the way to the end, that end being the end of Dad."

"Got that, baby," he said gently.

She nodded and wisely moved past that part quickly.

"Terrence is still tight with Perry and Nova, Nova being Anc's mom. Dad, Terrence and Perry, they came up in the business together. Out on the road, would run into each other. Worked on music together. At one point, bought houses in LA close to each other. That's how us three girls became such good friends. In the father stakes, Terrence was like Dad, Perry, as I told you, wasn't."

What he knew of Perry Constantine, lead guitar of the metal band Let, and his three-time wife Nova, was that the two of them were a mess, Perry being the bigger one. Their marriages, and the end of them, played out in such a way even Deke, who didn't give a shit about that type of thing, couldn't get away from it.

Perry had been in and out of rehab several times, all of them big splashes that included run-ins with police, photographers, fans...and his wife.

Nova, something he didn't know but learned through Jussy when she'd given him further details about Bianca last week, did one stint in rehab. She waited too long to do it but at least it took and that was the end of the on and off with Perry.

Nova was now married to some television actor and kept hold on her minimizing fame through him and doing guest starring stints on various programs or straight-to-video movies.

But regardless, according to Jussy, most of Bianca's parenting came from Johnny, Joss and Lacey's parents, when they were around, which, with their careers, was not much.

"Dad and Terrence, they could be *dads*," she kept going. "And they pulled those dad cards anytime we fucked up. But they were never assholes about it. That said, Terrence was an asshole about this. Making threats to Lacey that he was going to cut off her money, shit like that. Shit he *never* did. He wanted Tony gone and he made that so."

Now she had his complete attention.

"You reckon he knew something about this guy you didn't?"

She nodded, indicating her phone on the bed with her hand. "Or at least that's what Lacey thinks she figured out."

Her voice got even more serious when she carried on.

"Deke, honey, I haven't seen Tony in over a decade but I have spoken to him."

"Shit," he bit out. "When?"

"After Dad died. Not right after, a month or two, before I moved here. He called to give me his condolences. And he asked after Lacey. He also asked after Bianca."

"And you told him," Deke guessed.

"I didn't go into full details or speculate but I was worried about her and getting more worried. I knew he still lived in LA. Bianca was, and obviously is still back there. He had money back then, worked hard, nice clothes, nice cars, and we always got into clubs and places not only because we were who we were, but whenever we were with him it was because Tony had connections. Even better connections than us. So I told him and I think I even asked him to keep an eye out for her and let me know if he sees her or hears anything about her."

"So you think, he was into her back then so much he stayed into her, he heard she was in trouble, went in search of her, found her, cleaned her shit up and now they're together."

"That's Lacey's theory but I think it's a good one."

"Gotta tell Deck this, Jussy."

"Yeah, you do," she said softly.

"Lacey good to talk to her dad about what he knew about this guy to make her call it off with him back in the day?"

"That's what we're texting about now. She's not feeling a lot of love for pointing a finger at Tony if he has nothing to do with this. They ended but it wasn't ugly.

And Terrence has been talking with Perry and Nova, that's how Lacey heard about Bianca. Cops have talked with both Bianca's folks. If Lace brings Tony into it, shit might get said that shouldn't."

"Maybe smart. We'll see what Deck finds," Deke muttered.

He pulled out his phone, called Deck and relayed the information.

"Right, got a name, can get a lot further with that lead but I won't share with the cops. Not yet. Thanks, brother. Your girl thinks of anything else, I'm a phone call away."

"Right, later, Deck."

He disconnected and saw Jussy done with her sandwich but she was looking at him with an unsettled expression on her face.

"I know you're not okay, baby," he started. "This happening with your friend. But through that call, something make you less okay?"

"Dad took us on the road."

He nodded. "Yeah, you told me that."

"A lot of the time, we had tutors. He was home for a spell, we were in school, but that never lasted long. Except once, when he was on a huge tour, lasted a year, went over to Europe, Asia, Australia, he left us home and put me in school for what I think was the longest stretch I did. Bianca was in that school. Lacey at a private Catholic school. We were without a musketeer, I was the new girl with a famous last name and some girls fucked with me."

"Right," he prompted, seeing her focus on his shoulder, her mind was somewhere else.

Her gaze came to him.

"Bianca got suspended because she jumped them."

Deke knew nothing about girl world and how they dealt with their issues so he asked, "You were tight. Would you do the same?"

"Actually *jump* them?" She shook her head. "Maybe, though I can't say I would. I'm not about that kind of physicality. Doesn't matter, they got the better of her. There were three of them, one of her. And she was the one who started it so she was the one who got in the most trouble. I wasn't there but I told her between classes what happened and at the next break, she went for it."

"Jussy, why's this got you tweaked?"

"In the next month, those three girls had veritable shit storms consume their lives."

Deke was silent.

"I thought it was karma," she whispered. "But anything that could happen to them did. Boyfriends breaking up with them. One got her hair done at a salon and the bleach went wonky, most of her hair fell out during the rinse. Another got caught in the parking lot at a mall, mugged and roughed up. It doesn't end there, Deke."

"How old were you?"

"Fifteen, maybe sixteen."

He shook his head, uncertain she was going in the right direction.

"At that age, you think Bianca masterminded all that?" he asked.

"I think a guy in a biker bar touched me in a way I didn't like, she didn't like, and she lost her mind on him, Deke. She got the drop on him, got him on the floor on his back and did some major damage to his face with her fingernails before she was pulled off. Her dad had to buy her out of that one and that wasn't the first or the last. Some boy told stories about Lacey, I don't know, we were maybe only thirteen, and Anca *herself* went, staked out his parents' house, waited until they were all out and broke into his bedroom. She wrecked it completely and bragged about it to me and Lacey, proud she was looking out for her girl. No one ever found out it was her, because of course we'd never tell, but that boy freaked the fuck *out*. Nothing touched in the house but his shit, clothes, furniture, everything torn apart. The message was sent and it was clear. He didn't say shit about anybody again, as far as I knew."

"So she's got a highly-tuned revenge streak."

"Yes, I think so, but that kind of thing hasn't happened in a long time. And lately, the last few years…it's been that, honey, it's been years she's been folding in on herself…Lacey and me, we had shit going on. We didn't notice it at first. And then…"

She didn't finish that thought but Deke knew what she was saying.

It was too late.

He reached out a hand and touched his finger lightly to her knee.

That was all it took with Jussy.

She pulled in a breath and pulled it together.

"Don't tell that to Decker," she asked softly. "I don't…" She shook her head again. "Let me talk to Lacey. She's with her folks right now, went to them for her break instead of coming out here. They're upset about Bianca now, and were already upset about what happened to me. That's why she's texting. She doesn't want to talk in front of them. Especially about Tony. I'll text her and talk to her when she's alone and can do that talking freely."

"Text, gypsy," he urged. "Set that up so you can talk that out. Then, you already picked all your paint colors. Got the paint for downstairs, not the upstairs rooms. We'll go get it so I'm good to go when I'm back at it tomorrow. Sound like a plan?"

She nodded, picking up her phone.

He grabbed their garbage while she texted.

Then she dressed and he loaded her up in his truck and got them on their way.

Suddenly, she said, "Paying a stylist to make a sixteen-year-old mean girl's hair fall out is a far cry from finding a hitman, Deke."

Deke grabbed her hand, advising again, "Do not flip out until you know what you're flippin' out about."

"The guy strangled me, scared the shit out of me, I thought he was going to kill me. I cannot pull up a lot of emotion about the fact he's dead. It's not being vengeful or in denial. It's just that he doesn't matter to me. But if Bianca was behind that. If she was *there*—"

"Babe, what'd I say?"

She didn't answer.

"Justice."

"Do not flip out until I know what I'm flipping out about."

"Our focus is paint," he told her.

"Our focus is paint," she repeated after him.

"And you gotta decide what you want for dinner."

"But I decided lunch."

"And I decided how I was gonna fuck you before lunch. I'm tradin' my turn on dinner on deciding how I'm gonna fuck you tonight."

He glanced at her as he turned on County Road 18.

She was grinning at him.

When he looked back to the road, she said, "Deal."

That was good.

Because he'd already decided how he was going to fuck her and that goodness was happening for certain.

* * *

Deke drove into his Jussy on his knees, one of her legs pressed straight up his torso, the other leg curled around his hip, her hands above her head pushing into the headboard, taking him.

She was panting softly, a sound he felt drive through his dick. He could see through the moonlight that her eyes were hooded, her hair all over the pillows, her tits bouncing with his thrusts, and she was so gorgeous, he had to get her there.

Fast.

He pulled her leg off his torso, wrapped it around, bent over her and pulled her up into his arms.

He fell back to his calves.

Jussy swung her legs back around and hooked the tops of her feet on his thighs.

Deke wound one hand in her hair, the other arm he kept around her waist.

She curled both arms around his shoulders.

She bent her head to him, lips brushing his, pants blending with his rough breaths.

He drove up inside her.

She rode him hard.

"Need help gettin' there, gypsy?" he grunted, powering up faster.

She didn't answer.

Her head fell back, her tits pressed into his chest as her spine arced, and he felt her cunt ripple around his dick as she let out a soft breath with her orgasm.

He got her there.

So Deke plunged fast and deep, taking himself there with her, shooting into the condom, into his gypsy, his face buried between her tits.

Spectacular.

When he came down, she had the fingers of both hands laced together through his hair cupping his head.

He tipped it back and she dropped hers down.

He took his time kissing her, wet and deep, and she gave him her mouth for as long as he wanted it.

Eventually, Deke broke the kiss, slid a hand down to her ass and gave it a squeeze.

She got the message and climbed off him.

He angled off the bed, dealt with the condom and went back to her.

She curled in immediately while he pulled the covers over them.

"Back to the trailer tomorrow, babe," he murmured. "That's for the foreseeable future. Gonna be breathin' in paint fumes all day. Don't wanna do that at night."

"Good, I miss the trailer," she mumbled.

He could tell by her voice she was sleepy and he liked that she fucked, she got into it, she did it hard, no inhibitions, and she liked closeness after but didn't need to spend an hour on a run down blow by blow of their fucking, their day or any other crap that didn't require useless conversation in an effort to pretend it was sharing leading to closeness.

They'd already been close, that being fucking, and were going to remain close, that being sleeping together after fucking.

Justice got that.

She just, like always, got on with shit.

Now, since it was late, that shit was sleep.

And she "missed the trailer."

They'd been gone from it for two days.

Deke smiled into her hair.

"'Night, honey," she muttered.

"'Night, Jussy," he replied.

She snuggled deeper under him.

Within minutes, she was out.

It didn't take long for Deke to follow her.

CHAPTER FIFTEEN

Crock-Pot

Justice

"DEKE."

It was a plea.

I didn't know for what because I needed him to stop but I needed him *not* to stop.

Ever.

I'd never been afraid of an orgasm but the one Deke was building was threatening to tear me apart.

"Let go, Jussy," he grunted.

"*Baby,*" I panted.

"Christ," he growled and I distractedly heard the moist noises his cock made, sinking fast and deep into my pussy. "Your cunt. So goddamned tight. *Let go, Jussy*."

I let go, chest dropping to the mattress, cheek to the pillow, arms stretching out in front of me and experienced the heady ecstasy of an orgasm tearing me apart.

Deke's finger left my clit, his hand wrapped in my hair and he held it firm, driving me back into him as I climaxed and he kept thrusting, faster, harder.

My thighs quivered, my nipples dragged on the sheets, I whimpered and gasped as orgasm one was shoved out of the way so orgasm two could rocket through me as Deke kept powering inside me.

Finally I heard it and felt it, Deke losing control, bucking into me through his climax, doing it grunting, each thrust, each noise blasting up my pussy, exploding against my clit.

Enter orgasm three, not as soul-shattering but it was no slouch either.

I knew it was over when he slid in, stayed buried, his fingers sifting out of my hair, down my back and both hands coming to my hips, trailing, drawing mindless patterns as he started to glide in and out tenderly.

I heard his breaths even, felt the light, gentle beauty of his touch, the intimate caress inside me before he slid out.

He trailed a finger down my right thigh, over and then I felt a tug and the scarf he'd grabbed from my walk-in closet sometime before this morning came loose.

I did a full body shiver as he slid the silk away.

He'd woken me.

We'd had some fun.

Then he'd tied my thighs together and pulled me up to my knees, my legs bound tight together, and he fucked me from behind, his hand around to my front, finger digging into the close heat to manipulate my clit the whole time he did it.

It had been awesome.

He ran his fingers then his lips over one of my ass cheeks before he put pressure on my hip and I fell to my side.

He yanked the covers to my waist.

I felt him pull my hair aside, his lips touch my shoulder and then the bed move as he got out of it.

I watched his fantastic ass as he went into the bathroom.

My alternate and arguably better view was his cock as he walked out.

My head stayed down but my eyes aimed up as he sat on the edge of the bed. He twisted at the waist, bent and got close, one forearm in the bed, fingers of his other hand sliding slow and lazy up and down my spine.

"Can you move?" he asked, hazel eyes twinkling, cocky and hot.

"No," I gave him the truth.

And I got more cocky.

And hot.

"You gonna pass out?" he went on.

I gave him more truth. "Probably."

And from that I got more cocky…and hot.

I turned my head slightly so I wasn't looking into his face through the sides of my eyes but straight on.

"No one has ever tied me up," I whispered.

"Get used to that, gypsy," he whispered back.

I shivered.

And got more cocky and *hot*.

He bent deep, touched his mouth to mine and when he moved back, it was only half an inch.

"I gotta get to work. Go back to sleep, baby."

"Okay, Deke."

He went in for another kiss and I forced my body to use the small amount of energy it had left after being torn asunder through two massive orgasms (and a final one that was no slouch) to cup his bristly cheek.

He got my message and that kiss was not a touch. It went deeper and lasted longer.

He ended it lifting up and kissing my temple then pulling away at the same time tugging the sheets up to my shoulder.

I watched him walk back to the bathroom.

Deke was halfway there when my eyelids fluttered closed.

They didn't open.

* * *

Showered, dressed, phone in one hand, mug of coffee in the other, I walked out to the great room and found Bubba there working with Deke. Bubba was checking the plastic that had already been taped at the edges of the windows in preparation for priming. Deke was working on some equipment, getting ready to spray the paint.

"Hey, Bub, how're your two girls?" I asked.

"You're gonna see," Bubba answered, grinning huge at me. "Krys texted. Said you and Laurie are coming for a visit."

"Yup," I replied, this whole conversation happening as I made my way straight to Deke. I stopped close and tipped my head way back as he dipped his chin way down. "News that's not news, Lauren called while I was getting dressed. We're paying a visit to Krys. And she's letting me borrow her Crock-Pot."

His brows went up. "Crock-Pot?"

"You down with me going to the trailer after my visit with Krys and putting dinner in to slow cook for us tonight?"

He dug in his pocket, asking, "What's for dinner?"

"Steph's chicken."

"Who's Steph?"

"Some unknown, faceless but undeniably brilliant woman who came up with a killer Crock-Pot recipe for chicken."

Deke chuckled, taking a key off his chain and handing it to me, muttering, "Remind me tonight, Jussy. Get you a spare."

I went solid.

Deke shoved his keychain minus a key back into his pocket.

My eyes slid to Bubba.

He was still grinning huge but I had a feeling it was for a different reason because he was doing it staring at Deke.

"Want you texting me when you get to Krys's," Deke ordered and I looked back to him.

"Okay," I agreed.

"And when you leave."

"Right."

"And when you get to the trailer."

I stood there silent.

"And when you're on your way back here," Deke went on. "With sandwiches," he kept going. "Roast beef," he kept at it. "And Swiss," he finished.

"Uh…" I began, heard Bubba make a weird noise, looked to him, saw him widen his eyes to me, and I got it.

Bubba was a mountain man. Deke was a mountain man. Hence Bubba knew what Deke was doing. And what Bubba was communicating was that I should keep my mouth shut and text Deke incessantly so he didn't worry (even if there wasn't anything to worry about, it was still the first time I went out on my own after being strangled, the operative part of that was me being *strangled*).

I gave Bubba wide eyes back and looked up at Deke.

He still was eyes to me.

"You do know none of that between you and Bub was lost on me since I'm standin' right here," he noted.

"Um…"

"And you made a good call," he continued. "No sass."

I felt my eyes narrow.

"Don't start," he grunted. "Just text."

Before I could say anything, his gaze went beyond me toward the front door.

That was when I heard a car approaching.

I looked over my shoulder at the door but Bubba started moving, muttering, "I'll go see who it is."

Bubba lumbered away and I turned back to Deke.

"Key to your trailer?" I whispered.

He grinned down at me and I felt that grin *everywhere*.

"I like you," he whispered back.

Suddenly, I wanted to start crying.

Instead, I smiled so huge, it even blinded me.

Deke lifted a hand and captured a long tendril of my hair, twirling it around his forefinger.

He also bent his neck so his face was closer.

"We gotta talk tonight, Jussy."

That didn't sound good.

"Can't we just have amazing orgasms, banter, your cocky, my sassy and Steph's chicken?" I asked.

"We'll have all that too."

At least that was promising.

"Deke—"

"None of it'll be bad, baby," he said gently. "You think, what we found, it could be bad?"

I didn't think that.

But I wasn't the one who'd established boundaries blown through after assault, strangulation, a week of closeness, all this leading to amazing orgasms.

"Well…" I started.

"Jussy," Bubba called and I felt the pull on my hair, hair Deke didn't let go, when I twisted to look at the door.

Bubba was plodding back toward us and Mr. T was standing inside the closed door.

"Hey, Mr. T," I called.

"Justice," he called back, and even across the large space that was my great room, I saw he had attention keenly focused not just on me, but on me with Deke.

Deke gave a soft tug at my hair before letting it go.

I shot him a grin before I took off toward Mr. T.

"How's it hanging?" I asked when I stopped at him.

"Fine," he said crisply. He took a look around my now fully-walled space and then his gaze came back to me. "I came up here to tell you that, with your situation clearing up, I need to get to Nashville. Your aunt is going back into the studio and I have to make sure everything is as it should be."

That was a bummer.

I liked having him around.

Still, my situation had cleared up and Aunt Tammy, when recording (and performing, and breathing), could be a diva.

I nodded. "Okay," I said and grinned. "Back to regularly scheduled programming."

He nodded back. "Just so you're aware, I've had a word with a few people I know in Los Angeles and a few others who can pull strings here. They'll be expediting the DNA tests so we can be assured this gentleman in LA was the same as the gentleman who paid a visit to you."

Paid a visit to you.

Mr. T was a stitch.

I did not laugh.

I nodded again.

"I've also had a few words with the authorities in LA. I've not only been clear that what happened there has nothing to do with you, I've been assured there'll be no leak about any connection between what happened there and you."

"Right. Great. Thanks as usual, Mr. T."

"And Jacob Decker will continue to report to me as well as to you through Hightower."

"Sounds good," I approved, not that he needed my approval but I gave it to him anyway.

"Please continue to be careful, Justice," he warned.

"Not gonna be an issue since I'm going to visit my friend Krys and her new baby in about five minutes. Then I'm setting dinner up in a Crock-Pot at Deke's for tonight, where we're going to escape paint fumes. And then I'm back here with sandwiches and I've been ordered to text the progress of my travels so often, I might be able to get a few breaths in in between but we'll just have to see."

After I said that, Mr. T looked beyond me to where I knew Deke was.

"It pleases me," he started softly before he brought his gaze back to me, "that when the foundation of your father was pulled from under you, you found a safe place to land."

That gave me goosebumps.

"Pleases me too, Mr. T," I replied just as softly.

His lips moved in what was a semi-kinda-semblance of a smile.

That vanished and he stated briskly, "I must be on my way. My flight leaves in three and a half hours."

I nodded again and turned, calling, "Deke, Mr. T's taking off. He's gotta get to Nashville."

"Hey, dude. Cool to have you around," Bubba called while Deke headed our way. "Come back and visit Jussy soon. We'll make it a party."

Mr. T made no reply to Bubba and Bubba had been around him enough he didn't expect any. He just went back to checking the plastic taped on my windows.

Deke stopped close to me, throwing an arm around my shoulders and shoving out a hand.

"Bill," he said.

"Deke," Mr. T replied, taking Deke's hand for a firm squeeze before letting him go. "I trust you'll look after Justice," he said unnecessarily.

Deke just grunted unintelligibly. This was both his affirmative answer and an indication he was slightly insulted Mr. T voiced those words.

"Of course," Mr. T said to Deke then looked to me. "I'll be in touch."

"Can I get a hug?" I asked.

"If you must," he sighed.

Deke grunted again and that one was just masking a chuckle.

He let me go and I moved into Mr. T, wrapping my arms around him tightly, but carefully, still holding coffee and phone.

"Safe trip," I said into his ear. "Thanks for everything. And love you to pieces."

He gave me a short squeeze and stepped out of my arms.

Then he gave me a look that made my heart squeeze.

"Good-bye, Justice."

"Later, Mr. T."

He nodded once, turned, opened the door and moved through it.

Deke claimed me again and moved us into it before Mr. T could close it.

He glanced back only once before he walked directly to his rental car, got in and drove away.

"I'm gonna miss him," I muttered wistfully.

"Always tough to see the back of someone you love."

I looked up at Deke.

Deke was watching my drive, but when he felt my gaze, he looked down at me.

"Even far, babe, think you get, they never really are," he finished.

"Yeah," I said softly.

"Get to Krys," he ordered. "Her man's back at work, she's at home with a new baby, she's gonna need her girls around her."

I nodded and started to pull away.

"Kiss first, Jussy."

I looked into his eyes and just saw Deke looking down at me. It was not distant. There were no boundaries. He was close, his arm around my shoulders, waiting for me to roll up to my toes and give him a kiss.

I didn't know what this talk was going to be about that we'd have over Steph's chicken.

What I knew looking in his eyes was that, if Deke said it wasn't going to be bad, it wasn't going to be bad.

So I rolled up on my toes.

The kiss was hard, closed-mouthed, and not short, but also not long.

Deke had his fingers in my hair, his hand cupping the back of my head when it was over and he didn't let me roll back to my toes.

He commanded, "You're gonna be texting me."

"Yeah, I am," I agreed.

He gave the back of my head a squeeze, filtered his fingers through my hair and stepped away.

I went to dump my coffee in a travel mug and get my purse and keys. I called my good-byes, walked out the front door and got in my granddad's truck that someone somewhere along the way had driven back up to my place from the police station.

The last time I was in that truck, I was racing away, terrified of what had happened to me right along with being more terrified the guy was still around and could get to me.

I negotiated around Deke and Bubba's trucks and didn't give it more than a passing thought.

* * *

"Are you two boning?"

"Krystal!"

"What?"

"It's kinda not any of your business."

"Seein' as I'm gonna be kickin' some big white boy ass he doesn't pull his finger out, it *is* my business."

"Ladies," I cut in and when I had two sets of eyes aimed at me, I shared, "He's totally boning me. And it is seriously *fine*."

Lauren, holding Breanne, grinned at me.

Krystal smiled huge and said, "Well, all right."

Not all right.

Deke had tied my thighs together, fucked me hard, and through it, gave me three orgasms.

Totally not *all right*.

It was *fine*.

"Always wondered, he rough or can he be gentle?" Krystal asked.

"God, Krys!" Lauren snapped, cupping little Breanne's head like she could understand a word we said even if she wasn't right then fast asleep and all of about a day and a half old.

"Check and check," I answered Krys before they could get into it.

"Best of both worlds," Krystal muttered. "Surprising. Always figured Deke would fuck like a freight train."

"And check," I said, grinning at Krystal who grinned back at me.

"Lord," Lauren whispered, her head bent to Breanne. "Don't listen to your mommy. And you'll be spending lots of time with Auntie Laurie so you can learn how to be appropriate. Though I'll have to have a word with your Uncle Tate. He's got a mouth on him. But I suspect he'll curb it for baby girls."

Krystal rolled her eyes at me, but otherwise she was apparently unoffended.

"So it's good with you two?" she asked.

"Well, yeah, except he says we're gonna have a talk tonight over Steph's chicken."

Lauren turned her attention to me. "Talk about what?"

I shrugged. "I don't know. Maybe the fact that he wanted me at arm's length then lost his mind when I got attacked and wouldn't let me out of his sight, including us sleeping together every night since that night, though no nookie until

Sunday night. And now we're all, 'what's for dinner' and 'pick up sandwiches' without us even having a date."

"Deke doesn't date. He claims then he fucks," Krystal told me. "Though, not sure I know a single woman who spent more than one night in his trailer."

"Me either," Lauren muttered.

"That said," Krys carried on, "not sure more than a handful of women have even *been* to that trailer."

That made me smile.

"Tate called it," Krystal announced.

"He sure did," Lauren agreed.

"Called what?" I asked.

"You," Krys stated.

I was confused.

"Me?"

"You," Krys repeated. "Tate said later, after you left that first time in Bubba's, he saw Deke watchin' you talkin' to Bub and me. Said he also saw you lookin' at Deke. Said you two had a spark even if you didn't even share a look. Also said, if anyone could do it, it'd be a woman like you. Confident, got her act together, that would be the woman who could bring Deke to his knees. And he was right."

I was feeling weirdly like I was about to hyperventilate.

"I didn't buy it," Krystal added. "Hippie rock 'n' roll chick did not say Deke."

"I'm boho," I corrected.

"Boho is hippie, just less goofy," Krys returned.

She had me there.

But I had no interest in debating it anyway.

I was stuck on something else.

"Tate saw Deke watching me?" I asked.

"Says he did and Tate don't miss much, obviously, you two boning and talkin' over Steph's chicken, whatever that is," Krys answered.

Whoa. Whoa. *And whoa.*

Deke had been watching me?

"Are you nervous?" Lauren asked, taking me away from that happy thought.

"A little," I told her honestly.

"About what?" Krystal asked.

"Well, I like orgasms and Deke handing me the key to his trailer without blinking. And bottom line, I like Deke. He's...*Deke*," I said, not knowing how to explain it better.

I got nods like they both understood me (which, since they'd known him longer than me, I figured they did).

I still tried to give them more.

"I've been around. It's not like I've met every human being on the planet but there's no one like him. He's all...*mountain man*. And then he can be sweet. And he looks out for his friends. And he's funny. And he thinks I'm funny. And there's no denying he stepped up when shit got seriously crazy for me." I shook my head. "I don't want anything to fuck with that. Things have been a little bit rocky in my life lately. It's nice to just be...happy." I felt a tentative, hopeful smile curl at my lips when I finished, "Like, really *freaking* happy."

"Right, he's my friend and normally I would not lay him out there like this but, just in case you missed it, known him a long time and already said haven't known a single woman who's seen the inside of that trailer of his twice," Krystal shared. "And just sayin', he treats that land like its sacred so he usually doesn't take his hookups there at all. Not sure who makes that cut. Just know he's not ever once handed his key over to one of them to plug in a Crock-Pot."

Okay, now I was getting really, *really* freaking happy.

"Don't know his story," Lauren said. "Tate does but he hasn't shared and if it was open for Deke, which means Tate could share it, Tate would have given it to me. But him not sharing, well, don't want to wipe that look off your face, babe, but just be prepared."

Even with her words, I felt that look wiped off my face.

She leaned toward me in my armchair that was tilted toward hers, across from the couch Krystal was lounging on, reached out and touched my knee.

She drew back and kept speaking.

"We all have baggage. This does not negate all Krys said. I've known Deke a long time and he was so immune to connecting in any real way to a woman, it was troubling. Everyone knows he's a good man and for someone like that, you want him to find a good woman..." she gave me a sweet smile, sharing gratifyingly how she felt about me, "and get some of that happy. So just, you know, don't be nervous. But do be prepared. Because if Deke's gonna share, it's a gift, Jus. And he doesn't give that to everybody."

I looked to Krys and she shook her head.

"I don't know either, sister. And Bubba also doesn't. I'm not like Laurie. Somethin' that juicy about one of my people, I'd drag that out of him," she lifted her fingers and snapped, but not loudly in deference to Breanne, "like a shot."

"I can do baggage," and I damn well could, and *would*, "I just…"

I trailed off, not knowing what to say or maybe not wanting to put into words what was making me nervous.

"You're just fallin' in love with him," Krystal told me and I focused on her. "And in the beginning, that feels awesome and you don't want anything messin' with that."

Yep.

That was what I didn't want to put into words that was making me nervous.

I was falling in love with Deke.

"That's just what I'm feeling," I admitted.

"No sense in getting wound up about what you don't know, Jus," Laurie said and I looked to her. "Just go to the grocery store, get dinner cooking and get back to your guy with sandwiches."

"I will, after you give me Breanne for five minutes," I replied and grinned at Laurie. "You're hogging her."

We managed the handover without waking the baby girl and I'd just settled back, staring into her scrunchy face, watching her little red lips be all pouty when Krystal made her announcement.

"Makin' Bubba knock me up again first chance we got."

My eyes cut immediately to Krystal as I asked, "What?"

This I asked at the same time Lauren mini-shrieked, "*What?*"

Krystal tipped her 70's pinup hair (hair that was perfect, this because Lauren was there longer than me and looked after Breanne while Krys showered) toward the baby girl in my arms.

"That beauty we made? We're totally doin' it again," she stated.

"Uh, Krys, honey, Sunday freaked Bubba *out*. I'm not thinking—" Lauren started.

"I'll talk him into it," Krystal cut her off to say, her words like a wave of her hand.

"Honey, he was really worried about you," Laurie told her, glanced at me and asked, "Cone of silence?"

"Of course," I agreed.

She looked back to Krystal. "He got Tate by himself, Krys, and he lost it. Big, blubbering man tears. Tate didn't know what to do with him. All because he was worried with Breanne coming early something would happen to you. To the both of you. I think it was part relief because this happened with Tate after it was over. But it was mostly him getting out the worry."

For a second, I stared in astonishment at Krystal as Krystal did the same at Lauren.

Krys was the seen-it-all, done-it-all, fuck-the-T-shirt kind of gal. Not one who could be astonished by anything.

Then she straight up astounded me when I saw her face get so soft it was tender, love shining out of her eyes.

It was gone in a blink, like I'd imagined it, and she stated, "He'll have to man up. Bree needs a sibling and I ain't gettin' any younger." She lifted a hand, palm out toward Lauren who had opened her mouth to speak. "Don't worry. He won't be hard to talk around. Doin' the business that makes a baby is one of his favorite things."

"One of them?" I teased.

"He likes fucking a whole lot, but my man's addicted to blowjobs and that's me taking it in the wrong end to make babies."

"Good Lord," Lauren said to the ceiling.

I grinned at Krys.

She didn't grin at me.

She reached her arms out my way and stated, "Crock-Pot. You get on that, I can get my damned baby back."

I kept grinning as I got up, rounded her coffee table and gave her back her daughter.

I didn't straighten away for so long she looked up at me.

"Told you you could do it," I mouthed.

I didn't let her respond.

That was when I moved away, looking to Lauren.

"Crock-Pot," I said.

"Right, it's in my car," she replied, pushing out of her chair. "I'll be back," she said to Krystal.

"We'll be here," Krys said softly, her head tipped down to Breanne.

Laurie and I exchanged a happy look. Then we went out to her SUV and she gave me her Crock-Pot. I thanked her, making a mental note to add that to my shopping list of things to get for home when I had a kitchen (or after the painting was done, since I could plug it in in the laundry room, now my makeshift kitchen).

I then texted Deke I was leaving Krys's.

I went to the store, to Deke's trailer, and I got an electric charge (not quite like his kisses, bites, teeth grazing, mouth-at-nipple pulling, etc., but still nice) when I opened the trailer with his key.

I texted Deke I made it.

I started the chicken in the Crock-Pot.

And then I texted Deke I was picking up sandwiches and that I'd be home soon.

* * *

Surprise of surprises, walking into my house seeing Deke in white coveralls with a mask that had wings over his face, heavy straps at the back of his head around his man-bun, and noting he was still outrageously hot.

Bigger surprise of surprises, I hadn't paid a lot of attention when they were spraying the primer because I spent that time, to get out of the smell, in my bedroom or out on the deck. But it should have dawned on me spraying paint went lightning quick when they got it all done lickety-split last week.

So I stood inside my door, carrying bags of sandwiches, chips and La-La Land treats (the bruise under my eye wasn't gone, but it was gone enough for me to use concealer successfully, so Sunny hadn't so much as blinked at me—she and Shambles had just given me hugs and got me my treats while gabbling away like normal), my mind boggling because the whole downstairs was done, they were working upstairs and I hadn't been gone three hours.

That said, most of the walls downstairs were windows.

Still.

When my mind finished boggling, taking in the soft latte color of my walls and how it warmed the whole space, I saw Deke at the edge of the landing, having pulled his mask down to his throat (also hot) staring down at me.

"You all right?" he asked.

"Are you a wizard?" I asked back, swaying out a bag to indicate the space.

Another cocky grin.

God, the man killed me.

"Lunch!" I shouted.

"Right on!" Bubba shouted back, also in coveralls, mask at his throat, but no offense to Bub, he didn't make it hot.

"Bub, paper plates in the laundry room. Can you get 'em?" Deke asked as Bubba made his way off the ladder and Deke turned to follow him down.

"I can get them," I said.

"I got 'em, darlin'," Bubba replied and took off across the space.

I looked to Deke, having a weird feeling about Bubba's exit, which seemed pre-planned.

He finished climbing down the ladder and I slowly approached him as he not-so-slowly approached me.

"Is everything cool?" I asked.

He stopped in front of me and ordered, "Give me a kiss, Jussy."

I rolled up on my toes, he curled a hand around my jaw and we touched lips.

I rolled back and he didn't take his hand away.

"Okay, uh…kinda freaking here, honey," I whispered.

"Deck called."

Oh shit.

"And?" I prompted.

"Bianca and Anton Rojas left on a flight at ten thirty yesterday morning bound for Costa Rica."

"Oh shit," I said out loud.

Deke kept the information flowing.

"Thing that's sure was what freaked your girl Lacey's old man, Anton Rojas, when you knew him, had a very illegal business."

"Oh fuck," I breathed.

"Slow, steady growth, the guy played it smart," Deke shared. "When he got on radar with bigger fish who'd eat him whole, he made a wise decision that he didn't want things to turn messy. He merged operations with a very big player and took a mid-level management position."

"Tony," I said disbelievingly, because I could kind of believe it, I also just *couldn't*.

"Time in between, he worked his way up and he's heavy now, Jussy. He's also sharp. Everyone from the cops to the Feds know he's neck deep in some serious shit but they got nothing to tie him to anything."

"Right," I muttered just for something to say, totally flipped out at all Deke was saying.

"Now, they still got nothin'," Deke went on. "Those tickets were not bought yesterday morning. They were bought a week ago. Last Monday, precisely, the day after the shit went down with you."

I nodded, thinking this was not a coincidence.

Deke kept going.

"Anton's prints are in the system. Where they aren't is anywhere in that apartment. Only thing places him there is an eye witness and he's only one. No one else saw him or has ever seen him there."

"Okay," I said, again just for something to say because Deke stopped talking.

He started again.

"Sayin' that, no one saw Caswell go in. No one heard shit. No shell casings left behind. No signs of struggle. No mess like someone was getting out in a hurry. No one saw either of them leave. And no one can place those two there when Caswell was done. Outside the witness, who did confirm it was Rojas he saw entering the apartment, they got nothing else to put him there. Cops haven't approached Rojas's people but they suspect, when they do, they'll get alibis for him and Bianca. He lives closer to LAX. She could have spent the night at his place before they took off in the morning. Or someone could say that's the way it was even if it wasn't the way it was. And Bianca left clothes and other shit like she was coming back, just packing for vacation. Their tickets are return. They're set to come back next Sunday."

"Oh my God," I whispered, figuring my girl was going to step right into a shit storm when (if) she got off that plane.

Deke slid his hand down to my neck and bent closer to me.

"What I'm sayin', gypsy, is that good or bad, way it is right now, they got nothing to pin on either of them."

"Except opportunity and motive," I pointed out. "And them leaving the country right after the murder."

"Except that but, baby, that's dick without any physical evidence or eye witnesses. And those tickets were not purchased on the fly and they aren't one-way. They could say their vacation was planned."

"Caswell is linked to Bianca *and* me," I reminded him. "And his dead body was found in Anca's apartment."

"You're right," he agreed. "But just because she's got motive doesn't mean they can do shit about it. Deck says at this point, they don't even have enough to do anything but bring her in for questioning. She got bored, she could walk right out. They have nothing on either of them to hold them. As far as the registers go, your friend doesn't own a gun and never did. It's suspicious a known associate she owed money got dead in her apartment but that's all it is. By the time they get back, they'll have their stories straight, their alibis tight, and my guess, you'll hear from your girl who's clean and healthy and with a guy who does it for her. He's just a sharp-dressed man who's way the fuck dirty."

"So Tony is still playing it smart," I remarked.

"He did this, or arranged for it to happen, yeah. And to that end, Jussy, can't believe he'd even do him at her apartment unless there was a reason why. Could be he's settin' someone else up. Could be Caswell surprised them. Could be some other enemy was setting *him* up. Who the fuck knows? That's a loose end and this guy isn't about loose ends. He did Caswell there, he had a reason. We just won't know that reason until his play plays out."

"I don't know what to do with this, Deke."

"Only thing you can. If your girl was in on it, she took care of her problem, a problem she made yours. Not in a good way but that don't mean it isn't done."

"You're right," I mumbled. "That doesn't mean it isn't done."

But God, *what* was done was *crazy*.

"Jussy."

I focused on him.

"Likely she's never gonna share outright with you she had someone whacked, and there's still doubt, minimal but it's there, she actually did. She does, then *I* got a problem with her because that puts you in an uncomfortable position of keepin' your mouth shut about a felony which is another fuckin' felony. That swings your ass right out there in a way you got problems throwin' your girl under a bus *she* set in motion and doin' that gettin' you heat from whatever organization Rojas is running."

"God," I whispered.

"*She* caused this problem for you," Deke stated. "And her sharp-dressed man's got it together, no way in fuck he's gonna let her share anything with you, for her and, he cares enough to find you to call to offer condolences about your dad, for you. It's just done, baby, and you'll never know how it got done. Just move on."

"Move on from a friend having someone murdered for me?"

"Move on from some fuckwad breaking into your house and beatin' the crap outta you, choking you, scaring the shit outta you and you don't know dick about what happened after. But at least *that* shit's just done."

As totally fucked up as it was, Deke was right.

That shit was just done.

"A miracle has occurred. Something's actually put me off food," I declared.

He grinned at me, slid out his thumb and stroked my jaw. "You'll get that back."

I nodded, hoping that happened before Steph's chicken.

He bent and brushed his lips against mine before he straightened, moved away and yanked at his mask so he could pull it over his head, shouting, "Bubba, enough time!"

Yep.

It had been pre-planned.

"Thank fuck," Bubba said, walking into the room with paper plates, two cans of Coke and a Fresca. "I'm starving."

We headed to the ratty-ass furniture Jim-Billy rounded up for me.

Once there, I set about handing out sandwiches.

And there was me.

My bestie was tight with a criminal, linked to a murder, off to Costa Rica...

And I was doing the only thing I could.

Moving on.

CHAPTER SIXTEEN

Without You

Justice

I WATCHED DEKE haul his big body off his couch and head to the kitchen.

He'd cleaned his plate and was getting seconds.

I grinned down at my plate as I shoved more cheesy, chile chicken in my gob.

"My gypsy princess can also cook."

At his quiet words, I looked to him.

The Crock-Pot was steaming. The pot with rice at his stove was too. As was the plate Deke again had piled high.

"The recipe has four ingredients, not counting the rice," I shared. "It's hardly gourmet."

He moved back to the couch, folded into it and stretched out his long legs, his head turned to me.

"Not a big fan of gourmet, babe." He used his fork to indicate his plate. "But I'm a big fuckin' fan of this."

I smiled at him huge.

He watched my smile, his lips quirking before he turned back to his chicken.

But from the bent of our conversation, I decided it was time. Time to share what needed to be shared. The perfect segue into Deke knowing who the woman was he gave the key to his trailer so she could set up a Crock-Pot.

The woman he had to understand I was so he'd understand I was the woman for him because with each passing day it was becoming clear he was the man for me.

That woman being the woman he already knew.

The woman who was made for him.

"When I was eighteen, Dad did a huge festival in the UK. I went with him."

Deke turned eyes from plate to me.

"We stayed in Bristol," I went on. "Pretty harbor city on the Bristol Channel."

"Yeah?" he asked when I quit talking.

I nodded my head. "Yeah," I told him and carried on, "There was a promoter in the city. He really wanted to work with Dad. He took us out to this restaurant on the harbor, cool place, lots of windows, great views." I tilted my head playfully. "Though it was all boring to me seeing as, by then, eighteen-year-old girl who traveled everywhere with her rock star dad, I'd seen it all and knew everything. Very worldly."

"Bet you were," he said, his eyes crinkling with his tease in a way I'd never seen but I liked very much.

I drew in a deep breath to settle what that look and his tease did to the flutterings of my heart and kept talking.

"Opened the menu, didn't understand a thing on it."

His head cocked to the side. "Was the restaurant foreign?"

I shook my head. "Nope. Just everything was *gourmet*. It was like I opened that menu and it was one of those talking cards saying 'You are about to eat food that's way too good for the likes of you, for the likes of anybody, it should only touch the lips of God.'"

Deke gave me another smile with his eyes while he kept eating and I kept blabbing.

"I was embarrassed, you know, being worldly and knowing everything, so I didn't ask the waiter about anything because I didn't want to expose the fact I actually *didn't* know everything. Dad liked his food and didn't give a shit what anyone thought of him, so he asked. That was the only way I knew what to order. I got something that was chicken. I figured no one could really fuck up chicken."

"Let me guess, they fucked up chicken," Deke remarked.

I nodded, having a feeling I was at least twinkling my eyes at him because I felt them smiling.

"Yup. Totally. I took one bite of that stuff and my taste buds didn't know what to do with it. It was an explosion of flavors, not a pleasant one, everything trying to beat out the other. The sauce. The spices. The textures. It was terrible. I didn't finish it."

"Sounds shit," Deke muttered.

"It was," I confirmed. "Dad got something else and he didn't finish his either. Then after dinner we went back to the hotel and hung out, watching British TV. Rock 'n' roll lifestyle. Hard to beat."

That got me another grin but through it Deke just kept eating.

I kept blathering.

"There was a cooking show on, a famous chef, and at the end of his program, he had some celebrity in his restaurant kitchen for a cook off. The celebrity made something, a family recipe his mom made, and the chef made the same thing, except all *chefy*."

Deke shoveled more chicken in and did it watching me.

I kept talking.

"After they were done, they took the two dishes out to random people in the restaurant and made them taste test it. The celebrity made a chocolate pie. The chef made a chocolate hazelnut tart with some special crust and a dollop of some fancy cream. The random people tasted it. Everyone picked the chocolate pie. When they did, Dad said, 'Like that fuckin' restaurant. Stupid. Never overcomplicate somethin' that's good from the start.' And I knew Dad felt like me. It wasn't us that didn't deserve that food because we weren't connoisseurs. It was a menu that was a mess because it was created by a chef who'd convinced himself he was an artist above everybody, but actually, he had something to prove. All art should be accessible, even if the people consuming it don't quite get it. At the very least, they should get something out of it. No one is ever above it. If you think that, you're the one who doesn't get it."

"Jussy," Deke said softly, and I had a feeling he was getting me.

"But for Dad and me, it wasn't even about that."

Deke said nothing.

"We Lonesomes like simple pleasures," I whispered.

At that, he sat back and dropped the plate to his lap, his expression changing from warm and interested to closed off.

And it hit me what I'd said.

"I'm not saying that you're—" I started quickly.

"I get you, Justice," he interrupted me.

I leaned toward him. "No, I think you—"

"Babe, you think I didn't get you that first time you stomped out while I was buildin' your fire pit in those silly-ass boots to bring me coffee?"

I leaned back, not certain what he was saying.

Fortunately, it was Deke's turn to talk.

"There are folks who'd eat that chicken you ate, they wouldn't like it, but they'd say it was phenomenal just so people wouldn't think they didn't get it. Then there are folks who'd convince themselves they like it just 'cause, if they admitted they didn't, they think they'd be exposin' the fact that their lips are not the lips of God who deserves that kind of shit and they're sure their lips are the lips of God. And both those folks would look down on anybody who says they'd rather just have fried chicken because it is what it is. A whole lot better than some pretentious dish that tastes like shit."

"Right," I said warily.

"And you aren't either of those folks," he concluded.

I nodded. "I'm not. My dad wasn't. My mom isn't. Lacey appreciates good champagne and knows the difference between well vodka and top shelf. She'd still leave that restaurant and go get some fish and chips."

"I hear you, gypsy," Deke replied. "And what I hear from you sayin' this to me is you're worried we don't fit."

"No," I denied carefully. "I know we fit. What I'm worried about is that you don't agree."

"You aren't stupid," he muttered and my stomach dropped.

While I experienced that alarming sensation, he leaned toward me, grabbed the plate that I'd lost interest in and took it with his, dumping them in his sink. He then opened his narrow fridge and came back with two fresh beers. He twisted the caps off both, flicking them across the space. One hit the sink. One glanced off the side and came to land on the small counter.

I watched all this with distraction, not liking where he'd left it, not sure what to say next.

He handed me a beer before he put his to his lips and took a long pull.

When he lowered it, he also lowered his eyes to mine.

It was then I figured I'd instigated our talk and now it was time to get into it and get past it.

He just didn't say anything.

So I did.

"I am who I am, I do what I do and I can't change that primarily because I don't *want* to change that."

That time his head twitched as his brows shot together. "You think I want you to change that?"

I was now seeing my mistake.

I should have exercised patience and let him lead.

It was time to backtrack at the same time tell him where I was at so he could (hopefully) springboard from there.

"Actually, I think I just want you to talk about whatever it was you wanted to talk about so we can get it out of the way and go back to being Deke and Justice, the *new* Deke and Justice that I like better which includes orgasms, nighttime pizza and Butterfinger Cups added to our togetherness and banter. So I started this trying to explain that I am who I am, I do what I do but I'm still just the woman you know. I'm not anything else and I want you to go in understanding that in an integral way so down the line it doesn't come between us."

"It come between you with anyone else?" he asked.

I felt my face get soft.

"You've gotta know, honey, even before I got into the business, with the last name Lonesome, there were people who wanted to be around me not wanting to be around me, but wanting to be around *that*. That's why Lace and Anca and I are so tight. We all got that. And we could always trust with each other there were no ulterior motives."

"And you trust I got no ulterior motives," he stated, but in a way he wanted it confirmed.

"Of course I do."

"Babe, want nothin' to do with your money."

The way that was stated was not just a confirmation to my confirmation. It was almost harsh.

And because it was, it seemed borderline insulting.

"I know you don't."

"Want nothin' to do with your fame."

At that, my stomach clutched.

Money was money, everyone needed it and only fools would say life didn't get better in some ways the more you had of it.

Fame was something else.

Fame was something that, you got it, it was nearly impossible to shake. Degrees, maybe. But in some ways, it always followed you.

It was also something you could never control. It was an entity on its own, untamable, able to give good at the same time cause disaster.

You might not want any part of it, but once it was there, you didn't have a choice, whether it was yours or it was someone's you cared about.

And I knew with nearly everybody in my family having some level of fame, and having lived most of my life not actually having my own, it was harder dealing with it when it wasn't yours, but someone's you cared about.

"Those are both parts of me," I said, my voice sounding constricted. "I can't get rid of them, and like I said, I don't really want to. They come with the territory of not only who I am but what I love to do."

"You're not gettin' me," he declared.

I didn't want to be a bitch but he wasn't giving me anything and I felt it down to my bones that this conversation meant everything.

Absolutely everything.

I sensed Deke Hightower was my place in the world.

I'd sensed that all the way back in Wyoming.

So this conversation might be the most important one I'd had to that point or ever would have in my life.

Because of that, I laid it out.

"Well then maybe you should say more than a few words at a time because I was a bit nervous about whatever this talk was, honey, but now you're freaking me out."

We had been on opposite ends of the couch, but not far apart because the couch wasn't big but Deke was.

When I said those words, he reached out a hand, hooked it in the bend of my knee that was up on the couch and he used that to tug me closer so that knee was pressed against the side of his thigh.

And he didn't remove his hand.

"I'm not givin' you a lot of words, Jussy, because I don't know how to say them," he shared the instant he pulled me closer.

"I guess the only thing to say to that is to tell you that I like you, Deke, a whole lot. You know that but maybe you don't know how much. And how much I actually do like you, you should also know you can say anything to me."

He studied me a beat after I gave him those words before he opened his mouth to speak.

"Right, then, gypsy, you gotta know, it is not the fact that I drove up to work at the house of a woman who was the finest I'd met and saw police cruisers that put us here right now. It was the fact I wanted you before that and wouldn't let myself have you. And the reasons for that were not just because you're the woman you are, you got what you got, though, straight up, babe, that was part of it. It's because I'm the man I am and that's not gonna change either, and in my head, you're right. I was thinking we did not fit."

It was my turn not to have anything to say but it felt like something was crushing my heart.

"Then I saw those cruisers," he went on, "and I do not want your money. I also don't want the hassle that's sure to come from your fame. Not sayin' that to be a dick, sayin' it to be real but also sayin' it because I don't wanna have to watch *you* deal with the hassle that's sure to come from that. But seeing those cruisers got my head outta my ass about wanting you."

"Deke, this isn't really helping," I shared, no longer slightly nervous, I was downright anxious because he said this wasn't going to be bad.

But outside the him wanting me part—which I already knew, I just didn't know when that began—the rest just sounded bad.

And he was being weird, blunt, distant, and it was scaring me.

"My life, babe," he shook his head, "until I was about twenty, it was not good."

"Okay," I prompted carefully, not liking that.

"And because a' that, I got a way I gotta be and that's a way that's not gonna change."

"Okay," I repeated equally carefully.

"And Justice, bein' with you, bein' with any woman, but especially you, was likely gonna put the pressure on to change that."

"I don't want to change you either, Deke."

"I got no roots. I've never had any roots. And I do not fuckin' want any roots," he declared.

I just stared at him.

"And I do not like rich people. I do not wanna go to fancy restaurants, unless their menu is predominantly steak, more steak and a choice of sauce you can put on a steak, not that I'd ruin a steak with sauce. And I can go there not havin' to wear a suit, somethin' I don't own and never will."

"Right," I said just because he stopped talking but also because I couldn't say more since he declared he didn't like rich people and I was a rich person.

"No one has power over me," he went on. "And no one ever will."

I had nothing to say to that because I had no idea why he said it because I'd given him no reason to think I wanted that from him.

It was then he announced, "When I was fifteen, my mom and I were living on the streets."

At this news, my body turned to stone in order to conserve all its energy to battle desperate, miserable, soul-demolishing thoughts of the magnificence Deke and the mom he clearly loved a great deal, homeless, and I again just stared at him.

"That was on me. I fucked us up. I did somethin' seriously fuckin' stupid that got her fired and blackballed so she couldn't get another job. We didn't have a lot because she got paid shit at the job she had. She got paid shit, she ate shit and her life was shit until it turned shittier when I pulled my shit and our lives that were actually just garbage turned to full-on shit."

I kept staring at him but I did it feeling the wet hit my eyes.

"We got into a shelter, which was warmer than the streets, they had food so we weren't hungry all the fuckin' time, but the place still sucked. And she worked her ass off to get us out of there. She worked her ass off before we were in there and she kept doin' it every day of her life until workin' that hard killed her. Dead of a heart attack before she'd even reached sixty."

I could not believe this.

Hell, I didn't *want* to believe this.

But he was giving it to me, what Lauren had warned me I'd have to brace for, and she'd been right.

That said, it was no gift.

It was heartbreaking.

I felt a tear slide down my cheek.

Deke didn't quit talking.

"That was her life. My life, I started workin' at fifteen and I did everything I fuckin' could to take care of my ma. But when I knew she was set, decent place to live, job that was steady, money in the bank for a rainy day, I had to go. I had to get out and go somewhere where I wasn't covered with the shit of life and I could breathe easy. Between then and now, been a lot of places and there's only one place that happens. That's the road, Jussy. Only place I breathe easy."

"I understand that," I told him softly.

He nodded his head, his eyes on my wet cheeks but he didn't touch me outside the hand he still had tucked behind my knee.

He kept distant and he kept speaking.

"I know. You're my gypsy princess and you're a true rock 'n' roll gypsy. But what you understand, what made you a part of the road is not what made me."

"That's not what I meant," I said quickly.

"Tears in your eyes, Jussy, I get that you get me."

"I hate that happened to you and your mom," I whispered.

"Tears in your eyes, I get that too," he whispered back. "But it happened, baby, and that never changes. The road, it's in my blood not like you, born to it like you were. It's who I was driven to be. And it's that in a way it'll never stop."

"Deke, I don't get—"

"Come April, Jussy, snow starts thawing, weather turns, I'm gone and there ain't nothin' that can hold that back."

I slid away from him.

I had this reaction even though I knew this. He'd mentioned it during our night by the fire pit, how he'd take off, how he didn't stay put for long.

I just didn't know that it was something that might someday affect me.

I barely got an inch before his hand curled tight behind my knee and he jerked me right back.

"I go, Justice," he started, his voice low like a warning, "this keeps like it is with us, I want you with me."

I go, Justice…I want you with me.

More wet hit my eyes and didn't linger.

It slid right down my cheeks.

Deke watched it then looked at me.

"Think that's an answer, baby, but you gotta give it to me with words."

"I'd go anywhere with you."

It was then I felt Deke go solid as a rock.

"You make me happy," I told him something he knew.

But maybe he didn't *know*.

It was on the tip of my tongue to explain my poet's soul, to share that "Chain Link" was for him, when his hand left my knee. He bent to put his beer on the floor then he twisted to me, his hand coming up. He caught me at the back of my neck and pulled me to him. His other hand lifted and cupped my cheek, thumb sliding through the wet as he stared into my eyes.

"So fuckin' pretty, girl with all your hair, sittin' in a corner of a biker bar with her notebook, writing poetry," he murmured.

He was talking about way back in Wyoming.

His gaze shifted, watching his thumb move through my tears.

As for me, I was having trouble breathing.

His eyes came back to mine.

"You walked into Bubba's, you were different. Whole new girl. You'd come into you. Smelled the money on you, Jussy. Knew I wanted to tap your ass but was goin' nowhere near you because, I let you in, when I had to go, knew in my gut you wouldn't go with me and it'd tear me up, leavin' you behind, but it'd tear me up worse if I stayed."

"You thought that at Bubba's?" I asked breathlessly.

I watched his eyes grin. "Okay, maybe it was after your rant about buyin' me prime rib sandwiches, somethin' I'll note now, you have not done."

Mental note to take care of that ASAP.

"That first time at Bubba's, just wanted to tap your ass," he finished.

"You barely looked at me," I reminded him.

"Learned a long time ago not to look too long at somethin' you wanted you couldn't have. Served no purpose and only settled the shit in deeper that life was just mostly a lot of somethings you'd never have."

"Life's a lot more than that, honey."

He slid his thumb along my lower lip, not, I sensed, to shut me up.

Just to touch me.

And when he replied, he did it with gentleness, but the words still dug deep. "That right there, baby, is shit people like you say to people like me when we know more than you because we lived that difference."

It sucked, it sucked so huge it was impossible to process.

But I could not argue that.

"I don't want..."The words came out choked so I cleared my throat. "I don't want you to think you're a different type of people than me."

"Everyone's different, Jussy. That don't mean different is anything but that. Different. And I think we're proving that. And just to say, in order to make this shit clear we're talkin' about right now, I hope what we're proving keeps goin'. In other words, who we are might not fit but it can still work."

More tears filled my eyes and I didn't clear the hoarse from my voice when I said, "I hope that keeps going too."

"I get that, Justice. You haven't hidden you been into me from the start. Or, if you tried, you're shit at it."

That didn't make me keep crying.

I jerked my head back, my eyes narrowing.

Deke let my neck go but only to use that hand to grab my beer, put it on the floor and then he hooked me behind the back of one knee with his arm, scooping up the other along the way. He lifted from the couch as he did, taking me with him. He then dumped me on my back on the couch with him on top of me.

When I had his weight on me, his face in my face, he said, "Teasin' you, Jussy."

I wasn't in the mood to be teased.

I was in the mood to know for certain that Deke and I were where we needed to be.

Because I was falling in love with him.

And he'd given me indication that the same was happening for him with me and it was safe to say I loved that.

A *whole* lot.

But there were things unsettled, big things that might fuck up our future.

So now we had to get past that.

"So this talk you wanted to have boils down to something I already know, you like me," I declared. "And although you have some serious baggage in your life, stuff you lived through that breaks my heart, you're not letting it hold you back *living* that life. You do what you do and you want me to know when you get on with the part of doing that that puts your ass on the road, you want me with you."

"Pretty much, yeah."

"Something you knew I'd do because you knew I was into you."

"Yep."

"So I was nervous for nothing."

"Jussy, you're all about settin' up house. Can't say I didn't have a big fuckin' clue how you lived your life with your dad, all good with makin' home about him, that you get life on the road better than anybody. It still was not a given that you weren't done with that and ready to lay roots."

"So you were nervous too."

He grinned. "There was that, but mostly I figured I was good because you're really fuckin' into me."

"Sometimes your cocky is not hot," I snapped.

His brows went up. "There's times my cocky makes you hot?"

I didn't answer that.

He was sure of himself.

But I wasn't quite sure of *us*, what was happening in a future that I was hoping would be *our* future, and I really, really needed to be sure.

Or as close as I could get.

So I stated, "We've established you don't like rich people and want nothing to do with me being famous. I'm down with the road. It's part of my life and always has been. But, just to say, I didn't buy a house so I can leave it empty all the time."

"Settle in August, September, sometimes weather's good, October, Jussy. Sometimes that road comes with my trailer hitched to my truck so home goes where I go. Most of it's me on the back of my bike. Weather turns, most roots I got is me bein' rooted to Carnal for a solid six months. Sometimes more."

That was half a year.

I could totally do that.

"That's acceptable."

He grinned his cocky grin again.

"But you take me with you, Deke, just pointing out, the money, me being a Lonesome, that comes too."

"I don't have a crystal ball, gypsy. Cannot say however that hits me the first time it hits me I'm gonna know exactly how I'm gonna react. But I'm thirty-eight years old. I know the man I am. And this good we got keeps goin', it won't be about that. It'll be about you."

"That *is* me."

He shook his head. "Steph's chicken is you. Whatever went down with you and Krys in her Camaro is you. That isn't you. You now know the baggage I got that you've gotta put up with. That's the baggage you got I gotta put up with except part of it means you can lay down a load without blinking to buy a seventy-inch TV."

"So you want a future with me," I stated.

"No," he replied firmly, a strange look hitting his eyes.

It was a look I couldn't read, but it seemed unsure, and Deke never seemed unsure. So him giving me that answer to my question, that unsettled look in his eyes, my stomach clutched again.

But he wasn't done speaking.

"I'm gonna lay this on you and hope like fuck it doesn't freak you but you gotta hear it," he began.

I took a deep breath.

Deke kept going.

"I got a lotta friends I watched go down for the count and stay down because they like the feel of bein' stuck. And what I mean when I say that is they went down to the women they decided to spend their lives with. Watched that, dug that for them, straight up wanted it for myself. But I know the man I am and knew what that would take for it to happen to me. And never, not once, Justice, did I ever find one I even considered havin' this conversation with so the shit I'm tellin' you, baby, you gotta know up front not to take it lightly. And I'll share what I mean by sayin' that I don't want a future with you. Where I'm at right now, after seein' those cruisers at your house, is that I can't imagine a future without you."

I lay beneath Deke, staring at him, my mind filled with poetry.

Wither to dust, crumble like rust,
Only by your side.

Fresh air, cold beer,
Root myself in you,
Consider my life, you're all that's right,
Breathless to bring on the night.

Wither to dust, crumble like rust,
Only at your side.

Just what I need when I have everything,
The breath that I breathe,

I only get when you're laughing.
Chain links, worn jeans.

Wither to dust, crumble like rust,
With me at your side.

I could search 'til I'm done, 'til moon becomes sun,
To discover I know, you're the one.
There'll be only you, only you that's for me.
Through your eyes I finally see.
Holding your heart I can be.
At your side, I find peace.
Chain links, white tee.

Wither to dust, crumble like rust,
All I need is to be at your side.

"Jussy, need you to give me something, baby."

I focused on Deke.

He was watching me intensely and I still saw the uncertainty.

It was a thing of beauty.

God, he really, really, *so totally liked me.*

I lifted a hand and held it to his cheek as I whispered, "Please, honey, get off me."

Something passed through his eyes that I hated to see.

But I needed him up so I could give him something.

He angled off me and I wasted no time scrambling off the couch. I got my bag. I pulled my phone out of it and I dug in the side pocket to grab the wound-up ear buds I always kept with me.

I dropped the bag, plugged the ear buds into my phone and turned to him.

It took three steps to get to where he was standing, watching me, face blank, but I could see the distance forming. Perhaps he was confused at my movements but he didn't even want to give me that vulnerability.

He wanted an answer to the question he didn't pose but it was a question all the same.

One that meant everything to him too.

And I was going to give him one.

I got close, put my hand to his chest and put pressure on.

He was Deke so he gave me what I was asking for.

He sat.

I crawled into his lap and I saw relief strike through the blank as his arms started to curl around me.

That relief…

God, I was absolutely falling in love with this amazing man.

I lifted the ear buds, shoving one in his ear.

"Jussy."

"Shh," I whispered.

I put the other one in his ear, cued up my music, found what I needed and looked to him.

"Listen," I said, looking again at my phone, making sure the volume was right (because I could blast my music).

When it was all good, I played him "Chain Link."

Deke slid his hand up my back to curl it around the base of my neck while his other arm curved closer around my hip, his focus blurred and he listened to me singing in his ears.

I watched his face then I watched my phone and focused on breathing as the dot slid along the line.

When it was over, I hit pause and looked to him, lifting my hands to pop out the ear buds.

And when I did, he said quietly, "Heard that before, baby. Pretty song. You got a way."

"You were standing by a chain link fence wearing worn jeans and a white tee the first time I saw you in a biker bar in Wyoming."

The hand at my neck and the arm around me caused pain as both tightened with all the considerable strength Deke possessed.

I didn't share he was hurting me.

I stared in hazel eyes burning into mine and I whispered, "Told you, baby. Sitting there in that bar before you brought me a Jack and Coke, I was writing lyrics."

Suddenly we were up, me in Deke's arms, and I dropped my phone so I could hold on to him as he stalked down the narrow hall, doing it sideways to accommodate us both.

When we got to his bed, he swung me out so he was standing at the foot but I was on my knees on the bed in front of him.

"Get naked," he growled.

I stared for just a beat into the heat of his eyes before I hurried to do what I was told.

Deke didn't take that beat. At the end of that beat, his arms slammed into the ceiling of his trailer as he yanked off his freaking... *white tee.*

I started trembling.

Both of us naked, Deke hooked me at the waist, yanking me up so I slammed into his body and he was kissing me before he bent us over the bed, climbing in, taking me with him.

I went down and Deke came down on top of me.

I thought it'd go fast, be frenzied, rough, hard, deep, intense, amazing.

It was frenzied. Rough. Hard. Deep. Intense. *Amazing*.

But it was that as we took our time.

I got to drag my tongue tight against both his nipples (and more). I got his cock in my mouth. I tasted his neck. The skin around his navel. Grazed the insides of his elbows with my teeth. Touched my tongue to the lobes of his ears. Pulled each of his balls deep into my mouth.

Deke took in just as much as me.

We didn't give and take. We gave while taking. We took while giving.

And we were so into it...

No it wasn't that.

There couldn't be anything between us when Deke finally slid inside me, his cock unsheathed.

I held him close, I held him with everything I had, including holding his eyes as he moved over me, moved inside me, became a part of me.

The orgasm wasn't hard and soul-shattering, tearing through me.

It came slow, it lasted long, and through it, clutching him tight to me, it knitted Deke into every fiber of me.

Deke ended his with his neck bent, his temple pressed to the side of my head, his labored breaths sounding sweet against my ear.

"Wish like fuck, Jussy, I didn't stand you up."

I closed my eyes and kept him held tight.

He wanted that time back.

God.

God.

He wanted to know years ago I was a bear in the morning.

I'd wanted that too.

But now…

Now I was just fucking happy that there *was* a now.

"I wish like fuck, Deke, that I could erase the life that covered you and your mom with shit and you two had more than your fair share of happy, us visiting her at her cottage on a lake," I whispered back.

I opened my eyes when he lifted his head and looked down at me.

But I wasn't done.

"Though, that said, I'd do it so you'd still end up a travelin' man, because what can I say?" I gave him a slight shrug and a big smile. "I'm a gypsy."

I felt the beauty of his sharp bark of laughter all through me right before he took my mouth in a rough, hard, deep, intense, amazing kiss.

He ended it and kissed the mark that was still on my shoulder, except fading, and I wished he'd bite me again, had even thought about getting a tattoo of his teeth marks so I could have that memory of our first time, that mark that was Deke's with me always.

He slid out, rolled off and rolled me into him.

I rested my cheek on his chest, drawing mindless patterns through the hair there, staring at a wall filled with Deke's history.

"I wanna be a part of your trailer," I blurted.

"Say again?"

I lifted up, resting my forearm on his chest and looking in his eyes.

"The wallpaper history of Deke Hightower on the walls. I want to be a part of it."

His face got soft and his hand did what it did a lot. It trailed up my spine, and along its path, he tangled it in my hair.

This time he used that hair to pull my face closer to his.

"So I take it that's official you wanna see about lookin' into a future with me."

"Yep," I replied immediately.

"Fuck," he whispered, his gaze falling to my mouth. "No bullshit. Out there. Open. My Jussy." He looked again into my eyes. "Made for me."

I felt more tears sting my nose and combatted them by slapping his chest so hard, the sound cracked across the room and the surprise of it made him grunt and his body jerk.

I ignored that and ordered, "You have to stop saying shit like that because every time you do it makes me want to cry and now I'm thirty-four, I *am* worldly, worldly-wise and a little world-weary and as such, I'm *not* a crier. Except," I hastened to add, "when the man I like...*a lot*," I stressed, "tells me he and his mom were homeless. Then I'm allowed to cry."

He wrapped his other arm around me and hauled me up his chest so we were face to face.

He was grinning when he stated, "Can't stop sayin' it, gypsy. Honest truth. You seem made for me."

"You've said it. Sentiment communicated. It undoes me. Kindly stop because I can't handle it."

"Most women would like hearing shit like that."

"I think, me being the only one allowed to use your key and bring over a Crock-Pot, we've also established I'm not most women to you."

"This would be true," he muttered, his eyes again at my mouth, his mouth being where his hand at my hair was guiding me.

I pushed back. "Deke."

He stopped guiding my head and his eyes came to mine.

"Yeah, baby?"

"I'm being serious."

"So am I."

"If you don't stop being gushy, I'm going to have to write another song about you."

His eyes flared and he pulled my face closer in a way I couldn't resist.

"Baby, you think that's a deterrent, you are seriously fuckin' wrong."

I loved that he liked "Chain Link."

Loved.

Loved.

Loved that.

But it was time for more serious, that being him understanding what he just got himself into.

"The world finds out you're 'Chain Link,' Deke, I'm no Lacey Town. But still, just saying..." I let that hang.

"Justice, you felt the draw of me in Wyoming that I felt from you when you walked into Bubba's, you think I give a shit about the world knowin' that, you're wrong. When I say I don't want anything to do with your fame I say it so you know what we got don't got dick to do with that. That don't mean I don't get that you earned it and how you earned it. The things a man would be proud of his woman bein' able to do, know I'm proud of those things in you. It's just that a whole load of people know how good you are at doin' 'em too. And that worries me because some of those folks can think they own a piece of you. But mostly, it's just dead fuckin' cool that's a part of you."

God.

He was always just…so…damned…*Deke*.

I dropped my head, it collided with his jaw but was cushioned by whiskers, and I muttered, "Fuck, you're gonna make me cry again."

"Before you get mushy," he said in my ear, his tone changing, going low, "you protected against pregnancy?"

I closed my eyes. "Uh, not so much."

His hand still tangled in my hair wrapped around the side of my neck. "Right. Shit happens, we'll deal."

Whoa.

That was surprising.

That was it?

We'd just deal?

I lifted my head and looked at him.

"You got a problem with the Pill?" he asked.

I shook my head. "Only taking hormones when I'm not having sex regularly."

"Jussy, you're gonna be having sex regularly."

I pressed my lips together but still smiled through the press as I nodded.

Yeah.

We now officially were looking at a future together.

I guess we'd just deal.

He watched my mouth, his own lips quirking, but looked into my eyes when I quit pressing.

"You, um…protected against other things?" I asked.

"Didn't find her, that didn't mean I wasn't looking," he said strangely in answer. Then he went on to explain the strange. "She proved difficult to find. Still was lookin' and not about to bang some woman ungloved and pass on shit I wouldn't want her to have. This is good seein' as one day she just upped and walked into Bubba's." His hand (with my hair) shifted so he could stroke my jaw with his knuckles. "And now she's here and I got nothin' but clean to give her. And babies, if she doesn't get her ass on the Pill."

Babies.

I dipped close and touched my nose to his.

"You're doing it again, Deke."

"Whatever, Jussy," he muttered. "Get used to it." He then rolled me so he was on top and asked, "You bring the condoms?"

"Two boxes enough?"

He grinned at me.

"We'll make it work," he said, his mouth coming toward mine.

"Cocky," I muttered.

That was all I got out.

Deke kissed me.

The two boxes were definitely enough. Deke was a powerhouse in bed but he wasn't supernatural.

Still, I made a mental note until I got a doctor's appointment that we needed both locations stocked up so there were no worries.

Just happy.

CHAPTER SEVENTEEN

In Deep

Justice

THE NEXT MORNING, I got sidetracked from getting dressed to make the bed. Thus I had on my bra, panties and jeans while smoothing covers when I heard Deke get out of the shower, a place that was so tiny, no way we could share (the only strike against Deke's trailer). I even wondered how Deke could fit in there by himself.

He unusually didn't come right into his bedroom area to get dressed, but I was on a bed-making mission so I didn't look to see where he went.

I was busy fluffing and placing pillows when he came to me.

And when he did, he got right behind me, sliding a hand across my belly, slanting it up and pulling me to straight so I felt the heat of him, the hardness of him at my back before I felt something else.

Something cold with an edge that was scraping along the skin under the material of my bra between my breasts.

I looked down and saw the key Deke was positioning there.

I drew in a breath and forgot to let it go as tingles shivered at the skin there, over the tops of my breasts, up my shoulders, down my arms to sizzle all the way to my fingertips.

That was when I felt Deke's lips at my neck.

"Anytime you wanna set up the Crock-Pot, gypsy, or anything you wanna do. My space is yours and you're free to be here anytime you want."

That key was the key to his trailer.

The home he set up by a lake because his mom couldn't.

God, he was totally killing me. I knew it by the sting at my eyes.

Root myself in you

That was it. All I could think.

I wanted to root myself in Deke.

And it could not be expressed, even by the poet I fancied myself to be, how glorious it was that it seemed Deke wanted the same thing.

"Jussy?" he called when I said nothing.

"I'm gonna Crock-Pot the shit out of this winter."

He moved away but not far, only far enough to turn me into his arms again, this time front to front.

And when I looked into his face, I saw and felt that he was silently chuckling.

The breath I breathe I only get when you're laughing

"Crock-Pot is a verb?" he teased.

"It is now," I told him.

"Can you top Steph's chicken?" he asked with more than mild curiosity.

I could not. I knew one Crock-Pot recipe.

Plans for that day: Troll the Internet to find kickass Crock-Pot recipes.

"Not yet, but I will," I answered.

He was grinning but said through it, "We got a problem."

Problem?

There were no problems.

Another day had dawned where I wanted Deke.

And Deke wanted me.

And we were together.

There was no room for problems.

I felt the frown form between my eyes. "What problem?"

"When you're bein' cute, I wanna fuck you. Since you're cute all the time, this means I wanna fuck you all the time. This is a problem 'cause, when I settle in for the winter, I work and I work hard so I got money to hit the road when that time comes. And I can't earn if I'm not workin' and instead constantly fucking you."

I took this as good news, not a problem at all since I liked that he thought I was cute and I wanted him to want to fuck me all the time since he just had to breathe for me to want to fuck him.

To communicate that last part, I slid a hand up his back and pushed closer. "I think Max is the kinda guy who understands delayed start for morning nookie."

I actually did think this, though I had no idea if it was true. But if my theory was correct, that these mountain men had libidos that matched their good looks, his was as out the roof as Deke's. So I figured he'd not only understand that, he'd champion it.

Deke dipped his face closer and it had that soft look, that look I'd seen before. That look that right in that moment I knew I'd understand whenever he gave it to me. Which meant it was a look I treasured for more than one reason, because it meant I was cracking the nut that was Deke.

That look being the look Deke gave me when he was going to do something he didn't want to do. That being communicate he wasn't going to give me what I wanted.

"And I think that Max takes me on every time I come home," he said in a voice as soft as his look. "He pays good. He throws a shit ton of work my way. And he's been cool about all that's gone down, Jussy. But the bottom line of that is, I work for him. You bein' in a situation, he's gonna get. You bein' out of that situation, comin' out of it as my woman, he's not gonna be feelin' a lot of love that I'm bangin' the client and not gettin' work done."

I curled a hand around the side of his neck.

"Although I would prefer a delayed start, you're right." I grinned at him. "And you getting work done means me closer to having a kitchen where I can do more than kick the shit out of a Crock-Pot."

Deke grinned back at me, his arms tightened around me and I took his cue.

I lifted up on my toes as he dropped his head toward mine.

And he kissed me, as soft as his look, but wet, so also hot, and since he couldn't give me what I wanted—morning nookie—he gave me something else.

A long, soft, wet, hot kiss with Deke in nothing but a towel and me wearing no shirt but having the key to his trailer tucked in my bra.

It wasn't as fabulous as an orgasm from Deke.

But it was still a kiss I'd never forget.

* * *

Deke was alone upstairs with the paint sprayer, no help today.

But they'd finished the entire downstairs and one side of the upstairs yesterday. I'd eventually timed it, and not including setting up the sprayer, or cleaning it after, it took them all of nine minutes to spray an entire room.

Nine minutes.

That was it.

Awesome.

Deke at work, I wandered out to my deck, lit the fire pit and settled in with my phone.

It was early October, definitely chilly, but I was warm inside.

Warm inside because of what had happened last night. Because of Deke knowing "Chain Link" was written for him and how he'd reacted to that. And because Deke had shared with me his plans for the rest of his time working alone at my house.

This being, after he finished spraying the paint, he was going to lay the floors in my study, then hang the doors, finish off the outlets, put in the light fixture, install the baseboards—in other words, complete that room.

"Gettin' cold, Jussy," he'd said in his truck on the drive to my house. "Cold in the mountains can mean anything, including snow. You need a warm space to hang. Get that study done, you contact your designer today. Tell her to send the shit you ordered for that room. Boys'll be with me on Monday, work'll go a lot quicker. But you still got a few weeks before the majority of space is livable. You got another room, you can be inside, choice of change of scenery, close the door, you're all good."

That was Deke. Even in ways I didn't consider, he did and he looked out for me.

So I settled in beside my fire pit that Deke gave me, put my feet up on the edge so the pit toasted the bottoms of my cowboy boots, and I texted my designer that she could send the stuff for the study whenever she was ready.

Then I did what I'd been meaning to do for a couple of days.

I called Joss.

Surprisingly, since my mom was always busy, she answered on the first ring.

And she answered with, "Good timing. I'm at a photoshoot with Kenzie Elise, a woman who's decided to embrace the nonexistent rock chick within in the hopes of reinventing herself...again. A woman who also works my *last* nerve. And her manager gives me the serious creeps. So I'm not looking forward to today but I am looking forward to telling her she's gotta wait while I take an important call from my daughter seeing as it's high time you share with me all your Chain Link's talents."

Hearing her words I knew that I shouldn't have waited this long to call Joss. Like any mom or best friend (and she was both), juicy news like me hooking up with Deke wasn't something she'd be hip on waiting for.

And by the by, Kenzie Elise was an actress. Reportedly a difficult one to work with on all levels. Not Joss's usual client. She did musicians, mostly, not actors. But if someone was going to pay her, Joss didn't tend to turn any gig down.

We could just say she'd made shopping her living for a reason.

"You do know I'm not gonna go into detail about that," I shared.

"How 'bout you going into detail about how one second, the dude didn't know you and the next, he's so close to you when you're on the phone, I hear his voice like it's him on the phone?" Joss only semi-suggested since mostly she was demanding that I go into detail.

"It's a long story," I told her.

"The more I can make Kenzie wait, the happier I'll be. So spill," she told me.

I looked from the fire, turning my head to stare into the trees.

I had until April there. If Deke and I kept going as strong as we were (and stronger), when the weather turned, I'd be on the back of his bike.

That gave me a happy shiver and while having that I thought I had plenty of space at my place to park his Airstream.

Then again, if we parked his trailer here, we wouldn't have the lake.

I needed to give Deke his time at the lake.

"Justice!" Joss snapped, bringing my attention back to her.

"He likes me," I said softly, not able to stop my lips from curling up while saying it.

"You're likable," Joss replied. "Then again, you were probably likable the first second he clapped eyes on you again and didn't remember you."

"Well, uh…there came a point when he remembered me," I shared. "This point being before my drama with Anca's psycho."

"Let me guess, this was around the time you hit social media kicking the shit out of Ronstadt."

I blinked at the view before I turned my head again to not quite focus on my knees.

"What?" I asked.

Joss didn't say anything for a few beats before I actually heard her sigh over the phone.

Even though I heard that, she still didn't say anything.

So I repeated my, "What?"

"Baby, you sure this guy didn't remember you?"

I straightened in the chair at what she was insinuating and again asked, "What?"

"You know," she said gently and carefully, "there are those who can play the long game."

At that, mildly ticked, reminding myself that Joss had not yet met Deke so she didn't know what the hell she was talking about, I took my feet from the side of the pit and put them to the deck.

I leaned forward and put my elbow to my leg as I hissed, "That's not Deke."

"I hear you're pissed, Jussy, but I'm your mother. I worry. I have not met this guy. And you sound…" She paused before she went on, "I don't know how you sound because I've never heard you sound this way before."

This was because I'd never been in the throes of falling in love with a mountain man before.

Or any man, mountain or not.

I didn't tell her that.

"You think I can't spot a player?" I asked.

"I think he's 'Chain Link,'" she answered.

"As you know, he *is* 'Chain Link,'" I returned.

"And I think if he knows he's 'Chain Link'…"

She let that lie.

I did not.

"Joss, he's…" I shook my head and sat back, lifting my feet to the edge of the pit again, forcing myself to stay calm. "If you met him, you wouldn't say this kind of thing. He's not that guy."

"There are a lot of those guys out there, baby girl," she reminded me cautiously. "And they're all real good at making you think they're not *that* guy."

"Yes, and Deke's not one of them," I told her firmly.

"What does he do?" she asked. "Who is he? Because I know what you do. I know who you are. I know what you have. And some dude who works construction who knows that too can—"

I cut her off, informing her, "When Mr. T introduced himself to Deke, he did it as Bill."

"Holy fuck," Joss breathed.

Yeah, she knew how big that was.

"Unh-hunh," I mumbled. "And when Deke rolled up to my house the morning I got attacked, he saw the police cars and drove right back into town, right to the police station. And I don't know if they told him he couldn't see me or what. All I know was that I was talking to the detective and then I heard Deke shouting. Shouting for me. He was out of his mind with worry, Joss. The way you would be. The way Dad would be. The way Lace would be. I didn't recognize it when I ran out to get to him because I was out of my mind about something else. But I've looked back and he was *out of his mind with worry*. About *me*."

"Well, that's—"

"Beautiful," I whispered but spoke louder when I continued. "Romantic. *Amazing*. And from that point on, he barely left my side. He didn't even like me out of sight."

She was careful again when she started, "Justice, this can—"

I interrupted her.

"You know, everything I could tell you about him would support what you're thinking. He lives in a trailer. He's had a *way* tough life. He works construction and he's got a lot of skills, I figure he gets paid well, but he's not rolling in it. And as far as I can tell, he has that trailer, his truck, a Harley and some clothes, not many of the last, and not much else."

I drew in breath and kept at her.

"But that doesn't mean dick, Joss. Because I know he's a simple kind of man. He doesn't need much and life taught him not to want for anything because he wouldn't get it. He's not on the take. He's not setting me up to use me. He didn't remember me. He didn't know I was Justice Lonesome. All he knew, in the beginning, was that I was a rich chick setting up house in the mountains and he wanted nothing to do with me. But seeing as I *am* likable, I liked him and he liked me, he struggled with beating that back. When I got strangled, he lost that struggle. And now…now…well, now he knows he's 'Chain Link' because now he's mine."

He was mine.

I turned my head toward the house even if I couldn't see him.

God, I said it and I didn't say it wishing it was true.

I said it *feeling* it already was.

"So, what I hear in your voice is that you think he's the one," Joss noted.

"Yes," I stated, turning my attention to the fire. "That's what you hear."

"Girl, you gotta know, when this time came, I'd worry. I told Rod this progressed with you two and now he's worried. You can get caught up in someone and not see."

"When I first told you I'd reconnected with the man behind 'Chain Link,' you were excited," I reminded her.

"That was when I thought you might just be getting yourself some and before I heard what I hear in your voice. You might not have the celebrity of your father but you've always been a Lonesome."

"I didn't tell him my name at first," I shared. "Not my last, not even my first because I introduced myself back in the day. I worried he'd remember me and it'd be awkward, not to mention totally embarrassing he didn't remember me."

"He could still know you," she replied quietly.

"He didn't know me."

"Justice—"

"I'm falling in love with him, Joss," I told her bluntly and listened to complete silence on the line.

So I kept going.

"I was born into this life," I told her something she well knew. "I learned the lessons of Luna right along with Dad, and we both did it the hard way. Deke..." I looked beyond my deck to the trees, knowing what lay beyond was the town of Carnal, and shook my head. "No, not just Deke, these people, they're real, Joss. They know Dad. Some of them even knew me. And they've pulled me in. Made me one of their own. Took care of me when shit was extreme. For the first time in my life, everyone I meet, everyone around me is not about the Lonesome. I'm safe. I'm safe with them. And most of all, I'm safe with Deke."

She didn't reply immediately.

Then she did.

"Mr. T introduced himself as Bill?"

I drew in a calming breath, hoping I was getting in there, and informed her, "Before he left, Mr. T said that when the foundation of Dad was pulled out from under me, he was glad I found a safe place to land. He was talking about these people looking out for me. Staying up all night to stand guard over me. Pitching in to work on my house to make it so I'd soon have a home. Showing at my place to keep me company. But most of all, he was talking about Deke."

"I'd like to meet him," she said.

"And I want you to meet him," I replied. "Though that isn't going to happen soon, Joss, because me and Deke are just starting out, getting to know each other, doing this without Anc's psycho casting a pall over it and we need time to do that."

"Jussy, you gotta know, your mom and stepdad are not gonna be good with hanging tight while you get in deeper with some guy we've never met."

Okay, shit.

This was bad. Or a new kind of bad, maybe worse than Joss thinking Deke was what she thought he was.

This was bad because Joss was my mom and my best friend. That was a double doozy in the "look a guy over" business.

No way she was going to be easy to put off.

And when I shared how things were going with Deke, Lacey would be the same way.

So I had to nip this in the bud.

Immediately.

"And Joss, you gotta know, I'm thirty-four, not eighteen. I know what I'm doing and when it comes to Deke, *I know what I'm doing*."

The careful left Joss's tone altogether. "Justice, seriously. You've just told me you're falling in love with some guy I've never even clapped eyes on."

"Joss, if this works, it isn't *you* who's going to be falling asleep at his side every night. So you can clap your eyes on him when the time is right."

"The tone of your voice, the time is right right about now," she declared.

"The time will be right when I say it's right," I retorted.

"Girl, you hadn't even reached the age you could vote, not even close, before you declared every guy I dated had to have your stamp of approval."

This was true.

Shit.

"You're my mom," I returned.

Lame.

She caught the lame and ran with it.

"And you're my daughter," she snapped.

"When I did that, I'd learned my lessons from the nightmare of Luna," I stated.

"Yeah, I learned my lessons from that too."

Her point was well made.

Shit.

"Joss, I'm asking you, give us some time. Maybe come out for Christmas," I suggested.

"Are you high?" she asked, her voice rising.

Maybe I was. High on Deke. I knew no way Joss was going to wait three months to meet Deke.

"Thanksgiving," I bargained.

"Jus, stop."

I stopped.

"Marco is heading my way and he doesn't look happy. Since he has goons that are less Kenzie Elise bodyguards and more just plain goons, and they're following him, I think it's time to cut this chat short."

Too late for that.

And I got an alternate kind of shiver thinking about Marco, Kenzie Elise's manager. I'd never met him but Joss had a lot to say about him and most of it was creepy, but some of it was just plain scary.

"Okay, I'll let you go," I said.

"I'll talk to Rod. We'll see when we can pay you a visit."

At that, I sighed and requested, "Can you at least give us a few weeks? Deke and me time, and by then, my house might be set up to have guests."

"We'll see."

Joss was the coolest mom ever.

But still, like any mom, her "we'll see" totally meant "no."

I heard the door to the deck open and turned my head that way to see Deke coming out with a man I'd not yet met.

But he was clearly known by Deke, which meant he was a local, which meant his tall, dark hotness was off the charts.

And he was all those things, specifically tall. He was nearly as tall as Deke, though not as beefy.

"I gotta go too, Joss, I have company. We'll talk later."

"Right, baby, later. Your momma loves you."

"And I love you too. 'Bye."

"'Bye," she repeated after me and rang off.

I said all this with my gaze going between Deke and this new tall drink of hotness at the same time taking my feet.

"Babe, this is Jacob Decker," Deke said, getting close and claiming me with an arm around my shoulders, doing this then turning to face the man who was my private investigator. "Deck, this is Justice," Deke finished up the introductions.

I shoved my phone in the back pocket of my jeans, stuck out an arm, eyed him up as best I could without looking like I was trying to imagine him naked (it didn't take much to imagine, he'd be magnificent naked) and muttered under my breath, "Totally bottling the water out here."

"Sorry?" Jacob Decker asked, taking my hand.

I gave him a smile. "Nothing. Just cool to meet you," I said. "And cool to have the opportunity to thank you for all you did."

He nodded, giving my hand a firm squeeze before letting it go.

"Cool to meet you too, Justice," he replied.

"Jus, please," I invited on a smile. "Feel free. All my friends call me Jus or Jussy."

"Thanks, Jus," he muttered, looking between Deke and me like something was amusing.

Deke allowed him to have his moment of entertainment but it was only a moment.

When he was done allowing this, he prompted, "You came with somethin' to say, man."

"Right," Deck said, still muttering. He looked at me. "You got a minute?"

"I got a lot of them," I said on another smile.

"I don't," Deke put in. "Not to be a dick but got rooms to paint so let's hit this."

I looked up at Deke and asked impatiently, "Can I at least offer the man a seat?"

Deke looked down at me and grinned. "You can do anything you want just as long as I can get back to my paint and soon."

I fought an eye roll, lost and then threw out a hand to indicate the deck furniture. "Make yourself comfortable. I don't have coffee made but I could offer you water, Coke or Fresca."

"I'm good, Jus, thanks," Decker told me, moving to the loveseat which was opposite the fire pit to the loveseat where I had been sitting.

He sat.

Deke adjusted us and he also sat, pulling me down with him so close to his side, if it was possible, my hip and thigh would have fused with his.

But after my conversation with Joss, and getting over the hit of another mountain man hot guy, it was dawning on me Jacob Decker was here and that might not be a good thing.

So I asked quietly, "Should I brace?"

He shook his head immediately. "No, Jus. It's all..." He hesitated which took some of the meaning out of his finishing, "Good."

I didn't say anything, just held his gaze.

He took that as indication to keep going, thankfully, something he did.

"Okay, yesterday, a lot of shit went down with what happened at your friend's place."

I nodded.

Decker continued, "This bein' the fact that they got in touch with Anton Rojas in Costa Rica. He expressed alarm and concern about what happened at his girlfriend Bianca's apartment and shared that he and your friend would cut their vacation short so they can assist the police in any way. They're returning tomorrow."

So it was official.

Bianca and Tony were together.

And they were coming back home.

To a murder investigation.

"Oh boy," I whispered.

Decker shook his head. "Nothing to worry about, Jus, seein' as the police know Rojas's MO and knew this wasn't it so they started expanding their search. This included them getting a warrant to search several properties of a known enemy of Rojas. They got a big beef and it hasn't been quiet. These searches bore fruit. They found a gun that's a ballistics match on the slugs pulled out of Caswell."

"Holy shit," I murmured as Deke's body got tight beside me.

"This enemy of Rojas, he also known to be stupid?" Deke asked.

Decker looked to him.

"No idea," he answered. "Just know this guy also had a beef with Caswell. So this could be two birds with one stone, we just don't know who threw the stone. This guy orders the hit of Caswell to set up Rojas or mess with his woman to get to Rojas, or Rojas does the hit and sets up this guy. Doesn't matter. Rojas and Constantine both have solid alibis. Rojas's maid said they were at his place at the time of the murders, best she knows. She says they were watchin' TV when she went to bed at around eleven thirty. The timeline matches, plenty of time for them to have gone to his place after Rojas was seen entering Bianca's apartment."

Decker paused, like he was waiting for that to sink in, before he carried on.

"That journey from Bianca's to Rojas's takes an hour. The maid is live-in and her rooms are by the garage. She says if one or the other left, she'd hear. She didn't hear anything and even though they had time to get back there within what the ME says was the time of death, it'd be tight. This guy that's in custody does not have an alibi, so he has motive as well as opportunity, there's a reason why he'd do the hit where it was done and the police found the murder weapon in his possession. He's been charged and the case is strong. His attorney is already talking about a plea."

"So it's done," I said.

Decker's attention came to me and he nodded. "Yeah, it's done. Talked to Chace, DNA sample you gave is gonna have results tomorrow. LA's already sent theirs to the local lab here. They'll do the compare and Chace and me figure that'll draw a line under it."

I wanted to be relieved and I was relieved.

Kind of.

The part that made it only kind of was that this was way too neat.

Who murdered someone and kept the gun on his property?

Then again, what did I know? I wasn't in that life. Guns were expensive (I guessed). You probably wouldn't throw one away indiscriminately.

Then again, you committed a murder with one, that would be a discriminate time to unload it and do it in a hurry.

Deke gave my shoulder a squeeze so I tipped my head back to look at him, seeing his eyes on me.

"You okay, gypsy?" he asked quietly.

"It's too neat," I whispered my reply, not meaning to leave Decker out, just feeling freaked about saying it out loud.

"It is," Deke agreed. "And it's also what you said. Done. That's all that matters to you. The rest is not your shit."

I stared into his eyes, thinking that since we became friends, Bianca's shit was my shit. That was what being a friend was about.

But at the same time, Deke was right. When a friend's shit nearly got you strangled to death and someone got dead that might be the line in the sand of friendship that you didn't cross no matter how much you loved someone.

"The rest is not your shit, Jussy," Deke repeated on another shoulder squeeze, undoubtedly seeing my thoughts on my face, bending his neck so his face was closer to mine. "It's just over. Take that and move on."

I nodded like doing that could settle that idea in my head.

I also repeated after him with the same idea.

"Take that and move on."

At that point, Deke stared into my eyes.

This didn't last long before he announced, "Your girl gets back, reaches out, I get you've been carrying worry about her for a while. But gotta say, babe, straight up, I need you to tell her to stay distant. She made her shit your shit and whatever happened after that, it's over for you. But her shit was serious shit and she made that yours. So I'm not gonna be real receptive to her showin' and lookin' me over because I already know it's gonna take a while for me to look at her and like what I see."

At that, I bit my lip, not only at what he said but also at my earlier conversation with Joss.

Deke watched me bite my lip and through it muttered, "Fuck."

"Deke's got rooms to paint," Decker declared and we both looked to him to see him rising from his seat. We did the same, me giving him an apologetic smile that we'd left him out of the conversation as he finished, "And I gotta get back to my wife." He came our way around the fire pit, lifting his hand when he got close. "Nice to meet you, Justice."

I took his hand, shook it and replied, "You too. And, you know, for your efforts—"

"Thurston's covering that," Decker replied.

Mr. T always did.

"Great. Good to know," I said. "Thanks again. It...well, just knowing, however crazy it is, that Bianca's doing okay, it means a lot."

He gave me an intent look but simply said, "Yeah."

"Walk you out," I offered and Decker shook his head.

"I'll find my way. Take care." He looked to Deke and back to me. "And maybe we'll meet at The Dog, throw a few back not talkin' about hitmen, drug dealers or cartel members."

Cartel members?

Did that mean Tony belonged to a drug cartel?

Holy shit!

"Set that up, brother. And thanks for comin' out," Deke cut in. "Tell Emme she gets bored, she can come and help me lay Jussy's floor."

Decker gave Deke an annoyed look which, incidentally, made him no less hot (in fact, it made him hotter). "That's not gonna happen, man."

"She crawlin' the walls, pregnant and you sittin' on her not lettin' her do shit?" Deke asked.

"She doesn't need to do shit except take care of herself and give me a healthy baby boy," Decker returned.

"True enough," Deke muttered, his lips twitching.

I listened to this exchange wanting to meet Emme.

"Right, gotta hit it," Decker stated and looked to me, the irritation sifting out of his eyes. "Again, good to meet you."

"You too," I replied. "Take care."

He nodded, gave me a small smile, Deke a chin lift then he turned on his mountain man uniform boot and walked to and through the door to the house.

I watched him through the windows as he made his way to the front door the millisecond Deke gave me to watch this before he shifted so his big bulk blocked me, putting him smack in my space.

I looked up at him.

The instant he got my eyes, he asked, "You on the phone with your mom when we came out?"

Deke didn't miss much.

"Yep."

"Let me guess, you filled her in about us," he stated.

"Uh…yes," I replied.

"And that look you got earlier is about your mom comin' out here to give you her feedback before you get in deep with me."

I blinked.

"Um…how did you guess that?" I asked.

"'Cause you told me that shit went down with your girls and you talk about your mom like she's one of your girls and she knows about us so I figured one, the other, or both of them would be out to look me over."

Nope.

Deke didn't miss much.

"I think I've delayed her," I assured him.

"How long?" he asked.

"Maybe twenty-four hours," I said hesitantly, only half joking.

He lifted his eyes to the heavens and kept them there.

I pushed closer, pointing out, "Deke, we are where we are, you're eventually gonna meet both of them."

He lowered his eyes back to me.

"For the record," he began, "just in case you missed it, which I figure you haven't but layin' this out anyway, you're already in deep with me. I don't give a shit about them lookin' me over as long as I know you know that's where we're at."

I suddenly was having trouble breathing mostly because I wanted to laugh, cry, shout and maybe do a girlie happy jump all at the same time and the effort of not doing one (or all) was winding me.

So it sounded breathless when I said, "I know that's where we're at."

Though my response was more truthfully, *That's where I was hoping with all my poet's soul that was where we were at.*

Deke stared into my eyes. It took a moment before his warmed.

But when they did, he murmured, "Good," bent and touched his mouth to mine but didn't move too far away when he finished doing that. I knew why when he asked, "You okay with all Deck said?"

"Do I have a choice not to be?" I asked back.

"You can be anything with me," he returned.

At his words, I melted into Deke.

"And because of that, honey, I'm okay with what Deck said."

His arms gave me a squeeze.

I kept talking.

"But for the record, if I had the chance to look over Anca's guy and knew he was a member of a drug cartel, my feedback would be negative to the point of taking action, such as kidnapping and brainwashing just in case she didn't feel like listening. And I say that even liking Tony."

"Good to know you're not down with havin' a felon in the family," he remarked.

It was good to know that Deke understood the concept of friends being family.

I shared that thought with a big smile.

Deke enjoyed my smile for another millisecond before he kissed it off my face.

He went to work.

I went back to my phone, leaving a message for Lacey, doing this thinking I was glad she was on her tour. She couldn't drop anything to come and look Deke over.

Then again, I didn't want them to come not because I thought they'd see something I didn't see.

It really was just that I wanted time, just Deke and me.

I suspected I wouldn't get it.

So the time we did have, I was going to make the most of it.

Totally.

* * *

"Can I ask…?" I started, trailing off because with what I wanted to ask, I shouldn't have started in the first place.

It was late, after dinner of leftover Steph's chicken (just as good, maybe even better). After zoning out in front of the TV. After great sex. Deke and I were in his bed in the dark, me lying on his chest, Deke's hand playing in my hair.

It was mellow.

It was good.

I should leave it that way.

"Can you ask…" Deke prompted when I didn't go on.

I turned my head, putting my cheek to his chest, muttering, "Nothing."

"Baby, you can ask," he said quietly. "You can ask anything."

Yep. *So* falling in love with Deke.

"We're in a good place," I noted.

"What you're gonna ask gonna take us out of it?"

I lifted my head but only to put my chin on my hand on his chest. When I did I saw he was resting his head and shoulders up the wall behind his bed so I felt his eyes on me in the shadows.

"Yes," I answered. "Maybe," I went on. "Or I should say probably."

"Ask, Jussy."

"Let's just have a good night. I'll ask later."

"You wanna know somethin' about me, ask," he pushed.

"But we're mellow," I pointed out.

"Then we'll talk about whatever you wanna know and get back to the mellow."

I searched through the dark to find his face. I saw it, not clearly, but I felt the vibe was not upset, tense or irritated.

He wanted me to ask. He wanted me to know about him.

He liked my open.

He was offering the same thing.

And I liked that.

So I asked.

"You said you got your mom fired. You were fifteen. How did you do that?"

It took a moment before he rolled us, me on my back, his chest pressed to mine, his face much closer.

But that was all he made me wait.

Then he gave it to me.

"She was a live-in maid. We didn't have a lot, even before we lost Dad. But we had what we had and they went with it so she could stay at home with me. When he passed, they were also trying for another baby."

"Oh God, Deke," I whispered, unable to wrap my head around the idea of losing a husband at all, definitely not that young, not with a toddler in the house, not while we were looking to the future, trying to build our family.

"She didn't wanna work," he said softly. "Wanted to be at home with her kids until we got into school. They got together young. She didn't have a lot of skills. When he was gone, all she knew was that she had to do something that kept a roof over our heads and the only work she could find to do that was work that put a roof over our heads."

"Right," I replied when he stopped talking.

"She got that job and kept it for years. Wasn't a good one. Wasn't workin' for good people. We weren't like those TV shows where the help was a part of the family. We had our place, they had theirs and we did not mix."

I nodded, and I knew he saw it when he continued.

"We didn't mix but that didn't mean the daughters of the man who employed my ma didn't see me. They saw me."

Daughters seeing all that was Deke, perhaps with the understanding of all he was going to be?

This didn't give me a good feeling.

"Oh shit," I murmured.

"Yeah," he said, knowing I got it.

"Big, strapping, growing-up Deke, right?" I asked.

There was a smile in his voice as he tangled his fingers deeper into my hair and muttered, "Somethin' like that."

"Were they pretty?"

"They were cunts."

I felt my body stiffen beneath him at his blunt, coarse, offensive word.

"Treated me like shit," he went on. "Treated Ma worse. Until one of them got a thing for me. Then things changed."

Yep.

I got where he was going.

I also started to understand what kept him from moving on his feelings for me.

"She was into you and went for it," I guessed.

I saw his shadowed head move in an affirmative. "Went for it. I was fifteen, all about pussy. So she offered, I took her up on it."

"And Daddy found out and didn't like that," I said.

"No, Daddy didn't find out dick. She wanted more. I saw the error of my ways and backed off. She wasn't used to not getting what she wanted so she told her father I took her virginity. Said I did it without her consent, at first, but when he threatened to call the cops, Ma lost her mind. It wasn't like she didn't see what was happening. She didn't know where it went but she saw how that bitch was panting after me. And she had access to everything, including the girls' rooms. She got hold of her diary where that cunt laid it all out. So instead of calling the cops, he canned Ma's ass, kicked us out, did it without notice or severance and made sure she didn't get a job anywhere else, including agencies, and that was when the garbage that was our lives turned to shit."

This I wasn't understanding.

"And you think that's all on you?" I asked.

"Babe, fucked her," he answered.

"You were fifteen," I noted.

"Yeah, a fifteen-year-old kid who probably was a lot more worldly than you were. I knew better and fucked her anyway."

I shifted both hands to cup his jaw. "Baby, you were only fifteen."

"And I knew better."

Cautiously, I asked, "Did your mom blame you?"

"Fuck no," he answered immediately.

Of course she didn't.

She'd made Deke.

"She didn't because there was only one person to blame," I informed him. "That person being that girl for doing what she did. It should never have gotten that far."

"Right, and it was me who took it that far."

"You said she panted after you."

"She did."

"You return that?"

"Not until I fucked her."

"So it wasn't only you who took it too far. She instigated it."

"Jussy, I *knew better*."

"You know we had live-ins," I declared suddenly.

Deke said nothing.

I kept going.

"None of them had kids who lived with us but it didn't matter. We were different people, obviously, than these douchebags. I can't say we treated them like they were members of the family but this was because we weren't around often enough to make them that way. But that doesn't matter. You just know. You know there's a divide, at least with that," I said the last quickly so he didn't get any ideas. "You're just careful, not for your sake, for theirs. This is a job for them and it puts food on the table. You don't shit where you live and that goes both ways. But for her, this bitch who did what she did to you, an ending that disastrous, she had the greater responsibility."

I was speaking and while doing it, I was getting angry.

Really angry.

And I knew Deke was about to say something but I kept on talking.

Except it wasn't talking.

It had become ranting.

"And I can't believe she instigated that ending and sat back, watched it play out and didn't do anything."

"Jussy, she was sixteen and, like I said, a cunt."

I slid out from under him, sat up and semi-shouted, "You ended up homeless!"

Deke pushed up to a hand in the bed, reaching out with his other one to take the back of my neck in a firm hold before he replied soothingly, "Gypsy, it was a long time ago."

"It was whacked!" I snapped. "A, no way she should have gone there. I can imagine you were hot. You were even remotely as hot as you are now, I totally can see her wanting to go there." I leaned his way. "That doesn't mean she *should*."

"Jus—" he began, his voice trembling with what on that one syllable I knew was humor, but I didn't find anything funny.

"B, she couldn't control her base impulses, and obviously, I'm into you so I get that, still, she should have taken her shot and then let it lie. I mean, who accuses someone of fucking *rape* just because the guy doesn't want seconds?"

"Ba—"

"And C, she accused you of *rape*. Let's discuss that for a moment," I hissed. "I mean, what she did put you and your mother on the streets. But before she initiated that outrage, she accused an innocent fifteen-year-old boy of *rape*. What the *fuck?*"

Now I was definitely shouting.

Then I was moving.

Deke using his hand on my neck to yank me to him so my chest collided with his, he turned, flipping me over him so I was again on my back, but on his side of the bed, and he was again on me, but fully on me so I was taking a lot of his weight.

This silenced me, but it didn't calm me. I just had too much of his weight to breathe easily.

He took it off by putting it into a forearm but I remained silent because his face was so close to mine, I thought he was going to kiss me and I didn't want to miss that in order to keep ranting.

Unfortunately, he didn't kiss me.

He whispered, "You need to calm down."

"I'm not gonna calm down." I did *not* whisper. "This is despicable."

"Like I said, it was a long time ago."

"It could be fifty years, it could be two days, it doesn't change the fact it's despicable."

"Jussy—"

"You've been blaming yourself for twenty-three years," I declared.

Deke fell silent.

"Haven't you?" I pushed.

"It's on me," he said quietly.

"You're very, *very* wrong," I returned resolutely. "And my guess, your mother knew that. My guess, your mother knew just what a vile bitch that bitch was and she wished she'd been able to save *you* from that. So that makes what that vile bitch did even *worse*. Because you've held guilt for twenty-three years and your mother held guilt for not protecting you when both of you should have never been touched with that emotion because that *vile bitch* is a *vile…fucking…bitch*."

Deke said nothing.

I panted for a while, still pissed.

Then I realized he wasn't saying anything.

"Deke?"

"You done fuming?"

"I'm not fuming, Deke, I'm *ranting*."

"Right," more humor in his tone, "you done ranting?"

"No, I wanna know her name."

I felt Deke's body tense. "Jussy—"

"Tell me her name, Deke."

"Justice, it's long over. Twenty-three years. The damage is done and everyone's moved on."

"Except you who thinks that's on you."

Deke again went silent.

"Her name," I bit out.

"What do you think you're gonna do?" he asked curiously.

"Get Mr. T to find her and then I'll have a think and after I've had my think I'll activate Operation Fuck Up Vile Bitch's Life."

The bed started shaking because Deke's body was shaking because he was laughing.

Hard.

"I'm being deadly serious," I whispered and I sounded it.

He touched the tip of his nose to mine and whispered back, sounding just as serious (without the deadly part), "Fuck, you're cute."

On no he did *not*.

"Don't call a revenge-minded girlfriend cute, Deke," I rapped out.

He pulled away but only half an inch.

Then he stated, "Right, how's this for revenge? She's a cunt. She was a cunt when she was a little kid. She didn't grow out of that. And years later, when I went back thinkin' the same thing as you, watched her to find my way in to get mine back, I found she hadn't changed. She's got everything and she doesn't see it as bounty. She sees it as rightfully hers, and the more she's got, the more she wants. She'll never be happy. Not ever. Not with a man. Not with her life. So I took off and left her to her misery. And right now, lyin' under me is a pretty, sweet, cute woman with great fuckin' hair who digs me, is fuckin' phenomenal in the sack, and she's got more talent in her than anyone I've known or ever will. And she sees all God's seen fit to grant her as bounty. She doesn't expect shit. She lives. She works. She gives good to the people around her. And she gets that back. That's revenge, gypsy. I got a good life and I've had that for years. I made that life myself. She's entitled and miserable because she feeds off that and she'll have nothin' but that until the day she dies."

Sometimes it just plain sucked that he was so wise.

"I was thinking more along the lines of paying her stylist to make all her hair fall out and setting up her husband or boyfriend with a call girl and sending her the pictures, but your revenge works too," I mumbled.

"Glad you think that way," he mumbled back.

I kept up with the mumbling. "Though yours works, mine's better."

Deke's hand slid down my side, over my hip, in and he pushed my leg open so his hips fell through, doing this saying, "See? Jesus. She's cute and I gotta fuck her and I just got done fuckin' her."

"I support this option for our next activity because I have some residual Vile Bitch feelings to work out."

His mouth hit mine but when it did, he didn't kiss me.

He spoke.

"Just sayin', it wasn't actually me givin' you the option." And with that, I felt as he slid the tip of his hard cock through my gathering wet.

I suddenly decided I'd learned enough about Deke Hightower for one night.

"Are we done talking?" I asked.

More humor in his one syllable when he answered, "Yes."

"Then let's stop talking," I suggested.

Deke didn't reply.

He kissed me.

And we were done talking.

CHAPTER EIGHTEEN

Loss and Gain

Justice

THE NEXT DAY, I was in my truck on the way back from town with sandwiches when the call came in from Chace.

I took it, putting it on speaker, saying, "Hey, Chace."

"Hey, Justice, things good?"

"Yep," I replied, thinking that word was an understatement. "What's shakin'?" I asked.

"Callin' to let you know, DNA tests came in and they were a match. It was Caswell that broke into your house."

Everything had been pointing to that. But even so, I felt a profound sense of relief to know that was true.

That it was definitely over.

"You good?" Chace asked as I turned on to Ponderosa Road.

"Relieved," I answered. "So yeah. I'm good."

"That's good to hear, Justice. And was gonna call Deke but since I got you, Faye and me got a babysitter for Saturday. We're gonna hit Bubba's. She'd like to meet you. Maybe you guys could come into town and hang with us for a drink."

That pushed out the weirdness, even if it came with relief, and just left me with a glow because Chace was Deke's friend, he was going to call Deke, but since he had me, that me being Deke's girlfriend, he just asked me.

That had never happened to me before.

And it felt way nice.

"I'll talk to Deke but I'd love to meet your wife," I said to Chace.

"Great. You or Deke throw me a text when it's confirmed and hope to see you there."

"Right, Chace. And thanks."

"No problem."

"No," I said, my tone changing. "I mean thanks. Thanks for how you were at the station when I was flipped out. Thanks for working on this. Thanks for everything. It's your job but I hope you know how important it is. How much it helps knowing someone gives a shit, knows what they're doing and is doing something about it."

His tone had changed too when he replied, "It is my job, Justice. But I do it for a reason, me giving a shit is the reason I do it and the rest was nice to hear you say."

"I'll buy you a drink on Saturday," I offered, deciding it was time to get on to those cases of hooch, all around.

"I'll look forward to arguing with you about the fact you don't gotta do that."

I smiled as I turned on my indicator when the mouth of my lane came into view.

"Later, Chace," I said.

"Later, Justice. Take care and say hey to Deke for me."

That made my glow glowier.

"Will do. 'Bye."

He rang off. I drove down my lane and parked.

I grabbed the sandwich bag, the bag from La-La Land (Shambles had been in a ginger mood so it was ginger snaps for luncheon dessert, dee-lish) and hauled myself out of my granddad's truck.

I went into the house and found Deke in the study. A study that already had a full hardwood floor, the wood dusty but that didn't hide the beauty it'd have when it was polished. Deke was wearing protective coverings over his boots and squatting by an outlet he was working on.

He lifted his eyes to me at the doorway.

"Sandwiches," I said.

"Right. Few minutes, gypsy," he murmured and looked back to his outlets.

"Baby?" I called.

His attention turned back to me.

"Chace called. The DNA was a match for Caswell."

I watched the same relief I felt flare in his eyes so bright, I could see it even from a distance.

But he only said a soft, "Good."

"And Faye and Chace want us to meet them for drinks at Bubba's Saturday night."

"You up for that?" he asked.

I nodded.

"I'll text Chace," he said, looking back to the outlet.

It hadn't even been two weeks since my assault. Since my world changed. Since Deke, who had already been in it, came roaring into it, thundering my name.

And here we were, making plans for drinks with his friends like this was what we did. Like this was a part of life. Like this was the natural order of things.

I'd flown around the world and back again, the kind of girl who did that sort of thing and didn't bother to count how many times she'd circled the globe.

And twice, those meanderings put me in Deke Hightower's path.

It was clear that Deke thought it uncommon for someone like me to recognize life's bounties.

But watching him work on my outlet, the sandwich I bought him in a bag curled in my fingers, knowing I was going to share one with him, and by the end of the week, I'd have a study (though, for me it'd be a music room) where I could hang and stay warm because he'd made that so, I wondered how he thought I'd ever miss them.

* * *

"Selfie!" Lauren yelled. "Everyone, back of the bar."

The music was loud. Bubba's was packed.

It was Saturday night in Carnal.

"I don't do selfies," Jim-Billy declared. "I don't even do pictures," he went on.

"C'mon, Jim-Billy," Lauren cajoled. "I'm gonna send it to Krys. She won't be back in for a while, she's already stir crazy, and we should let her know we're thinking of her."

"Right, I don't do selfies but more, my ass doesn't leave this stool," Jim Billy retorted.

Lauren was undeterred, ordering, "Everyone, surround Jim-Billy."

Jim-Billy looked unhappy, but considering his ass actually *didn't* leave that stool, he was not about to vacate it to avoid a group selfie.

"Specific kinda torture, the genius who decided to put a camera on a phone. Fuck," Tate muttered but he did this doing as his wife told him.

I gave Faye, sitting beside me, a smile, not for the first time since I met her several hours before thinking that Lauren was the perfect match for Tate, Lexie's lush gorgeousness the perfect match for Ty's outrageous handsomeness, but Faye's redheaded sweetness was beyond the perfect match for Chace's lawman with an edge.

I did not know Chace and Faye's story. I knew she was the town librarian. I knew he had the same mountain man good looks that it seemed all of Deke's friends had (though his was the only one that was fair rather than dark). And I knew she was the one who'd been buried alive.

I hadn't thought about it, considering most of my interactions with Chace were during my drama or on the phone (after my drama).

But seeing him with his wife, I realized there was something different about him.

It had been Faye who'd been buried alive, but chatting with her, I'd noted that utter insanity seemed not to have touched her.

It was Chace who had somehow been broken and you could see the shards that had been carefully glued together.

Unless he was with his wife, who was definitely pretty but in a much more subdued way, not to mention a lot shier and more soft-spoken than all the rest.

But when Chace was with Faye, only then was he whole.

It was a beautiful thing.

And they were both so cool, I was glad they had each other. That Chace's obvious strength led Faye to seem completely unfazed by an event that would probably break most people, and Faye's clear but quiet love was what smoothed out the dents in a knight's armor.

I stopped thinking this when Deke claimed me with an arm around my chest, pulling me off my stool, shifting me and securing me in front of him, my back pressed close to him, Deke not a guy, I was noticing, who had a problem with having his picture taken.

Lexie pressed in at my right side in the same hold with Ty behind her. Lauren had handed her phone off to Tate, a good choice since he had a long arm. She then curled both her arms around Jim-Billy in front of her, Lexie sandwiched in between Laurie and me.

Faye and Chace got close at Deke and my other sides and Tate leaned over his wife as he held the camera out in front of us.

"Give Krys a big, fat smile!" Lauren yelled.

I had no idea about the others, but in our huddle, mellowed by several beers, in good company, it was not hard for me to aim my eyes at the camera and give Krys a big, fat smile.

I saw the screen snap a bunch of images before Tate dropped his arm and we all shifted, separating, the men going back to their drinks, the women forming a new huddle around Lauren so we could bend over her phone and check out the pictures.

But when I caught sight of the photos, my body stilled and I stared.

Everyone had given Krys a big, fat smile. Even the men hadn't held back.

Drinks and bonding in a nowhere biker bar in the mountains of Colorado.

Me right there in the middle surrounded by these good people, smiling huge.

Me.

Jussy.

There it was in that picture.

Proof.

Here, I was not a Lonesome.

In Carnal, I was just me.

I was just me, and in that instant I understood something that I was getting, but it hadn't quite come to me.

After a lifetime as a gypsy, I'd found home.

"I'm so totally printing this out, framing it and putting it up behind the bar," Lauren declared then her gaze came to me. "If you're cool with that, Jus."

Not only taken out of my thoughts, also taken aback by her saying that, I asked, "Why wouldn't I be?"

"Don't want to raise a profile you want to keep low," she replied.

Good people.

Surrounding me.

Home.

"I'm totally cool with being a part of this bar, Laurie," I said quietly. "And can you text those to me?" I asked, not sharing I wanted them not only because I dug those pictures, me surrounded by friends, but also because they were the first pictures taken of Deke and me.

"Sure," she replied.

"Me too," Lexie put in.

"And me," Faye added.

Laurie bent to her phone, mumbling, "On it."

"Cool, thanks, Laurie," I murmured, intent on moving back to my beer, and Deke, who had been standing behind me while I sat on my stool gabbing to Faye on one side, Jim-Billy on the other, Lexie beyond Jim-Billy. Deke had been standing in a man cluster, talking with Ty and Chace, as well as Tate, when he wasn't with Lauren working the back of the bar.

I got close to my man. Putting my hand on his waist, I circled him from behind, trailing that hand along the small of his back in order not to interrupt the conversation he'd returned to with Chace and Ty.

And as I did, he automatically lifted his other arm high so I could duck under it. When I made it to his other side, still with his attention on the men, he curled his arm around my shoulders, pulling me in for a sideways hug before he released me so I could hit my seat.

All this participating in a chat with his buds.

But doing it managing to let me know he knew I was close. He liked me close. And he wanted me to know that.

And when I took my stool, he shifted into me so I could use his long body as a seat back then I felt his hand weave through my hair and come to rest, lightly fisted, on my shoulder.

This wasn't claiming. Deke did not have to claim me around these people.

This was entirely affectionate.

This was just Deke being Deke.

I felt Faye climb up on her stool beside me but I didn't look to her. I memorized the feel of Deke behind me, his hand in my hair, thinking for me, but also for Deke, that we came easy. That this came easy. That the lives we'd led brought him to me so he could give me this easy.

But more, so I could give that back.

On this thought, I felt something funny, lifted my gaze and caught Tate's eyes on my shoulder where Deke's hand lay.

He must have sensed he had my attention because I'd barely looked at him before his gaze came to me.

He did not smile. He did not lift his chin. His face didn't soften. He looked reflective, actually borderline brooding. And when he looked in my eyes, he didn't wipe any of that to hide it.

From what Deke had said, it was clear of all these folks, he was tightest with Tate.

And that look, I knew, was the look I could not see that Joss had when she was talking to me on the phone about her concerns I was getting in deep with Deke.

Catching Tate's eyes, knowing this, I didn't know what to do. I'd never been on the receiving end of a guy looking over the chick his best bud was into, wondering if she was right. Wondering if she'd make his friend happy. It had always been me that had to be cautious, my loved ones a hundred times more cautious than me.

But I was rich. I was famous. I was settling into a big house in the mountains.

And none of that fit with the man who was Deke.

My guy was thirty-eight-years-old and he'd looked, he'd been open to it, and he'd waited for the right woman who fit into his life as he liked to live it.

Tate was sharp. Tate was a man who cared about the people who meant something to him.

So Tate knew that.

He just didn't know how I fit.

I didn't suspect dudes had in-depth conversations about the women they chose to make their own, so Deke wouldn't be sharing this with him.

And I knew there was no way for me to put Tate's mind at ease. I couldn't say anything that would make him know how I felt whenever I made Deke laugh. How I felt sitting right there, Deke's hand on me, Deke doing something so casually thoughtful as positioning his body so I'd be more comfortable on a barstool.

I could not give him a big cocky smile. It was way too much to put in a look. And there were no words I could say that would put his mind at ease that I not only had this, it was beginning to mean everything to me.

The only thing I could do was sit there and hold his eyes, accept his challenge and walk the walk to give Tate the things he needed to know that I not only meant to make Deke happy, I was made to do it.

For the first time in my life, I had something to prove.

And staring into Tate's eyes, I was intent on proving it.

I knew he understood his challenge was accepted when he reached out a hand and rapped his knuckles once on the bar in front of me before he broke eye contact and moved away.

Yes, Tate was sharp.

And Deke had good friends.

I had thought they were coming to be mine. Hell, Lauren wanted me in that photo at the back of the bar.

But I knew then I still had to earn it from all of them.

And I was going to accept that challenge too.

* * *

Late that night, Deke opened the door to my house and moved in in front of me.

He had a habit of this, both house and trailer.

It wasn't ungentlemanly. I knew that by the way he blocked the door so I couldn't get in and he didn't shift aside until he'd done a scan of either space with his eyes.

This he did right then before he got out of my way by turning to the alarm control panel and punching in the code.

I closed the door, locked it and was caught by Deke with a hand at my neck.

I looked up at him, mellow, not tipsy, but I had a sweet buzz on that meant our next activities were going to rock.

Sex with Deke with a sweet buzz?

I couldn't wait.

I must have communicated this to him in some way because his lips quirked and his eyes heated before he muttered, "Gonna turn off the lights. Meet you in the bedroom, yeah?"

I nodded. "Yeah, honey."

He bent deep and brushed his lips against mine before he let me go.

He moved to the study, which was done, but my furniture and the rest of the stuff that I'd chosen for that room wasn't going to start getting there until Wednesday.

But still, that room was fab, it was ready and waiting for me to make it into my music room where I could work the laidback way I liked to do that and it was just one more thing Deke had given to me.

These thoughts in mind, I moved through the space that now had a partial floor laid because Deke had finished the study mid-morning Friday, Bubba had been in that day, and Deke didn't mess around. Bubba didn't either.

Deke and Max had both told me that, with the added crew starting on Monday, it still would take at least two, maybe three weeks to finish the rest of the house. There was a kitchen to install. Acres of floor. Stairs. Bathrooms. The chimney hood.

And as I wandered to my room, it was the first time I thought I could wait. I could wait to have it all.

And I could do this because getting it in two to three weeks meant it would no longer be just me and Deke.

Then again, as the days got colder and shorter, cuddling with Deke by an inside fire after having eaten some magnificent Crock-Pot recipe I'd made for us wouldn't suck.

I hit my room, lifted the strap of my bag over my head and went to a nightstand. I twisted the light on but only to a dim glow, moved to the dresser, dropped my purse to it but did this only after I pulled my phone out.

I engaged it, went to my texts and saw Lauren had sent me four versions of our group selfie, only slight nuances of differences in each, in all of them I was surrounded by people that were coming to be my people and smiling.

I had it, it was within my grasp. Hell, I was holding the evidence of it in my hand.

My less that was more.

I was living it and all I had to do was take care of it, nurture it, make it stronger.

Then it always would be mine.

Everything I'd ever wanted.

My place in this universe.

And it felt amazing.

So much so, my thumb started to move over the picture in order to save it to my phone so I could forward it to my dad and do what I always did with Dad. A habit. The habit we both had.

The habit he'd taught me because he'd started it, sitting under stars, on tour buses, in dressing rooms, whenever we had a quiet moment.

And when our lives led us separate ways, we kept at it with texts, sending photos.

Sharing our blessings.

My thumb stopped and I felt a sharp stab of pain pierce clean through my heart.

I lifted my head, turning it to look into the night. All I could see was the faintly filtered silvering of moonlight on pine trees.

My feet took me to the light on the nightstand I'd switched on so I could turn it off.

They then took me to the windows and I stared into the dark.

And for the first time since he passed, having held it back, unable to cope, terrified it would crush me, the full weight of his loss bore down on me as images assailed me.

These images were photos that would never be taken, all of them chasing themselves in quick succession through my mind.

Dad on my deck, the fire pit blazing, a big smile on his face, his feet up on the flagstone, a guitar on his lap, pads of his fingers on the frets, the other hand to the strings.

Dad in the morning—his morning, like mine, that being late morning—slouched over the marble I'd chosen for a countertop for the kitchen island. His hair a mess, his face creased with sleep, the fingers of one hand hooked through the handle of a coffee mug, his other arm wrapped around the hips of Dana, who always stood close to Dad like Deke had that night stood close to me.

Dad in my study, making music with me.

Dad at Bubba's, telling stories of the road, making everybody laugh.

Dad at my dining room table, shoveling Thanksgiving turkey and stuffing into his mouth, his favorite holiday, his favorite meal.

Dad sitting on one of the couches I'd ordered for the great room, a bottle of beer in his hand, Dana curled into his side, his eyes across the space, a smile on his face.

This smile would not be aimed at me.

It would be aimed at Deke, who I was curled into on our own couch.

It would be a smile of male camaraderie. A smile of happiness. The smile a dad would have that I'd never see. A smile he'd have safe in the knowledge his only daughter had found the man who'd make her happy until she was no longer breathing.

A hand touched my waist lightly and, caught up in these images, I gave a slight twitch in surprise at the touch when Deke called softly, "Baby?"

I stared into the dark, into trees my father would never wander through, not able to see through the dark to the river that he would have sat on the deck, listened to and known peace.

"That night, back when, when we were in Wyoming," I spoke to the window, "before I saw you at that fence, I was moving out of the bar to get some air. To take a breather. Get away from my thoughts or maybe give into them because my head was fucked up and I needed to clear it. Or at least sort it out."

I felt Deke get close to my back, felt his words stir the top of my hair, heard in his tone that he felt my vibe and was falling into it, so I knew he'd bent to me there when he asked, "How was your head fucked up?"

It would be hard to share this, especially with Deke, all I'd had, all he didn't.

But even knowing it would be hard, deep inside I knew he'd get it.

"It sounds bad," I told him. "I know it does. But that doesn't make it any less true that at that bar, I'd begun to realize that in all I had, I didn't have what I wanted."

I shook my head, still staring at the night, Deke's hand moving from my waist to my belly, his other arm wrapping around my ribs below my breasts.

I felt his chin hit my shoulder and I kept talking.

"The thing is, it wasn't about what I wanted. It was about what I needed."

"Yeah?" he asked when I didn't go on.

"Yeah," I said. "I had it all. I was uneasy because I had it all in a way I had it but I wanted something else. Something more. And I was uneasy because it felt like I was being ungrateful. All I had, all I could get, and I wanted more."

Deke's hold on me tightened. "Did you know what you wanted?"

I nodded to the night and answered, "Less."

His deep voice had been restful, quiet.

He sounded puzzled when he asked, "Say again?"

I curled my fingers tight on the phone I was still holding, lifting my free hand to trail Deke's forearm, over his wrist, until I could lace my fingers with his.

Then I repeated, "I wanted less."

"You wanted less," Deke murmured, and I knew he still didn't understand.

"Less is more," I told him. "You can have it all, but if you don't have the things that are important, you don't really have anything."

I felt his fingers tighten in mine but he didn't say anything.

"I had good friends. A good family. But I didn't have…"

You.

I left the word unsaid.

Deke kept tight hold on my hand.

"I have it all now," I whispered, the words thick. "I have it all and he'll never know. He'll never see. He'll never get that peace knowing his girl has everything."

There was a beat of silence, it was heavy, weighing further down on me before Deke asked gently, "You talkin' about your dad, baby?"

I nodded, my throat sounding clogged when I said, "And the fuck of it is, I found it *because* I lost him. I found it because losing him meant I needed to find my peace in a world without him in it. But I got more than that. I got my less that's more. I found my place. I found my oasis. I found home. I found where I'd be safe and looked after. I found peace. And he'll never know."

Deke made no reply.

But he didn't let me go.

He held me to him, my fingers laced with his as I stared into the night, and he did this for a long time.

Then he lifted his chin from my shoulder and put his lips to my ear.

"Come to bed, Jussy."

I nodded again and Deke let me go.

He moved. I moved.

I had shit on my mind, and as I put on my pajamas, more shit crowded in.

Like he said we would, and I knew we would (which was why I had a doctor's appointment the next week), Deke and I had sex regularly. Always before we went to sleep. Most of those times we did it then we cuddled and chatted and did it again. There were times, rare and only happening when we spent the night at my place where I could go back to sleep when we were done and not have to get up and get in Deke's truck to come to my place, he woke me early in the morning and took us there.

But right then, I was not in the mood.

Right then, I was coping with a clash of emotions I was having difficulty processing.

Loss and gain.

Profound joy and acute sorrow.

Feeling this, all I wanted to do was climb in a warm bed, try and hold on to the remnants of that mellow buzz I was quickly losing and go to sleep, wake up with that all gone and face a new day when I had the energy to bury the bad again and focus on the good.

What I didn't want to do was have sex with Deke.

I wanted to hold tight to my big, warm teddy bear that came in the form of a mountain man and use his strength to take me where I needed to be.

But Deke might have other ideas. He always had other ideas. Ideas I'd always had too. And I didn't know what I'd do if he acted on those ideas or how I'd feel if he tried.

I climbed into bed, unsure how to share what I needed to share, equally uncertain how he'd take that, and scared of how I'd feel if his reaction wasn't what I needed it to be.

Then I lay in bed, Deke claiming me, turning my back to his front. He curled into me, yanking the covers up to my shoulder then burying his face in the back of my hair.

And like that, he held me. His hands didn't wander. His lips didn't search for anything. I didn't even feel the hardness of his cock against my ass.

He was just Deke, sensing and then giving me what I needed.

And doing it, he opened that place inside me. That place I'd closed after I lost it the day I heard Dad had died, needing to shut it away so it wouldn't crush me. That place where I'd buried everything and turned into Deke after I'd been assaulted. That place where I didn't go when I found out one of my best friends might be pulling her shit together, but she was doing it with someone who was not the man I'd want her to have, so much so, her future terrified me.

It started with my body rocking.

The sob came only when Deke's arm around my waist slanted up so he could curl his fingers around the side of my neck and whisper into the back of my hair, "Let that shit out, gypsy."

God, *God*.

I hoped I was made for him.

Because he sure as fuck was made for me.

I lifted both hands and curled my fingers around his strong wrist and did what he invited me to do.

I let go.

He didn't turn me into him. He didn't say words that might soothe me and I was glad because there were no words to soothe me.

No.

Deke just held me while I cried, first for the monumental loss of my dad and all he'd never see, all the things that would happen without him being with me.

Walking me down the aisle. Holding his grandchildren. Meeting the man who'd been made for me.

And then I cried for Bianca, how she'd been cast adrift a long time ago by parents so caught up in their own shit, they didn't notice she had no anchor. How Lace and me, Dad and Joss had tried to keep her on course, steady, loved, and how we'd failed and now…

Now…

Now she'd found her course but it was just as stormy.

Then I cried for all I'd gained, all of it encompassed in the big, warm body curled close and holding me.

This meant I cried a really long fucking time.

Eventually, the sobs tapered into hitches.

And through it all, Deke kept holding me.

Finally, I quieted.

And Deke kept holding me.

I drew in breath and burrowed backward.

Deke kept holding me.

The dark room was quiet and I blinked slowly, exhausted by my tears, my eyes losing focus on the silver of moonlight on my sheets.

"Better?" Deke whispered.

"Yeah, honey," I whispered back.

"Been through a lot. You've needed to let go for a while. Good you did that, gypsy."

I drew in a soft breath. It broke twice as it came in.

It flowed out easily.

He didn't think I was weak.

He didn't think anything but giving me what I needed.

I bent my head and kissed the apple of his palm.

He followed my movement, keeping close, his face in my hair.

"Sleep, Jussy."

"Okay, Deke."

His fingers still at my neck gave me a squeeze but otherwise he didn't move.

And I lay in bed while the silver of moonlight vanished, giving way to sleep.

But I fell into it knowing one thing.

There was no falling in love with a man like Deke.

If you had him, he had that.

And I had him.

So he had that from me.

* * *

When I woke, I felt bright sunlight on my eyelids, so I took it slow in opening them.

After a couple of blinks, I saw sheets and sun and trees.

But all I felt was Deke.

We hadn't moved in sleep, except his arm was no longer slanted up, fingers curled around my neck. It was resting heavily along my waist.

I attempted a small stretch of my back, not wanting to wake him if he was still asleep.

"You up, gypsy?"

He was not asleep.

And God, I loved his voice in the morning.

Or any time, really.

I turned in the curve of his arm and he straightened his legs for me so I could press in, front to front.

I tipped my head back and looked at his face.

He was awake but the life he'd lived that he normally wore on his face was still smoothed out. There was a tranquility there I wished I could give him so he had that look throughout the day. So he felt that serenity every second he was awake.

An impossibility.

I still wished I had it in me to give him that every breath he would take, even when he was awake.

"You doin' okay this mornin', Jussy?" he asked quietly.

I nodded, tangling my legs in his, pushing closer. "Thanks for last night, Deke."

He dropped his head and I felt him run the tip of his nose along mine, from the bridge between my eyes all the way to the end.

I closed my eyes at the marvel of how this big, rough man could give so much with a simple touch, and when he pulled back, I dipped in and pressed my face into his throat.

"You wanna get up, shower, go someplace and find breakfast?" he asked the top of my head.

He was still being cool with me. Giving me the affection I needed after my emotion last night. Not doing what I suspected he wanted to do on a morning when we had time, no work to get to, nothing.

I drew in breath and slid my hand over his waist, to his back, up his spine as I touched my lips to the base of his throat.

Once I'd done this, I answered, "Later."

He got me and I knew this when his hand moved too, under my cami and down, so just his fingertips were inside the waistband of my pajama bottoms.

"Watcha want now, baby?" he murmured.

I pressed my breasts to his chest and slid my lips up his throat.

In response, his hand glided fully into my pajama bottoms.

"Anniversary fuck," he mumbled.

I tipped my head back and caught his eyes. "Sorry?"

"Last night, Jussy," he started, "we're a week old."

He was keeping track.

That was sweet.

But I thought back, my attention turning vague, as I said, "Seems longer."

I lost the vague when Deke replied, "Figure we can celebrate a lot of different anniversaries. Wyoming. You walkin' into Bubba's. Me walkin' into your house. First night we slept in the same bed."

I felt my lips curve. "That's a wide variety of anniversary fucks."

He rolled into me, his eyes dropping to my mouth, his lips muttering, "Absolutely."

Feeling his gaze on my mouth, I was done talking.

So I lifted my head and kissed him.

It was a soft, warm morning kiss.

Until Deke slanted his head and it was no longer that but instead a deep, wet, start-of-foreplay kiss.

When he ended it, his mouth went to my neck.

My hands drifted all over.

His hands didn't drift. They shifted up into my cami, then he arched away from me and my cami was gone.

I decided to let my hands get busy too, so I pushed them into his shorts. His mouth now at my throat, he angled his hips away so I could pull them over his ass and push them down. Deke lifted a knee, catching them with a foot and shoving them all the way off.

His hands then went back, both of them, in my bottoms and this time my panties. They spread to the sides and down, grazing over my hips. He rolled his legs to the side so I could windmill them off and they were gone.

Naked.

One of the top things on my list of how I liked to be with Deke.

He slid his mouth from my throat, down to my chest, between my breasts, to my midriff where he kissed me then lifted up, hovering there.

I looked down at him to see his gaze on me, his hazel eyes firing, the smooth of sleep still there but mingling with the dark of hunger.

A good look on Deke.

Though, for me, every look was good on Deke.

"Be back," he whispered, and I watched him bend again to me, touching his mouth to my belly before he rolled off me and the bed.

I turned to my side, cheek to the pillow, arm under me curled, the other arm straight out. I hitched a knee and watched Deke go to his bag. He pawed through it and I pressed my lips together as my clit contracted when I saw he had a blue bandana in his hand.

He hadn't tied me since that one time with my scarf.

I was getting the feeling anniversary sex was going to rock.

But I had no idea.

No idea it wasn't going to rock.

It was going to change my world.

He climbed back into bed, crawling into it on hands and knees, his eyes locked to mine, his movements predatory, and I swallowed, my fingers reflexively clenching into the sheets, heady prickles radiating from clit, through cunt, over my ass and up my spine.

When he reached me, he yanked the covers totally off me and hooked my waist with an arm. He pulled me up, coming up himself, so we were both on our knees, facing each other.

Then he trailed the hand with the bandana down my arm, to my wrist, where he circled it and lifted it up.

Only then did he take his eyes from me so he could watch as he threaded the rolled bandana between our wrists.

When his head moved that way, I turned my eyes and watched him secure a knot he'd done one handed, tightening it with his teeth.

At feeling the material constrict, anchoring me to Deke, a spasm exploded between my legs, another one close on its heels at the sight of his strong teeth, the feel of our wrists bound snugly together.

His gaze came to mine and I got lost in it, mired deep in the heat of his eyes, so in the thrall of Deke sharing his need for me stark, right there to see, to *feel*, I lost track of where his other hand was until I felt it in my hair. Up it went until it was close to the scalp where it gripped, yanking back.

The pain at my scalp translated to pleasure as it raced over my body, my back arching at his demand, then his mouth captured a nipple and sucked hard.

"*God*," I breathed, my arch pushing deeper, offering more to him as he took our bound wrists, twisting my arm, pinning it behind me.

He worked my nipples, one, the other, back, and again, until I was whimpering, my free hand fisted in the back of his hair, my lower body pressing hard into his, feeling his rigid cock snug against my belly.

I rubbed into it, needing the feel of it, wanting to give him something while he was giving to me.

Then suddenly his hand at my hair wasn't tugging back, it was pushing down and Deke shifted as he forced me to bend. Drawing our tied wrists around, his hand covering mine over his cock, his other hand still in my hair, tugging it back now to arch my neck, he drove the head of his cock through my lips and I took him. I took him with my mouth as both Deke and I jacked his dick.

Damn.

Amazing.

Never anything like it.

I'd never had anything like Deke.

I planted my free hand in the bed to keep steady in order to give him more while I took what he was giving. I closed my lips tight around the rim of the head of his cock and sucked hard. His fingers around mine gripped firmer, moving faster, pumping harder.

I was moaning against his cock, the insides of my thighs quivering, feeling the wet gather, desperate to put my free hand between my legs, unable to because I needed it for support, this making the desperation more acute, phenomenal, turning the noises I was making into verbal keening.

Deke heard it, pulled our hands from his cock and started fucking my face in earnest and I rocked into him, meeting his thrusts, hollowing my cheeks to draw him as deep inside as I could get him, feeling the rumbles he was making sound around my heart and tremble in my womb.

I thought he wanted me to take him there with my mouth but abruptly I was up, both our bound hands between my legs, Deke's middle finger pressing mine to my clit, circling, twitching, his mouth slamming down on mine, his tongue invading.

I kissed him back as I rode our hands and I kissed him harder as I rode us urgently when he slid both our fingers inside and started finger fucking me.

He took our fingers from clit to cunt, back and again, until I was so gone, I couldn't take his mouth anymore.

I tore my lips from his and shoved my face in his neck, moaning, "*Baby*."

"Do not get there," he growled.

"*God*," I breathed, holding on, fighting my orgasm, unable to stop my hips moving feverishly against the manipulation of our fingers.

I took all I could take and when I could take no more, with my free hand, I reached and cupped his balls. Not able to control it, I squeezed him maybe a bit too roughly.

In reaction, on a grunt that blistered through me, Deke sunk his teeth just beyond where my neck met my shoulder and he did it hard.

Right where he'd marked me.

And I knew he'd again given that to me.

"*Deke*," I whimpered.

At his name, our hands went from between my legs. He twisted my arm behind my back again and used both our arms to lift me, swinging me around, and he fell into me. My back was to the bed, my head hanging down the side, Deke's weight on me. He shifted his hips and I read what he wanted, opening my legs for him to fall through.

He reached to the nightstand.

I lifted my head.

And his hand came back just as his mouth crushed down on mine for a wet, bruising kiss.

He pulled away and I watched, squirming under him, as he used his teeth to rip open the condom packet.

"Hurry," I begged.

His eyes caught mine and I saw he was right there with me, gone like me, nothing existed but Deke and me, what we were doing, all we were feeling.

I felt his hand work between us and repeated my plea.

"*Hurry*."

He yanked our bound wrists from under me, twisting his, lacing his fingers in mine, pressing our hands into the bed as I felt the head of his cock slide over my clit that was so sensitive, my entire body jerked underneath him.

I needed him to slam inside, to fuck me hard, but when Deke caught at my entrance, he didn't thrust deep.

He pressed only the tip in and whispered, "Jussy."

I was concentrating solely between my legs, my neck straining to hold my head up, eyes to his face but not taking him in.

When he whispered my name, I focused on him.

And I watched his face as slow, so damned slow, so beautifully slow, so goddamned Deke, he slid in…and in…and in, taking his time, until finally, blissfully, he was filling me. A part of me.

Mine.

My fingers spasmed through his.

"Made for me," I whispered, trailing my fingertips down his spine to the small of his back.

He made a noise. Not a growl, not a rumble, not a groan, a sound that gave me all three before he dropped his head, took my mouth in a slow kiss, and took his time moving in and out of me.

As he did, it felt like he was memorizing my pussy, every centimeter. Not claiming it as his, exalting in what he knew he already possessed.

Adoring it.

Worshipping it.

Worshipping me.

I'd never experienced such beauty. In all I had, in all I'd earned, in all I'd been given, never, not in my life had I received such splendor.

I wrapped both legs around his thighs, trailing my fingertips on the swells at the top of his ass, lazy then faster as his movements came more quickly.

Faster, using my purchase on his thighs to lift my hips to take his thrusts deeper.

Faster, my hand now clutching the hard cheek of his clenching ass.

He broke the kiss. Bending his neck at a sharp angle so his forehead was pressed to my shoulder, my head fell back off the side of the bed. His fingers in mine grasped so hard they brought slight pain as his other hand went between us, his thumb skimming through the hair between my legs until it found my clit.

It pressed and rubbed.

And I was done.

My head shot up and I turned my face into Deke's neck and cried out when I exploded, my eyes closing, my breath suspending, my vision detonating in bright, my body arching and tightening.

His hand laced in mine jerked both up and I felt him grip my hair as his hips bucked punishingly into mine and my breath came back as I gasped through the final throes of my orgasm, hearing him grunt and feeling him rear through his.

It took a long time before he slowed and settled inside. I felt his hand loosen in my hair so both our hands were just tangled in it, his other hand sliding out from between us to wind around me at the waist. He used that to tug me into the bed so my head wasn't hanging off.

Through this, he kept his face in my neck and I felt his labored breaths breeze against my skin.

We lay there and another thing that was so Deke, something that made me know he was mine, meant for me: we did it in silence. He didn't feel the need to rush to speak. Ask me if I was okay. If I came (though he couldn't miss that, still). If that did it for me. If I needed anything.

He just knew I was okay, he'd made me come, everything he did did it for me and I didn't need anything but to feel him connected to me, covering me, warming me, reveling in all he'd just given me.

Eventually, he started to work my neck with his mouth, lazy and tender, at the same time he pulled our hands out of my hair and held them to the bed, his thumb idly stroking the side of my palm in casual affection.

Finally, he nipped my earlobe with his teeth before he asked there, "Ready for some breakfast, gypsy?"

This was Deke giving me unconditional beauty and then Deke and me getting on with our day.

"Mm-hmm," I mumbled my response.

He lifted his head and grinned down at me.

I lifted my head and touched my mouth to his.

I dropped back and saw his face was as it was when Deke woke from sleep. Smooth. Untroubled. Content.

Happy.

I knew the edges would come back. Life was like that. You couldn't avoid it. You couldn't erase history.

But I'd take that. I'd take giving him that for even another minute. I'd do anything to give it to him for as long as I could make it last.

And not just because I knew he'd do the same for me (though I loved knowing that).

Simply because he was Deke.

And he was mine.

CHAPTER NINETEEN

Overalls

Justice

JUGGLING FOUR BOXES of pizza, I opened my front door.

I barely got through before Bubba was there, grabbing all four boxes.

"Thanks, Bub," I muttered.

"You feedin' me, least I can do is carry the boxes," he replied.

I gave him a grin and turned to the hubbub that was eight men working in my house.

I did this shouting, "Soup's on!"

While I shouted, my eyes caught on Deke, who was in my kitchen. A kitchen that was actually beginning to look like a kitchen. I had an enormous island that nearly spanned the space (no countertop), base cupboards (no countertops) and Deke with another dude was setting in my hutch that would sit opposite where the range and the fridge would be.

Bubba went to the counter-less island.

I went to Deke.

And Deke came to me.

We met halfway.

He stopped in my space and bent his neck to look down at me.

"Again, you do not gotta buy these boys lunch," he said low.

As the word "again" would attest, he'd said this before. Every day now since the boys had come to work. It was Friday so that "again" consisted of him saying this (now) five times.

"And again, I'm not gonna bring us lunch and not do the same for the guys," I replied.

"And *again*," he stressed, "you don't gotta buy *me* lunch."

"And *again*," I stressed as well as drew the word out, "I like buying you lunch. You give me a hutch, I buy you lunch. And so it goes. So seriously. Shut it about lunch."

His head went back an inch. "Did you just tell me to shut it?"

"About lunch, yes," I confirmed.

"Justice."

"Deke."

We grew silent.

Then his eyes traveled the length of me and he got a look on his face I didn't get.

It seemed like a sneer at the same time it seemed like he wanted to drag me to my bedroom and have his wicked way with me.

This meant my back went up at the same time I experienced a lovely shiver.

"Something on your mind?" I asked when he said nothing.

He looked to me.

"Hate those overalls," he stated bluntly.

Well!

"So gonna like strippin' 'em off you after the boys leave."

Right, one could say that explained the look.

He leaned in, his eyes again aimed low, and muttered, "Fuck, can see your panties."

I leaned in and muttered back, "Deke, don't turn me on when seven men are horking back pizza in my kinda kitchen."

Deke stayed where he was but his attention came back to my face. "Then don't wear shit that's gonna make me fight gettin' hard when the boys are horking back pizza in your kitchen."

"And what would you like me to wear?"

"I'd say those overalls because they're butt-ugly but since that only makes me think of how fast I'm gonna get them off you after the guys leave, that doesn't work."

I tipped my head to the side, prompting, "So?"

"So, I got no ideas because pretty much anything you wear makes me think how fast I wanna strip it off you, even if it's cute." The look in his eyes changed, I felt that change in my pussy, and he finished, "Especially if it's cute."

I got closer to him and hissed my warning, "Deke, this is not helping."

He grinned at me. "Like how easy it is to get my gypsy hot for me."

"Put a lid on it, baby, or your comrades in hammers are gonna know how you sound when you come." I paused before I finished, "*Hard*. And how you can make *me* come. *Harder*."

"Fuck," he growled, that look in his eyes intensifying.

It was my turn to grin.

"I'm gonna get pizza before the good shit is gone and before I miss it altogether 'cause I gotta take a cold shower," he muttered.

My grin got bigger.

Then I remembered my chat with Sunny and Shambles.

"Go eat," I ordered. "But before you go, think about dinner tomorrow night at Sunny and Shambles's place. They asked while I was in today and I promised them after my drama was done, we'd get together."

His expression lost the look I liked and got a different one I'd never seen when he declared, "Babe, we're goin' to The Rooster with Max and Nina tomorrow."

We were?

"We are?" I asked.

"Max called while you were pickin' up pizza. Said Nina sorted a sitter and they got a reservation. We're meetin' them there at seven."

"She got a babysitter and made a reservation?"

"Told you Max said he wanted to take us out. He mentioned it earlier this week, said they might not be able to hustle a sitter, but if they could, we were on."

I felt my brows go up. "Did you think of telling me this?"

"You got plans tomorrow night?" he returned.

"I didn't. Now Sunny and Shambles want us at dinner tomorrow night."

Deke put a hand light on my waist, getting deeper in my space to do it. "No offense to them, Jussy, like 'em. They're good people. But they're vegetarians."

"So?" I asked.

"I'm not. You aren't either. And The Rooster does a kickass steak."

I heard *that*.

And Lauren had also waxed poetic about The Rooster's talent that could be appreciated most by carnivores.

As did Faye.

And Lexie.

Still, even if Shambles was unlikely to make us meat, he'd probably kick ass with whatever he did make.

"I like Sunny and Shambles," I told him. "I barely know Max and I don't know Nina at all."

"And Sunny and Shambles asked if we were free. They didn't have to hustle up a babysitter or make a reservation. They want, we can come to their place next weekend. Fuck, by next weekend, you might be able to make them Steph's chicken here." With his hand still at my waist, he swung his other one behind him to indicate my space.

"They're vegetarians, Deke. I can't make them Steph's chicken."

Though I liked the idea of a dinner party here.

That said, I might have a kitchen next weekend but I might not have any furniture. Apparently, a lot of the shit I ordered took weeks before it would be delivered.

Even more weeks than it had already taken.

Regardless, my afternoon plans just changed. It was time to hit the home store and buy a Crock-Pot.

I was close and getting closer. It was happening.

So it was time to start nesting.

Maybe I could get Krys and Breanne out of the house and they'd come with me.

Deke cut into my thoughts of nesting.

"Then make me Steph's chicken and make them something with tofu."

Just Deke uttering the word "tofu" made me start giggling.

He had a small smile on his face when he asked, "What's funny?"

"You saying tofu."

"Think that's the first time that word left my mouth," he muttered.

I started giggling harder.

Deke's hand that was light on my waist slid around to the small of my back, doing this inside my overalls, pulling me close so our bodies were touching.

He waited until my giggles subsided before he stated quietly, "Max and Nina tomorrow night. If Sunny and Shambles can do it, we go to them next weekend. And next time I hear we might have plans, even if they're not certain, I'll share that with you."

I was still smiling from my humor but what he said made that smile fade.

Although I'd had relationships that had lasted, they'd lasted months, not years. This meant I was an amateur at this. Having a home. Having a man. Making plans this weekend, the next, doing that taking into account there was another person involved.

Still, it was not lost on me that Deke didn't share something that involved me, he wanted one thing and I wanted something else.

It happened. There was a solution. We came to it quickly (or Deke did) and Deke saw without me having to point it out that he'd made a (minor) mistake.

I liked this and how it ended, with me giggling and Deke getting it. No escalating into an argument, no disagreement about what we were going to be doing.

Just...

Us.

I felt pressure at the small of my back and focused on him again when he asked, "That doesn't work for you?"

"Works great, honey," I answered quietly. "Call Max and confirm. I'll talk to Sunny and Shambles."

He flattened his whole hand at my back as he murmured, "Right."

"Now, go get pizza," I ordered.

"Right," he repeated, bending his head and touching his mouth to mine.

We broke, but he didn't remove his hand from the small of my back as he turned away from me and started guiding both of us to the kitchen.

"Next single, famous hottie Max has got on the rotation that he wants to send a man out alone to get work started on her place, I'm volunteering to go in," Scott called as we moved to the guys huddled around the open pizza boxes at my kinda kitchen island.

Scott was one of Max's crew. The one who I guessed was the youngest of the lot and him saying shit like that out loud was why I'd guessed it.

"Bud," Bubba said so low I wasn't certain anyone but me heard him.

"Next time you think about runnin' your mouth about my woman in front of my face, and hers, you don't want my fist down your throat, you think again," Deke returned conversationally over Bubba's one word.

He spoke conversationally, but the edge of his tone not being a threat, but something else a whole lot stronger, was still there.

Scott read the conversational tone and not the other, clearly, for he replied affably through a mouth full of pizza, "It's a compliment, bro."

Deke said nothing but I saw Scott's expression shift so I peered up at my man, catching the tail end of the look he'd sent to Scott. Even fading, I read it and felt a tingle trail down my spine.

I did not share with Scott I didn't mind a little razzing about anything, and through that sharing the same with all the boys. Boys who I was facing at least another week of them being in my house. Including razzing me and Deke about hooking up and the way we did. Because I really didn't mind it. I'd grown up around men, these men being my dad's band and his friends. I knew how it was.

I didn't share because, for whatever reason he had, Deke didn't like it. Most likely he didn't like it because he thought it might bother me. Therefore he wanted it shut down so he shut it down and it wouldn't be cool for him to make that point and me to contradict it.

I did not have a problem with this. It was my lion protecting me, even against things that I didn't need protected from.

You didn't mess with a lion, especially my lion, who was so badass he could shut someone down with a look.

I reached for a slice of pepperoni and did it trying not to smile.

Deke reached for the same.

I decided to eat one slice with the boys and take my next slice to my music room so not only was the client not there, hanging with them, but also the client who one of their own was banging wasn't there, making things weird for everybody.

I had floors. Nearly had stairs. There was now more than one working toilet in my house. And I was edging in on having a kitchen.

None of this sucked.

Still, I ate my slice, grabbed my next one, gave my man a look that included a small smile, and wandered to my music room, wishing it was just Deke and me, sandwiches and La-La Land treats with the occasional Bubba mixed in.

But it wasn't.

Whatever.

I had afternoon Crock-Pot plans that would lead to nesting.

So I had good waiting for me.

All I needed to make it better was to coax Krys into coming with me.

* * *

"Jesus," Deke called as I struggled in the door with some of my many purchases.

It was late.

The guys were gone.

But Deke was doing his usual overtime.

And I saw I not only had my built-in hutch, I had my stone backsplashes and patterned copper oven back.

So I was smiling hugely even as I dumped my bags with a loud thump to the floor and announced, "Crock-Pots are heavy."

Deke moved to me, asking, "How much you still got out there?"

"Um…a lot," I shared.

We'd just say Deluxe Home Store had a good day.

And I had plastic spoons that were actually awesome spoon/scrapers that Lauren talked me into getting—in three colors.

Amongst other things.

Deke stopped close. "You leave anything in the store?"

"Barely."

"Krys good?"

I kept smiling. "Yup. And Breanne was perfect her first time shopping. And Lauren is the master homewares shopper. And I'm more than good. I'm nesting *and* I just *knew* that copper oven back would be *the bomb*."

Deke grinned down at me but the grin slid from his face, his expression turning serious just as his voice dipped. "Jussy, just to say, you got a lot of shit to haul in, you grab a coupla bags, get inside and tell your man you got a lot of shit to haul in. Then I go out and get it. Yeah?"

"Deke, I can carry in—"

I stopped talking when he gave me a look. It wasn't the kind of look that he gave Scott, but it shut me up all the same.

He knew I got him when the seriousness of his face lightened, he bent in, gave me a lip brush then pulled away and moved away, ambling to the door.

I decided to take only a few bags to the laundry room at a time, though I only got my few bags in there. Deke brought the ones in from the truck while I was doing this and when we both went back to the great room, he grabbed all the handles of the ones I'd dropped to the floor and took them there for me.

In the time we'd been together, we had not gotten into past relationships. This last week, we just…were. I was either working or setting up my music room while Deke worked. We did dinner. We had sex. We slept. We woke up together. And repeat.

But I didn't think this was about some woman training him how to be the man of the house.

This was about him growing up from two-years-old being the man of the family with his mother, even when they didn't live in their own house.

The man Deke was demonstrating he was going to be for me made me happy. Ecstatically so. It wasn't that I couldn't haul my own bags. It was that he got something out of doing it for me that was sweet, taking care of me even in minor ways that were only minor for me. For Deke, they had a deeper meaning.

But this came with the reminder that what I'd lost with my dad passing, Deke had lost with his mom too. Knowing she'd never see the fruits of the upbringing she gave her son, doing this miraculously even as life beat them down. Understanding the kind of man she'd made. Having her look at me and me being able to share with just my manner how much she gave through her son.

"Feelin' Rosalinda's then a drink at Bubba's," Deke declared as he walked back into the great room. "You in?"

I pulled myself out of my thoughts and nodded, asking, "You wanna shower here or go to the trailer?"

He kept coming at me, answering, "Here."

He had a big bag packed for here, but it wouldn't matter. He left his clothes on the floor, and if I was doing laundry, they got laundered and I didn't put them back in his bag. I put them in the closet and dresser.

Deke did not protest this. Deke didn't say shit.

Deke just went to the closet to get jeans, and if there weren't clean ones there, he went to his bag.

I had left a few things at his trailer. Deke did not hang them up. But he did toss my bag onto the floor of his tiny closet.

In other words, for whatever plans we might have, we were both good either way.

Again Deke pulled me out of my thoughts and he did it then by getting deep in my space.

I tipped my head way back.

Then I dragged in a ragged breath when all of a sudden his hand dove right into my overalls, right to my ass.

Lightly, the touch chasing a tickle between my legs strong enough to make my knees start to get weak, he traced the edge of my panties under my ass as he lifted his other hand and cupped the side of my neck.

"Been thinkin' of doin' that since I first saw you in these fuckin' ugly things."

The part about him thinking about having his hand in my pants was good.

His insult to my overalls was not.

"They're comfy," I snapped, though it wasn't as sharp as it could have been considering Deke was leaning in closer so his fingers could move deeper.

"You got a fantastic body, gypsy, and they do shit for it."

"Would you prefer I wander around in a bikini?"

"Babe," he stated simply, his eyes lighting.

"I take it that's an affirmative."

"Jussy, I got a dick and that dick likes to be in you. You show skin, it reminds me, and specifically my dick, how good that skin feels, and tastes, by the way, which reminds me how much better you feel inside."

That "inside" liked how he was pushing deeper, trailing his fingers along the edge of my panties between my legs. Because of this, I lost track of the conversation so I could instead concentrate on spreading those legs for him so he had better access.

His thumb pressed against my jaw, tipping my head farther back, and his face got close to mine.

"You wanna shower with me?" he murmured.

Unlike Deke, who'd been engaged in manual labor all day, I didn't need a shower.

"Yes," I breathed.

His fingers went from panties' edge to panty gusset and started stroking lightly.

Wow. That felt nice.

So nice, a soft wisp of breath escaped my mouth and wafted across his lips.

Those lips came to mine.

"Or you want me to make you come right here?" he whispered.

"Your choice," I exhaled, though at that point, I wasn't sure how I'd make it to the shower.

Or if I'd be able to remain standing in it.

Gently, he pushed the gusset of my panties aside, dipped his body deeper into me, and slowly slid one long finger inside.

I fought panting.

"Soaked," he growled.

He slid his finger out, glided it to my clit and started circling.

He also kept growling.

"Make you come right here, put on a show for me."

"Okay," I agreed.

"Want you comin' hard for me, Jussy."

I found my hands were curled into the material of his tee on either side of his lower back.

I kept them there so I could continue standing as Deke continued circling.

"Okay, baby," I blew out.

Deke went in harder with his finger.

I arched into him as he bent farther over me, his hand at my neck sliding to the back.

"Let me hear you," he rumbled.

A whimper I didn't know I was holding back slid out of me, my legs trembled and Deke shifted his arm so his hand was still at my neck, but his forearm was running along the middle of my upper back, supporting me.

"Work that," he ordered roughly.

I ground into his finger and another wilder, hungrier whimper escaped.

"There you go, gypsy," he murmured approvingly.

He slid his finger back, it was joined by another one, they thrust inside and his thumb hit my clit.

I gasped and kept doing it, my eyes half-closed, my hands dragging his tee up his bowed back to find better purchase.

"Deke."

"Fuck, nothin' more beautiful."

I tried to force my eyes wider so I could watch him watching me as my legs began to tremble beneath me when it started coming, I knew the force of it was going to rock me, and I needed him to keep me safe so I could ride that storm.

"Deke," I repeated, the only way I could communicate all those things.

But he understood me.

"I got you, Jussy."

He had me.

He always had me.

With a soft cry, I let go.

And Deke had me, holding me up, his fingers relentlessly working me, pushing me further, the orgasm burning through me, making me shudder in his hold, and only when the burn started to subside did he gently slide his hand away, cupping my ass with it.

His other hand sifted into my hair to cup the back of my head and that was when he kissed me.

When he was done kissing me, I was done coming, and as he slowly lifted his head, I slowly opened my eyes.

"Think I might like these fuckin' butt-ugly things now," he teased.

My eyes narrowed.

He grinned, pressed his hard cock in my belly and put his mouth to mine. "Shower blowjob payback, baby."

My clit convulsed.

His grin got bigger like he felt that happen himself.

Cocky.

Hot.

Fuck me.

Deke.

He pulled his hand out of my pants and grabbed mine.

He then dragged me to the shower.

I had a big one, room enough for four of us.

Definitely room enough for a shower blowjob.

If that was in question, Deke and I answered that question.

There was room enough.

Definitely.

* * *

The next night, I walked out of the bathroom dressed for dinner at The Rooster, my high-heeled western boots dangling from my fingers, but I stopped on a stutter step when I saw Deke.

Apparently, although Deke said he'd never wear a suit, that didn't mean he wouldn't spruce up.

And Deke Hightower spruced up was a sight to see.

Dark-wash jeans and a forest-green, button-up shirt that skimmed the lines of his torso, that narrow waist widening to broad shoulders, a powerful upper-body V highlighted by that amazing shirt doing a number on me.

Not to mention, even from across the room, I saw that shirt made the hazel of his eyes a lot less hazel and a lot more green.

He had his man-bun up as usual and his beard was way bushier than it had been when first I saw him again. Actually, as far as I knew (and I definitely knew once we got together), he hadn't trimmed it once.

It looked awesome.

"Wow," I said, moving my gaze from his feet in boots that were also better than the normal ones he wore that I'd seen (these being work boots and motorcycle).

Although I'd recovered enough to speak, the look I caught on his face again winded me.

And I knew I'd chosen the right dress.

Now that I was settling in, the house getting done and I'd begun nesting, Joss, who always held on to a lot of my stuff considering I never stayed anywhere long enough to keep it all with me, had promised to send it.

So I didn't have a lot of clothes Deke had not seen.

The dress I was wearing was, as far as I knew, the only remaining piece.

It was a soft taupe with a muted pattern of rust, orange and turquoise. It had an empire waist, the cleavage cut to it. It was formfitting from midriff down to my waist, flowing out at hips. It had long, three-quarter sleeves that gathered at the ends and the dress fell to my ankles.

It also had a deep slit that was more than a slit. It was a rounded opening that started at mid-thigh.

This was the best part of the dress, I thought, especially when I moved, the skirt flowing out behind me, exposing boots…and legs.

It was sexy boho rad in the extreme.

Deke might not like my baggy overalls.

But he felt differently about that dress.

He didn't need to say it, his look did.

But he said it anyway.

"Nice dress, gypsy."

The words came out in a thick rumble that, coupled with his look, completed what he didn't say. A line used so often it had long since lost its hotness.

A line left unsaid but spoken nonverbally the way Deke was doing it that was hot in the extreme.

That being he liked my dress.

But he was going to like it more when it was on the floor.

I was going to like it more when it was on the floor too.

Tangled with his fucking shirt.

"Are we gonna jump each other and be late for dinner?" I asked.

"Tempting," Deke answered.

We stood there staring at each other.

"Baby, put your boots on," he eventually ordered. "I can see with that hair and that dress that those boots are gonna torture me all night. But to do all I'm gonna do to you later, I need steak."

That sent a tremor through my whole body.

"You like my hair?" I asked.

I'd done a lot of braids falling and twists back from my face, but the back fell free in natural waves and curls to my waist.

"Babe."

He said no more.

He liked my hair.

I lifted up my boots. "You like my boots?"

"Jussy," he growled.

I grinned.

"You do know we're goin' to dinner with my boss," he noted.

My grin died along with my fun.

I needed to be cool and we needed not to be late.

"Sorry, honey."

Deke moved to me, got close and put his hands on my hips.

"You're a sweet tease. I like it like that. And that's to say I like it like that only from you. I still like it. And you know Max is a friend. But just sayin', the man's still my boss."

"Right," I whispered.

"So put your boots on, gypsy. Yeah?"

I nodded.

He gave my hips a squeeze and let me go.

I walked to my bed, zipped on my boots then went to my dresser and added a turquoise statement necklace, switched out some earrings, threw on some bangles, loaded up with rings, then I was done.

I turned to Deke, who was coming out of the bathroom, shrugging on a nice leather jacket, another item in Deke's wardrobe I had not seen.

He looked to me, his eyes warmed and his lips muttered, "And she makes sweet sweeter."

I gave him another grin.

"Jacket?" he asked.

"In the closet, I'll go get it."

"Meet you at my truck."

"You got it."

Deke didn't meet me at the truck.

He met me on his way to the door while I was on my way to the walk-in closet.

He caught my wrist, stopped me, bent to me and we touched mouths.

With that, he let me go and moved away.

And I got my jacket and met him at his truck.

* * *

"You gonna tell them or am I?"

We were at The Rooster, a somewhat rustic but mostly elegant restaurant nestled into the side of a mountain that was made almost entirely of glass.

Deke and I were in a booth sitting across from hot guy, mountain man Holden "Max" Maxwell, and his pretty blonde wife, Nina, who had a hint of an English accent and a manner that said she was full of attitude.

I liked her on sight.

The question was asked of his woman by Max.

The full attitude hit Nina's pretty face as she turned it to him. "We're not going to tell them at all."

"Duchess, anyone sits opposite us at The Rooster should know," Max returned.

Duchess. Cute nickname. She was *so* a "duchess."

"Not even sure how I got talked into comin' here," Max stated and looked to us. "Vowed never to step foot in this place again after the last time. I wanted you to come to our house and make you a meal. My wife can cook. Her fish pie is the best thing I ever tasted. But she wanted to get dressed up. So we're here."

That didn't sound good.

That said, it was sweet Max came out so his wife could get dressed up.

"Tell us what?" Deke's deep voice sounded.

Nina looked to him and said quickly, "Nothing."

Max turned his attention to him, and after his wife said that, he said, "Me and Nina hit The Rooster, shit happens."

"Like what?" I asked.

"Once, a brawl," Max answered.

Say what?

A *brawl*? In a fancy steak restaurant?

Yikes!

Nina, across the booth from me, leaned in. "Tables turning over, ketchup and horseradish sauce everywhere. It was insanity."

"Holy cow," I whispered. I slid a quick glance Max's way, Max being a man I could totally see involved in a brawl, before I asked Nina, "Were you involved?"

"Mildly," she murmured, giving the impression she was fibbing.

A giggle escaped me.

"Though, Max didn't do the brawling,' Nina clarified. "Not that night. He'd beaten the absolute crap out of another guy earlier in the week though."

There you go.

I was right.

Max was a brawler.

Another giggle escaped me.

"Luckily, I don't see anyone in here who might have somethin' up their ass they feel the need to share at our table," Max declared, eyes still on Deke. "And you may be the only man I know who's got no enemies."

I looked to Deke, finding this fascinating in a very good way.

Fascinating and believable.

His circle was small and tight. He lived. He worked. He kept himself to himself but did all he could for the people who meant something to him.

That was his life.

That was who he was.

That was part of what was now mine in having him.

Nina broke into these happy thoughts by snapping to her husband, "You're intimating, darling, that that someone who might have something up their ass would feel that way about *me*."

I didn't think he was intimating that at all.

Max looked down at his wife at his side. "Baby, you're an attorney and one who kicks ass. Anyone on the other side is gonna have something up their ass about you and a lotta them *do*. Was at The Mark with you just last week when I had to deal with one of them who felt the need to share that with you."

Apparently, he *was* intimating that.

"It's my job," she retorted.

Max grinned and did it well. So well, I was surprised Nina, watching him do it, didn't instantly lose her snit and melt into him before asking if we minded if they vacated the table for half an hour to take care of business in their car.

He then said with obvious pride, "Yeah it is and you kick ass at it." He looked to Deke and me. "But just sayin', be prepared in case shit goes down. My duchess isn't the type to let things go. So if that happens, and she blows, just hold on. It'll happen, and unless our table is across the room when it's over, we can just finish our steaks."

Nina was glaring at her man. Though I noted she was just glaring, she didn't deny anything he said.

"Consider us prepared," I replied after swallowing another giggle, actually kind of hoping shit went down. It'd be fun to watch Max deal with it.

More fun to see how Deke would wade in.

Our waitress in black trousers, white button-up shirt, long, thin black tie and longer, crisp white apron dangling down her legs approached, asking, "Have we decided on drinks?"

We had so we ordered drinks. We got our drinks. And we gabbed.

Through this, alas, no one approached our table to cause a scene.

We ordered dinner. We gabbed more, Nina sipping her martini, me doing the same with my Jack and Coke, both men got beers, and I learned the stories about Nina and Max's altercations at The Rooster (amongst other scenes—Nina seemed like a scene magnet, not (all) her choice).

Our appetizers came, and by then I was glad we decided to go out with Max and Nina. Firstly, because I'd seen Deke spruced up and he probably wouldn't do that to go to Sunny and Shambles's. Secondly, Deke got to see me spruced up, he liked it and I liked how he liked it. And lastly, I knew I liked Max, but Nina was sweet at the same time being funny as hell, sharp as a whip, and her banter that was more like loving bickering with her husband was fun to watch.

It all seemed to be going well and it wasn't until the waitress whisked away our appetizer dishes when it seemed like things were going to turn.

This started when I was smiling at Nina as she spoke animatedly and with a great deal of love about her and Max's children and I caught something out the side of my eye.

Before I even looked that way, I felt it like I always felt it the rare times it happened.

I knew I'd been spotted.

And when my gaze hit a table in the center of the restaurant, I saw four sets of eyes on me, with one of the women at the table's hand falling after what appeared to be her pointing at me.

As they got my attention, the two women and one of the two men smiled at me, big and excited. And the woman who hadn't been pointing lifting her hand for a shy wave.

I felt my muscles get tight as I tipped my head and gave them a look that I hoped communicated I appreciated that they knew who I was, were excited to see me sitting there, but it wasn't an invitation to come to the table for a chat or to ask for an autograph or picture.

If it had just been me, I wouldn't care. For me, it would be far worse if no one ever recognized me, and especially looked excited when they did, because it would mean they hadn't heard my music, liked my music, and last, probably *bought* my music.

Even without my earnings, thanks to Granddad (and eventually when the shit with Mav and his mother was over, Dad), I'd still be in my oasis tucked in pine and aspen.

But what I earned was what *I* had earned and it meant a lot to me.

However, it wasn't just me. It was me with Max, Nina...and Deke.

Max and Nina had warned us they were a magnet for drama at The Rooster (or at least it seemed Nina was, and not just at The Rooster). So they'd had practice and might be able to ride whatever wave was approaching.

But Deke had said he didn't know how he'd handle facing the hassle that came from my fame.

I didn't think this was a hassle. Connecting to people who connected to me through something that was a deep, emotional part of me, truth was, if it didn't get weird, I loved it. I didn't mind scribbling my name, smiling at someone's phone, having them tell me I'd made their night, knowing even if I said it they wouldn't believe that they'd made mine too.

Deke might not agree.

And we were having a great time. The food good, the company—as ever in these Colorado mountains—stellar. I didn't want that to turn.

In other words, I didn't want to learn that Deke, who was the mellowest man I'd ever met, would react negatively to something that might not happen every day, or even frequently, but it happened.

So after I gave them their look, I looked away, hopefully communicating that I was pleasantly occupied and would rather not be disturbed.

No one at our table seemed to notice this and I was relieved, primarily because part of that no one was Deke.

I'd rejoined the conversation and the waitress came, bringing Nina a glass of wine and me another Jack and Coke, when I felt Deke's arm that was lying on the booth behind me, curl around me.

He pulled me into his side.

I looked up at him.

"Babe, folk at that table over there know you," he said quietly.

Of course, Deke had noticed.

"They're takin' pictures, tryin' to be cool about it," he went on.

Shit!

"Maybe not somethin' you wanna do but think it'd mean a lot to them, you went over, had a word before our steaks get here," he advised.

I felt my mouth drop open.

Deke looked to my mouth then back to my eyes.

"Your call, you don't want to," he said.

"You're okay with that?" I asked.

"Be more okay with that than them getting a picture of you shovin' a huge bite of steak in your mouth, somethin' you might not like, and that shit's all over Twitter or whatever by morning."

I'd feel better about that too.

"I, well, if I go over there, honey, they'll want pictures and other people might notice and it might get around that I'm, well…me."

"You *are* you," he pointed out. "So be you, give 'em you, and get back here before our steaks get here because you won't want to eat yours cold."

My mouth didn't drop open then.

I just stared.

"Is everything okay?" Nina asked.

Deke looked her way and did it sliding out of the booth. "Jussy's got some fans here. She's gonna go see to 'em."

I cast an uneasy glance at Nina and Max as I slid out behind Deke, wondering if they'd be annoyed at possibly having their dinner delayed, our night interrupted.

But Max was just looking at me benevolently and Nina was looking over her shoulder. She'd clearly caught the table where the patrons knew me because she was waving.

They were waving back.

Okay, not annoyed.

I took my feet next to Deke and looked up at him.

"I'll try to be fast," I assured.

"Do what you gotta do," he muttered, his head coming down to do what he often had to do.

Touch his lips to mine.

They were almost to their destination when I whispered, "Baby, they could be taking pictures."

His head halted its descent and his gaze lifted from my lips to my eyes before he whispered back, "You mine?"

Oh yes.

I was.

Abso-fucking-lutely.

"Yes," I answered.

"Then who gives a shit?"

He asked that and didn't allow me to respond. He went in for the lip brush, hand on my hip giving me a squeeze.

When he pulled away, I wanted to grab him on either side of his head and yank him back. When I'd accomplished that, I wanted to kiss him hard.

In absence of that, I wanted to smile at him huge to tell him how much his reaction to this scenario meant to me.

And last, I wanted to tell him I loved him.

I didn't do any of these things.

Instead, I gave him a look that I hoped shared all of that, a small smile curving my mouth, lifting my hand to trail my fingers along his at my hip.

He caught them, twisted them in his for a beat before he gave them an affectionate tug and let them go.

I looked to Max and Nina. "Be back."

"We'll be here," Nina replied brightly.

My smile to her was grateful, I turned it on Max and then I moved on my high-heeled boots through the restaurant to the table.

The women were nearly bouncing in their chairs.

Both men were standing by the time I made it to their table.

I spoke with them. I signed two cocktail napkins, personalizing them. And I stood and scrunched together for four pictures, one taken by a waitress.

Other patrons watched, none gawked (fortunately) and no others approached or cast certain kinds of glances that would mean I'd be taking a tour of the restaurant that would last an hour before I went back to my dinner with Deke and our friends.

We were undisturbed through steaks, more beverages (for Nina and me) and desserts.

But when it came time to pay the bill, it was the manager who showed, looking at me and saying, "It's our pleasure you joined us, Ms. Lonesome. So much so, The Rooster is covering your meal." He slightly bowed to me, Deke and then to Max and Nina before he looked again to me. "Please come again."

He then glided away.

"Um…" I mumbled to the table at large. "Weirdly, that comes with the territory, the people most likely to be able to afford steak dinners in nice restaurants get them for free."

"Free food at The Rooster. Never wanted to be famous, suddenly I want to be famous," Nina remarked, again smiling at me. "Do you get designers sending you free clothes?"

Her manner made it easy not to be embarrassed by an embarrassment of riches.

"When I was touring, yeah."

"Okay, now I definitely want to be famous," Nina decreed.

I smiled back.

"This means I get nothin' but the tip which means we didn't take you two out for dinner at all which means," Max was speaking to Deke and me but he turned to Nina and said his last, "your fish pie at our place and you and Jus can dress up all you want to sit at our table with our kids. But I'm not puttin' on boots."

"No. Next time our turn," I butted in, thrilled by the possibility that I could actually take that turn. "At my soon-to-be-done house, that being soon thanks to Deke and Max."

"We accept," Nina said instantly.

"Can she cook?" Max asked Deke.

"Yup," Deke answered Max, again curling his arm that was behind me on the booth around my shoulders and pulling me in close.

"Then we accept," Max confirmed to me.

"Awesome," I replied.

And it was awesome.

An embarrassment of riches.

But this time, the important kind.

* * *

"Grace."

We were halfway home from the restaurant, this journey made in silence.

Content after a nice night with good food in our bellies, the silence was about that.

But it was more.

It was just the way of Deke and me.

"Sorry?" I asked, turning to look at his profile lit by the dashboard lights.

"Your dad see that?" he asked the road.

"See what?" I asked back.

He didn't glance at me when he explained, "Way you were tonight with those folks. That grace you got in you."

I felt my breath catch in my throat.

Deke's obviously didn't because he kept talking.

"For them, a nice night out turned into a memory they won't forget. They'll be tellin' that shit to their grandkids. You made it that way, walkin' up to them, givin' 'em your time, givin' 'em all the good you got in you. Watched you do it, Jussy. You just bein' you lit up their worlds for as long as you were at their table."

As I tried to regulate my breathing which had gone erratic at Deke's compliment, Deke reached out, found my hand, curled his around it and pulled both to his thigh.

And his voice was lower, filled with sheer beauty when he continued.

"Don't think I've ever been prouder in my life than watchin' you handle those people. No way to describe it. 'Cept pure grace."

I squeezed his hand and my voice was different too, lower, but husky when I replied, "Thank you, baby."

"Your dad see that?" he asked.

I cleared my throat and looked to the dark road. "Kind of. Usually it was him giving that to people."

Sweet memories filled my head of watching him do just that for as long as I could remember.

Memories that I noted were just sweet, without any of the sting that memories of Dad had been causing since he'd passed.

And that sweet was something else Deke had given me—keeping me together even as I fell apart, letting me get things out it was unhealthy to hold in, paving the way for me to move on, release the bitter, keep the sweet.

"He taught me how," I finished.

"Born to it and still, both a' you know what it means. Don't take it for granted."

"No, we both know what it means," I confirmed.

Or Dad knew. And he'd taught me.

Deke was silent. This stretched and I let it.

Deke ended it.

"One album, Jussy. You say you like what you do but, baby, you haven't explained to me what it is you're gonna be doin'."

This was noted conversationally. I felt no tension in the cab, heard none in his words.

He wasn't asking to gather information, assess if our paths would down the road divide.

He was just asking.

"I write songs," I answered. "Sometimes, if I like the artist, I produce. It's rare, though, that I go in to do that. Produce, I mean. It takes a lot of time and," I rubbed my thumb along the side of his hand, "until recently, I wasn't big on staying in one place for very long."

"Yeah," he murmured, amusement and approval in his tone.

That was when I fell silent.

Deke didn't fall into it with me.

"One album, babe."

I looked to him. "What?"

"It's been a while. When you gonna do another one?"

When my hand squeezed his that time, it was involuntary.

"I don't record anymore," I shared.

He shot a glance at me.

"Say again?" he asked the road when his eyes went back to it.

I looked back to the road too. "I don't record. Like I said, I just write. And sometimes produce."

"You don't record."

The way he said that made me turn my head his way again.

"No, Deke. Not anymore."

There was no pause before he asked his next, but when he asked, he asked gently.

"You wanna tell me why?"

I looked back out the windshield. "It wasn't for me."

"What wasn't?" he asked. "Parts of it or the whole thing?"

A wise question.

"Parts of it. I..." I hesitated then noted, "You read up on me."

"I did."

"So you know the story."

"Read it but didn't think it was the whole story, Jussy, seein' as you're young and you got amazing talent. Thought there were more chapters to be written."

"I lost my drummer to an overdose," I announced. "He was Dad's drummer before he went on the road with me. So he was family. And I was the leader of the band then. That means I didn't take care of one of my boys. I didn't look out for him."

Before Deke could put his two cents in, I went on hurriedly.

"I know it wasn't my fault. I get that, really. That doesn't mean there isn't a part of me that feels I hold some responsibility. And, well…that happening shook me."

It was then his hand tightened what seemed like involuntarily in mine.

But I gave him more.

"And the schedule, Deke, it's insane. On the road. On a bus. On a plane. In a car. In a hotel room. Up early for press. Interview after interview trying to answer the same questions that are asked over and over again, doing it in different ways, trying to seem engaged. Dog-tired by sound check. Amping for the performance to be so jazzed at the end you can't sleep. Booze all over the place. Drugs easy to get. Everything. Illegal. Prescription. And everybody wants to be your friend because you can get them backstage or get them introductions to the people who'll make their dreams come true or they can just take off with all the shit folks shower on you for no reason, just because you can sing and you have a famous last name. You're open to being used, open to shit that is seriously unhealthy for you, finding yourself needing it just to get through the day, doing your best to deny that, turn your back on it and keep going."

I looked to him, took a breath, but I wasn't done.

"All that happens and if you're lucky, it grows. Then you need to build a wall to stay behind, to keep away from all that shit, to stay safe. And suddenly, you're behind that wall. What I do, Deke, it isn't about being behind a wall. It isn't about keeping myself shielded from the people who love the stories I tell. It's about us being two halves of a whole. I love what I do and I'd be happy doing it just for me. But they love what I do too and it's indescribable how amazing it is that what I give is something they want to take. It isn't like there would be no me without them, yet it is. We're one. You remove yourself from part of that, you're missing something crucial to the process. No one can live without their other half."

I watched as he lifted my hand but he stopped in mid-air. I didn't know what he intended to do and it seemed for a moment that he didn't know either.

He decided and I had to turn to him when he lifted my hand farther up, pulled me closer, and pressed it to his chest.

I felt that hit me in the throat in a way I liked.

And with that warmth right there, I kept sharing.

"The more success you get, the more there's a need for that wall. Then you start needing that wall reinforced until you're so far away from your other half, it's like they don't exist."

"Your dad had to have that wall, baby," he noted softly.

"He did," I told him. "That's why he always toured. He might take a break for a few months but only to plan the next tour, record the next album. He was always on the road because he needed those times when he could tear down that wall. Be onstage with his fans a sea of faces in front of him, singing right along with him. There is no greater beauty in a song than thousands of voices singing it. I know it might piss some people off when artists onstage turn the microphone to the audience. But I can say there is nothing a songwriter can experience in the art more beautiful than shutting your mouth and hearing your work sung to you by thousands of voices. Knowing something that came from your soul is embedded in someone else's."

"You miss it," he noted.

I turned back to the windshield. "Some of it," I told him.

A lot of it. I heard whispered in the deep recesses of my mind, this surprising me.

Deke took me out of that thought when he fully lifted my hand and I felt his lips touch my knuckles before he dropped it back to his thigh.

I didn't watch that. It felt beautiful. If it was as beautiful to see as it felt, I'd unravel in the car.

We were driving down Main Street in Carnal when Deke spoke again.

"Want you to think on that, Jussy."

"Think on what?"

"You have way too much to give to let others offer it for you, baby," he said carefully, quietly.

Marvelously.

And he wasn't done.

"It's your choice. You want your less that's more, I get that. I do. But you miss it, you feel the need for that connection direct, you should go for it."

I didn't know what he was saying.

But what I thought he might be saying concerned me even as it bizarrely elated me.

And I focused on the part that concerned me.

"And if I went for it, where would you be?" I asked.

He shot me another glance before he asked back, "Where would I be?"

"That's what I'm asking."

"No, babe, where *would* I be?" he asked again, but it was a statement as much as a question.

I just didn't know what he was stating.

"Yes, Deke, that's what I want to know. Where would you be?"

It was more than a glance, he gave me a full look before he shifted his attention back to the road and put on his indicator to turn left on County Road 18.

He did this saying, "With you."

I gripped his hand so tight I felt his bones dig into the pads of my fingers.

"If…if…" I swallowed and forced myself to finish. "If something like that happens, Deke, and I'm not saying it will, but if it does, that's a lot to ask of you."

"And me makin' it clear I want a future with you, doin' that tellin' you you gotta leave your home to be on the back of my bike with me half a year wasn't askin' a lot of you?"

This was true.

Though I wasn't certain he really understood.

But maybe he did.

"Jussy," he gave my hand a light tug, "this works with us, there's gonna be a lot of times I'm gonna ask a lot of you and I'm gonna get the same back from you. I got no experience with it. Longest I've ever been with a woman was a three-month stretch up in Idaho. But my boys all got women and I see that's the way it goes. Shit, wait until Christmas. Laurie goes absolutely fuckin' nuts at Christmas. She's a grouch with a mission until she's baked every cookie and sent every card, and the woman bakes and sends thousands, no fuckin' joke. Tate and Jonas, they put up with that. Think it's hilarious but they don't get up in her shit about it. They keep their heads down and let her have at it because it's important to her. And that's it. The way it goes. You just gotta go with it."

I was all for just going with it.

But Lauren being really into Christmas was not exactly the same as being on the road with your woman the rock star.

"Well, I'm not getting back into that," I told him.

"Maybe," he replied. "Don't close that door, even in your head."

"Deke, there's more to me leaving that life than what I said. I was in a relationship with one of my band. He was deep into shit I wanted no part of."

I got a hand squeeze where Deke probably felt my bones at talking about my relationship but he didn't say anything about it.

So I carried on.

"Honestly, baby, it wasn't who I was. It didn't feel right. None of it."

"Unless you were on the stage."

He was freaking me out, how he seemed to be able to read things.

It was frankly a little scary.

"Unless I was on a stage," I agreed.

He must have read my freakout because he explained, "Not hard to see, gypsy. Only saw you once and it was clear. That was your place. That's a big piece of who you are. Couldn't miss it."

Right, well, that made sense.

"Your choice, Jussy, like I said," he continued. "Just want you to know you got that choice."

And I wanted him to know I loved him. I also wanted him to know all the reasons why.

But he was making a turn so I didn't say it to him.

And we'd been *together*-together not very long so I didn't want to share that and completely tweak him.

So I kept my mouth shut about that and just said softly, "Thank you, honey."

He rubbed my hand on his thigh then kept holding it tight.

And without another word, Deke drove us the rest of the way home.

* * *

The next morning on the way to the bathroom, my foot got caught in something and I tripped.

I righted myself before going down and looked at what caught me.

My dress tangled with Deke's green shirt.

And I stared at that dress Deke had thrown aside and the shirt I'd thrown aside last night, both lying on my bedroom floor, thinking distractedly I still needed a rug in there.

But mostly what I thought was, that dress and that shirt could be on that floor in that house.

Or it could be on any floor, if there were wheels underneath it or if it was in a motel in Idaho.

Wherever.

Be that on the road with Deke.

Or Deke on the road with me.

Staring at our tangled clothing, something slithered over me, every inch of my skin, like a protective sheen.

This was the understanding that Deke had found the woman who could handle the road, the only place he could breathe easy.

But it was also something I hadn't thought about.

This being that I had found the man who breathed easiest on the road, something that was in my blood, something that was a part of me, something that could mean something deeper again someday without me having to worry about where the man in my life would fit if I took to that road.

My choice.

I felt no anxiety around this train of thought, a train I hadn't taken in a long time.

I felt only ease.

My choice.

I had that choice. I had it when I didn't have Deke and that had not changed like it most likely would have with another man.

I still had it now that I had him.

So I didn't think of it at all.

I just smiled at my awesome dress tangled in his kickass shirt, remembered how both pieces got where they were and kept walking to the bathroom.

CHAPTER TWENTY

Root Myself in You

Justice

Standing in the chill outside by his SUV, I handed the clipboard with the paperwork that I'd just signed back to Max's foreman, a guy named Deacon Gates.

He'd been around occasionally, helping out sometimes the week after I'd been attacked. But mostly, after the boys had come, he let Deke take care of managing them, showing only when inspectors came to sign off on things.

But now Deacon had just completed the final inspection, an inspection I'd trailed him through and just signed off on.

This was because my house was all done.

Done.

"Right," Deacon's rough voice came at me and I focused on him in the ample glow provided by the outside lights at the door to my house.

He was definitely of the gorgeous variety of mountain man.

But he was different.

The first time I'd met him my poet's soul had started keening. Not like it did for Deke. It was something I'd never experienced.

Chace, I sensed, had been broken. Meeting Faye, I knew she was the one keeping him together. More, it felt like Chace would give his all to keep himself together…for Faye.

This man, Deacon Gates, had not been broken.

He'd been destroyed.

I saw it in the backs of his eyes. A deadness there that was chilling, heartbreaking, even frightening.

This would have worried me, even so far as obsessed me, driving me to my notebook to pen a dozen songs he'd never know were for him even if I wrote them in an effort to heal him.

Except I'd caught him catching a call.

He'd been removed from me so I couldn't hear what he said and I didn't know who he was talking to, but whoever it was, they wrought miracles. As he spoke on the phone, his entire demeanor changed. He morphed before my eyes from a standoffish, taciturn man who was well-mannered and respectful but didn't invite friendliness, becoming an average, everyday hot guy who you wouldn't hesitate to invite over to watch a game.

He'd fascinated me in the few times he'd been around, because it was the poet in me who saw this. Everyone else treated him like he was that everyday hot guy, maybe not exactly of the Bubba bent, but definitely like Deke. A good guy. One you'd want to be your friend. One who was open to being just that.

It was me who saw into his soul and I suspected he felt it. To protect himself from me learning more, he kept distant, this being one of the few times we'd spent any amount of time together. Mostly, he dealt with Deke.

"Max has a twelve-month guarantee," he went on, cutting into my thoughts. "That may seem like a long time, Justice, but that time flies. You got a lotta house for just you. I advise you use it. Even the parts of it you won't be in very often. Plug things in outlets. Flush toilets. Run faucets. Leave overhead lights on. Fire up that fireplace. Do a walkthrough if we get a big rain, make sure the roof is good. You find anything, you give me a call."

He said his last reaching behind him to pull out his wallet. When he got hold of it, he extracted a business card and offered it to me between two long fingers.

I took it just as I noted flurries were starting to fall.

I tipped my head back and looked to the night sky.

The flurries were light but there they were.

My first snow in the mountains.

"Probably best to get those pumpkins in tonight," Deacon stated and I looked back to him. "Mountain freeze this time of year can come with a thaw. And repeat. Those pumpkins could be goo in days."

I turned my head and stared at the cornucopia of autumn delights I'd arranged up my front walk. Real pumpkins. Strings of kickass electronic luminarias. The awesomest Halloween decoration I'd ever seen that I'd found in a gift shop in town: a stuffed, cackling witch on a broomstick decorated with leaves and glittery twine that Deke had mounted on my door.

I turned back to Deacon. "I'll take them in."

He nodded and asked, "You got any questions?"

I shook my head.

He looked over that head to my house and muttered, "You got 'em, you got answers a lot easier than callin' me."

Deke was in my house so he was absolutely right.

"The guys were great. It looks phenomenal. Thanks so much," I told him.

His attention came back to me. "Our job, Justice, but glad you like how it turned out."

Oh, I liked how it turned out.

It was perfect.

I grinned at him.

"Gotta get home to my wife," he stated, and with the flurries falling around us, the space lit by my outdoor lights, with an abruptness that was startling, I saw life flash bright in his eyes in such a way, I felt my heart squeeze.

Death resurrected, right there for me to witness.

So *that* was who the call was from.

God, this man existed. He did his thing during the day, going through the motions.

His life began again every time he went home.

That so totally needed to be a song.

"And you gotta get outta this cold or Deke's gonna kick my ass," he finished, a (very) small smile playing at his attractive mouth.

Deke was bigger than this guy. Even so, I wasn't sure it'd be easy for my man to kick Deacon Gates's ass.

Or anyone to do it.

"Right, thanks again, Deacon," I said.

He jerked his head to the house. "Inside, Justice. And you're welcome."

He moved to his truck.

I moved up the walk, bending to gather a few pumpkins on the way.

I stopped at the front door and turned back, juggling pumpkins to lift a hand to wave.

Deacon was down the lane, his SUV shrouded by dark. I couldn't see if he waved back.

But I doubted he did.

He was on a mission.

Go home so his life could begin again.

I opened the door on that thought, felt the wave of warmth hit me, squatted and put the pumpkins on the floor by the side of the door.

I didn't go back for more. I couldn't see Deke but if he knew I'd gathered all the pumpkins without him helping, this would not make him happy.

As I closed the door on the cold behind me, I took in all that lay before me.

This was obviously not the first time I saw it. I'd watched it all coming together. And that day, as the finishing touches were done, the guys going around sweeping and vacuuming (I still had a cleaning service scheduled to come in the next day and do a full clean—the dudes tidied but they were *dudes* so they weren't real good at it), I'd not once but several times wandered around, taking it all in.

Though now it was vacant and quiet and I could do it without distractions or getting in anyone's way.

It was everything I imagined it to be and more. This more coming from the long copper hood over the center fireplace that was a showstopper. It also came from a set of wide, open-backed stairs set at the landing to the right. The treads of those stairs were the only thing in the house carpeted—thick, cream wool wrapped around each tread. The elegant yet rustic railings were pure artistry. And the inviting widened swirl bottom landing was something I couldn't envision from looking at the plans. Something that was startlingly beautiful in reality.

All building materials had been taken away but my garage was still filled, now with furniture and décor my designer had been sending, deliveries I'd been getting from hitting go on weeks of online shipping, bags of stuff I'd been buying.

It was now Tuesday, a week and a few days after Deke and I went to dinner with Max and Nina.

Tomorrow morning it was the cleaning service and me unearthing purchases from bags and boxes. Tomorrow evening, Deke had arranged for the guys to come around and carry in the furniture that had been delivered.

And my house would start becoming a home.

The only pall on this was that Deke was scheduled to hit another job Max was working on tomorrow. I would no longer have him at my house all day.

Weirdly, we didn't get on each other's nerves with all the time we spent together. Granted, he was working and I also was doing my thing so we weren't in each other's presence 24/7, but we spent a lot of time together.

More weirdly (but this weird was wonderful), the way that was felt like it wasn't going to change. Not that what we had was new and we were in the throes of that—when every second you spent with a lover was fresh and exciting so you wanted to spend every second you had with them.

No, it seemed more like this could be us. *Was* us. We could be that couple who worked together (if we had a business we both could do together), spending nearly every waking and sleeping moment in each other's company, that coming natural, being easy, never getting old.

I'd already found that we could do our thing, me going shopping with the girls or into town to get food or a mani/pedi. But there was a settling when I got back.

Not like I couldn't wait to get back, hated to be away from my man.

Just that, when I was with Deke, everything that was me settled into the fact I was back where I belonged.

So I wasn't real hip on him being gone all day in a way I couldn't get to him and ask what he thought about the towels I was buying for the guest bathroom (or whatever).

But this was life. This was its rhythm and would be the months we stayed put.

I needed to get used to it.

I didn't have to like it, but I needed to get used to it.

Thinking of Deke, it came to mind that he'd disappeared. There was a lot of house, all of it easily accessible now with the stairs and all.

But I had dinner in the Crock-Pot, a pulled-pork recipe that had filled the house with delicious smells all day. Smells Deke had told me he was looking forward to experiencing.

And it was time to experience.

So where was he?

"Deke?" I called, moving farther into the space.

"Yo," he called back, sounding like he was in the bedroom.

I headed that way but stopped when he emerged through the doorway to the hall.

He did this with snowflakes quickly melting in his hair and on his shoulders. And with the chill setting in, even if he worked inside still only wearing a tee, now he had a padded flannel shirt on over that.

He also emerged with a bottle of champagne in his hand and a Deluxe Home Store bag dangling from the other.

He moved right to the black, toffee and cream-veined marble-countertopped island that easily could seat six, even eight.

Though there were only six stools wrapped and waiting to be brought in from the garage.

We'd see how they fit. I might be doing more ordering.

He shrugged off his flannel shirt and tossed it on the island. He put the bottle and bag on the island and dug into the bag.

"Not sure in all the shit you bought that you got champagne glasses, or if you can even find them in that mess in your garage, so Lexie handed these off to Bubba and he stashed them outside."

After unearthing them from white tissue, he set the fluted glasses on the marble, tossed the bag aside and commenced unwrapping the foil on what I could see was a very good bottle of champagne.

I stood immobile, watching him.

The cork popped.

I didn't so much as twitch.

Deke turned to me.

I stared at his face.

"Jussy?" My name was a question.

"It's snowing," I whispered.

"Yeah," he replied quietly, being Deke, reading my mood and falling right into it so he could be there with me.

Right there with me.

"I need to get the pumpkins inside," I shared.

"Do that for you, babe, after we toast your place."

Yes, he would. He'd do that for me. He'd buy me champagne. He'd go on the road with me like Mace did with Stella and the Blue Moon Gypsies. Mace and Stella taking their kids along like Dad used to do with me.

Fuck.

Fuck, fuck, *fuck*.

"Gypsy," Deke said, calling my attention back to him.

"I needed you…on the road," I blurted.

"Say again?" he asked.

"I could have done it," I shared, knowing this to be true straight to the pit of my heart.

That place where my dad lived, Granddad, Joss, Lacey, Bianca, Mr. T, even Mav.

Where Deke lived.

"I could have made it," I told him. "I could have handled it, all of it, if I'd had you."

His face changed, and immediately I memorized that change, the magnificence of it.

A magnificence of feeling.

"Get over here, Justice," he ordered roughly.

I didn't get over there.

I turned my gaze out the windows and saw through the dark that the flurries were falling thicker.

I saw it but I thought about Chace having Faye. Deacon having whoever he had at home.

And me.

I'd drifted here, anchorless without my father.

And I'd found Deke.

Hell, I'd nearly been strangled to death on my own bed.

But somehow, that dramatic, life-altering event barely touched me.

Because I'd found Deke.

And now I was standing in my newly-finished house with a man who lived in a trailer. But he was a man who knew what this house meant to me and thought enough about me to plan ahead, have a friend bring glasses, buy a bottle of champagne and toast the beginning of a new chapter of my life, *our* lives, doing that for me.

I had not found my oasis. I had not found a home.

I'd stumbled into Heaven on earth where miracles could happen.

I knew this because I'd sensed this in Chace. In Deacon.

But I *felt* it in me.

"Justice," Deke rumbled.

I started, shifting my eyes to him.

Then, slowly, I walked to him.

When I got close, Deke, so damned *Deke*, curved an arm around my waist and pulled me tight, my front to his side, his bearded chin buried in his neck to hold my eyes.

His held concern.

"You okay, baby?" he whispered gently.

"I bought champagne glasses," I whispered back.

Deke said nothing.

"And red wineglasses," I carried on. "White wineglasses. Martini glasses. Bourbon glasses—"

Deke cut me off. "I'm catching your drift."

I nodded.

"Talk to me," he ordered.

I did not talk to him.

Oh no.

A moment like that was not for words.

It was for song.

So I didn't talk to him.

I sang to him.

"Wither to dust, crumble like rust, only by your side."

His arm got tighter and I felt it before I heard the noise that reverberated from his gut, through his chest and out between his lips.

But I kept singing.

"Fresh air, cold beer. Root myself in you."

"Stop it, gypsy," he growled.

I didn't stop.

Couldn't.

He knew the words were for him.

But I'd never given them to him, straight from me.

"Consider my life, you're all that's right, breathless to bring on the night."

Deke shuffled us around the corner of the island, clear of the glasses and bottle of champagne.

And I kept singing.

> "*Wither to dust, baby, crumble like rust, only at your side. Just what I need when I have everything.*"

I stopped to gasp as his big hands spanned my hips and I was up, ass to the counter, Deke pushing his hips between my knees, those knees spreading so he was pressed to the heart of me.

Then I was staring at nothing but hazel when his mouth came to mine.

"*Chain links, worn jeans,*" I crooned there. "*I could search 'til I'm done, 'til moon becomes sun.*"

His hand slid up in my hair, bunching it at the back of my skull, his other arm banding across my back, the pads of his fingers digging into the sides of my ribs.

> "*Chain links, white tee.Wither to dust, crumble like rust, all I need is to be at your side.*"

I stopped singing.

"You done?" he asked, his voice thick, his hold on me fierce, his eyes burning.

"Thank you for my house, honey."

"You're done," he muttered.

I was done.

But we were not since he kissed me.

While he did, he pushed me so my back was to the counter, his tongue in my mouth a sensual assault, an intimate branding, more potent than his mark, the one he often found times to renew on my shoulder.

Through it, he yanked at my belt, jerked down my zipper, pulled at my jeans. As I felt wet flood between my legs, I also felt cold marble hit my ass. But even cold, it heated me as Deke angled away. He lifted one of my feet, yanking off my boot, my sock. To the other, they were gone. With a vicious sweep that pulled my ass to the edge of the counter, forcing a gust of electrified breath from my lips, my jeans were torn away.

I watched Deke straighten, his hands to his own jeans. He pulled them down over his hips, his hard cock springing free.

Then he surprised me.

He didn't bend over me, take my mouth when he took my cunt.

He reached to me, wrapping his hand around my throat. Collaring me with his touch, scalding me with the look in his eyes, he caught the back of one of my knees in his hand, yanked up as his hips pressed in.

They rolled and his cock head slithered, fixed on its target, and then he drove in.

Taking him, feeling the exquisiteness of Deke filling me, my neck arched back, the weight and warmth of his large hand spanning my throat splitting my avid attention from that to the force of his thrusts pounding into me.

"Eyes on me, Justice," he ground out.

I righted my head, looked into his eyes, watched the ferocity of feeling etch in his face.

That ferocity for me.

All for me.

I trembled on marble.

"Root myself in you," he grunted, doing just that and grinding.

Oh God.

God.

I lifted the leg he didn't have hold of and pressed the inside of my thigh to his side, everything quivering, legs, belly, lips, fingers, pussy.

"Deke."

He pulled back, but not out, and again started thrusting.

His fingers tightened on my neck even as his thumb slid up, wedging against the hinge of my jaw. Trembling more violently, I felt the pad of it pressing there, searing, certain after we were through I'd look in the mirror and see the burn of his print there, scorched into me.

"Anyone but me ever gonna get in this cunt?" he asked.

I tensed around his driving cock.

Yes.

I was right.

He was searing himself into me. His. For his use. For him. No other.

I was Deke's.

"No," I whispered.

"Ever?" he clipped.

"Not ever, baby," I promised breathlessly.

He pounded into me, my body wrenching with each thrust, held steady only by his hand at my throat, his other one gripping hard at my knee.

Suddenly he jerked up that knee, slamming my pussy into his driving cock, each lunge colliding with my clit, pulsing through me. I lifted one hand to wrap my fingers around his wrist at my neck, holding him there, keeping him there, submitting to all he was doing, communicating I was his to claim. The other hand I slid between my legs, fingers separating, feeling in another way the beauty of Deke claiming me, marking me as his inside, all his, a place no one else would ever be.

It started sweltering over me. I lifted my head, pressing into his collar at my throat, looking under my lashes right into his eyes, moaning raggedly, "Baby, fuck me. Keep fucking me, Deke. Don't stop. Never stop."

He'd been taking me roughly, but at my words, his growl drove up my cunt as it rolled out his mouth and he bent slightly into me, his eyes locked to mine, and the silken violence of his fucking turned to velvet savagery.

"Yes, baby," I panted. Pulling my fingers from between my legs, I lifted that hand and caught it hard around the back of his neck. "That's yours. Make it yours, all yours, Deke."

"Come, Jussy," he grunted.

I didn't want to come. I wanted my grip on him, his grip on me, his eyes like that, his face like that, his cock marking me deep, and I wanted it for eternity.

"Goddamn it, *come, Jussy*," he snarled.

I was panting, soft moans escaping each time he plunged deep, filling me, connecting with me, knitting himself stronger in everything that was me, my eyes pinned to his.

It was time.

"Love you," I whispered.

"Love you too, gypsy, now fuckin' *come*," he growled back.

I came. My spine arching off the marble, my leg winding around the small of his back, my fingers curling, my nails sinking into flesh, I cried out, first his name then soft noises escaping me as I felt my pussy undulate around his still thrusting cock, my clit contracting, throbbing, my breath finally suspending.

"*Fuck*."

That came from Deke and it was a muted roar as he continued to pound into me, the feral sound of his release scraping into my skin, driving up my cunt, prolonging my orgasm as I felt him shoot hot and wet and deep into me.

When he collapsed on me, forehead to my temple, forcing my head to the side to cushion him, he didn't let go of my throat or my knee.

I struggled to modulate my breathing and felt it against my ear, my cheek, as Deke did the same, his cock planted deep, rooted in me.

Rooted in me.

Love you too, gypsy…

Love you too, gypsy…

Love…

You…

Too.

I felt the tears gather in my eyes and I was too spent, physically and emotionally, to fight them back.

With Deke sense, he knew they were there the instant the first one slid over the bridge of my nose.

I knew this when he lifted his head and noted, "Baby, for a woman who says she doesn't cry, you're a serious fuckin' crier."

I righted my head and looked up at him.

"You just told me you loved me," I pointed out in a reverent whisper.

Deke wasn't in the mood for reverence.

"Yeah, and you just told me you loved me. But after the best fuckin' orgasm I've ever had in my goddamned life, this besting the one you gave me last night, which, babe, was off the charts…remind me to tie you face down again and soon…you don't see me cryin'."

I watched his eyes turn glazed as my pussy shivered around his cock at the reminder of last night.

But my lips still hissed, "You're a mountain man, Deke. It's a guess, but a good one, that mountain men rarely cry. Even after avowals of love."

He again focused on me. "You're now a mountain woman, Jussy, a world-weary, worldly-wise, rock gypsy one, and, drop of a hat, you're blubbering like a baby."

Was he giving me shit about crying after he just told me he loved me?

"And I'll repeat, this is because you just told me you loved me," I declared. I lifted a hand, finger out, indicating my face. "And just to note, you giving me shit at this juncture, I'm no longer crying," I pointed out, then complained, "You've totally ruined the moment."

A playful light hit his eyes which caused another pussy shiver that in turn caused his lips to curl up.

"Totally?" he teased.

"Totally," I snapped, though it was a little breathy.

Suddenly, his face was closer and his thumb was sweeping my jaw, my chin, and up, catching on my lower lip.

"Totally?" he whispered.

Okay.

Not totally. Nothing could ruin this moment.

Not a thing.

Being Deke thus being awesome, he didn't push it, make me admit it out loud.

He just asked, "You love me, Jussy?"

Now I could say it. I could say it not in the middle of fantastic sex through which Deke was claiming my pussy, my body, *me*.

I could just say it, right out, all for him.

For Deke.

"Yeah, baby, I love you."

I watched that settle in his face, and doing it, I watched the miracle of this place that gave things like Deke to me and things like me to Deke at work.

This latest miracle being watching the edges life had cut into his face smooth out, not from sleep, not from sex.

All from me.

Shit.

I was going to start crying again.

To control that, I pulled in a ragged breath while Deke ran his thumb from my lip, over my chin, down my throat. "Thinkin' a' buyin' you champagne every night."

"I like champagne, honey, but you *really* wanna get in there, you get me bourbon."

He pressed his hips into mine, my lips parted at the sweet feeling, and he asked, "Can I get in deeper?"

I was utterly serious when I looked right into his eyes and answered, "No."

He read my serious.

Totally.

"Rooted in you," he stated, his eyes gleaming, predatory, possessive, making the point he'd made with his cock, his hand around my throat, everything he'd just done to me.

The point he'd made our first time, sinking his teeth into my skin.

I'd been his then.

We were just making it official.

"Rooted in me," I breathed.

He wrapped the leg he had hold of around his back and used his now free hand to slide up my neck, his fingers going into my hair, his other hand leaving my throat to follow suit on the opposite side.

"Only roots I want, me in you, you in me," he said quietly.

Fuck.

He was going to make me cry again and I wasn't going to be able to control it.

He watched my face.

Then he said, "Shit, you're gonna start up again."

"Am not," I snapped, though the words were shaky.

He grinned at me teasingly, but that was a front, giving me what I needed to pull myself together. I knew this because I also felt both his thumbs stroke behind my ears soothingly.

"I need champagne," I declared.

"Yeah," he replied.

"Do you drink champagne?" I asked.

"Tonight I do," he answered.

Tonight he did.

Tonight, a night for a lot of celebrating, for me, Deke drank champagne.

I lifted up and touched my mouth to his before falling back into his hands in my hair. "Then pour, honey. I'll get cleaned up. We'll toast my pad being done then pulled pork."

"You got it," he murmured. "I'll grab the pumpkins then hit the champagne."

He slowly slid out and then pulled me up so I was sitting on the counter.

He kept us there, me in his arms, my head tipped back, his chin dipped down.

He studied my face, liked what he saw, showed me that with his expression, and then he kissed me, long and sweet.

When he was done, he helped me off the counter, yanked up his jeans, tucking his cock inside, but helped me grab my jeans and panties before he did his up.

"Be back," I told him.

"Gotcha," he replied.

"Always, Deke."

It came out as a blurt, and his gaze, having roamed to the bottle of champagne, came to mine.

"Yeah, baby," he whispered, his mouth soft, his look warm.

I gave him that back.

Then I dashed to the bathroom to clean up. Having had my period in the interim (so no baby after the time Deke did me ungloved), I was now on the Pill.

No more condoms.

Just Deke and me.

That was good since we'd run out.

This thought gave me a grin.

Thoughts of the last twenty minutes made that grin turn into a big, fat smile.

Thoughts of pulled pork made my stomach start grumbling.

So I cleaned up, pulled on my clothes, grabbed a new pair of warm socks and tugged them on.

I took only a second to look out the windows to the flurries that had become full-blown snow falling down, thick and heavy, on my patch of mountain.

"I'm happy, Daddy," I whispered.

The snow kept falling quietly, beautifully, peacefully.

I took that as Dad's answer that he was glad.

Then I did what I said I would do.

What I would always do.

I went right back to my man.

* * *

Deke

Later that night, Deke felt Jussy relax in his arms and heard her breaths even out in sleep.

Lying there, holding his gypsy close in her big, expensive bed in her big, expensive house in the mountains after what they'd shared on her island, he felt a stillness his entire life he only felt while doing one thing.

Being on the road.

It did not tweak him.

It made complete sense.

Deke was in love with her.

So it was no surprise she brought him this peace.

Deke did not look out the window.

Instead, he buried his face in Jussy's hair.

And he did not speak out loud.

He thought the words inside his head.

I'm good, Ma.

Then, falling deeper into that place, holding Jussy to him in that big, expensive bed in that big, expensive house in the mountains, Deke closed his eyes and found sleep.

CHAPTER TWENTY-ONE

Not Ever Again

Deke

DEKE FELT JUSSY plant her hands in his gut, her hair sweeping across his chest as she arched back, the nectar of her flooding his mouth as she came on his face.

He took it in, kept her there as long as he could before he had to give himself what he needed.

Gripping her hips, he hauled her down his chest, slid her off him and rolled into her as he pulled her to her side, her back to his front. He grasped his dick, shifting down. Guiding his cock, he drove inside, and as he took her, he felt the hot, sleek of her clutch him while she kept coming.

He dug one arm under her and angled it up, spanning her throat, pushing it back as he bent his neck so her head glided up his cheek, her hair tangling in his beard. He buried his face in her neck and his other hand between her legs, pushing in, finding her clit with his finger, rolling hard.

"Get there again, gypsy," he growled, thrusting into her tight pussy, feeling his own orgasm gather in his balls, his cock.

She panted softly, moving her hips to rock into his thrusts at the same time grind into his fingers.

"God," she whispered.

"Get there," he ordered.

"*God*," she blew out.

"Baby..." he slid his hand up her throat to wrap it under her jaw, "*get there*," he grunted.

Her head pressed back into his shoulder as she stopped panting and started mewing. He felt the rush of the wet of her second orgasm coat his cock and he couldn't hold back.

He shifted his hand from between her legs so he could wrap his arm around her belly and drove her down. Grinding up, he felt the sweet release, his cum jetting inside her, his world narrowing to only that. His dick buried deep in Jussy, her slick, snug, sweet, hot cunt clutching him from root to tip, milking him dry as he felt her body judder, not with her orgasm, with the power of his body taking her along the ride with his.

It took its time moving out of him and just as slowly his world expanded. He felt her softness tucked against him. He smelled her hair. Tasted the essence of her skin drifting into his mouth as he breathed hard against her neck. The sun shining against his closed eyelids. The sound of Jussy's breaths starting to even. The feel of her soft sheets, firm mattress, both made warm by their bodies.

Not satisfied with what he was getting, Deke went in direct, touching his tongue to her skin, tasting Jussy. His hand still at her jaw pushed her head back farther as he turned his, gliding his mouth up her neck to work just under her ear, knowing she liked what he was giving her as she relaxed in his hold.

He trailed his other hand up her belly, over her tit, up her chest, around her neck and back into her hair. He gathered it there, up high, feeling the tangle of curls drag up his chest as it went, and he shoved her head forward, shifting his lips to work the nape of her neck.

She shivered against him, a soft noise escaping her that he felt tighten in his balls, but she stayed still, taking what he was giving, getting off on it, her cunt contracting around his still-rooted cock.

He filtered his fingers out of her hair and lifted his head slightly, tracking his lips to her other ear.

He sunk his teeth lightly in her earlobe, tasting the metal of her earring, before he released her and whispered, "Love my gypsy."

The shiver that got was bigger, inside and out, forcing him to press his hips into her ass, deepening the connection they were losing as the hard went out of his cock.

"Love you too, honey," she whispered back, finding his hand, covering the back of it with hers, lacing her fingers through his.

Deke moved minutely to kiss the skin where her shoulder met her neck, before he settled in behind her, face in her hair, holding her close, doing that until he naturally slid out of her wet, glazed in him, glazed in her, in them.

And he still held her.

It was Jussy who moved first, but only to turn in his arms, look into his face and do what she did a lot.

She scrutinized it, her attention acute, but as usual, it didn't last very long before whatever she found there settled her. She melted into him and lifted a hand to dig her fingers lightly into his beard where she left them.

Post-fucking, holding her, their quiet, her peace, he didn't want to leave that bed. It was the Saturday after Jussy's house got done. The client Max had him working for didn't want overtime. So they had the whole weekend.

They also didn't since she didn't waste any time asking everyone over for a housewarming party, no gifts allowed, and she was making a vat of Steph's chicken.

Not to mention, he knew his girl. Sex helped shear off the edge of her morning mood. But it didn't eradicate it.

"You want coffee?" he asked.

"Yeah, baby," she answered.

"You want pancakes?" he went on.

Her eyebrows lifted. "You can make pancakes?"

"Babe, you bought Bisquick, along with everything else the market had on offer. Add eggs, milk, stir, pour, cook, eat. Not hard."

She grinned. "Then yes, I want pancakes."

He grinned back, dipped in, brushed his mouth to hers and pulled away. "Then I'm on coffee and pancakes. You get cleaned up."

"Right, Deke."

He gave her a squeeze then dipped in again, this time the touch of their mouths lasted a lot longer and included a healthy taste of his gypsy.

When he finished it, he rolled, careful to keep the covers over Jussy. He hauled his ass out of bed, twitching them higher on her, knowing she'd laze, not for hours but as long as she needed.

He bent, grabbed his fleece sweatpants he'd taken off in order to fuck his woman and tugged them on. He then grabbed the band Jussy always pulled out when they fucked before sleep from the nightstand and used it to secure his hair.

On the way to the door, he twisted to catch sight of her, the jumbled mess of dark curls all over the bed and pillow behind her, her eyes on him, her look lazy and cute.

She hitched up one side of her mouth.

He shot back the same, turned to face where he was going and walked out of the room.

Moving into her living space, Deke looked to his right and saw what Jussy had created with her designer.

She might have had the help of a designer, but what she made was straight-up Jussy.

Two full couches flanking the fireplace parallel to the house, both covered in soft faded denim, four chairs in distressed brown leather with brass buttons marking their edges, two with their backs to the front door, two across with backs to the kitchen.

In the corner by the front windows at an angle, another big couch, slouchy, in a dark brown, one red armchair to one side, a bright blue one to the other side, matching ottomans, but switched, blue in front of the red chair, red in front of the blue. Large square coffee table. More tables between chairs and couches. Standing lamps around so nothing got in the way of setting down a bottle of beer, a glass of bourbon or a finished plate of food.

She had another seventy-inch TV fixed on a kickass mount that pulled out, angled up, down and sideways. That was Deke's suggestion, giving her the opportunity to push the TV flush to the wall so it could be seen from the seating at the fireplace, or angled where it was closer to the corner space and watched from there, or again angled so it could be seen from the kitchen.

The doors to her music room were open, that room painted black and he could see her guitar on the stand in there, the curvy couch covered in some hide that was dark-chocolate-colored and had a sheen. She also had curved chairs in there with cream backing, zebra print on the front. There was a big rug in a muted red design. Plus there were dark wood cases of different sizes holding a top-of-the-line stereo and speakers she'd set up as well as her CD collection, which her stepmom had mailed, something that was expansive. And last, a feminine, almost delicate desk with a leopard print chair where she'd put her laptop.

He moved to the kitchen and looked into the opened doors of her dining room. One side of that room was curved and she'd gone with a massive, round table surrounded by twelve chairs. Some had arms, oval backs, and were covered in tiger print. Others had high backs, inwardly sloping at the top, covered in wine red velvet. The last, again with high backs, these curled back, the deep purple velvet upholstery buttoned.

The chandeliers, light fixtures and other lighting she chose were made of branches or iron, large statement pieces that, along with all the rest, drew the eye so you didn't know where to look, but it all was such the shit, you wanted to take everything in at once. Including the four dangling pendants over the island that ended in large, flawed, oblong globes that looked almost like drops, the glass blown so bubbles were trapped inside.

The island was also flanked by six stools running the edge, low backs, seriously deep seats, comfortable and covered in a paisley that brought all the colors into play. Rich colors. Warm colors. Rock 'n' roll colors. Jussy's colors. Red, blue, brown, purple, black.

There were rugs on the floor (and finally one in her bedroom, even if it took him, Ty, Tate, Bubba and Chace to lift up her huge-ass bed while Jussy and Lauren rolled it out underneath). There were throws tossed around she told him were mohair. Sheepskins draped here and there. Soft, fluffy toss pillows in every shape imaginable all over the fucking place.

Not to mention, each room upstairs was furnished all the way down to bed linens and towels in the bathrooms. Up there, though, there were wall hangings.

Downstairs, Jussy had things of hers, her father's and her grandfather's that for the first, she was waiting on her mom or stepmom to send, the last, she was waiting for the nuisance shit that her half-brother was pulling to be over to get them so she could mount them where she wanted them when that happened.

She'd told him what they were. Framed concert posters. Gold and platinum records. Original album cover art. One-of-a-kind photos of her dad, grandad, aunt and uncle onstage or candid on tour and at home, with family.

This thought brought his eye to the only empty space left, the room she wanted her father's collection in. The broken window had been replaced and Deke had adjusted the doorframe, this being the only thing left to finish since Max had had to custom order folding doors that worked with the space, Jussy's vision of the place (which meant they were dead cool) and they wouldn't be in for another two weeks.

He'd also had the boys build a double platform in there, that platform running along the entire back of the space. And he'd ordered illuminated bookshelves fitted wall to wall, floor to ceiling on either side, putting in the ceiling lighting himself of small spots that would highlight the guitars when they were where they were supposed to be. All of this so she could display those guitars and her grandfather and father's awards that she and Dana had divvied up that were in her father's possession.

Deke stopped at her brushed stainless steel fridge and gave the entire space a sweep.

It was Jussy, end to end, top to bottom.

It was huge.

It screamed money.

And outside his trailer, he'd never felt more relaxed in a space in his entire life.

It didn't feel like it was hers. Since his hands touched nearly every inch of it, each sweep of paint, every nail and floorboard—with the addition of the fact that not a stick of furniture, even a goddamned toss pillow, was chosen without his approval—it felt like it was theirs.

His mother had never owned a home. Not even when his father was alive. They'd rented, saving meagerly to buy when they had the chance, this savings the only reason she was able to keep a roof over his head for the months it took her to grieve at the same time find a job.

Now he felt like he was home.

He hadn't sunk a penny into Jussy's place, but his energy and sweat put it together.

It wasn't even that.

It was Jussy, almost from the first—before they got their shit together to be together—making him feel like this was his space, a part of him as it was a part of her.

Deke felt this in a way he knew, when they got back from the road to settle in for winter, he'd go to his lake. He'd fish. He'd take his woman to the trailer to have her with him, fuck her there, let her put her stamp on it with shit they collected along the way, sticking her part of his history that was now starting to be their history on the ceiling, the walls.

But this would be where they would be so Jussy could have her father close to her through his guitars and all his other shit and Deke could be in the place he gave her—not offering it up with money—piecing it together because that was his job.

And that was the way he could give her what she needed.

He shook himself out of his thoughts, as good as they were, because he needed to make his woman coffee.

He had it brewing, had pulled out the Bisquick, eggs and milk and was reaching for a mixing bowl out of a drawer when he heard someone driving down her lane.

He looked to the front door, knowing it could be anybody. Even though those anybodies were all invited to her place that night, that didn't mean one (or several of them) wouldn't be at her door for whatever reason they had need of Jussy.

This had just become the way. Jussy was a part of Carnal now and when the folks of Carnal accepted you that happened.

Deke left the shit on the island, moved around the marble and made his way to the door.

He had it open and stood in it. The sun was bright in the sky. The snow that had stuck, stayed through the chill of Wednesday, then disappeared by afternoon Thursday after warm rushed back in meant his woman's pumpkins were again out.

There was a shiny black Escalade in the drive.

Out of it stepped a woman, long legs, great ass, big head of auburn hair, a profile that was a mirror of Jussy's.

She turned to him full face with sunglasses on. He couldn't see her eyes, but he still knew she was Joss.

She slammed the door, and on high-heeled boots, her rounded hips incased in faded denim, a feminine-cut sheepskin jacket that looked torn off the likes of Carly Simon and transported straight from the 70's on her shoulders, huge shades covering her eyes, shades locked to him, she moved across the gravel like she was gliding gracefully along ice.

When he sensed movement, Deke's attention shifted to the man rounding the hood of the SUV. Tall, seriously lean, his head a mass of long, tangled, spiked-out-at-the-top, dirty-blond hair. He was wearing a black leather jacket that was a lot of zippers and snaps with a dangling belt at the bottom, black jeans, motorcycle boots with rings at the sides, wraparound black shades covering his eyes.

Roddy Rembrandt.

Without notice, Jussy's family was calling.

Fuck.

He didn't move even as they made their way up the front walk and stopped in front of him.

"Jesus, you're a big boy," Jussy's mom muttered.

And looking at her close, Deke was straight up stunned.

Not a line on her face. The shades still on, he couldn't see her eyes but from what he could see, he knew the woman was fifty-three, and she looked, tops, like she hadn't even hit forty.

"You're Joss," he stated.

"Yup," she declared. "And you're Deke."

"Yup," he replied, turned his attention beyond her to Rembrandt, who was standing close to his wife's back, and he greeted, "Rembrandt."

"Dude," the man greeted back.

Deke moved out of the way, opening the door farther as he did, indication they should come in.

No hesitation, they came right in.

He shut the door behind them and turned, seeing they were already planted inside, facing his way.

Jussy's mom had her sunglasses pushed up in her hair and he saw gray eyes, not Jussy's brown, and still no lines.

These were aimed at his chest.

And her mouth was curled up.

"Jussy's lazing," he shared. "I'll go rile her ass," *and get a fucking shirt*. "Coffee's on. Take off your coats, come in, get comfortable. Be back."

Rembrandt had kept his shades on, as apparently rockers did, even inside, but he didn't hesitate to shrug his coat off. When he did, Deke saw a long sleeve tee that had seen better days, was faded from its original black to a dark gray, and had big, cracked white letters on the front that said, IT'S ONLY ROCK AND ROLL. BUT I LIKE IT.

Joss kept smirking at him.

Jesus.

Deke moved and was halfway to the door to the back hall when Jussy came out of it, dressed in a new pair of ridiculous pajamas she'd unearthed from a box that came the day before from an online order.

Bottoms long, gathered at the ankle, a peachy-cream with bright embroidery across the front of the hips and down one leg, waistband so loose, it didn't sit at her waist but hung on the tops of her hips. Top, a tight-fitting, army green thermal with a dizzying pattern of stars on it that in no way matched the pants, but came with them.

Deke had learned to look on the bright side with some of Jussy's clothing. A lot of it rocked because it showed tits, legs, or if he got close, panties and/or bra. The rest of it, there was always something good about it, even if he had to dig to find the good.

This was no exception. The top fit snug at her tits which were clearly not bound by a bra. The bottoms had slits all the way up the sides from gathered hem to waistband.

In bed, and out of it, his hand could find itself in very good places with the slits in those pants. And starting about five minutes after she'd put them on last night, they had.

Almost as good, her nipples were showing through the thermal, she didn't give a shit, he liked that and he liked the view.

"Uh…what the hell?" she asked, her eyes aimed beyond Deke to her mother and stepdad.

"Surprise," Joss answered on a drawl.

Jussy's face screwed up.

Deke stopped at her side and put a hand to her belly.

She tipped her pissed-off expression to him.

"As you can see, your family's here. Gettin' a shirt. Makin' pancakes for four. And it's all good," he stated.

She clearly didn't agree.

So he pressed his hand light into her stomach and repeated, "It's all good, gypsy."

She drew in breath, doing it pulling a Jussy, which meant pulling her shit together.

Seeing that, Deke let her go and kept moving.

But he'd find she hadn't pulled her shit totally together because he heard her mother asking, "My baby girl gonna come and give her momma a hug?"

"Yes, she is, because she loves you. But first, she's going to ask if your fingers have all been broken, and Roddy's, so you couldn't text me to tell me you were showing first thing on a frickin' Saturday morning."

That's all he got before he was in her room and the voices became less distinct.

So he was grinning when he hit her room.

He grabbed his own thermal, pulled it on and moved his ass back to where Jussy was with her family.

When he got there, he saw Joss's sheepskin jacket was off, it and her bag thrown on one of the denim couches. This exposed a bright red tee, barely-there sleeves, a dead-fucking-cool Chinese dragon stitched on the front.

Rembrandt's jacket was on the couch too, and Jussy was giving him a hug. It was a jerky, short, annoyed one, but it was still a hug.

Deke's lips quirked as he moved to the side of the couch opposite them and leaned against it.

Jussy pulled out of Rembrandt's arms and turned Deke's way.

"I take it you met Deke," she remarked, throwing her hand toward him.

"That we did," Joss replied.

"And Deke's a mellow guy, so he's always laidback, so I can't tell from him if you were cool when you met him," Jussy went on.

Joss's eyes narrowed on her daughter. "We've barely been here five minutes, girl, *and* I've barely said five words to him."

Jussy lifted her brows to her mother, not missing a beat. "And were those five words cool?"

Joss seemed like she was fixing to blow when Rembrandt skirted the couch, put his back to the arm, and collapsed into it, still wearing his shades, announcing, "Took the redeye here. Got fuckin' six fuckin' suitcases, four of 'em filled with your shit, Jussy, in that SUV. Wrangled that crap myself because your mother wanted to arrive without *an entourage*," he said the last like this was a sticking point on a variety of things between Joss and Roddy. "Now I'm bone-tired, need coffee, food, to bonk my wife and then pass out."

"Rod!" Joss snapped.

"What?" he asked, looking up at her through his shades from his position on the couch. "That's not all gonna happen?"

"All of it *would* have happened if you hadn't announced in front of Jussy's new man that you were gonna bonk your wife. Now that particular part is *not* gonna happen," Joss returned.

"The dude's a dude," Rembrandt shot back, turning his head on the couch to look at Deke. "A *big* dude." He aimed his shades back up at his wife. "We dudes don't get offended by that shit. He's cool."

"So, say, *Jussy* doesn't feel like carrying the knowledge her guest room bed is gonna get broken in by her stepdad bonking her mom," Joss retorted.

"Jussy's cooler than her dude, I know that for sure," Rembrandt muttered, something that was absolutely correct, and he did this folding his hands on his chest like he was a vampire in a coffin except his coffin was a couch his legs were dangling off the side.

Deke was having a fuckuva time controlling his need to bust out laughing.

He looked from Rembrandt to his gypsy and found that effort easier when he saw her neck bowed, shoulders slumped, head shaking side to side.

"Baby," he called softly.

Her head came up and she turned her eyes to him.

"I *am* a dude but you know I'm cool."

"I need coffee," she replied.

"Gotcha," he murmured, turned and moved into the kitchen.

"Did I hear pancakes?" Rembrandt called.

"Those are coming after coffee, Roddy," Jussy declared, and when she did, Deke knew she was on the move toward him.

"Rod, get your ass up and go bring in the suitcases," Joss ordered.

"Fuck that," he replied. "Nothin' in them is gonna go bad. They can wait until after my nap."

"Rod—"

"After pancakes, I'll get 'em," Deke injected into their exchange, fingers through one of Jussy's new mugs, other hand reaching toward the pot.

"I'll help," Jussy decreed.

"No you won't," he told her.

"Yes, I will," she returned.

"Justice," he said low.

She looked into his eyes, sighed and shifted to the fridge, undoubtedly to get her creamer.

"I take mine dollop of cream, no sugar," Joss announced.

"I take mine black and I hope like fuck that shit's strong," Rembrandt called from the couch.

"Rod, you wanna cut back on the language?" Joss suggested, sliding her firm ass on a barstool, doing this with torso twisted to the couch.

Turning his shades his wife's way, Rembrandt fired back, "Babe, the *dude* is a *dude*. Relax."

Joss twisted to her daughter, sharing, "I knew I shouldn't have brought him."

Deke handed Jussy her mug, seeing by her profile she agreed.

He beat back a chuckle and reached for another mug.

"You think I'm gonna get left out of lookin' over Jussy's boy, think again, somethin' I told your ass when you tried to elbow me outta this trip," Rembrandt said.

Deke was pouring and through it he heard Jussy's audible sigh.

Christ, he hadn't been called a "boy" since his mother's dickhead employer referred to him only that way from the time he could understand English to the day the motherfucker fired his ma.

He had this thought and still, Rembrandt doing it, Deke felt his mouth twitch.

"Just so you don't get peeved, I'm officially ignoring you for the next half an hour," Joss told her husband.

"I'm down with that," her husband muttered.

Deke couldn't beat back the strangled noise that was a swallowed laugh.

"We're so totally going to need more coffee," Jussy mumbled.

He turned a smile to her.

She caught it, her face softened and she gave him a small smile back.

"Girl, get your ass over here," Joss ordered. "Sit by your momma. And tell me about this place which…is…*fine*. The dining room, baby girl…*inspired*."

Jussy's look to him lingered before she moved to her mother.

A minute later, Deke was sliding her mug across the island toward Joss, who now had Jussy on a stool by her side, when she aimed her eyes to his.

"She wouldn't let me come. We had to surprise her. She asked for some time. We gave her some time. Time was up. I'm sure you get it."

It wasn't asking for a confirmation. She was telling him he'd better get it because it was the way it was, for more reasons than the fact they were actually there.

"I get it. And it's all good. Soon's she gets some coffee in her, she'll beat back her morning mood and she'll get it too," Deke replied, pulling away from the island to go back to the mugs.

"He's good-looking," Joss shared openly.

"Please don't talk about him like he's not here," Jussy returned.

"You're good-looking," Joss stated loudly, this Deke knew was aimed at his back.

"Gratitude," he muttered, the word sounding tortured because it *was* torture trying not to laugh.

"And he's big," Joss went on. "You're big," she called immediately so Jussy wouldn't get in her shit about it. "Though I already told you that."

He turned and looked at her. "You did."

Then he started to walk a filled mug toward Rembrandt on the couch.

"You told him he was big?" Jussy asked.

"Baby, he was standing in the door when we got here. I couldn't miss that. There are people in the space station who didn't miss that."

He had Rembrandt's eyes on him so he caught the big, professionally-whitened smile the man returned to the one Deke could not bite back.

"No, you're right. It's impossible to miss. But that doesn't mean you should *say* something about it," Jussy retorted.

"I did, and he doesn't care."

Jussy's tone tightened when she noted, "So you *weren't* cool in those five words you gave him."

"Justice, drink your coffee. We'll resume communications in five minutes when the caffeine has started working its way through your system," Joss declared.

Deke thought this was a good play.

"Thanks, dude," Rembrandt muttered as Deke handed him his mug.

He didn't wait to watch after the man started curling up to take a sip. He turned back to the kitchen.

He'd poured his own cup by the time conversation resumed.

"How long are you staying?" Jussy asked her mother.

"I have a client to see Monday afternoon. Rod's got shit on too. So we have to leave Sunday, late afternoon."

He watched his woman do another shoulder slump. Now that they were there, she was getting past the surprise, her irritation they showed and why they did, she didn't like the short visit.

"Though, this place is the…fuckin'…*shit*," Rembrandt decreed from the couch. "We're totally coming back."

"Next time, though, we'll let you know," Joss said to her daughter quietly.

It was and was not an apology.

And while Deke watched her, moving back to his bowl, he saw his gypsy accept it, doing this inaudibly.

"Dude, you're hittin' the pancakes, just to say, I like mine doughy, by that I mean, medium rare on the inside," Rembrandt placed his order.

Deke looked to Jussy and grinned.

She grinned back, shaking her head.

Joss twisted toward the couch.

"First, Rod, his name is not *dude*, it's *Deke*. Second, you aren't in a restaurant. You're in Jussy's home."

"Thought you were ignoring me," Rembrandt noted.

"Fuck, I forgot," Joss muttered.

Deke couldn't help it. His shoulders shaking, he failed in holding it back and released the chuckle.

"Just so you know, I'm normal," Joss stated. "He's not, but I'm so normal, I can often balance us out. I'm unable to do that right now since his not normal is in overdrive due to the fact he's tired, hungry and horny."

Jussy looked to the ceiling.

Deke's shoulders kept shaking as his laughter got louder.

Through it, he looked at Joss and saw a beauty that hadn't even started fading in a way she'd be that kickass bitch at seventy that twenty-year-old girls looked at and vowed they'd be like her when they got that age.

This boded well for him because he could tell already she'd passed that down to his girl.

When his laughter died down, he said, "No offense but you aren't normal either, Joss. But just to say, that's good. Normal sucks."

Joss took him in and she took her time doing it before she turned to her daughter and said, "I give preliminary approval."

"He can make a doughy pancake, I give full approval," Rembrandt called from the couch.

That was when he heard it, Jussy's giggle, starting the way it always started, with a tinkling sound, before it became full-throated laughter.

And then Deke watched her fall forward into her mother, who caught her in her arms as Jussy wound hers around Joss.

"You're a pain in my ass," she said in her mom's neck, voice muffled by a shit ton of auburn hair that was second only to her daughter's. "But I'm glad you're here."

Deke kept watching and while he did, Joss Rembrandt did not get his preliminary approval.

She got it full, the way her profile gentled, love saturating her face, her eyes slowly closing in a way that looked like she needed to do it in order to fully focus on a moment of bliss, her arms visibly tightening.

"Missed you, baby girl."

"Missed you too, Joss."

They held on to each other.

Deke turned from mother and daughter to find the measuring cups.

* * *

Late that afternoon, the countdown at two hours before everyone was going to get there, Deke sat at the end of one of Justice's denim couches, Jussy curled up to his side.

Rod and Joss sat across from them in the middle of the couch. Rod slouched into the side of his wife, his stocking feet on the edge of the fireplace, legs at an angle. Joss was slouched too, down in the seat, her legs in front of her bent, soles of her feet to the fireplace.

It was after pancakes, Rod and Deke hauling in the suitcases, Joss and Rod disappearing upstairs for their nap and possibly other activities, which fortunately, if they happened, he and Jussy didn't hear.

With Deke helping, Jussy got on starting Steph's chicken. And with Deke lazing on the bed he'd helped Jussy make, he kept her company while she unpacked a variety of shit from the four suitcases. Most of it was clothing, some shoes, sandals and boots, some small cases of jewelry, all of it a headache-inducing variety of colors, patterns, feathers, metals, beads and tassels, and she put them away.

After that, they took a shower, and just in case the distance and shower sounds didn't muffle it, Deke did so her family couldn't hear their activities.

When Joss reemerged from the guest room, leaving her husband up there, Deke took stock of the situation in fridge and cupboards that Jussy had already covered at the market. And even though it was unlikely they needed more due to two extra people considering the slightly alarming amount of provisions Jussy had already stocked, he headed to town to augment it.

He did this so his gypsy princess had time with her mother and because Joss had explained both she and Rod were also bourbon drinkers. So even though they had two bottles, he figured another two wouldn't hurt.

He came back and found Rod had roused. Jussy made them all grilled cheese sandwiches, which were the best he'd ever tasted. Simple flavors, three different types of cheese melted together, the fresh bread coated in real butter that crisped and flavored the bread.

Now they were kicked back, Steph's chicken not labor intense, only needing to pour out chips, nuts, fill dip bowls and start the rice since Shambles said he and Sunny were bringing dessert.

Conversation was mainly about the folks Joss and Roddy would meet, folks Jussy had spent time texting to share the heads up that they'd be at a housewarming party that included a famous member of a metal band and her mother.

Thc mood was casy. It was as hc'd told hcr it would bc, all good. Joss and Rod had come to look him over, but more, they'd come to be with Jussy and they were tight. They settled into that quickly, clearly happy to be spending time together, especially after all that had happened from losing Johnny to Jussy getting attacked.

Unfortunately, although that ease seemed stamped on where they'd fallen into after an unexpected arrival, Joss was Joss, Rod was Rod, so in a way Deke figured it frequently was, that ease evaporated.

It did this when Rod suddenly twisted his neck to look at his wife and stated, "We should tell her. Talk about it now before her friends show."

Jussy's loose body lost some of its looseness at his side as Joss looked at her husband, declaring inflexibly, "We'll talk about it tomorrow."

Rembrandt either had a habit of ignoring or not caring about his wife's inflexibility, even when it pertained to something that had to do with her daughter.

"We should get on it now so she can think about it. I gotta tell Ricky. He's taking this on. More time he has to deal with shit, the better and, baby," Rembrandt's voice had dipped to quiet, "even if it's only a day, with this kind of shit, you know that."

"She doesn't need to have it on her mind when she's looking forward to a good time with her friends," Joss returned.

That made Jussy's body lose all its looseness and tighten at his side.

Which made Deke straighten in the couch and pull her closer.

"Shit needs to get done, Joss, and she's not gonna think it's a bad idea," Rod retorted.

"We can talk about it tomorrow," Joss stated.

"We should talk about it now," Rembrandt fired back.

"You're gonna talk about it now," Deke cut in after feeling Jussy get more and more tense. "Now that it's out, she needs to know. And whatever it is, she's Jussy, you know better than me that she'll deal."

Both Joss and Rembrandt looked to him, Rembrandt nonthreateningly.

Joss's face was getting hard.

"My daughter can speak for herself," she snapped.

Deke felt Jussy turn to stone.

He strengthened his hold on her and said to her mother, "She can. But she isn't 'cause you two are doin' your thing, and I can feel it's tweaking her. So just say it so she can have it and do whatever she needs to do with it."

Joss opened her mouth to say something but Jussy got there before her.

"Not another word."

That made Deke's body tense and he looked down at his woman to see her face was as rigid as her frame.

"Do not ever speak to Deke that way again, Joss," she ordered, her voice firm, authoritative, not like a daughter talking to a mother, but like a friend laying out to a friend what needed to be laid out, something important to her, something she wanted to make sure wasn't missed.

"Justice—" Joss began.

"Not ever again," Jussy whispered angrily.

Deke looked from her to her mother to see Joss's face was now also stiff. He also saw the one thing other than the man's clear affection for Jussy that made Deke know he was not only going to like Rembrandt, but respect him.

Rod had straightened, shifted, took hold of Joss, and was now offering her what Deke was offering Justice with his arm around her.

The men remained silent as mother and daughter went into staredown and Deke was not even a little surprised when Jussy came out the winner, Joss turning her attention to Deke and saying, "My apologies, Deke."

"No worries," he murmured, gave his woman a squeeze and looked down at her. He waited until she aimed her irate eyes to him and he repeated, "No worries, baby. Yeah?"

She studied his face and must have gotten what she needed because she mumbled, "Yeah."

"Dana called," Rembrandt put in and both Deke and Justice turned surprised eyes to him.

Deke didn't miss that Joss noted both their expressions, which communicated to her all Jussy had shared with Deke, the breadth of it and the depth.

With his look, she knew that Deke was fully aware that there were four people in her parents' separate relationships, two who didn't belong, these two being the ones who belonged to the wrong people. It was fucked. It was sad. But the ones who didn't belong loved the ones who belonged to each other so much, in a sad, fucked-up way, it worked.

So Dana, who they all knew had no business being with Johnny when he belonged to Joss but the man died with her as his widow, calling either Rembrandt or Joss was news.

Surprising news.

"Dana called?" Jussy asked.

Rembrandt nodded. "She had an idea, darlin'."

"You don't have to do it," Joss put in quickly.

"You don't," Rod confirmed. "And you decide that way, girl, that's the way it's gonna be and it's all cool."

"What are you talking about?" Jussy asked.

Rod looked to Joss, she looked back, and Rod got more respect from Deke when he took the reins.

He turned his attention again to Jussy and said quietly, "She wants to do a tribute concert. For your dad. To benefit his music program. She's asked Terrence, Lace, Perry, Jimmy, Tammy, me. We've all agreed to do it. Back in Kentucky. Big thing. Jiggy and my manager, Ricky, are gonna sort everything. Thurston's also involved. But Dana, well, all of them wanted your mom and me to ask you."

"You don't have to do it, baby girl," Joss said gently. "But we'd love to have you there, if not onstage, just there. For your dad."

More respect from Deke, when Joss said "your dad" in a way her grief clung to those two words openly and Rod pulled her tighter into his hold.

Jussy said nothing for so long, Deke looked down at her.

She was staring in a fixed way at the cold fireplace.

"Gypsy," he called.

Her eyes instantly flicked up to him.

Even though they did, they were still blank.

"You okay?" he asked.

"Did I tell you about Dad's music program?"

She had. She talked about Johnny all the time. She did this because he prompted it as smooth as he could. And Deke did that because she needed to talk about him. She needed him to be a part of her life in the new way he was. She needed to get used to that way, celebrate him, keep him close in mind and memory.

So he knew Johnny Lonesome had started a charity where they raised money to give to schools, rec centers with kids' programs, boys clubs, girls clubs, anyone who had music programs so they could pay for instructors, equipment, rental blocks for space.

"You told me," he confirmed.

"It'll die without him," she said, a tremor of sorrow in her voice it fucked him to hear. "I hadn't thought about it."

"It won't."

At Rembrandt's declaration, both Deke and Justice looked to him again.

"Dana talked to us about that too," he shared. "All of us. She asked us to take places on the board. All of us." He gave Joss a shake and Deke felt Jussy take a deep breath at this additional surprise, Dana offering Joss the opportunity to work together on something that was Johnny's, Rod along for that ride. "We gotta sign contracts as members of the board that we'll raise or donate a certain amount of cash every year, do shit to keep the profile high, recruit donors that'll keep the accounts rockin'. We all agreed."

"She wanted us to talk to you about that too," Joss said softly.

Her mother spoke but Deke knew Jussy didn't hear her because she said in a choked voice, "Rod."

Rod straightened uncomfortably on the couch, cleared his throat, but still only muttered, "Fuckin' fine musician. And the man made one of my girls happy for a spell. That bein' only a spell means I get the privilege of doin' the same. And just plain played a part in *makin'* my other girl. And that program does good work. So..." he shrugged with forced detachment, "I'm in."

It took a few long beats before Jussy replied.

"You're the shit, dude."

Her words made a shit-eating grin spread on Rod's face. "Know that, sister."

Deke looked down at Jussy and saw she was grinning back.

"Take your time," Joss cut in and got both Deke and Jussy's attention. "You don't have to answer now."

"I'm totally on for the board and I'm totally on to perform. You tell me when, I'll be there," Justice declared.

That had Deke grinning.

But it was clear both Joss and Rod were surprised.

Joss looked from her daughter to Deke, assessed his grin, her face blanked and she looked to her girl.

"I'm pleased, Jussy."

"Me too, darlin'. A shit-hot lineup just busted out," Rod stated.

"Will you be there?"

Even if he wasn't looking at her when she asked it, Deke knew Joss's question was for him.

"Yes," he answered.

"We're thinking April, Johnny's birthday," she told him like it was a warning.

"Great idea," Jussy muttered.

Deke didn't respond to the warning.

He had Jussy's love so he had nothing to prove.

Her mother still thought he did but there wasn't shit he could do about that except giving it time.

He'd have that time.

And she'd see.

But straight up, he wouldn't have it any other way. Not for Jussy. Just for her but also for all she was, all she had, the best of it being family that would show to look a man over who was becoming a part of her life, sleeping in her bed, all but living in her home.

He could easily be some jacktard player, getting in there for the sole purpose of all she could give, that being all he could take, none of this all she really had to give. All that was Jussy.

So yeah. Deke didn't give a fuck. They felt he had something to prove, he'd take his time.

And he'd prove it.

"I'll call Ricky and Thurston," Rod muttered, leaning forward, pulling out his phone at the same time he pulled his ass out of the couch.

"I need a drink," Joss declared.

"I'll get it," Jussy said and he felt her eyes on him so he gave his to her. "Beer, honey?"

"Yeah, babe."

She grinned, a light in her eyes, excitement shining there.

Seeing that light, Deke had no choice.

He smiled back.

She got up.

He settled in and looked to her mother.

Not a surprise, she was watching.

"Want some chips with your bourbon?" he asked.

"You getting them?" she asked back.

"Wouldn't offer if I wasn't," he told her.

"Then not chips, crackers and cheese," she ordered like the diva she was that she covered up in jeans and a rock chick top.

"On it," he murmured and pulled his own ass out of the couch.

"Deke?" Joss called when he was around the side of the couch.

He stopped and turned back to her.

"Pancakes were the shit, big man. Thanks for breakfast."

A peace offering. Détente. She loved her daughter, that daughter threw down at the barest hint of attitude aimed her man's way, she was good to settle in and give Deke that time to prove what she felt he needed to prove.

He made no reply, just lifted his chin, changed the direction of his body and went to the kitchen to get crackers and cheese for Jussy's mother.

He did this not thinking about Joss or Rod or the crew of people showing in less than two hours.

He did it thinking that Jussy had just agreed to take a stage, a big one, for her dad.

And she was excited about it.

So he did it not smiling on the outside.

But he still had that smile for his gypsy.

It was down deep in his gut.

CHAPTER TWENTY-TWO

Deke Watched

Deke

DEKE WALKED THROUGH the room, six open longnecks dangling from his fingers, scanning the space and realizing something he didn't have to ask to know Jussy understood it before she put money down on the place.

It was perfect for a party.

There were a fuckload of people there and everyone fit, everyone was comfortable, everyone could see the others, drift from group to group, plant their ass in a seat, kick back, relax and enjoy.

He stopped at Ty, Tate, Ham, Decker and Wood, handed out the fresh beers and stood in their huddle, but he wasn't paying attention to their conversation.

He looked out the windows to the back, saw the fire pit glowing, Shambles wearing his round sunglasses, the lenses red, a big grin on his face, his hands moving while he obviously told a story to Dominic, the guy who owned the salon in town, Nadine, a regular at Bubba's, Faye, Bubba himself, and Decker's wife, Emme.

Lauren was holding court at the kitchen island, surrounded by folks on stools, Max's friends, Mindy and Jeff, Zara, Ham's wife, their kid on her lap, Maggie, Wood's wife, and Daniel, Dominic's partner.

He turned his attention all the way across the space and caught Rod in Jussy's music room, smiling and nodding his head at Tate's boy, Jonas, who had Jussy's guitar on his knee. It looked like Rod was giving Jonas a guitar lesson.

Deke then took in the corner seating area and saw Max and Chace had kids crawling all over them, this overseen by Nina and Lexie.

And in the center area, the fireplace blazing but set low, Justice sat with Sunny, Jim-Billy, Twyla, Twyla's lover, Cindy, and Krystal. This with the addition of Joss, having commandeered Breanne, the baby was up against Joss's chest, her little face in Joss's neck, looking, even in the muted clamor of conversation with music playing in the background, like she was getting ready to fall asleep.

There were bowls of chips and dips and nuts placed around seating areas, used paper plates and plastic utensils that Deke had talked Justice into buying (just barely) with the residue of fully-consumed Steph's chicken set down wherever the person who finished it was sitting.

Deke had noticed that Jussy unsurprisingly wasn't a rush-around-and-clean-up-after-everyone type of person, making folks think they needed to walk their shit to a trash bin or giving them any indication they should do anything but relax. She made certain if bowls got low to fill them, and if she happened to be walking somewhere she (or anyone) would grab a plate to take it to the trash.

But it wasn't about keeping tidy. It was clear the place could look like a festival lineup of rock bands partied in it after everyone left and she'd just deal with it in the morning.

Like she felt he was looking at her, Jussy's eyes came to him.

Seeing as Krystal, Sunny and Joss were in deep conversation and Cindy was giving Twyla longing looks at the same time patting Breanne's diapered tush (with Jim-Billy just sitting there because he'd planted himself there when he'd arrived and hadn't moved), Justice didn't say anything when she pulled herself out of one of the armchairs.

She came to him, but as she did, her gaze drifted to her music room and a sweet smile started playing at her mouth.

He lifted his arm high when she got close and the men took this hint and shifted to accommodate a new member to their crew. She ducked under it, pressing herself to his side as he curled his arm around her shoulders.

"Chicken was the shit, Jus," Ty decreed.

"Thanks," Jussy replied.

"If Zara hasn't asked for that recipe already, give it to me before we go," Ham said.

Jussy looked up to him. "I should have printed out twenty of them."

"There's time," Wood put in.

Jussy grinned at him. "I'll get on that."

Wood winked at her.

Her grin got bigger.

The men's conversation resumed and Deke found himself surprised as time passed and she did nothing but rest deeper and deeper into his side, doing this not joining in.

He looked down at her and called low, "Gypsy."

She tipped her head back and caught his eyes.

She looked content, but still distant.

"All good?" he asked.

"I wish Lace was here," she answered, then gave him a small smile. "And even though you don't wish the same and she'd have some 'splainin' to do, I wish Anca was here too. Without Tony, of course," she hurried to say the last.

He knew she wanted this.

Rock star and stylist to the stars or not, Joss and Rod fit in with this group with ease.

Joss had made Jussy, and Rembrandt had been in her life for a good chunk of time, so this wasn't totally a surprise.

It still was a surprise how down to earth they actually were, demonstrating this immediately when folks started showing. Putting people at ease. Making it clear this was a party, not a party with a famous rock star and his wife in attendance.

So Deke had no doubt her girl Lacey would be the same.

Bianca, he didn't know and hoped it'd be a while before he found out.

What he did know was, for Jussy, it was about wanting her girls with her.

She still left something unsaid.

He dipped closer and noted quietly, "And your dad."

She nodded. "Yeah, and Dad. Though if he was here, Dana would be here, him and Joss would get into a rip roarin', Rod would get shitfaced and Dana would spend a lot of time in her room."

"Right," he said through a short chuckle.

Her eyes coasted to her mom. "Sucks, they got all their shit together after he was gone."

He knew their conversation with her mom and stepdad earlier had been playing on her mind.

"Bottom line, they got their shit together," he stated and she looked back to him. "You know, baby, it wouldn't have happened any other way. But now you get to know these people where they always were but history wouldn't let them go there. They have it in them to pull it together to keep somethin' alive that meant somethin' to your dad, they always had that but couldn't go there when he was here. Now you have that. And that does not suck."

She turned slightly to him and pressed closer, now with her front to his side, and the smile she had wasn't bright, but it was better than the ones he'd been getting.

"You're giving me a complex," she told him.

His brows went up. "How's that?"

"You're too wise for my own good."

"You wanna wallow?" he asked.

She shook her head, her smile brightening. "Nope."

"Then I'm just wise enough," he said.

"You're wiser than that, honey," she returned.

He loved it that she thought that.

To share that with her, Deke bent in and kissed her nose.

When he straightened, she slid an arm around his stomach and put her cheek to his chest as they turned back to the huddle.

He saw Tate's eyes on Jussy, his look sober in a way Deke didn't get and didn't much like but he didn't say anything about it because he heard another car on the lane.

He glanced around the space then down to Jussy. "Anyone else you ask to this shindig?"

She tipped her head back. "No. Why?"

"Car comin' up the lane."

Her head twitched and she separated just enough from both of them to look through their bodies toward the front door, Jussy murmuring, "That's weird."

Deke started to move but stopped when he saw Chace heading to the door, two empty wineglasses in his hands, and he was shaking his head at Deke.

"Catch it on the way for refills," he called.

Chace had heard the car too.

Deke nodded.

"Maybe someone invited somebody," Jussy remarked and Deke looked again to her. "Though, no one said anything."

She was detaching, getting ready to head to the door Chace was arriving at in order to offer her greeting.

Deke started to move with her when he saw the door was open and he heard Chace, who was partially blocked by the open door, saying loudly into the night, "Can I help you?"

"Who're you?" a voice came back, sounding distant, and Deke figured Chace spoke before whoever it was made a full approach.

But Deke had tensed because the question was asked, it wasn't voiced nice, and most importantly, it made Jussy get tight at his side.

"That's my question but I asked it a different way and I'd like you to answer it," Chace pointed out and Deke saw his body had switched from cool to alert.

"Outta my way, I wanna talk to Justice," the voice from outside said, definitely closer, and Deke noticed Jussy hurrying toward the door but doing it glancing at Joss.

He also distractedly noticed their friends becoming aware of the situation and conversation beginning to falter, attention shifting, as well as bodies.

These the men's.

And now Chace was not alert at the door.

He was barring it.

"I'm afraid that's not gonna happen until you tell me who you are."

"Don't know who the fuck you are either but do know whoever you are, you got no right to stand in the way of me havin' words with my sister."

Hearing this, blood rushed to Deke's head, a sensation he hadn't felt since the last bar fight he'd been in over half a decade ago.

He and Jussy were almost to the door and he had just enough of his shit together to push her back gently, but not enough not to put some serious pressure behind the grip he took on Chace's shoulder to tell the man to get the fuck out of the way.

Chace's head jerked to the side at the contact but he read Deke and got the fuck out of the way.

That was when Deke was confronted with Jussy's near-twin, the male variety, a boy who refused to become a man who looked a fuckuva lot like a young Johnny Lonesome.

He took that in in half a second before he got right in Maverick Lonesome's space and used his bulk—this mainly being his chest, he didn't lift his hands—to shove the shitheel back.

"Hey! Fucking shit! What the fuck?" Maverick shouted.

Deke kept bumping him back then lifted one hand to plant it in his chest and give him a shove that sent him sailing four feet.

Only then did he turn and growl to Chace, "She stays inside."

"Deke—" Jussy started, already one step out the door and still on the move.

That's all she got out. Chace pulled her back through the door and shut it behind her.

"Seriously, dude, *what the fuck?*" Maverick clipped and Deke turned his attention to the kid.

He heard the door open behind him, tensed, felt it wasn't Jussy just as he heard her protesting deeper inside the house, and knew someone he didn't mind joining them was joining them.

Other than that, he didn't take his attention off Lonesome.

"First, you're gonna tell me why you're here," Deke informed him. "I'm good with what I hear, you'll get to talk to your sister. I'm not, you'll get in your car and drive away."

"Who the fuck are you?" Maverick asked, his gaze skidding from Deke to whoever had joined them.

From the fear that instantly glinted in his eyes, Deke guessed it was Ty, definitely. Decker, probably. Tate, undoubtedly, because Tate would always be at Deke's back. Also Twyla, because, she'd deny it to her dying breath, but the woman would take a bullet for any of them. And with the length of the kid's sweep, Deke figured, maybe Ham.

"I walked out of that house, kid," Deke reminded him. "That house bein' your sister's. Not me that's gotta explain what I'm doin' here."

He pulled himself up, giving himself the impression he didn't have to look so far up to keep Deke's gaze.

"I'm only talkin' to Jus," he stated.

"Think I covered that," Deke told him.

His face screwed up. "I don't even know who *you* are, so I'm not sayin' *dick* to you."

Deke heard the door open again, he tensed again, but he didn't hear Jussy's voice so he sought patience and kept at the kid.

"Like I said, you are not gettin' anywhere near your sister unless I got an understanding what you're doin' here and I'm down with you gettin' to her. She's havin' a good night. You been shovelin' shit at her, what I can tell from what she tells me, since you came out bawlin'. But the shit you've been shovelin' since you all lost your old man is not on. And no way in fuck I'm gonna let you upset her more than you already have just showin', no notice. You tell me what you're doin' here, I'll tell her, she decides if she wants you in her space."

Maverick opened his mouth but Deke leaned in, the kid's eyes widened, but his mouth shut.

"I'm not repeating myself and I'm not negotiating. It goes like that, no choice, or you got men who'll walk you to your car. You put up a fight, man who opened the door is a cop. He'll have Carnal officers escorting you off the property and do not," he leaned deeper, "fuckin' *test* me. You fuck with Jussy, you resist attempts to remove you, your ass is in a goddamned cell."

He stared in Deke's eyes several beats, swallowing, his Adam's apple bobbing, then his gaze shifted to the side and his face went hard.

Deke's body got even tighter when he felt a light hand on his forearm.

He looked down and saw Joss standing there.

Her face was harder than the kid's, brittle, the anger in her profile so intense, just looking at her Deke tasted it in his mouth.

"Do as you're told, son," she said quiet, her voice as brittle as her face.

"Not talkin' to *you* at all," he spat. "And I sure as fuck am not your *son*."

She nodded, curled her hand firmer on Deke's forearm and pulled at it like she was telling him to step aside.

He didn't move.

She did, looking over her shoulder at whoever was standing behind them.

"The man who lives in this house doesn't want this boy here. I think it's time he's shown to his car," she said.

Deke felt the men move and he started to move with them but Joss kept her grip fixed on him.

He looked down at her, but before he could say shit, she did.

"Jussy will not like you being involved in what those boys might have to do," she said softly. "That kid's a stubborn ass. Let your friends play that out." She tipped her head to the drive. "You go talk to Chace. He's in with Rod and some of the girls, got Jussy in her music room." She got closer and went up on her toes. "And she's watching, Deke."

He nodded, indicating her message was clear, but he didn't go in.

He looked to the folks hustling Maverick to his car and saw he was right, Tate, Ty, Decker, Twyla and Ham.

"Fuck you!" Maverick shouted, pushing off on Tate.

It was like the kid didn't touch him. Tate's body didn't even sway.

"Get off me, man!" Maverick yelled, scuttling away from Ty.

"Deke, this may need the cops," Joss warned.

"Got Johnny in him," Deke muttered.

"What?" Joss asked.

He looked down at her. "Kid's got Johnny in him. He's here for a reason. He'll get his head right and we won't need the cops."

Joss studied him as the situation escalated loudly in the drive.

Then she whispered, "My Jussy girl. Always had hope for that boy. Gave that to you." She shook her head as if this made her sad.

"Fuck you! *Fuck*! Fuck all of you!" Maverick shouted. "Right! Fuck! Okay! Goddamn shit! Okay, I'll tell you what I wanna talk to Jussy about!"

Deke and Joss looked his way.

The men had him pinned to the driver's side door, not deep in his space, but he had nowhere to go but in his car.

He was looking over the roof to Deke.

"I...God!" he yelled angrily. "We don't got any money, man. Froze our assets and Granddad's royalties don't come but every six months and they don't...for Mom and me they aren't..." He shook his head like he was trying to keep in the dickhead but was losing hold on it and Deke knew he lost hold when he said, "I gotta talk to my sister."

"You gonna hit her up for money?" Deke asked.

"I..." He shook his head again. "No, man. I just need...I can't lose what I was supposed to get."

"So you're gonna drop the suit," Deke surmised.

Maverick took a few beats to answer. "I just can't lose what I was supposed to get."

Deke's voice was a warning when he repeated, "So you're here to share you're dropping the suit."

Maverick was silent and this time it lasted longer.

Then he said, his voice a lot more calm, "Just tell her Mom doesn't know I'm here."

Deke looked down at Joss. "That good enough for you?"

She was looking up at him so he caught her mouth going slack at his question.

"Joss, Jussy's probably pissed as shit in there. Answer. Good enough for you?" he prompted.

She nodded.

He turned on his boot and prowled into the house.

He was barely through the door before Krys was on him, holding her daughter, at his arrival clearly caught in the middle of pacing.

She immediately demanded to know, "I gotta get my shotgun?"

"We're good," he muttered, walking right by her, direct to Jussy's music room where she was pinned in by Rod, Chace, Wood, Bubba and Shambles, all of them standing sentry at the open double doorway. But she was being kept company inside by the whole girl posse.

The room was a big room but it was fucking crowded in there.

Jussy was already facing the door and the second he saw her through the men, he knew he was right.

She was pissed as shit.

"Okay, my lover, we'll be talking about that macho bullshit *a lot* after whatever the fuck is happening is no longer happening," she declared, her face flinched weirdly comically and she looked down at Lella who was standing close to her legs. "Sorry, baby. Don't say the F-word. It's very bad." She started to look at Deke but then jerked her attention back to Lella. "Or the B-S-word. That's bad too."

Fuck, only Jussy could make him want to bust a gut laughing when he was this pissed.

"Says his mom doesn't know he's here and he's got money problems, babe," Deke told her after she returned her gaze to him. "Think he's calmed down and good to talk. You're doin' that on the back deck. I'll have the boys escort him around."

"He can come through the house, Deke," she retorted.

"No. He can't," Deke stated.

It was then she really looked at him and it was then he knew she got him because she lost the attitude and nodded.

And what she got was the fact that Deke was not allowing that pissant into her house until he'd earned the right to be in her space, even in order to walk through it.

Deke looked to Rembrandt.

"Rod, you wanna keep Jussy company outside?"

"Yeah, man," he muttered and looked to his stepdaughter. "Let's get out there and get this shit over with, darlin'." Not missing a beat, even though he had a hand extended to Jussy, he looked to Lella. "And don't say the S-word either, gorgeous. It's also bad."

He heard some swallowed laughter that sounded amused, but nervous. He didn't take it in. He waited until Rod took Jussy's hand and then he moved back to the front door.

He went out it and stood again next to Joss, who hadn't shifted an inch.

"Bring him around the side of the house to the back deck," he called. He dipped his chin and said to Joss. "You're with me through the inside."

"Aye, aye, big man," she murmured.

"I can walk my fuckin' self," Maverick snapped.

"Guess that's right, still not gonna happen," Ham told him.

Deke let Twyla and the men deal with it, and once they'd both turned to the house, he took hold of Joss's elbow. He guided her through the door and gave looks to key people as he moved through the house. They'd do what Jussy needed and Deke didn't even know what all that was. He just knew they'd be doing it.

He got to the back of the house where Chace was at the door. The men nodded to each other as Deke led Joss out.

"Do you all inject extra testosterone or is this just a Colorado Mountain anomaly?" Joss joked.

He shifted his gaze again to her.

She took in his face.

"Right," she whispered. "Time for fun and laughter later."

She gave wide eyes to her daughter.

Jussy wasn't in the mood either and Deke knew it when she smiled a half smile to her mom that she didn't mean and then looked into the dark where Maverick was being escorted on his approach to the deck.

Jussy remained standing by a chair while Rod draped himself casually over another one opposite where Jussy was at the pit. One of his long legs over an arm, the other leg splayed in front of him, back to the corner of the chair.

But the rock-god-on-a-throne bullshit was all a show. His attention was fastened to the kid coming up the steps and his mouth was tight.

Maverick made his ascent glaring at Jussy the whole time, which moved Deke to her back, and close.

The men and Twyla retreated but stood in the yard not near, not far.

"Right, now that I did all that to get to the great Justice Lonesome, what next? You want me to jump through burning hoops?" Maverick asked snottily.

The blood rushed to Deke's head again as he growled, doing it beginning to move around his woman, "That's it. You're done."

She caught his hand and did it tight.

That wouldn't have stopped him.

But she also said in a voice that held persuasion and deep emotion, telling him she wanted him to drop the macho bullshit and let her guide this from here on out.

"Deke, baby. Please."

He halted at her side, his eyes locked to Maverick.

He heard Justice take a deep breath, releasing his hand, before she stated, "Okay, Mav, you've got five minutes. You can be a douche or you can explain why you're here. I would advise against being a douche for a full five minutes, though. Deke kinda likes me which means he definitely doesn't like it when people do shitty things to me so I'm not sure how long I can hold him back."

Maverick opened his mouth but before a sound came out, Rod spoke.

And he got more respect because Deke didn't think the man had that pissed-off, kinda-dad, do-not-fuck-with-my-girl-or-I'll-make-you-hurt tone in him.

But he seriously fucking did.

"For once in your life, son, be smart. And take that advice seriously, hear me?"

Maverick looked to Rod, to Joss, to Deke, and finally, like it took effort, he turned his attention to Jussy.

"It shits me to be here," he declared.

"You've kinda made that obvious," Jussy returned.

He shifted on his feet, a full shuffle, casting his eyes down to them, pulling his shit together, and he looked back up.

"Mom doesn't know, but talked to Mr. T. He says the terms are ironclad. We…I mean, *I* contested the will so I've lost everything. And he isn't backing down on that. So I need you to…to…I need you to talk to him, Jus."

Jussy didn't reply and the kid waited for it but not long enough to get his head straight, read the situation, and not give too much away or make himself seem like an even bigger dick.

"We had three attorneys that advised—" He cut himself off then kept going, "The one we got, I, Jus, seriously, I didn't like him from the start. And I think he just wanted to take Mom's…I mean, *my* money. I talked to Mr. T, said I'd drop the suit, he says he can't do anything to help me. He says it's all Dad. He says it's all legal-like and the suit was filed so I relinquished all claim and now I have to pay back the money that's frozen in my accounts or I can go to jail. But I know Mr. T can do anything and I know, if you talked to him, he'd do anything for you. So I need you to talk to him."

When Jussy remained silent, the tension thick around the fire pit, his situation clear that he was not amongst friends, far from it, Maverick stupidly rushed to fill the void.

"I…I…well, I thought on it and I don't even mind that…that…*woman* gets her piece." He shook his head and right in front of Deke's eyes, dropped more than a decade, turning from a boy who refused to be a man right into a stupid, selfish kid. "But, even you gotta agree that…that…*woman*…that it's not fair, not right that she gets a third. A third of what's *ours*. Yours and mine. I mean, that's crazy, right?"

Finally, Jussy spoke.

"It's clear it hasn't dawned on you, Mav, that the money Dad worked his ass off all his life to earn is *his* money. It'll always be *his* money. Even after he's gone, it's still his. And we don't have fuck all to say about what he wants to do with it. He's shared explicitly what he wanted to happen with that money and it's not for me or you or Dana or Joss or anyone who loved him with all their heart to say anything different."

The stubborn hit his face when he turned his eyes to Joss. "Even you gotta agree with me about her."

"I don't gotta do anything, boy," Joss said quietly. "And for the record, I *don't* agree. She loved your father, loves him in a way he's gone and that's never gonna die. She treated him right. She believed in him. She stood by his side no matter what, and I'm glad he had that, at least with one of the three women he let into his life."

At her mother's words, Deke felt Jussy's hand brush the back of his in a searching way.

So he twisted his wrist and closed his fingers around hers tight.

She didn't close hers around his the same way.

Her grip was like a vise.

"Come here, baby," Rod murmured gently, pulling out of his rock star sprawl and reaching a hand to his wife.

Joss moved to him and took his hand. Then she took a visible deep breath and stood by his side, still holding his hand but turning her gaze back to Maverick.

But Maverick gave up on her and went back to Jussy.

He also switched tactics.

"I need you to talk to Mr. T, Jussy." His tone was now whiney and wheedling. "I know…I know you're not big on Mom but she depends on me and, sis," he swallowed and finished on a whisper, "I'm hurting."

Jussy's voice was quiet and almost gentle when she said, "I warned you, Mav."

He skated around that. "I just need you to talk to Mr. T."

"I know this hasn't occurred to you but Mr. T cares a lot about you. He was very patient about all the shit you pulled. But if it's out of his hands, and I can believe if he could do something he'd do it, then it's also out of my hands."

"He can do anything and he *will* do anything you want him to do," Maverick returned.

"He can do anything and *does* do anything a *Lonesome* wants him to do. So when Dad asked for his will to be written a certain way, Mr. T saw to that." Her voice turned full-on tender. "And you knew the consequences of butting up against that, Mav. Dad told you, and even if he didn't, Mr. T did and so did I. Repeatedly. You made your decision, and if Mr. T says there's nothing we can do about it, there just isn't."

He started to take a step to her, didn't miss Deke going alert, jolted to a halt and made do with leaning her way.

"Then you gotta…you and her…you gotta decide and you gotta talk to her because if the courts won't…then you have to, Jussy," he begged.

Deke felt Jussy's fingers go limp in his before they again squeezed hard and she asked disbelievingly, "Are you telling me you want me to give you your third and ask Dana for the same?"

"It's mine," he stated. "Dad wanted me to have it."

"You keep her, don't you?" she asked, abruptly changing the subject.

Maverick straightened. "This isn't about her."

"Baby brother," Jussy said softly, "the fuck of it, the shit that tears me apart, tore Dad apart, is that through you, it's always been about her. I never had you. *He* never had you. Not without her coming in between even when she wasn't even there."

"I don't wanna talk about my mother," he snapped.

"And I'm not about to give Dad's money to her," Jussy returned. "And Dana's a soft touch. You go to her and act all wounded, even though you've not once been kind to her, or even decent, she will. She'll see Dad in you and she'll do anything for you. So I'll advise her and give a heads up to Mr. T so she doesn't fall for your mother's shit because you are not here for you. You're here for her. And don't," she bit out her last, lifting her free hand, palm out her brother's way, "deny it. Your share of Granddad's royalties will not keep you on yachts. It's enough to get by and well, unless your mother is going through it like she went through the divorce settlement, your child support—"

"I said we're not talkin' about my mother," Maverick hissed.

"Then we're not talking at all," Jussy returned, her voice now fragile, sad, heartbroken.

Deke used her hand to pull her closer.

"God!" Maverick said loudly. "He's gone and you still think you can get me away from her. Like I'm tied to her apron strings or something. Newsflash, Jus, I'm a grown man."

Deke bit his tongue.

Literally.

So hard he tasted blood.

Jussy didn't do the same.

"No, what you don't get is that when you came to visit and I was there, I wanted my brother. Not my brother acting like a dick because his mother filled his head with bullshit the entire time he was gone. Dad would get you there, Mav, a day or two before you had to leave us again. You'd see he wasn't all she said. You'd see he loved you more than life. And *that's* what I wanted. That's the brother I wanted. That's the *son* he wanted. Then you'd go back to her, she'd launch right in to fucking with your head, and when he got you back, he had to start all over again. And now he's gone and all you've got is her filling your head with bullshit you *know* is bullshit because we've proved it time and again. And if you were as grown up as you say you are, you'd think for yourself for once and see it."

"Not bullshit, you tellin' me you're not gonna help me out. If Mom knew I was here, she'd say this," he swept his hand to the deck, "is exactly how this would go down."

"And what you don't see," Jussy shot back, "is that for weeks, showing at your place, call after call, I *did* try to help you out by telling you *not* to pull this crap and you didn't listen to me. You dug your own hole. And, baby brother, *newsflash*," she rapped out, "a grownup stands on their own two goddamned feet, no matter who's whispering in their ear. And a grownup is smart enough to think before they do stupid shit and not do it. And if emotion trips them up, they own up to their fuckups. This is your fuckup. Not mine. You wanna lay that trip on me, do it. But I won't lose any sleep over it because I know it just plain isn't true."

"Wasted good money on a goddamn plane ticket and rental car," he muttered, burning an angry glance his sister's way and looking like he was about to stalk off.

"You don't know," Joss began, and Maverick jerked his pissed-off eyes her way, "that mere weeks ago, an intruder broke into this home, kicked the shit out of your sister and nearly strangled her to death."

The vibe on the deck instantly shifted. Tense still, absolutely. High alert as well.

And tweaked.

"What?" Maverick asked.

"Joss," Justice said low.

"He did," Joss confirmed casually, eyes locked on the kid. "The man is no longer a threat but not far from where you're standing, Jussy nearly lost her life to a maniac."

"That isn't even funny," Maverick bit out.

"No," Joss said, dead calm, dead serious, her gaze flint. "It isn't."

Maverick took her in long beats before he slowly turned his gaze to Jussy.

"Did that really happen?" he asked.

"Yes, Mav, but—"

Deke prepared to move when he watched the kid's entire body wind up before he roared, "*Why the fuck didn't you tell me?*"

Deke got closer to his woman, doing it stepping slightly in front of her.

When he did, Maverick's eyes slashed up to him, he took a step back and then he jerked his head so he was looking over his shoulder at the people in Jussy's yard, keeping watch over his sister.

The fullness of the situation he couldn't totally understand because he didn't have the information dawned and Deke watched the color drain from his face.

"She didn't tell you because you'd hurt her so badly, she didn't feel you had that right," Joss announced.

"Dammit, Joss—" Jussy tried.

But Joss kept talking.

"Mostly, that was her excuse for not telling you because, first, it'd freak you out and she's your big sister, she wouldn't want to do that to you. Second, because that would open the door to more of you and your mother's shit and she'd nearly lost her life, she didn't need to deal with that."

"That can't be why you—" Maverick began, eyes to Jussy.

Joss spoke over him and he looked back to her.

"My point in telling you this is, in all you're missing in all that's happening, in all you've missed for as long as you've been alive, when you lost your father, you missed learning a very valuable lesson. The people you love will not be around forever. They won't be there to catch you when you fall. They won't be there to listen to your shit when you have to unload it. They won't be there to laugh with you or give you hell or help out when you need it. So you spend every goddamned second on this earth treating the people you love with the respect and affection they deserve. Because if you lose time with them because you didn't offer them that, the only person you'll have to blame, should something happen to anyone else you care about, will be yourself. I sense this will be lost on you as it seems it already has. But it bears saying anyway. I miss your father even if he wasn't in my life any longer. He meant a lot to me. But months later, I nearly lost my fucking *daughter*, and I'd already learned that lesson. But I learned it again, fuck yeah. And I'll never forget."

"Joss," Jussy whispered.

Joss turned fierce eyes to her daughter. "Tore me up not to be with you. But Rod says you're me with longer hair and a few less years. And if I told you what I needed to deal and you went against that, I'd lose my mind. He knows me. He knows you. And he was right. He said I had to do what I'd want you to do. Do what I told you to do. So I did that." She drew in an audibly harsh breath. "It still tore me up."

"I was taken care of," Jussy replied.

Joss's eyes flicked to Deke before they went back to her girl and she returned, "I'm seeing that."

"Jussy, who did this shit?" Maverick demanded to know. "And where are they? Did the cops catch him? What the fuck?"

"It's taken care of, Mav."

"What the fuck?" he repeated.

"It's over. I'm healed. Breathing. Safe. It's all good."

"What the *fuck?*" he repeated, his last word emphasized at the same time it broke.

Deke went still.

Jussy shifted closer into his side.

"What the fuck?" Maverick whispered. "You didn't call me? Some fuckwad *strangled* my sister and you *didn't call me?*"

His gypsy pulled at his hand, Deke let her go, and then she was gone. To her brother. In his space. Both her hands to either side of his head, pulling it down so his forehead was to hers.

"Breathe, baby brother, look at me. I'm right here."

"I miss Dad," he said suddenly, his voice hoarse.

"I do too, Mav," Jussy replied, her voice husky.

"I miss you," he kept at her.

"Me too, Maverick," she whispered, pulling him into her arms. "I missed you too, brother."

"You got hurt and you didn't call me," he said on a croak.

"I'm seeing I probably should have done that," she kept whispering.

He shoved his face in her neck, Deke saw his shoulders heave and he looked to Rembrandt.

The man gave him a chin lift, pulled himself out of the chair, and with a tug on her hand, pulled his wife to the back door.

Deke followed them and with a look to tell Chace he was off duty, he took Chace's place, leaning against the counter, arms crossed on his chest, eyes out the glass watching Jussy with her brother.

She got him to sit down with her.

And Deke watched.

They started talking.

Deke watched.

The men and Twyla came in the front door, everyone started cleaning up.

And Deke watched.

Joss and Rod took care of dealing with everyone leaving.

And Deke watched.

Finally, Jussy and Maverick got up from the chair and moved to the door.

Deke got out of the way but he didn't move far.

She came in, eyes to him.

"We're gonna go out and get Mav's bag, honey. He's gonna break in one of the other guest rooms. You cool with that?"

He examined her face.

She wanted that.

She wanted her brother near.

"I'm cool with that," he said.

"Can you turn off the pit?" she asked.

"Yeah, gypsy."

"Dude, I was—" Maverick started, looking younger than his already young, the guilt heavy on his face, grief weighing there too.

"It's done. Let it be done," Deke stated.

Maverick stared at him a second before relief started to slide in and he nodded.

Jussy moved him into the house.

Deke watched them move through to the front door.

His body jerked in surprise when Joss sidled up the counter beside him.

He looked to her.

"Full approval," she whispered, stared into his eyes, did it a long time.

Then she winked at him and glided away.

Deke watched her go.

Then he went out and turned off the fire pit.

* * *

"I think something's happened with Roddy and Joss," Jussy whispered into his throat late that night in the dark while they were lying in her bed, front to front, limbs tangled. "I've never seen them like they were tonight, dealing with Mav."

She stroked the skin of his lower back and kept whispering.

"On the outside, he's the quintessential rocker. Sex, drugs and rock 'n' roll, the more of all of that, the better, in his case, drugs being booze. But he loves her. He loves her so much, honey. And he's never even looked at another woman, as far as I could see. He'd never step out on her. I think she sees that. I think she sees how deep that feeling goes for him. I think she understands how precious it is. I think she finally gets it."

"Yeah," Deke murmured, drifting his fingers through her hair.

"It worries me," she went on. "What she said, making it sound like she should have stood by Dad even though he shredded her trust. She's not that woman. No woman should be that woman. She believes in herself enough to know she doesn't have to take that."

"Love is strong enough to find forgiveness, gypsy," Deke told her. "Even in extreme circumstances like that. Bubba cheated on Krys repeatedly. Let her down so many times, hard to count. She got shot of him, he loved her enough to turn that around. Loved her enough to prove that to her. Pulled out all the stops. And she loved him enough to find it in her to forgive. Been years now, those two are as tight as Tate and Laurie. Lexie and Ty. They put it behind them and now they got that. Your mom, lookin' back, maybe she's seein' what could have been if she was strong enough to forgive at the same time seein' what she got out of that, realizin' it's far from a raw deal."

She pressed her face deeper into his throat, muttering, "Yeah."

She fell silent and he fell into it with her, running his fingers through her hair, the curls, like always, wrapping around like they had minds of their own and didn't want him to let go.

"I'm not giving him any money."

These words were so quiet, Deke automatically dipped his chin in an effort to hear them all.

"Maverick?" he asked.

She nodded against his throat. "I decided. I'm not giving him any money."

"You share that with him during your talk?"

She nodded again, saying, "He's good at a sound board, Deke. Like, *really* good. I was all about the music, playing guitar with Dad, Granddad, Aunt Tammy, Uncle Jimmy. Maverick, when he was on the road with us, he was always with Gordon, Dad's sound guy. Always up in the booth or wherever the board was set up. I think he needs direction. He definitely needs to grow up. And he needs money. I think he'll feel good, being in the business, his family's business, doing something he's talented at doing."

"Think you're right, Jussy," Deke agreed.

"Yeah," she replied. "So I told him I'd call Gordon. Mr. T. Make a few other calls to people I know. See if I can get him some gigs. Paying work. Get him started. He can launch from there and I told him I wanted him to do that, to find his way, but I'd be there for him. Sound folk, good ones, they don't make millions, but they do all right. He won't be able to keep his mom the way she's used Dad through Mav all his life to keep her. Not if he wants a good life himself. He needs to cut himself loose. And I think he's seeing that and that's good too."

"That's definitely good," Deke confirmed.

"So, I'm not gonna give him any money. I'm gonna help him find his way. Help him grow up. And then, if he pulls his shit together, maybe," he felt her shake her head, "I won't ask Dana to do it but maybe I'll give him his part of my share of Dad's money."

Deke didn't say anything to that.

She tipped her head back and asked, "Do you think that's right?"

He looked down at her. "I think it's your money, gypsy, your brother. So I think whatever you decide is right."

"Okay," she returned, giving him a light squeeze of her arms. "But if it was you. Your dad. Your brother. Your money. Do you think it's right?"

"Yes, Justice, I think it's right."

He saw the flash of white of her smile in the dark.

"I knew it. Totally. I sat out there with him, listening to him, getting the gist that he was realizing his mom was playing him, maybe not all these years, but definitely with this latest fiasco. And I got a definite hint that he knew after those three attorneys advised against it that shit was not going to go right, but she kept pushing it and it was just habit for him to let her. Now he's lost so much, not just the money, but being with people who loved Dad while we were all grieving so that could help him, he could help them, that 'them' being me, he's beginning to see. And it's cutting deep. But I knew I couldn't give in. I shouldn't prop him up. I had to guide his way. And I knew this because the whole time we talked, I thought, if my man was in this situation, what would Deke do?"

Deke let out a low bark of laughter and pulled her deeper in his arms, twisting her hair in his fist.

"You're so full of it," he muttered.

"No. Totally. I'm getting a bracelet with W.W.D.D. embroidered on it," she stated, a smile in her voice. "I'm gonna look at it every time I'm in a situation, which seems to happen a lot in my life, even though I try to keep my head low."

"Shut it." He was still muttering, but doing it grinning.

"I am. I'm special ordering it tomorrow."

He smiled down at her even as he used his fist at the back of her head to gently shove her face again in his throat, repeating, "Shut it, gypsy."

He felt her kiss the bristles of his beard there.

They had a quiet moment before, her voice sounding drowsy, she said, "Downer end to a good party."

"We'll have another one."

She snuggled closer. "Yeah. We will."

He bent his neck and said into the top of her hair, "Go to sleep, baby."

"I will if you will," she replied.

"I will," he promised.

"Okay, Deke. Love you, honey."

"Love you too, gypsy."

She kissed his throat again and settled in.

Not long later, he felt her body relax into sleep.

And once he felt that, Deke followed her there.

* * *

"Stings a little," Joss stated late the next afternoon, and Deke tore his eyes from Rembrandt and Jussy across the drive, their backs to Joss and Deke.

Rod had Jussy in an affectionate neck hold and they had their heads bent together.

Deke looked to Joss to see her looking at the house.

That was when Deke turned his attention to the house and he could see Maverick through the window, sitting at the couch in the corner, the TV on and slanted his way.

He'd given his somewhat stilted and totally awkward good-byes at the door. But he wasn't an asshole. Didn't wake up as one. Was quiet, watchful, but cool all day. There was definite affection between him and Justice that he was out of practice giving to his sister, but since she never was out of practice with that, he warmed up quickly.

With Joss and Rod, he was wary, but that started to go too as the day progressed because Joss and Rod guided it there. What was done was done, they were moving forward, and they communicated that to him.

Deke saw the routine playing out and he suspected that routine was not lost on Jussy, Rod or Joss. The kid emerging out from under the bullshit his mother piled on him, seeing the people around him for what they were. And it said a lot about Rod and Joss (Deke knew Jussy would give that to her brother) that they didn't give up, thinking it wasn't worth the effort since he'd go back to the woman who'd twisted his head and fucked up the entirety of his life, and he'd allow himself to get piled in it again.

Now it was up to him to go back and not allow himself to get piled in it again.

"Joss?" he called when she said her words and didn't continue.

She started and looked up at him like she forgot he was there. Then she gave an apologetic smile.

"Sorry. Just that," she tipped her head to the house, "he looks so like Johnny did at that age."

Yeah, that kid looking like the man she loved deeply, gave him a beautiful baby girl, then lost him for decades. That would fucking sting.

She shot a sidelong glance at Rod and Jussy, who were still in their huddle, before she turned her back on them, got closer to Deke and dropped her voice.

"That kid, maybe he's got good in him," she began. "He's got Johnny in him somewhere so that could be. But, Deke, get me, he plays this game a lot. Always has. I wanna hope for Jussy, and also for him, that this latest bullshit is gonna get his head out of his ass. But history has proved that could very well be an impossible task. Jussy's gonna give it her all. You gotta—"

"Joss," Deke interrupted, also saying her name low, but he didn't go on.

She stared in his eyes before hers started shining.

"Right, you got this," she murmured.

"Yeah," he stated. "I got this."

Her lips curled up in a smile that was natural, but it was uncomfortably too sexy considering the woman was his woman's mother. But Deke figured it was the only way she could do it.

She lifted a hand to his shoulder, moved into him and slid her hand across, getting up on her toes.

She gave him a hug.

He gave her one back.

They separated but stayed close.

"Look after my girl?" she asked, knowing she didn't have to ask it, and she was beautiful, young in a way she'd never get old, but she was still a mother. So she asked it.

"You got my promise," he answered.

She grinned, gave his biceps a squeeze and turned, calling, "Rod, baby, we gotta get this show on the road."

Not letting her out of his neck hold, Rod swung Jussy around.

"Right there, beautiful, two secs," he replied, bending back to Jussy, taking two seconds, and then in their huddle, their faces still close, Rod started walking Deke's gypsy back to her man.

They arrived and broke off after turning into each other and having a long hug.

Rembrandt stuck a hand out to Deke.

"Good pancakes. Good friends. Cool dude. Glad to know you, man," he said.

Deke took his hand, both got firm before they let go and he said, "Same. Though you're on pancake duty next time."

"Deal," Rod said. Claiming his wife and pulling her close, he invited, "You two should think of comin' to Malibu for Christmas."

"Beach at Christmas sounds good, but I work winters so I got good weather off," Deke told him, doing that also claiming Jussy. "That happens, Jussy can go out. I'll meet you there day before Christmas Eve, but I'll have to get back day after Christmas."

"Not to invite ourselves after a surprise visit, but I'm thinking Jussy'll wanna be in her new pad at the holidays," Joss put in, looking up at her husband. "And it'll be a white one."

"You're welcome here anytime," Jussy said. "You know it. *Except* when you show no notice." She grinned. "But once I get over being pissed, you're welcome then too."

Mother and daughter shared smiles. Rod and Deke shared looks. Then mother and daughter separated from their men to fall into each other's arms for a hug that lasted a fuckuva lot longer than Jussy and Rod's did.

Deke stepped away. So did Rod.

They gave them time.

The women took that time.

Then they moved out of each other's arms with soft faces, warm looks, and low murmurings that Deke didn't try to hear because it was none of his business.

Rod opened Joss's door and she moved there. Jussy came to Deke. He slid an arm around her shoulders.

Joss threw her daughter a kiss, Deke a smile and got in.

Rod gave Deke a hand to forehead salute, shifted his hand in devil's horns and stuck his tongue all the way out at Jussy, making her giggle, all this as he rounded the hood.

Joss waved at them all the way down the lane and Deke knew she did because Jussy pulled him to the center of that lane, making him walk with her, following the car on slow feet, watching and waving back.

When the SUV turned right on Ponderosa Road and they lost sight of it in the pines, they stopped.

"Right, Mr. T down. Mom down. Mav down. You just have Lace, Dana, and when you deem it time, Bianca to go," she declared.

He looked down at her.

She was looking up at him and still talking.

"And in case you already hadn't noticed, which you being you, I'm sure you have, the tough ones are done. Lace will definitely try to get you drunk and pry out your innermost secrets, but she'll see you make me happy so she'll be totally down with you. Dana will fuss over you like she's your mother when she's only a year older than you. And Bianca will like you on sight, but warning, she's now tied to a cartel member so if you ever hurt me, with her revenge streak, shit could get nasty."

Deke started chuckling and he did it curling her into him.

He stopped doing it halfway through the kiss he gave her.

When he pulled away, she took an arm from around him and started stroking his beard.

"Roddy wants me recording," she told him quietly.

Deke's arms tightened. "Yeah?"

She gave him a big grin. "Says I'm denying the history of rock 'n' roll their next generation of Lonesome."

Deke knew Rembrandt wasn't wrong.

But he said nothing because that had to be entirely Jussy's decision.

She didn't go there when she went on.

"I'm gonna offer Mav staying here for a week or so. Until I got him a firm gig to go back to in LA. Just, you know, see if I can give him what he needs to get to know for certain what he's got from me so when he gets back to his mom, he's got that down deep."

Deke had a feeling she'd done that countless times before but he just said, "Cool with me."

She tipped her head and her gaze went intense. "You sure?"

"Babe, he's your brother. He's in a situation. And you wanna look after him. I'm sure. He starts playin' you, I sense that, we'll have another conversation. But now, I don't sense that. So yeah. I'll repeat. I'm sure."

Her eyes lit, she rolled up on her toes and slid her hand from beard to the back of his head to pull him down to her.

They kissed again.

After they were done, she murmured, "I need to start dinner."

"Jussy, we had a late lunch," he replied. "And it's not even four o'clock."

"I still need to start dinner," she returned.

Her repetition of that was suddenly intriguing.

So he tilted his head. "What's for dinner?"

That's when her face lit.

"Prime rib sandwiches."

Deke burst out laughing, doing it turning her, curling an arm around her shoulders, and he put her in a neck hold that was a lot like Rod's and still totally different.

Then he walked his gypsy back to her brother, the warmth of her house…

And her preparations for prime rib sandwiches.

CHAPTER TWENTY-THREE

"Come to Me"

Justice

"GORDON WANTS ME to go on the road with him. Be his assistant. But I got the offer of that gig from The Wash. They want me regular. The money's better at The Wash, Jussy, permanent gig so it's stable. But Gordo says that, even if it's tough on the road, the money isn't all that great, I'll be meeting a lot of people, something I won't do with a gig at a club. Need the money. But need the connections too. Fuck, I don't know what to do."

I was standing in the kitchen, listening to my brother talk in my ear, but I was watching Deke go to the door because someone just knocked on it.

And I was ecstatic Mav was asking me for advice.

It was now mid-December. Joss and Rod were descending a couple of days before Christmas to spend the holiday with us, all the way through to the New Year. Lacey had a long break from her tour and was spending Christmas with her folks, but coming out to my place for New Year's.

Therefore, Deke and I were going to throw a big New Year's party.

I couldn't wait.

I'd offered Mav the invitation to come too, but he didn't have the money to spare and I was vacillating on giving it to him.

He was getting his shit together, even though, suffice it to say, things did not go well (understatement) when he got home, told his mom about his trip, told her he was pulling the suit, no longer paying an attorney who only took the case to fleece them.

She'd lost her mind, unsurprisingly. She'd laid into Mav and then she'd laid into me and Joss.

I'd had a feeling that would be the end. He'd buy her bullshit and I'd lose him. Lose him in a way I wouldn't get him back because Deke would not put up with him yanking my chain time and again. And I wouldn't want to make Deke put up with my brother yanking my chain time and again.

Not to mention, it didn't feel all that great when he yanked my chain.

Mav pulled a few shitty maneuvers after that. But through them he nearly lost a gig Gordon got him, and he'd shot a wad flying out to be with me, a wad he did not have.

In the end, he realized he needed to eat. He had a lifestyle he was accustomed to as well, one Dad, when he was alive, gave to him regardless of the fact he knew in doing it, he was also giving it to Luna. Mav had blown his chance to continue to live that way and definitely couldn't be the conduit to give his mother the same.

So he sorted his shit out, saved the gig, and made peace with me.

He currently was not speaking to his mother because she wasn't speaking to him.

She did speak to the press, airing all this shit bitchily, making another play.

This backfired very badly.

The fortunate part of that was, while that brief maelstrom hit us, including smacking Maverick in the face, my brother saw deeper into his mother's black soul. The other fortunate part of this was that there was no way for Luna to spin it, no matter how hard she tried, to make her look like anything but the greedy, grasping bitch she was.

She'd been torn apart by the media.

Lacey had gleefully sent me YouTube tidbits of gossip shows ripping her to shreds.

Joss had done the same.

The unfortunate part was, we were all dragged along for the ride, even if it wasn't big news, lasted what seemed like a flash and nobody's reps took a hit that shouldn't have (Mr. T saw to that, letting it slip to the press how "Justice Lonesome and her team" attempted to save her brother's inheritance, this confirmed by a short interview Mr. T made Maverick give).

Being dragged along for that ride didn't make Deke happy.

But as fast as that storm stirred up, it died away when Luna shut her mouth, tucked her tail between her legs and went dark.

So things were all around good.

Deke was working. I was in my music room a lot, fiddling with a variety of songs, all of them not songs I was going to sell.

All of them songs I was considering recording.

Deke knew this and he listened a lot to things I was doing.

He liked it all but then again he would. He was my guy and I hadn't come up against there being anything he didn't like about me.

We talked about it, not a lot but more than a little, and Deke listened. Through all this, he made it clear he was with me whatever way I went, back in the biz or just Jussy on the back of his bike.

Yep, he'd take me either way. He'd be beside me either way. He'd champion me either way.

That was Deke.

More good in my life, I had Dad and Granddad's collection on display. I had their things on the walls and shelves. Dana and Joss had sent all my belongings to me.

So I was nested.

I was home.

And Christmas was coming. Deke would meet Lacey. And Dana said sometime in February she was coming out for a visit.

"I hate to say this, baby brother," I spoke into my phone, my eyes still on Deke, "but I don't know the answer to that."

"Fuck," he muttered.

"I know who does, though," I shared. "And that would be Gordon. He's lived the life. Been at that job for decades, Mav. So if he's advising you go on the road, he wouldn't fuck you with that advice because he wants a good assistant. He'll look out for you." I took a deep breath, watched Deke sign for something and finished, "And if you still have concerns, the person we both know that knows the business inside and out and can advise the right path is Mr. T."

"I'm not his favorite person, Jus," Mav pointed out.

"He might have been angry at you, but you're a Lonesome and he'll take care of you until the day he dies."

I watched Deke accept something, nod, move out of the door and close it, turning carrying a stunning spray of Christmas greenery. So wide it had to be four feet across, thick and downy in both depth and breadth, decorated in pinecones, rusted bells, with a big rustic star in the middle that had etched in it the word BELIEVE.

As Deke moved to me, I could smell the scent coming off it, filling the big space with the aroma of Christmas.

When my eyes lifted to him, I saw him looking at me.

I drew up my brows in question.

He gave a one shoulder shrug, so I looked back down and caught sight of one of those plastic fork things with a little white envelope stuck in the piece, the opening of which Deke was obviously going to leave to me.

"I'll take Gordon's gig," Maverick said in my ear, and when he did, I noticed he'd been silent. Thinking. His voice was softer when he finished, "But I'll call Mr. T. Ask him if he thinks that's the way to go."

Maverick doing that, going so far, extending that olive branch, that made my decision for me.

"Right, good," I said. "Think that's smart, Mav. And just to repeat, this tour of Gordon's starts in the New Year. I got a room open. Joss and Rod and Lacey will all be here. We're having a big New Year's Eve party. Would love to have you for Christmas and New Year's."

Deke's face got soft because he knew I'd been struggling with this decision, and in starting this conversation again, knowing that Mav had earned the end of that struggle. He also knew what the way that decision had swung meant to me.

"That'd be cool, if Joss and Rod are down with that," Mav said, his voice still soft. "But, Jussy, like I told you last time, got some gigs happening to keep me going, don't think I can swing heading out that way."

"Christmas present," I shared. "Plane ticket and someone will be at the airport to pick you up. You'll have to make do with Granddad's truck, if I'm not using it, you wanna get around town."

"Jussy, I can't do presents and—" Mav started.

"Having you with me the first year we don't have Dad, Mav, will be the only present I need. Hell, having you with me anytime is a present for me. Seriously."

He was quiet.

Deke set the boughs aside, took the big cylindrical glass bowl filled with layers of limes, cranberries and oranges with their array of pine boughs coming out the top that I got in town at Holly's Flower Shop to the hutch, came back and put the centerpiece where it should be.

In the center.

Through all this, Mav stayed quiet.

Then he said, "Let me think about it."

He'd have to give up his mom on Christmas, this was a concern. They might not be speaking but I had people. As far as I knew, Luna didn't have anybody. Mav would feel that.

And Maverick was beginning to understand how it felt to stand on your own two feet, so accepting a plane ticket from his sister when he'd have no problem doing that a year ago was a hit to the manhood he was seeking.

But he was figuring shit out.

So I suspected he'd understand what was important and end up sharing Christmas with his family.

"Right, brother, I gotta go. They're having the annual Christmas party at our local and we gotta get to town," I said.

"Okay, Jussy."

"Call me and let me know what you decide...about everything," I ordered.

"Will do and...um...well..." he trailed off. I waited. Then he finished it, "Say hey to Deke for me."

"I will. Love you, Mav."

"Back, Jussy."

"Later."

"Yeah. 'Bye."

We hung up and I looked to Deke.

"That sounded like it went good," he remarked.

I nodded, reaching beyond him to the envelope sticking out of the delivery. "He's now got multiple offers to consider." I pulled the card to me and grinned at my man. "Told you he was talented."

"Not like I didn't believe you, babe," he muttered, his mouth twitching.

I bent my head, opened the little envelope and pulled out a florist card with a Christmas design on it.

The message read:

Jussy,

Love you. Miss you. You're always in my heart. I hope I'm still in yours. We'll talk in the New Year. Merry Christmas.

Bianca

"Who's it from?" Deke asked.

I looked up to him and didn't answer. I handed him the card.

He read it and even through his beard I saw his jaw get tight.

But the irritation disappeared when he looked back at me.

He got close, lifted a hand and cupped my jaw.

"I should tell her she's in my heart," I whispered, my voice gruff.

"Probably," Deke murmured.

"I'll find a way to do that at the same time sharing I need a little more time," I told him.

"Good idea."

My grin was shaky.

This was because I worried about her.

But I was glad she'd reached out. I was glad she seemed to have gotten it together. I didn't know exactly how that was, but from what I did know, I wasn't certain I agreed with the path she was taking.

That would never negate the fact that she was, indeed, in my heart.

And always would be.

"I'll text her tomorrow. Let her know her delivery arrived," I said to Deke. "But we should go now, honey."

"Yeah," he got closer, his expression shifting the mood as it filled with amusement. "Warning, Jussy. You're about to get a full-on blast of Laurie at Christmas."

He thought this would freak me.

He wasn't the only person who'd told me Lauren Jackson Christmas stories so it might.

But still.

I couldn't wait.

* * *

"Okay," my voice was shaking with suppressed laughter, "never in my life would I think Laurie could best Twyla."

We were on our way back home from Carnal's Christmas party at Bubba's and doing a debrief.

It seemed the whole town showed up, the place jam-packed, the outside strung with so many lights, it was certain they could see it in the next county. The inside decorated, every inch, in Christmas.

There were deli trays all around and a big vat of eggnog that I avoided because it was spiked so deep, one sip of it, I couldn't taste nog, only rum and it went right to my head.

I didn't want to be hammered. I wanted to be buzzed sweet and enjoy every second of my first experience with what had become Carnal's official kickoff for Christmas.

Lauren, however, got sloshed out of her mind. And when she went to the jukebox, pulled the plug (on Christmas songs, she'd filled the damn thing with nothing but starting on December first) and demanded loudly everyone needed to start singing—you guessed it, Christmas songs—Twyla declared that, at least for her, would not be happening.

Laurie got in her face. Somehow it was decided an arm wrestling match would determine the winner, and then to everyone's surprise, with a lot of hilarious grunting, Twyla's eyes getting bigger and bigger in her head as it came clear the way it was going, Lauren's Christmas monster came out and she beat Twyla at arm wrestling.

An amazing feat.

Thus Twyla sang "Holly Jolly Christmas" and "It's the Most Wonderful Time of the Year" with Lauren while Jim-Billy put in his astonishingly good baritone, a bunch of three-sheets-to-the-wind bikers and their babes and another bunch of locals chimed in.

But not Deke, Tate, Ty, Chace, etc. because mountain men apparently didn't sing Christmas songs in public, but they did laugh their asses off watching Twyla do it.

Twyla then exited the premises pronto, dragging a giggling, waving and drunk-off-her-ass Cindy behind her.

It.

Was.

A *blast*.

The whole night.

The best kickoff to Christmas I'd ever had.

Truly.

Even besting the ones Dad and Joss initiated, and they were both holiday fiends.

But not like Lauren. I swear her breath smelled like peppermint, that's how deep she lived and breathed Christmas.

This could have been Schnapps, though.

"Told you," Deke said, his voice a smile.

"Yeah," I agreed, watching him turn up my lane.

"Good night," he whispered.

I reached for his hand, gave it a squeeze and agreed, "The best."

He squeezed my hand back, parked outside my door, and through my buzz I decided to have another conversation with him about the garage.

My truck was parked in there. The second bay was taken up by Deke's Harley, which he'd moved there from his trailer.

There was a third, kinda-half bay where you could store ATVs or snow mobiles, if you had them (and I wanted to get them) but now it was stacked with Deke's tools and some of the construction stuff left over from the house. Extra tiles. Floorboards and bags of grout not used. The remnants of the slabs of marble my countertops were cut from. All of this Deke suggested (this more aptly described as demanded) I keep, at least for a while, just in case I needed to switch something out, do a repair, and simply because I bought it so I owned it.

Since I was closing on the extra property soon, I was having a stable built come spring. Max was having it designed. It'd have a big tack room, four stalls, and a large storage space.

We'd move that crap out there when I had the stables, Deke's Harley to the half bay of the garage and Deke could park inside.

Something he should be doing now.

His truck was newer, nicer, and he had to go out in the cold to get in it to go to work in the morning. I did not have to do the same thing.

But he wouldn't hear of me not parking Granddad's truck inside. We'd had words. I recognized that meant something to him, so I'd backed off.

That said, it was cold, there was a lot of snow on the ground, we kept getting it regular, and I figured if Deke and I spent a few hours in the garage, we could stack the house stuff in a way we could move his Harley over and get his truck inside.

That would be our conversation tomorrow.

After sex, coffee and breakfast.

After that, our plans were to go get our Christmas tree, a live one, and decorate it with the ton of Christmas stuff I'd bought.

But right now, it was about getting inside, sex and sleep.

Deke cut the ignition. We got out. I waited for him at the head of my front walk, the outside arch of my front door draped with fake Christmas boughs, lit and now illuminated, the side points of the draping decorated with big gold and white bows, the middle point having a lit star. And beyond, on the door, there was a fat, brightly lit wreath.

Deke had put that all up.

For me.

It looked gorgeous.

When we got to the door, walking hand in hand, he put his key in and I moved closer to him in an effort not to waste a second in getting out of the cold the minute he allowed me entry.

My mind focused on that, therefore it missed his body stilling.

I didn't miss it when he used his hand in mine to push me slightly back.

"Deke," I said.

"Shush, Jussy," he muttered, bending low so he could peer through the center of the wreath to see into the front door window while slowly turning the knob and pushing in.

What happened next happened so fast, it was almost like it didn't happen.

But it did.

Fuck me.

It did.

All of it…

Did.

Deke pushed me off, turned to me, bit out, "Run!" then entered the house, slamming the door behind him.

I heard the lock go.

I stood there, stunned immobile, then I heard the gunshots.

My body jerked in shock, instantly electrifying, and my feet moved without me telling them to do it.

In my cowboy boots, I ran along the snow at the front of the house, dodging pine, naked aspen, my hand finding its way into my bag, curling around my phone.

I took the corner of my house on skid through the snow that nearly brought me down. I righted myself, yanked out my phone and I didn't think. I couldn't. The house had good insulation, double-paned windows.

But I heard men shouting.

Luckily, I recognized one of those men was Deke.

Extremely unfortunately, he was unarmed and in my house with someone who had a gun and *used it*.

Looking down at my phone, running blind, pine boughs fluffed with snow stinging the skin of my face as I ran through them, for some reason, I didn't call 911.

It seemed too much effort, too much time.

I hit contacts.

I hit "K."

And I hit Chace.

I put the phone to my ear and heard it ringing as I rounded the far end of the deck by the river, cleared it and started racing up the incline toward my private deck.

"Jussy, hey," Chace greeted in my ear. "All okay?"

"Deke," I wheezed, hitting the steps to my deck, starting by taking them two at a time.

Slipping on ice, the sole of my foot went out behind me and I went down hard on my shin on the edge of the step above.

"Justice," Chace growled in my ear.

"Someone in my house. Deke pushed me back. He's inside. I'm not," I panted, righting myself. The burning in my shin not fazing me, I leaped to the top step. "Gunshots, Chace."

"Get safe," he ordered urgently. "I'm calling cruisers now. On our way."

"Deke…has a gun," I puffed, my hand back in my purse, finding my keys. "I…"

"Get safe, Justice."

"I have to get it to him," I finished, pulling out my keys.

I dropped the phone from my ear, dimly hearing Chace call my name. I focused, not about to waste time like I did, freaked out when I was strangled, dropping keys, chasing them around.

I found the key to my house, a master that opened all the locks, and slid it in. I unlocked it, pulled it open and rushed inside.

I tossed my phone to the bed. Pulled the strap of my purse over my shoulder, threw it that way too and darted to Deke's side of the bed.

I yanked open the drawer to his nightstand, where he kept his gun at the back.

Always close.

Just in case anything threatened his gypsy.

I nabbed it and pulled it out, hearing sinister murmurings in the other room.

I sprinted first to the panic button, not that I didn't think Chace didn't have cruisers heading our way about ten seconds after he lost me, just to make sure they knew the situation continued to be critical.

Then I sprinted to the bedroom door and stopped on the wet heel of my boot, sliding a few inches, halting with my hand thrown out to catch the jamb, taking time to pull my shit together.

One breath.

Two.

Get the gun to Deke.

They were armed. He was not.

That was what I had to do.

Get the gun to Deke.

I shoved the gun in my back waistband and bent, tugging off my boots as quickly but as carefully as I could so I didn't make any noise doing it.

When they were off, I grabbed the gun and slid out on my stocking feet, moving surely but cautiously. I didn't have a plan. There was no light coming from the great room but moonlight. Maybe I could use shadows. I knew where the rugs were, muffle my footfalls, the furniture, crouch behind it, find my way to Deke, get him his gun.

Or use it if needed.

As the case may be.

Time.

Just time.

That's all we needed.

The cops would be there soon. They were probably halfway there already.

We just needed time.

My heart racing, I walked into the hall, through the doorway to the great room. Hunkering in a shadow, I stopped dead.

The moon on the snow coming in my window illuminated the scene.

Boxes on the floor, the headstocks and necks of guitars sticking out the top.

A bundle on the floor, halfway from collection room to front door, a human one, not moving.

And my fucking cousin Rudy, standing inside the doors to where now only half of my dad's collection still stood displayed.

He had a gun aimed at Deke.

And then there was Deke, not far from the human bundle on the floor.

And even in the moonlight, I saw the red stain of blood marring the right upper chest of his white tee.

"Down, man, on your stomach," Rudy ordered, his voice thin, strained, weak.

The same could be said for his body.

He was strung out.

Wasted.

Half a man, reduced to that through addiction.

Thoughts quickly chased their way through my head.

The last time I saw him, he didn't look as bad, but I knew by his eyes that he was gone. Lost to that world. Lost to his need.

The last time I talked to him, the last four times, actually, all phone calls, asking me for money, eventually begging for it.

The last time I was there when his name was uttered around my Aunt Tammy, the grief in her eyes, like he was already dead.

My cousin Rudy.

Here to steal. Steal from me. Take a Lonesome legacy so he could smoke it, inject it, whatever the fuck he did to feed his need.

Here to steal.

Steal my father from me.

"Like I said, I'm not lettin' you take that from her, bud," Deke returned.

At that, I knew. I knew why Deke looked into my house and didn't take us right back to his truck, get away, call the cops.

He saw they were taking my dad from me.

So he pushed me to safety and he went in.

God.

Deke.

"Just *get on your fuckin' stomach!*" Rudy suddenly shrieked.

I shoved the gun up under my jacket and in the back waistband of my jeans.

"Rudy," I called softly, lifting up from my crouch and moving into the room carefully.

Rudy's attention, and the barrel of his gun, swung to me.

Having a gun pointed at me sent surges of adrenaline screaming through me and it did not feel good.

"Jussy," he whispered.

"Justice, get in the safe room," Deke growled. "Now."

Rudy swung the gun back to Deke because he'd started moving toward me.

Having the gun aimed at Deke felt worse.

Deke stopped.

"Rudy," I called again, wanting his attention on me.

He was fucked up, wasted by a life he shouldn't have lived, brought low not realizing when the time was right to give up the dream and try for a new one.

But he'd never hurt me.

Steal from me, sure.

But we were Lonesomes.

We got it.

We were family.

No way he'd hurt me.

"Jussy, goddammit," Deke bit off.

"How'd you get in, honey?" I asked Rudy.

"Not hard, Jus, code was your dad's birthday," he said.

"I coded it European," I said, like he didn't know that since he'd obviously figured it out.

"Yeah, that was what we got. Fourth time was a charm."

"Justice," Deke cut in.

"Put the gun down, Rudy," I ordered.

"You need to get this guy to back off, Jus," he returned, indicating Deke with the gun.

"Please, Rudy," I started moving cautiously forward.

"*Justice*." It was a muted roar from Deke, a command not to be disobeyed.

But Deke was bleeding.

And this was my cousin.

I shifted farther forward.

"Fuck," Deke hissed.

"We'll talk this out, you need something, we'll talk it out, see how I can help you," I lied. No way I was talking shit out with him. He'd sunk this low, like Mav, he had to face the consequences. He could straighten out in jail. "But you have to put the gun down first."

He turned it to me. "Stop moving, Jus."

I stopped but he instantly aimed the gun back to Deke.

"You stop moving too, asshole."

Deke lifted both hands in a placating gesture.

"Fuckin' shot him, he still charged in like a maniac, took out my boy," Rudy clipped, attention on Deke, but he was telling me this story.

I didn't doubt that from Dckc.

But I didn't think on it.

I could see Rudy's hand shaking and I didn't think that was a good thing.

Deke started shifting to me.

"I said *stop fucking moving!*" Rudy screamed.

"Take it," I said quickly and Rudy's attention came back to me. "Take them. Get your guy. Both of you get out. Take them. All of them. Let me and Deke walk out of here and you just take them, Rudy."

Rudy thought about that for a second before his face twisted in the moonlight and he snapped, "You're not gonna just let me walk outta here."

I was.

The cops that would be here in about two minutes would not and I needed Deke and me in the safe room when they rolled up and took care of business.

That said, Rudy could have the guitars, the house, I'd cut off my hair and give it to him if that meant Deke was safe.

Safe with me.

"The most important thing in this room to me is Deke. Take the guitars. Take the awards. Take the records. Take whatever you want. Just let us walk away."

Rudy looked again at Deke and screeched, "*Motherfucker! I said stop moving!*"

The next moments happened in a flash that still played out like a drawn-out nightmare that lasts for decades, centuries, all of it you know you can't escape by waking.

Because it was real.

The guy on the floor that Deke had taken out had come to and he was turning. I noticed. I cried out Deke's name.

Deke moved, fast, to me.

I pulled out his gun.

And the room exploded in ear-splitting noise. Gunshot. Lots of them. So many, I couldn't hear a thing but the blasts and ringing.

Deke tackled me and I hit the ground with a jarring thud, Deke on me.

He wrested the gun from my grip, rolled, his weight full on me, back to my front, my back pressed to the floor, and he fired.

And fired.

And fired.

I felt his body jerk unnaturally, no thoughts about that except it being the kick of the gun, my hands moving to his waist, holding on.

Then, silence.

Nothing.

"Deke," I breathed.

He rolled again, to the side, sliding off me.

Other than that, he didn't move, his back to my side now.

I smelled gunpowder mingled with pine and lay still.

No movement, no sound.

Not from Rudy. His partner.

Not from Deke.

Not from Deke.

I sat up fast, scanning, seeing both other men. Rudy was on his back, not moving with a stillness that was eerie. The other guy was on his side, the same way.

I thought fast and my first thought was, alleviate the danger. Get us safe. So I got up, raced to them, saw the blood spatter on walls, floors, the pools of it growing around their bodies.

I snatched up their guns, ran back to Deke, tossing them in the fireplace as I went.

He was still on his side.

I fell to my knees, put my hands to him and gently rolled him to his back.

His white tee was no longer white.

It was dark.

Covered in blood.

My insides started burning as I moved my hands to him, feeling nothing but warmth too warm, all of it wet, my eyes shifting to his shadowed face.

His eyes were on me.

"I called Chace," I said, finding the source of some gushing, pressing in, still searching, my eyes not leaving his. "He's coming."

"Good, baby," he whispered, the words faint.

Faint.

Not Deke.

So not Deke.

"Stick with me," I ordered, finding another source, pressing in. The blood flowed over my fingers and I beat back a whimper, bending close to him. "Stick with me, baby."

"With...you," he pushed out.

There seemed to be more sources of blood. Fuck, blood everywhere.

I put my chest to his, covering more area, resting my body on him, putting pressure on.

My face close to his, I saw his eyelids slowly closing.

I put my bloody hands to both of his cheeks, sensing company, someone coming in from the back stealthily.

I didn't look.

I shook Deke's head and demanded, "Stick with me. Stick with me, baby. Stick with me, goddammit."

His eyes slowly opened.

"Justice," Chace said.

"Wither to dust," Deke whispered.

No.

Nonononono.

No.

My nose stung, my eyes filled with wet.

"No," I bit out. "You're with me. Stay with me."

"Ambulance, immediately. Man down at ninety-seven Ponderosa Road. Get them here *now*," Chace bit out.

"Do it at your side, gypsy," Deke said softly, his voice fading.

"Yes," I whispered. "Yes, honey. Yes. Wither to dust. At my side."

"Yeah," he breathed out.

His eyes closed.

"Deke," I called.

"Jussy, roll off, let us get in," Chace said, hand on my shoulder.

I ignored Chace, shook Deke's head, called out, "Baby."

"Jussy, need you to roll off, sweetheart."

I shook Deke's head again.

His eyes stayed closed.

"*Deke!*" I shrieked.

His eyes stayed closed.

Chace pulled me off, up, into his arms.

I struggled and screamed.

But fucking fuck, he was stronger than me.

Two officers went in and worked on him.

I kept struggling.

The ambulance came.

I got my shit together so they wouldn't think I'd lost it and they'd let me ride with him.

It didn't matter. Chace made them let me ride with him.

So, rushing out behind the gurney still pulling on my boots, I rode with him.

They took him from me at the hospital.

The whole time going there, they worked, they did it urgently, the words they said to each other and in their radios I blocked out because I could feel it.

I could feel it.

And Deke didn't open his eyes.

* * *

Tate

Tate heard the woman screaming the minute he hit the doors of the emergency room.

It sounded nothing like her.

He still knew it was Justice.

His stomach dropped for the second time that night, the first one happening when he got the call from Chace.

Pulling his wife with him, feeling Jonas at his heels, with fast strides, he moved to the noise and stopped dead, his woman at his side, when he saw Justice, covered in blood, cornered, eyes wild, mouth a snarl, squaring off against three members of the hospital staff.

"Sir, please move away," one of them said, catching Lauren, Jonas and Tate there.

"We're friends of hers," Tate told him.

"Tell them to get away," Justice snapped. "Tate, tell them to leave me alone."

Tate looked to Justice.

"They want to clean my hands," she bit at him. "They want to take him from me. They don't get him. I'm keeping him." She wrapped her arms around her middle. "I'm keeping him until they give him back to me."

He heard Laurie make a noise, felt her make a move but he looked down at her and shook his head.

"She needs to get cleaned up, sir, and she needs a sedative. She was there when—" one of the staffers started.

"Leave me with her," Tate ordered.

"She's exhibited signs she might get violent," the man went on.

Tate spared him a glance and clipped, "Leave her with me."

Tate felt the man's gaze. He hesitated, but backed off, though only a couple of steps, the other two following.

Tate went to a standing gurney not close to Justice but closer than he'd been.

He hauled his ass up on it, opened his thighs, doing all this eyes locked on Justice.

When he got there, he said gently, "C'mere, Jussy."

"Don't make me wash him away, Tate," she snapped.

"Honey, come here."

"I'm keeping him with me," she shot back.

"Jussy, right now, where would Deke want you to be?" he asked. "Who would he want minding you? Tell me."

She did a shuffle step away from him, turning her shoulder, keeping eye contact over it.

Fuck, she was fucked up, in shock, way beyond tweaked.

"Deke was here right now, Jussy, who would he want taking care of you?" Tate asked quietly.

She hesitated, looked around, took in the staffers, Lauren, Jonas, then back to him when she answered, "You."

"Yeah. Me. Now c'mere."

Another shuffle step, this one toward him. And another.

Then she turned fully to him. Ducking her head, her long hair falling down either side, she hit him head first, right at his collarbone, and drove in.

He wrapped his arms around her.

Lauren got close behind Justice, lifted her hand, hesitated, looked at her man and Tate gave her a short nod. Jonas just got near, and when Tate glanced at him, he saw his boy's eyes locked to his old man.

Laurie moved in closer and started stroking Justice's hair.

Her touch set Justice to talking.

"I don't know if I did wrong. He told me to run. But I heard gunshots. I called Chace. But Deke was in there. Unarmed. They had guns. And I wanted him to have his gun."

"You didn't do wrong," Tate said, not knowing what went down, if what he said was a lie, or the truth.

What it was was what she needed to hear right then.

Though calling Chace was the right thing.

"Then I saw it was Rudy. My cousin. I thought I could talk him down. We're Lonesomes. He wouldn't hurt me. No matter how fucked up he was, he wouldn't hurt me."

"I can see you thinkin' that."

"He...he...didn't mind hurting me."

Tate knew that to be true but he didn't say anything.

"I got Deke the gun," she whispered.

"Right, honey."

"But I'm worried I did wrong."

"Got lots of worries right now, Jussy. Why don't you let that one go for now?"

"He tackled me."

"Who? Your cousin?"

"He tackled me," she repeated.

"Jussy—"

She burrowed in, fuck, so strong, she almost took his back to the gurney.

Tate braced, wrapped her tight and shifted his gaze to his wife's anguished eyes.

"He didn't tackle me," Justice whispered, her voice fracturing. "He shielded me."

That was when she went down, knees failing.

Tate caught her as she fell, pulled her up, swung her out and settled her in his lap.

She cried in his neck, holding on tight.

She was limp, almost lifeless when she'd cried herself out.

He coaxed her to take the sedative. As she got drowsy, he and Laurie helped her wash her hands. As she'd been crying, Lauren made the calls, got through to Twyla who hadn't left yet. When she arrived, they got Jussy's jacket off, her bloody shirt, and changed her into one of Twyla's sweaters.

She didn't lapse into sleep until they were in the waiting room and she did this collapsed into Tate's side, holding the bundle of her bloody clothes tight to her chest like a child would a teddy bear.

He moved her head to his thigh, Krys shifting in to lift her legs, curl her up on the seat beside him. And Lexie covered her with Ty's jacket.

Everyone showed, including Chace.

He reported the two men who invaded Justice's home were both DOA.

Eventually, a lot of the folks who showed left. They had little kids. They had to get home.

It was the early hours of the morning when the surgeon came out.

Deke pulled through. But he'd lost a tremendous amount of blood, took four bullets, the damage was extensive, and he was in critical condition.

As he spoke carefully, uncomfortably, words he didn't have to say because his manner screamed it, the surgeon shared they could not make any guarantees. If he lasted twenty-four hours, something left unspoken but it was clear the doctor did not think that would happen, then there *might* be hope.

"But, think it's best, if he's of that religion, that you call for Last Rites," the man finished solemnly.

This made Nadine, Cindy and Lauren all lose it, Twyla, Jim-Billy and Jonas moving in to give them comfort.

They all did that quietly.

Tate couldn't offer his wife that comfort.

He just felt his stomach squeeze, the intensity of the pain forcing sick to surge up his throat.

But he swallowed it back and did what his brother would want him to do.

He sat immobile, Jussy's head still on his thigh, his fingers shifting through her hair soothingly even though she was still fast asleep.

At least she'd missed that.

At least.

* * *

Tate woke with a start, his body's movement bringing Laurie's head up from his shoulder.

He stared into the room, not knowing where the fuck he was for a moment before he saw Jim-Billy, head bowed down, baseball cap pulled over his eyes, asleep in a chair in the hospital waiting room across from Tate, Nadine tucked to his side. And down from them, Jonas stretched out on chairs, arm over his head to block out the light, asleep.

He looked right and saw Krys walking in, her movements agitated, Bubba following her, Breanne strapped in swaddling to the big man's chest.

For a second, Tate stared at Krys, thrown. He knew where he was. He knew why he was there. He hated it like fuck.

But he'd never in his life seen Krys without makeup, her hair straggling down straight, looking just washed, dried, but untouched.

He got over that, turned his head left and saw Twyla standing at the end of the row of seats, eyes aimed out the window, Cindy in a seat, eyes open, on Krys, but she was leaning into her woman.

"Word?" Krys rapped out.

Fuck, he was going to have to tell her.

Fuck.

She'd been gone, home with Bubba and their new baby, when the surgeon came.

Tate started to get up but felt Lauren's hand curl on his thigh.

He looked to his wife.

"Where's Jussy?" she asked.

His head shot around to the row of seats behind him.

Ty's jacket laid there, the bundle of bloody clothes there too.

No Jussy.

He looked to Twyla.

"You see her leave?" he asked sharply.

Twyla's face shifted, mouth opened, but it was Cindy who answered.

"We both woke up a couple of minutes ago. Didn't think, Tate, except maybe she had to go to the bathroom or something."

Jim-Billy was stirring, pushing his ball cap back, Nadine lifting from his side sleepily, Jonas hearing the conversation, pushing up into a hand, and Tate rose from his chair.

He headed to the hall, knowing from the sound of footfalls there was a parade behind him.

He hit the nurse's station outside the Critical Care Unit.

"Can I help you?" the nurse there asked.

"Jussy—" he bit out, stopped abruptly and started again. "Deke Hightower, a friend of mine, he's here."

"I know, sir, he's still—"

Tate interrupted her. "His woman was sedated when the doctor told us his condition. We've been in the waiting room, woke up, she's not with us. Have you seen her?"

Her expression altered to understanding as she said quietly, "Ms. Lonesome has been informed of his condition and she's in with him."

"Dammit," Tate muttered under his breath.

It was him who should have told her.

It was him Deke would have wanted to tell her.

Fuck.

"Take us to him," Krys demanded. "Take us all to them."

The nurse shook her head. "Only one visitor at a time in this unit, sorry."

Laurie pushed closer to the station. "You need to take us all to him."

"It's policy that—"

"He needs his friends around him," Laurie whispered, a hitch in her voice, and Tate rounded her belly with an arm, pulling her back to him.

"It's not—" the nurse began.

"Please," Lauren begged.

The nurse took them all in and Tate was grateful at the same time agonized at what it meant when she slowly nodded her head.

"I'll need you to be as quiet as you can. I'll also need you all to wash your hands and put booties on. And I'm sorry, sir, no babies."

"You all go. I'll take Breanne," Cindy said hurriedly, already coming forward, helping Bubba unwrap the swaddling.

The handoff happened. The nurse took them to the sterilization station. They washed their hands and put on booties.

Tate was holding Lauren steady as she put hers on when the nurse murmured, "What's that?"

But he heard it.

And Tate knew what it was.

He moved swiftly toward the sound, followed by Laurie, Jonas, Krys, Twyla, Jim-Billy, Nadine and Bubba.

He stopped just in the door.

They pressed in behind him.

The nurse got there before him, was deeper in the room, and she opened her mouth to speak.

Tate darted out a hand, curled it on her shoulder and her eyes came to him.

He shook his head and mouthed, "Please."

She didn't look like she liked it but she said nothing and turned her eyes to the bed.

Tate did too.

Deke was in it, the bulk of his body, his hair and his eyes the only way Tate knew that it was his brother in that bed. His face was mostly obscured by the apparatus at his mouth, a tube down his throat, more leading to it, more in his arms, the back of the bed slightly elevated. He had no hospital gown, sheet and blanket around his waist, his upper body naked but there wasn't much you could see since all of it was wrapped in bandages.

Jussy was seated in a chair at his side.

She was leaned into him and she was singing.

He'd never heard the song and would only know what it was and who sang it days later, when Laurie would find it, play it for him, and they would listen to it, his wife weeping in his arms.

The Goo Goo Dolls, "Come to Me."

Lauren couldn't watch. Tate knew it when she curled into his front, shoving her face in his chest, and it didn't take long for the wet of her silent tears to soak his Henley.

But Tate didn't tear his gaze off Jussy, a woman so in love with her man, in this situation it was so difficult to witness it actually made his eyes hurt, keeping them on her. Listening to her beautiful voice wrapping around words, each one full of love and hope and belief, each one spearing right through his fucking heart in a way it was a wonder the wet of his life blood didn't mix with the salt of his wife's tears.

He curled a hand around the back of Laurie's head, his other arm around her waist, pulling her closer right before Jussy reached out and picked up Deke's hand.

She brought it to her mouth and she started singing in husky, broken whispers when the lyrics became about getting to the church on time.

Tate watched her open his hand, curling it on her face, singing into his palm like her song could keep the pulse beating at its base.

Suddenly, she slumped forward, forcing Deke's hand to sift into the hair at the back of her head. Her forehead hit the side of his bed and she finished the song, the lilt of desperate hope gone in her voice, nothing but sorrow remaining, as she sang the final words, all this clenching Deke's fingers with hers in the back of her hair.

Something struck him.

Tate tore his gaze off Jussy and took it to Deke.

His friend had his eyes open and there was no missing the question in them.

Tate nodded his head slowly, sharing that yes, he was taking care of Deke's woman.

Deke nodded back more slowly, only once, then his eyes shifted down to the woman he called his gypsy.

He must have done something, moved his fingers in her hair, because Jussy's head shot back so fast, all that hair went flying.

Tate let out a tortured breath.

The one he pulled in felt a lot fucking better.

And then he smiled.

CHAPTER TWENTY-FOUR

I Know

Wood

"THE SMALL TOWN of Carnal, Colorado is back in the news today with a fatal shooting happening at the home of critically acclaimed singer-songwriter, Justice Lonesome, daughter of rock legend, the late Johnny Lonesome," the newscaster said.

Looking into the camera, pictures on the screen to the right side of her head shifting from Jus, to Johnny, the newscaster for the Denver station kept speaking as the picture again switched to one of a wiry guy who could have been good-looking, if he wasn't so gaunt, being led somewhere by a cop with his hands back in cuffs.

"Rudy Lonesome Smith, the estranged son of Justice's aunt, Tammy Lonesome, allegedly broke into Justice Lonesome's home in order to steal the fabled collection of Johnny and his father, Jerry's guitars. Rudy Smith has become well-known in the media the last decade through a variety of run-ins with the law, all of them drug related. It's been confirmed that he was killed at the scene, along with a partner, currently unidentified, after firing on Justice Lonesome and her live-in boyfriend, Deke Hightower, Mr. Hightower reportedly firing back in self-defense."

The screen flashed to footage from down Jussy's lane, only the front of her drive visible, her house hidden by trees, as uniformed officers stood sentry at the mouth of the lane, keeping the reporters and cameramen back. In the distance, cops milled around in the drive.

The newscaster's voice kept coming.

"A statement from the hospital reports that Mr. Hightower was shot four times during the clash. He's survived surgery but is currently listed in critical condition. A statement from Carnal Police notes Justice Lonesome called the report in, squad cars were instantly dispatched but the two intruders were dead on arrival of the police. Carnal authorities also report that preliminary findings indicate that Mr. Hightower shielded Ms. Lonesome while the shots were being fired in her home, which was why he sustained so many injuries, however Ms. Lonesome is said to have been unharmed."

The screen went back to the newscaster as she kept reporting, a picture now of Jussy's aunt next to her head.

"Tammy Lonesome's people have released a statement on her behalf, sharing her deep sadness at this heartbreaking end to her son's life, a man who has been riddled with troubles due to drug addiction, these starting after a failed attempt to find success in the family business. She and her husband are now on their way to Colorado to claim the remains of their troubled son and join her brother Jimmy there so they can also be with their niece during this terrible time."

The picture that had changed to Jimmy Lonesome disappeared and the camera centered on the newscaster.

"No word as to if it's expected the gravely injured Mr. Hightower will pull through. Ms. Lonesome has been sequestered in the hospital and has not been seen. It's been a difficult year for the Lonesomes, with the unexpected loss to an aneurysm of Johnny Lonesome earlier this year, and now the tragic end of Rudy Lonesome Smith. We'll report further when we know the identity of the second intruder and the condition of Mr. Hightower."

She looked to her right, the male newscaster came on with a graphic beside him of a different story, and Wood lifted the remote and switched off the TV.

He dropped the remote to the side, took his boot off the edge of the coffee table and pulled his ass out of the couch.

He went looking for her and found her in the room in the basement where they kept a lot of shit they didn't use often and a crap ton of the kids' stuff they'd grown out of, his wife convinced some day one of them might want some of it and she didn't want it to be gone if they did.

After he opened the door, he leaned against the frame and saw her at the long, folding table he'd set up for her, her sweet, round ass in a steel folding chair, the entirety of the table filled with wrap, tape, ribbon, bows, boxes, the cement floor all around her covered in bags, snippings of paper and ribbon and stacks of wrapped presents.

"You want help?" he asked, only because he knew her answer.

"Like you're gonna wrap a present," Maggie replied.

Yeah, that was her answer.

He grinned at her.

Her hands arrested, blade of scissors to the end of a ribbon, her eyes on him, she did not grin back.

"He's gonna be okay," she whispered.

She saw right into his soul.

She always did. Christ, even from their first date, he'd felt that.

He'd forgotten it along the way.

Staring in her warm eyes in her pretty face that topped her curvy body, ass to a chair in the basement of his house, back again where she belonged, it was fucking good he'd remembered.

"I know," he whispered back.

"They're moving him out of Critical Care tomorrow," she told him something else he knew.

"I know," he repeated.

"He's a strong guy, sweetheart. He'll be back to normal in no time."

"I know, baby."

She gave that time then she asked quietly, "Do you think, Deke finding Jus, all that happened happened, it's all going to be all right...*again*...that all the drama is finally going to be over?"

Wood gave his woman the truth.

"It's never over, baby."

Still watching him, she gave up on the present, got up and walked to him.

She didn't stop, fitting her small, soft body into his long one, wrapping her arms around him.

He did the same with her, bending his neck, putting his lips to the top of her hair.

"You wanna go to bed?" she asked his chest.

"Fuck yeah," he answered.

Maggie tipped her head back and smiled.

And Wood felt better.

EPILOGUE

"I'll Crawl Home to Her"

Justice

"YOU LOOK *SHIT hot*," Krystal declared and I looked through the mirror at my girl walking into my dressing room, Bubba following her carrying Breanne on his hip.

"Krys, shi-ee-oot," Bubba growled, curling his free hand around one of Breanne's ears.

She tossed a glance over her shoulder at him. "Worse could happen, her first word bein' shit."

"How about we still avoid that, yeah?" he asked.

She turned to me, rolling her eyes.

I looked up to the makeup artist at my side and gave her a grin.

"You're done anyway," she muttered. "Come back to do a touch up and put the headpiece on before you go on."

I nodded.

She wended her way through the bodies crowding my dressing room.

"Champagne, champagne and more champagne," Jim-Billy called out, having instantly found his way to the refreshment area, a table laid out with snacks and big bowls filled with ice. Bottles of water and soda were stuck in one, champagne in the other. He looked to me. "Got beer, sweetheart?"

"Mini-fridge, Jim-Billy," I told him.

"I'll take champagne," Lexie called out.

"Me too," Faye said.

"Beer for me,"Twyla grunted.

"Yo." I heard Lauren greet.

"Yo." I heard Deke reply and I turned my attention to the couch where Deke had been sprawled since even before the stylist started working on me.

Lauren had thrown herself down close to him, in the opening of his arm stretched at the back.

Once down, he curled it around her.

I found Tate and saw him grinning at his woman with his friend. He felt my gaze and gave his to me.

I smiled.

Tate didn't smile.

He walked right to me, lifted his hand and slid it inside my hair to the back of my neck. He pulled me down as he bent and I felt his lips touch my forehead.

The pressure at my neck lessened, I drew back and looked up at him.

"You ready for this?" he asked.

I nodded. "It's gonna be great."

"Yeah, it is," he murmured, finally giving me a smile before he slid his hand back out and moved away.

"Just FYI, the rest of 'em are in the VIP section, savin' us seats," Krystal informed me.

"Cool," I replied.

"Can we take beer to the VIP?" Jim-Billy asked.

"You can do anything you want," I answered.

He gave me a broken grin.

"You decide if you're gonna announce tonight that you're recording again?" Laurie asked.

I nodded my head, though I answered, "No announcement. I think we'll make it low-key. Drop the album. While Deke and I are on the road, I'll hit some bars, honkytonks. Nothing planned. Still, it'll hit social media, create buzz. Mr. T said that when the stuff was downloaded when I played at Bubba's, my sales didn't skyrocket, but they did get a push. It'll be more fun that way and low pressure. I don't need another gold record, just..." I shrugged, turning my eyes to Deke who had his warm on me, "to make music."

"Sounds fuckin' cool," Twyla decreed.

"Uh, would everyone stop cussin' around my kid?" Bubba asked impatiently.

"Dude, you're bringin' her to a freakin' rock concert. And whatever Lacey Town does. What's that called?" Twyla asked me. "Hip hop?"

"R&B," I answered.

"And that," Twyla said to Bubba.

"She likes loud music," Krys declared, moving to her baby girl, putting out a finger that Breanne instantly grabbed. Krys dropped her face in her little one's, sing-songing, "Don't you, Bree? You're like your momma. The louder, the better."

Breanne giggled her agreement, shaking her momma's finger excitedly then letting her go and reaching out with both hands.

Krys took her. The handoff complete, Bubba moved to the refreshment area.

He grabbed a Coke and popped it open.

"Lotsa flowers," Ty muttered, having lounged in an armchair, his arm curled around Lexie's hips where she was seated on the arm at his side.

"Yep," I agreed.

"Folks wantin' you back in the business?" Chace asked.

I shook my head and started pointing, counting them down.

"Dana, for doing this. Joss, to break a leg. Lacey, because we do that, big gig, a massive spray of flowers. I did it for her too. Mr. T, because his assistant sees to that kinda thing for him. Mav, because he's finally got his head out of his ass." My voice dipped and I pointed to some exquisite red roses, but my eyes shifted to Deke. "Deke." I grinned at him before I pointed to the last. "And my girl Bianca because she's not gonna be here but she wants to be here in spirit."

"This is probably good," Chace muttered.

"This is definitely good," Deke muttered back.

In the interim, especially after what happened at my house, calls had been made and texts had been exchanged between me and Bianca. Once Deke was firmly on the road to recovery, a short conversation had been had that didn't say a lot over the phone because I suspected she *couldn't* say a lot over the phone and wouldn't do it in person either.

But she was keeping her distance. For me, because at first I needed that to see to Deke. Then I'd shared it'd be best simply in regards to Deke.

Not to mention, because Joss had eventually phoned her, chewed her ass out about what happened to me and said she didn't want to see her face again until she was ready (this, I figured, would last another week or so before they sorted it out and all was good).

And Lacey wasn't speaking to her at all.

She'd get over it too.

Time.

Time healed.

I looked back to Deke, my eyes skimming his chest covered in a chocolate-brown, button-up shirt that looked hot on him.

Yeah.

Time healed.

"We should have bought her flowers," Faye whispered to her husband.

"Next time, sweetheart. This time, looks like she's covered," he whispered back.

A knock came at the door and Twyla moved to open it.

The gal with a mouthpiece wrapped around her cheek looked at Twyla, swung in, found me and said, "Ten minutes to go time, Justice."

I nodded. "I'm ready."

"Grab some brews, we should get to our seats," Jim-Billy ordered Tate, who now had his own beer and was standing by the mini-fridge. "I don't wanna miss anything."

"You need anything, Jussy?" Lexie asked.

I shook my head. "All good."

"Right." She jumped from the chair, grabbing Ty's hand. "Up, Mr. Humongo. I don't want to miss anything either."

I slid off my seat, gave out hugs, cheek kisses, and when Krystal came to me, I said, "Love the hair."

"Had to go rock 'n' roll," she replied and looked in my eyes. "For you." A pause as the attitude she held up as a shield to hold others back melted clean away and the love she had for me swept in in its place before she finished, "And for Johnny."

I felt a lump hit my throat, bent into her and touched foreheads.

"Straight up, he'd love it," I shared.

He would. She'd gone full-on 80's video vamp, all blonde frosted flips and curls, teased so far out, it was ratted in some places.

She rocked it.

Dad would have loved her hair, but he would have loved her better.

She was his kind of woman.

She shoved her forehead in mine. Breanne beat my chest, Krys pulled back and I shot Breanne a wide-mouth-and-big-eyes goofy face.

She giggled again.

By the time they were all gone, the makeup girl was back and she slid on the headband which was a patterned scarf with a hint of braiding that had long ends that mingled with the back of my hair. The front of that hair was plaited in a fat braid from one temple across my front hairline to disappear behind my opposite ear.

The rest hung long.

While she did this, I didn't pay attention to what she was doing.

I was alternating between watching Deke grin at me in the mirror and looking at the photo I'd stuck into the side of it, one of the photos from that night months ago at Bubba's.

The first photo of me and Deke.

The first photo of me with my new family.

The stylist finished up by hitting my cheeks with some dewy peach and doing another swipe of lip gloss before she pulled back, scrutinized me from crown to shoulders and declared, "You're good." She straightened and bid, "Kick ass out there."

"I will," I assured.

She took off.

I twisted my seat to Deke who was still in the couch.

"So?" I swept up a hand to indicate me.

My outfit consisted of rust-colored short shorts that had a subtle gold glitter to them, but that subtlety would be lost when the lights hit them onstage. Also a lacy cream bra. None of this was seen very well because I was wearing a huge smock that hung down below my shorts with a scalloped hem that was made of a netting of delicate lace. It had a gathered, scooped neckline and scalloped, full sleeves that hit at my elbows. There were cut outs at my shoulders.

I'd accompanied this with lots of dangling necklaces, long hoops in my ears, as well as the studs up the shells, lots of bracelets on my non-strumming wrist, a thick band of Native American beading at that wrist and my beat-up, fawn suede cowboy boots.

"You wanna wear that top anytime, gypsy, without the shorts and bra, feel free," Deke replied.

Approval.

I felt my mouth curl up, slid off the seat and went to him.

I put one knee in the couch at one of his hips, the other on the other side and settled down, straddling him, my hands to either side of his neck.

"You decide if you're gonna stay backstage or go to VIP?" I asked quietly.

"VIP, Jussy," he answered, his eyes lighting. "Don't wanna miss anything."

He wanted to watch me perform, be out there where the beauty happened.

I got that.

"Then you best go," I told him.

He nodded. "Yeah."

"You can't mess anything up," I warned at the look in his eye. "There's twenty thousand people out there and my lip gloss has to be just right."

This was less about Deke messing up my hair and makeup and more about him having that look in his eye, me wanting to give into it, which meant the start of a huge, multi-act concert in tribute to my father would be indefinitely delayed.

He shook his head, his eyes still lit, and then ducked it, going in to kiss my throat.

He pulled back, rested his head on the back of the couch and whispered, "Love you, Justice."

I knew he did. I knew it before he'd nearly died for me.

Now, I *knew he did*.

"I love you too, Deke."

"Proud of you, baby."

My voice was husky when I replied, "Thank you, honey."

"Like that girl said, kick ass."

"I will."

Suddenly, we were both up, Deke surging out of the couch, his hands on my waist lifting me with him.

He put me down on my feet and I bent my head way back to keep his eyes.

He dipped his chin deep into his neck to keep mine.

Then he lifted his hand, forefinger extended, so he could slide the tip of it from the top of my throat along the soft skin under my jaw to the point of my chin.

I drew in breath and held it.

He'd touched me, *a lot*.

A lot, a lot.

But he'd only ever done that to me once before.

The night we met.

In Wyoming.

He remembered.

Everything.

"Give 'em hell, baby girl," he said softly. "See you on the other side."

Baby girl.

He'd called me that only in Wyoming too.

"Yeah, Deke."

His eyes crinkled, one side of his lips hitched up, and I pivoted as I watched him walk out of the room.

I drew in breath and stared at the door.

Twenty thousand people.

I'd never played to a venue that big.

All of them were there for Heaven's Gate. Let. The Chokers. Uncle Jimmy. Aunt Tammy. Lacey. And the final act who came in after I'd asked their band leader: Stella and the Blue Moon Gypsies.

All of them were there for my daddy.

A knock came on the door, it opened before I called out and Mav swung in.

"They're ready for us, Jussy," he said.

I nodded and walked to him.

He took my hand when I got close.

We wound our way through some serious backstage activity to the side stage.

Dana was standing there.

She turned and smiled at us. Reaching out a hand.

It wasn't me who moved us forward to take it.

It was Mav.

For several long moments we all did nothing but stand there, linked together, looking at each other, holding on tight.

And then, at Mav tugging Dana and my hands, we started to move onstage.

But something made me look back.

When I did, emerging from the shadows and hubbub backstage, Mr. T appeared.

He had eyes on me.

And my heart squeezed when I saw on his lips that he was smiling.

Out and out smiling.

I shot my smile back and then faced forward.

And the three people who meant the most to Johnny Lonesome in his life at his death walked onstage hand in hand to start a kickass party.

* * *

I looked back to Dad's band, smiling so huge it hurt my face, as we all lifted then fell to the final note of one of Dad's most kickass songs.

I turned back to the crowd of screaming, clapping, shouting fans, the chant of, "Lonesome, Lonesome, Lonesome," coming in a beautiful wave, undulating all around me.

I swept my smile through them, but at its end, I looked home.

This being to the right side of the stage, cordoned off, fitted with padded seats that were all empty because everyone was standing.

I saw a lot of people I knew who didn't belong to me.

But with Deke, I saw a lot of people who did, including ones who hadn't come in to check up on me and raid my mini-fridge: Max and Nina, Sunny and Shambles, Wood and Maggie, Dominic and Daniel, Ham and Zara, Decker and Emme.

Home.

My smile lingered on them before I moved back to the standing microphone.

I'd already sung "Chain Link," glancing at Deke occasionally throughout as I did.

I did that because Deke knew that song was for him. I didn't need to make a point of it.

But it was more.

In all that had played out, no one was going to get that. That was only his.

And I wanted to keep that only for Deke.

For him and for me.

I'd also sung Rondstadt's "It's So Easy." I did this for Deke too, liking the curve it put on his lips. But, as ever, I also did it for Joss.

I'd sung others of mine. But that wasn't the vibe I wanted to give. The slow and the sweet.

No.

I wanted to give them Dad.

So, with his band backing me, we did lots of covers of Dad's music. And halfway through my set, Lacey, Perry and Terrence (my girl was on after me, Dad's buds had already done their sets), came out to the crowd going wild, and together we did Dad's most well-known rompin', stompin' rock anthem.

And now it was time for me to wind up so Lacey could do her thing and then Stella and her boys could finish the night off.

I drew in breath and looked out into the dark sea of faces.

Then I said into the mic, "My father was Johnny Lonesome to you. But he was Dad to me. The best dad there could be." The crowd roared but I kept talking and they quieted quickly to hear me. "I miss him. I'll always miss him. And part of that is missing the fact that he was gone before he saw that I'd found my peace. But I know he knows that peace is with me. So I figure he'll like me ending my time with you, singing the words to a freakin' awesome song to share with you the peace a life of bounty saw fit to give to me."

I felt the shift in the crowd as I spoke.

They knew, with the media all over it for weeks, what Rudy did, how Deke saved me, Aunt Tammy's haggard face, Uncle Jimmy's tight one, Tate, Ty, Wood, Chace, Bubba crowding me, trying to hide me from the cameras as they rushed me to and from cars and hospital.

They knew.

Everyone knew my bounty.

I stepped back, looked over my shoulder, nodded, giving the beat, one, two, three and four and…

I went back to the mic and it was me who flicked my fingernails on the strings for the first notes of Lynyrd Skynrd's "Simple Man."

The crowd went crazy.

My dad's band kicked in behind me.

I shifted my eyes to the right and started to sing that song.

And that song I sang right to Deke. Unlike "Chain Link," I didn't take my eyes from him when words flowed through my mouth.

Every word, I gave right to my man.

I didn't care that twenty thousand people saw. I wanted them to. That's why I was doing it.

I was proud to share the best way I knew how, through music, the kind of man I had. How much there was of him. How he made less so much more. How he redefined the word "simple" in glorious ways.

Dad's band rocked it while the darkness in front of me lit with the pinprick lights on cell phones.

And I prayed to God my voice raised to the heavens so my dad would hear each word and truly know just the man who had given me peace.

That said, I knew he was watching over me.

So he already knew.

When the song was over, I pulled my guitar from around my neck and walked sure-footed to the side of the stage. You know, just in case some in the upper decks missed it.

I got down on my knees, put my guitar on its back to the stage and bent way forward.

Because Deke was right there.

His head tipped back, his hand slid into my hair, and I kissed him, long, hard and wet.

I knew pictures were taken. That would never stop.

Even with his long hospitalization and recovery, Deke did not escape the fame his actions settled on his broad shoulders. Mr. T gave his most valiant effort, but with what Deke did, the way Deke looked, the perfection that was him and me, to that day, they still hounded us.

Deke took to fame a lot better than me.

It happened.

And at my side, he just kept being Deke.

When our kiss ended, the roar of the crowd was deafening.

But me and Deke, we just touched noses.

I looked into his eyes and whispered, "Bounty."

His teeth caught his lower lip and his hand in my hair spasmed.

I pulled away, got up and sauntered with guitar back to the mic.

"Time for Lacey," I told the crowd, lifted my guitar and felt the wave of love hit me. "Thanks for spending time with me. And more." I put my hand to my chest. "Thanks for being here for my dad."

More love blasted over me as, lifting a hand in a wave, carrying my guitar with me, I walked off the stage followed by my dad's band.

* * *

Justice Lonesome with her father's band doing a rendition of "Simple Man" wouldn't be the video that Mr. T's people uploaded from that night on YouTube that got the most hits.

No.

Because the best was yet to come.

* * *

I stood backstage, touched up and ready to join everyone else at the end of the concert when we'd all jam to Dad's "Never Missin' Home."

But I was watching with some confusion as the setup for Stella's set included the stage lights going purple and the stagehands setting up eleven microphone stands up front.

I felt someone join me and looked right to see Joss slide in there.

She never liked to miss anything either so she'd been in VIP.

"Hey, what're you doing here?" I asked.

She just gave me a look I felt in my belly and around the rims of my heart.

She took my hand just as more fingers slid around my other one.

I looked left and saw Dana.

Oh shit.

"What's going on?" I asked, my body bracing.

Dana turned her head toward the stage.

I looked that way too.

The stagehands were gone.

And filing in solemnly were Perry, Terrence, Lacey, Rod, Uncle Jimmy, Aunt Tammy, Stella, and her band, Hugo, Pong, Buzz and Leo.

They each took a microphone.

The crowd seemed to sense something was happening. The buzz was low and attentive, when, even after this array of artists took the stage, it stayed purple.

"Bear with us, folks, we've had a request," Stella said into the microphone. "There's a man who wants us to sing a song to his gypsy."

My vision instantly went watery, but my eyes shot to the right, where I could see the front of the VIP seating.

Deke was already looking at me.

That was when the humming started, like a funeral dirge, somber in its beauty.

And the punctuated clapping.

A low, perfect harmony.

My gaze cut back to the stage.

And beats after it did, a cappella, Rod started singing Hozier's "Work Song."

My knees got weak.

Dana and Joss held me up, their hands in mine tightening, their bodies shifting into my sides like they felt it happening.

As for me, I felt. A lot. Too much. Such beauty, making my skin seem too thin to contain it, hold it in. My heart working hard in the effort to draw it deep inside me, absorb it, keep it forever there, filling me. All this as the fat drops of wet slipped from my eyes, gliding down my cheeks and I saw Rod turn his head and sing his words to his wife.

So beautiful.

I loved my mom had that from Roddy.

But still.

Those words were for me.

Those that didn't have hands raised, cell phones up, dotting the sea of dark faces with thousands of slowly swaying stars started to add to the slow clap as well as giving stomps of their feet. Thousands of hands striking and feet landing, the noise reverberating through the arena, each one thumped against my flesh, beating the emotion I was feeling right to the pit of my heart where I'd always hold it.

Always.

I looked again right, catching Krystal grinning so huge at me, it was like her smile was a flash of a cell phone.

But I only spared her a glance in my search for Deke.

He was still watching me.

Perry sang. And Terrence. And Hugo. And Buzz.

Everyone on stage sang the chorus and consistent humming.

Uncle Jimmy finished the song.

Through it I studied my man's face. Unsurprisingly, the lines of life had tunneled deeper after he took four bullets for me and had months of painful recovery.

Now, for the first time since it happened, they were gone.

His life had smoothed out of his face once again, finally, as he watched me receive the second most beautiful gift I'd ever received…that one and the first both coming from Deke.

And at that end the song, Deke's lips moved.

I watched them form one word.

Bounty.

It was a miracle of music. It was a moment a music fan wished for for a lifetime. The kind they'd tell their friends, their kids, anybody who would listen, sharing it over and over until the day they died.

That day eleven legends took the stage and sang the most beautiful love song ever written.

A song whose astonishing, exquisite words, for me, from Deke, months before came nearly literally.

So yeah.

That got the most hits on YouTube.

Absolutely.

And Dad would have absolutely *fucking loved* every second of it.

* * *

Deke

Body bent back, knees in the bed, Deke smoothed his hand over the ceiling of his trailer.

When he was sure all the edges were glued down, no bubbles, what was there fixed there being *fixed* there until that trailer was no more, he dropped his hand and looked up at the poster for the Johnny Lonesome tribute concert, one of several made up, this one with a picture of Jussy at a mic with her guitar.

He looked down at her lazing on her back on their bed.

"Good?" he asked.

Her eyes went from the poster over their bed to him.

"Perfect," she whispered.

Not exactly, he thought. *But it's the perfect start.*

He twisted and went down on her, taking her mouth.

Jussy opened for him.

Deke slid his tongue inside.

There it was again.

Perfect.

* * *

Twang Magazine

Rock's Gypsy Princess Makes Miracles

Justice Lonesome's comeback tour is not what you'd expect it to be.

Unlike what came from Lonesome's debut, Chain Link, *after dropping her remarkable second album,* The Miracle Mountains, *she did not hit sold-out venues and press junket after press junket.*

She went on the road.

Not on tour.

Just on the road.

Apparently, you can be anywhere from sea to shining sea, and if the music stars are aligned, shining on you the fortune of Lonesome, you might be having a beer at a bar and suddenly a woman, sometimes with a full band, sometimes with just a guitar and a microphone, will start singing.

And that woman will be Justice Lonesome.

She'll rock her signature covers of Rondstadt. She might sing any of her father, Johnny's, songs. However, as old fans and the new ones Lonesome is claiming along the way are avidly keeping track of on social media, she always sings Johnny's "Never Missin' Home."

And, of course, each time she'll hand you the jewel that shone in her first album, that album's title song, "Chain Link."

She'll also do her new stuff and you will not be disappointed.

Lonesome stamped her talent of penning a rock ballad all over her first effort.

Spreading her wings, showing growth and maturity, the ballads from The Miracle Mountains *are more nuanced, have more passion, more pathos, and clearly demonstrate from debut to album two that Lonesome has honed already epic storytelling chops, including "Knight in Dented Armor" and "(Ev'ry Time I Come Home) Life Begins Again."*

But The Miracle Mountains *gives us even more.*

Emerging from the very long shadows of the two legends who came before her, Jerry and Johnny, Justice Lonesome's signature ballads this time are mixed with twangy, foot-tapping, knee-bouncing country rock Ronstadt herself set the standard for with Lonesome's new singles "Pleasure and Pain" and "Gypsy Princess."

The Miracle Mountains *is not a successful second effort.*

It's transcendent.

But it's not only that.

It's the way she's going about spreading that love that's refreshing and unique.

With her current level of popularity and a loyal, solid fanbase who've been waiting over half a decade for her second collection, Lonesome could easily fill event centers and smaller arenas.

Instead, seemingly randomly, with no notice, no promotion, no press, and most surprisingly, no ticket sales, wherever the wind takes her, she's walking into saloons or honkytonks and letting fly.

But Justice Lonesome is not crazy nor is she stupid. It's not just handheld phone video that's hitting download sites. Professionally shot videos are also spreading wide. Even so, the production is minimal. It's Lonesome, perhaps backed by her band or just rock 'n' roll's gypsy with her guitar.

If your stars have aligned and the fortune of Lonesome shines on you and you find yourself in that bar having that beer and Justice Lonesome takes that mic, request her rendition of the Zac Brown Band's "Free." Buzz backed by fan video is that it's wicked good. Added bonus, every time she sings it, her eyes never stray from the man who took four bullets for her, a man who never leaves her side, her fiancé, Deke Hightower.

Unlike her grandfather, Jerry, who worked the road and the business with smarts, screaming talent and downhome sensibility, earning his crown as a rock god. And unlike her father, Johnny, who took up the family mantle, followed his father's path and soared even higher, earning his own reign. In one fell swoop, Justice Lonesome has seized a new crown: Rock's Gypsy Princess.

Long may she reign.

* * *

Heart

Out in the middle of nowhere, nothing there but silver steel blinking in the bright sun, the door to the Airstream opened and the woman stepped out, the heavy waves and curls of her beautiful, long, dark hair lifting at the sudden warm wind that swirled around the trailer.

She wore a flowy, sleeveless, lacy top that hung down low over her hips in four points. Cut-off shorts frayed at the hems. Square-toed, dark-brown motorcycle boots on her feet, flowery socks you could see over the top rims.

She hopped down and a big man followed her, his beard thick, his hair long, pulled back in a mess, fastened at the back of his head.

The man stopped, one hand in hers, the other one lifting to lock the door of the trailer.

Dipping his chin, he looked down at her as he turned, tugging her along with him as he moved them both to the motorcycle parked six feet away.

He strode.

She skipped.

He grinned.

She giggled.

Positioning her out of the way, he threw a long leg over first, lifting the bike from its stand, kicking that stand back.

She mounted behind him with practiced ease, instantly pressing close, wrapping her arms tight around his stomach.

He fired up the bike, lifted a hand. Pulling some shades from the collar of his white tee, he flicked them out, slid them on.

She unearthed her glasses from that mess of hair and positioned them over her eyes.

Blue-lensed Ray-Ban aviators.

The Heart approved.

The man bent slightly to take hold of both grips.

The woman went with him.

His hand moved minutely and a fog of dirt kicked up as the bike shot forward, roaring out of the dirt right to the road.

The Heart moved.

Hovering in the middle of the road, he leaned forward and blew lightly.

Another gust of warm wind raced down the road, hitting the man and woman in the back, blowing her hair even more wildly than it was already moving around the man's face.

The man smiled white at the horizon.

The woman rested her chin on his shoulder, pressed tight and sighed deep.

The Heart watched.

And he watched.

And when they were no longer a dot on the horizon, the rider and his gypsy disappearing into the sun, the Heart looked up.

And he went home.

The Colorado Mountain Series will conclude
with the story of Wood and Maggie.

Printed in Great Britain
by Amazon